Emily

by

Mirabelle Maslin

Mirabelle Maslin

Augur Press

EMILY
Copyright © Mirabelle Maslin 2007

The moral right of the author has been asserted

Author of:
Beyond the Veil
Tracy
Carl and other writings
Fay
On a Dog Lead

British Library Cataloguing in Publication Data.
A catalogue record for this book is available from the British Library.

ISBN 978-0-9549551-8-2

First published 2008 by
Augur Press
Delf House,
52, Penicuik Road,
Roslin,
Midlothian EH25 9LH
United Kingdom

Printed by Lightning Source

Emily

With heartfelt thanks to my editors, and to all those who encouraged me to write this book. In particular, I would like to thank Elizabeth, Alexandra and Vanessa for their unfailing interest in the story.

Joanna Thomson of Joanna Thomson Jewellery was the maker of the brooch that appears on the front cover of this book, and I have obtained her permission to use that image.

Author's note

Although this book is complete in its own right, it is the consequence of a much greater endeavour.

I wrote most of my first novel – *Beyond the Veil* – in the autumn and winter of 2002-2003. During the following winter, I wrote several books, one of which was *Fay*. By that time, I was receiving requests to write a sequel to *Beyond the Veil*, but I was too involved in ongoing projects.

At the end of 2006, I made a start on the much-requested sequel, but as the tale began to unfold, I realised that it was to be the culmination of the story that had emerged in *Beyond the Veil* and the quite separate story that had evolved in the writing of *Fay*. It was then I became aware that those two novels were 'companion' books – their content running in parallel, never touching, yet expressing many of the same positive qualities of human experience.

The characters in these books express attributes to which many of us aspire – kindness and concern, compassion, honesty, co-operation and commitment. Although faced with much adversity, in situations that cannot be readily explained, they do all they can to support one another, and what springs from this experience is beyond price.

Emily is a character in *Beyond the Veil* who was then but a toddler, and she made only a few appearances. In this book – *Emily* – she is the central character. It is not long before she becomes aware of something that links her to the core of the story of *Fay*...

Chapter One

Only another few days until it's my birthday, thought Emily happily as she jumped out of bed to wash and dress herself in plenty of time for school. One of the best presents this year was that her dad would be at home. He had managed to arrange a weekend off especially for her birthday. She and her mum would collect him at the station on Friday, and then he was to be at home for the whole weekend before he had to go back to his job on the oil rig. He had promised to go shopping with her on Saturday, and Mummy and she had invited friends round for Sunday, her birthday, when she would be eight at last.

Her mother, Clare, had laid out her clean clothes. She put them on carefully, checking her appearance in the mirror to see that the collar of her blouse looked neat.

Emily was mature for her years. She was bright and enthusiastic, and she was unsophisticated. It was as if she knew not to waste her energies on anything that was of no real value. She lingered in her room for a few minutes, enjoying the way that it had been decorated. Her mum and dad had repainted it only three months ago – using the exact colours that she had chosen. The walls were pale blue, and the blue on the woodwork of the window frame and the door was a little darker. That colour reminded her of the forget-me-not flowers that grew in the garden every year. She had some posters on the walls that showed named pictures of birds, butterflies and trees, and she loved lying in bed looking at them.

'Nearly ready now,' she said aloud. She gave her room a final glance, and left the door ajar as she made for the stairs. She was tall for her age. Despite her slender build she was quite strong, and she moved confidently. She prided herself on standing up straight – the way that she was taught in class at school.

'Hello,' said her mother, smiling warmly as Emily went into the kitchen. It never ceased to surprise her how Emily seemed to know instinctively when it was time to get up each morning. It was almost as if she had an internal alarm clock that she could reset at will.

'Hello, Mummy,' she replied, running to her and throwing her arms round her. 'Mummy, what time do we meet Daddy on Friday?'

Clare laughed. Her daughter knew the answer to that question very well, but she asked several times each day just for the pleasure of talking again about exactly how that day was going to be.

'You know already,' she replied.

'But I want you to tell me again,' Emily insisted.

'I come up to meet you from school at half past three, and then we go straight to the station in time for Daddy's train.'

Emily sighed contently and counted the days. 'Today's Tuesday…' she began.

Clare waited and watched her daughter intently while she worked out that Friday was now only three days away. She thought how much Emily's appearance reminded her of her sister, Jane, when she had been that age. Clare was only eighteen months younger than Jane, and she remembered well Jane's athletic build, which in addition to her head start in years, meant she had quite an advantage in their rather frequent battles.

Even the grey November sky looked full of interest and promise to Emily as she ate her breakfast, her mind going over the events of the weekend to come.

Clare watched how her daughter seemed to drift into a kind of reverie as she ate, and she knew that her mind must be full of happiness.

It was not long before their neighbours, David, and his mother, Asma, were knocking at the door.

'Come on, Emily,' David shouted. 'We'll be late.'

Emily turned her head instinctively at the sound of her friend's voice and called, 'Co…ming.' She stood up, hurriedly put on her coat, and then picked up her schoolbag, her eyes scanning along the kitchen worktop.

'It's all right,' Clare reassured her. 'I've already put your packed lunch into your bag.' She winked, and added, 'Including the dried apricots you wanted.'

'Oh, thanks, Mum,' said Emily smiling.

Clare gathered her into her arms and gave her a close hug, just as David appeared in the kitchen.

David was stockily built, with the same very dark hair and eyes as his mother, although he had inherited his father's square features rather than his mother's oval face.

Clare gave her daughter's hair a quick brush. Silently she admired the waves in it, and the way that it shone. Its dark nut-brown colour was certainly quite unusual, she reflected.

She followed Emily to the door, and then waved to the three as they set off down the road to join the walking bus at the crossroads. After that she quickly got herself ready to cycle to her part-time work about two miles away in the opposite direction. At forty-two, she was fit, and thought nothing of the distance. A few grey hairs had begun to intrude in her thick brown hair, but she rarely noticed this, as she felt as well as she had ten or more years ago.

David had been Emily's friend since they were both very small. He was only a few weeks younger than Emily. The two families lived next door to one another at the bottom of a quiet cul-de-sac in a small development of modern houses, and they had always got on well. Asma's husband, Bill, had worked at the local hospital for many years, and was now a consultant in A&E, working long hours, often on call. There were never really quite enough staff at the unit, and he dedicated his energy to doing all that he could to keep everything running as effectively as possible. He and Asma were in complete agreement about this, and she supported him unfailingly in their decision.

When Friday morning came, Emily could hardly sit still on her chair.

'I don't think I need any breakfast this morning, Mum,' she said, her face glowing with anticipation.

'I think you should try to have something,' Clare replied wisely. 'I remember when I was young, if I was excited I often felt as if I couldn't swallow anything. But about two hours later, I'd be starving!' She smiled ruefully as she remembered how uncomfortable she had felt as a result.

'All right, then. I'll try.'

Emily put on a determined look, and chewed her way through a slice of toast.

'Will that do?' she asked proudly, as she finished the last corner.

'Of course,' replied Clare, smiling. 'By the way, I've got a surprise for you.'

'*Another* surprise? Tell me, tell me.' Emily's eyes were sparkling.

'Your Auntie Jane will be coming on Saturday morning, and she can stay until Sunday evening.'

'Auntie Jane!' Emily flung herself into her mother's arms and hugged her tightly. Afterwards, a serious expression came over her face as she said, 'Auntie Jane is special.' She paused, and then added, 'She helped Daddy to understand what I needed.'

'I know. Somehow she seemed to know things about you right from when you were a baby.'

They looked at each other for a little while, and then Emily collected her things and was soon off with David and Asma.

'See you at half past three,' she called back down the road.

Clare hurried to tidy away the breakfast things. She did not like to leave anything lying around in the kitchen when she set off to work.

Suddenly the phone began to ring.

'Drat!' she said, grabbing the tea towel to dry her hands. 'I wonder who on earth that can be at this time of morning.'

She lifted the phone.

'Hello,' she said a little stiffly, as if expecting to hear the voice of an unwanted salesman.

'Is that Mrs Foulds?' said a man's voice.

'Speaking.'

'My name is Colin Brand, and I am speaking on behalf of Britoc Oil.'

Clare caught her breath, but said nothing.

The man's voice continued. 'I'm afraid I have some bad news for you.'

'What is it?' she asked urgently.

'I'm afraid to have to tell you that your husband is missing.'

'Oh!' Clare felt as if her body was turning to ice. She tried to say something, but no sound came from her open mouth.

'Mrs Foulds, are you still there?'

Clare gathered herself. 'Yes,' she managed to say. Her voice disappeared again, but she made an enormous effort and added, 'There must be some mistake.' She paused, before repeating in uncertain tones, 'Yes, there must be some mistake.'

'I'm afraid not, Mrs Foulds,' said the voice.

'But there must be,' she insisted. 'He's on his way home. I'm to meet him at the station around four.' She could hear her voice wobble, and she could feel her heart pounding.

4

The voice pierced her rising panic.

'When did you last speak to him?'

'Yesterday... At about lunchtime.' By now she was almost stuttering. She realised that she felt very weak. She was leaning on the table, but could hardly stand. 'I need to sit down,' she said.

'Of course.'

She took the phone to an upright chair and perched on the edge of it, keeping hold of the table with one hand. 'What happened?' she asked, trying to steady her voice. The words had felt as if they were going to choke her.

'I'm afraid we don't know. The only information we have is that he is not on the rig, and there's no record of his having left. He was last seen at around two, just after he packed his things.'

'Have you got them?' Clare was filled with horror at the thought that they too might have disappeared.

'Yes.'

Clare sagged in her seat. She could tell that this man was thinking exactly the same as she was – that George hadn't merely forgotten to log off the rig – an action in itself that was inconceivable – and that he had somehow ended up in the sea.

'Have you any other information?' she whispered.

The man seemed to have heard her and said, 'None at present.' There was silence between them, and then he asked, 'Have you got anyone with you?'

'Not at the moment,' Clare replied dully.

For the first time the man's voice took on an insistence, and it penetrated her shocked state. 'It's important,' he said. 'Who can you ask?'

'Er...' Clare felt paralysed. Important? Yes, she supposed that it might be important. But surely the most important thing was to find George. Yes. 'What about finding George?' she demanded determinedly.

'We will do everything we can,' said the man, who had quickly retreated to the use of formality. 'Mrs Foulds, I must ask you to decide who you can contact to sit with you.'

Clare sagged in her seat. 'I can watch out for the neighbour who's just taken the children to school,' she said, trying to contain the turbulence that she could feel surging inside her.

He continued. 'Can I give you contact details?'

'Yes. Yes… of course. You must. I'll get something to write on. Hang on a minute.'

Clare's thoughts were whirring. George… drowned… But no one knew what had happened… so maybe he was alive somewhere? She grabbed a pad and pen, and returned to the phone.

'Can you give me your name?' she began.

'Brand. Mr Colin Brand.'

Dimly she realised that he had already told her this, but exactly when she did not know or care.

With shaking hand she wrote: *Mr Colin Brand*, and then said, 'Right, can you give me your number.'

He gave it to her slowly, digit by digit, before instructing her to repeat it back to him. Then he added that it was an emergency number that was manned day and night.

Clare heard herself say clearly and deliberately, 'Be sure that I get any news straight away.'

'Of course.'

There was an uncomfortable silence, and then she asked, 'Why did no one contact me immediately?'

'I'm afraid I don't know the answer to that,' he replied, with obvious discomfort in his voice.

There was another silence, and then Clare said with dignity, 'I think I'll ring off now. Please leave any news on the answering service at this number if I am not in.'

She put the phone down. She was breathing heavily, and her heart was still beating rapidly. She realised that she was deeply shocked, but also intensely angry. Why had they not contacted her straight away? And where was George?

She looked at her watch. If Asma was coming back home, she should be here soon. She stood at the front window, motionless, looking up the street, waiting to catch sight of her friend.

Asma had said goodbye to the children at the school gate, and was about to continue on to the shopping centre, when she heard a voice. 'Go home,' it instructed. She turned to see who was speaking to her, but saw no one. All the other parents and carers were fifty or more yards down the road, with their backs to her. She shook her head as if trying to clear it, and began to walk towards the shopping centre.

'Home,' came the command. It wasn't loud, but it was very clear.

It was then she realised that it seemed to be inside her head.

Feeling alarmed, she took her mobile out of her bag and rang Bill at the hospital. His secretary informed her that he was in a meeting, and wouldn't be free for a while.

Reassured, she tried once again to continue to the shops, but she was consumed immediately by an overwhelming desire to go straight home. Having decided that she could manage for now without the items on her list, she retraced her steps, and was soon walking down the cul-de-sac where she and Clare lived. From a distance, she could see Clare standing at her front window.

That's strange, she thought. Surely she should be at work by now? Then she added aloud, 'Maybe she's taken the day off to get ready for meeting George. It's funny she didn't mention it, though.'

On impulse, she decided to speak to Clare, so she passed her own house and returned to Clare's front door. She rang, and when Clare did not respond, she went to the front window. She could see that Clare's face was pure white. She tapped gently on the window. At first, Clare stared at her apparently without recognition, but then went to the door and let her in.

'What is it, Clare?' asked Asma in gentle tones. 'What's happened?'

'A man phoned. George is missing.'

'Oh, no!' Asma took Clare's arm. 'What did he tell you?'

'Nothing much. But I've got his number here.'

'Clare, you must tell me everything about that call. Let's sit down, and you can tell me exactly what happened.'

'Thanks, Asma.' Clare took a deep breath. 'I'm so glad you're here.'

'So am I,' said Asma. 'Clare, are you supposed to be at work today?'

'Yes.'

'Can I phone them to say that there's a problem and that you'll be in touch?'

'Please.' Clare wrote a number on her pad and handed it to Asma.

After she had made the call, Asma put on the kettle and said, 'You're shivering. I'm going to make a hot drink for you, and then you can tell me exactly what happened.'

Clare explained everything that she could remember. Asma sat quietly, apart from offering gentle prompts in the form of simple questions.

When Clare had finished, Asma said determinedly, 'I'm going to leave a message for Bill with his secretary, and I think that you and I had better stick together until we know more.'

Clare did not resist. She realised that she desperately wanted the companionship of her friend. Dimly, she knew that later today they would collect the children from school, but she had no idea how she was going to explain to Emily that her daddy was missing.

Asma's voice broke into her thoughts. 'What's the exact time of George's train?'

'He's not coming!' Clare's voice rose to a kind of screech. 'Not coming!'

Asma took hold of her hand. 'I know.' She squeezed Clare's hand gently, and repeated, 'I know,' before adding thoughtfully, 'but I think it would be wise for us all to go and meet the train.'

Clare stared at her friend. 'You're right,' she said without emotion.

They sat quietly together for a long time.

The silence was later punctuated by the ringing of the phone. Asma answered it, and found that it was Bill.

'I got back to you as soon as I could,' he said. 'What's happened?'

'Clare's had a call from George's company. He's missing. I think it's best if you talk to her yourself. She's very shocked.'

She handed the phone across to Clare, who haltingly explained everything to him. Asma noticed that she also spoke about some other thoughts that were in her mind, and she was glad that she had initiated that conversation for her.

When Clare put the phone down she said, 'He says he should be home before six, and he's going to try to arrange cover so that he won't get called out this evening.'

'That's good. I hope he manages. Friday evening can be so busy,' said Asma. She looked at Clare intently and said, 'Look, I know you probably won't want to eat, but I think we should try to have some soup at least. After that we must talk about meeting the children. I've been thinking that we should get a taxi.'

'But it's only a few minutes walk,' Clare burst out.

'I know. But I think we need privacy at the moment.'

'Yes,' she whispered.

'In fact, I think I'll phone the school and see if we can collect the children five minutes early.'

'What will you say?'

'I don't know, but we can think of something while we're having our soup.'

Clare managed only a few spoonfuls, but she did feel a little helped by it, and thanked her friend for insisting. After that, they decided what Asma should say to the school, and she made the arrangements.

The rest of their time was spent going over and over the last words Clare had had with George, and the content of Colin Brand's call.

At ten past three, the taxi drew up outside the house, and they arrived at the school in good time. A teacher appeared with both the children, and Asma guided them into the taxi.

David and Emily were full of suppressed excitement.

'What is it?' they demanded in chorus. 'Why are we getting a ride in a taxi?'

'There's been a change of plan,' said Clare confidently, in a voice that surprised her. 'Daddy can't come today, but I think that we should go and see the train that he would have come on.'

'When *is* he coming?' asked Emily eagerly.

'I don't know yet,' her mother explained gently. 'I'll tell you as soon as I have any news.'

Asma was watching her friend's face throughout this interaction, and she marvelled at her composure. She was being completely honest with her daughter, and in a way that was entirely appropriate for her age and the situation. It would be wrong to tell Emily that her father was dead if there was even a small chance that he was still alive. Both David and Emily were used to sudden changes of plan because of their fathers' employment, and although they often had to suffer sudden disappointment, everyone had always acknowledged this, and had talked about it in a realistic way.

'I wish Daddy was coming on this train,' said Emily sadly as it drew into the station.

'I wish he was too,' echoed David. 'Mummy, when did you say that my daddy was coming home?'

'Quite soon,' replied Asma.

'But he might have to stay at the hospital if someone very sick comes?'

'Yes, that's right.'

'Well, if he comes home, I want Emily to share him, because she's sad that her own daddy can't come today after all.'

Asma smiled. She and Clare had often noticed the way each child was quick to share whichever daddy was there, if one or the other was upset. 'I'd like that too,' she replied. 'It's a very good idea.'

Emily watched intently while all the passengers disembarked, and then she turned to Clare and asked again, 'When *is* my daddy coming?'

'I don't know,' Clare repeated, 'but I promise I'll tell you as soon as I know.'

After the children were in bed that evening, Asma stayed at home with David, while Bill went to sit with Clare. She was standing in the hall when he rang the doorbell, and she opened the door immediately. Her face had taken on a greyish hue.

Bill took her hand warmly and looked straight into her eyes.

'Clare,' he said. 'I'm terribly sorry about all this, and I'll do everything I can to help.'

'Thanks Bill,' she replied. 'I think I know that, but it's good to hear it too.'

She took him to the sitting room, but he made no move to sit down. Instead, he turned to her and said bluntly, 'I'd like to phone the number Brand gave you. If there's been no more news from that end, I think we should make contact now.'

Clare nodded. She handed the number across to him, and Bill picked up the phone extension that was on a side table. Clare remained standing, and watched him intently as he keyed in the number.

'Hello... My name is Dr William Blane... I'm phoning about George Foulds... Yes, I'm sitting with his wife at the moment... Security details? Look, I'll hand you over to her so that she can verify who I am.'

Clare took the phone and said through clenched teeth, 'Clare Foulds speaking. You'll know the number because you'll be able to see it on your equipment. I authorise our friend, Dr Blane, to speak to you.' Despite the turmoil that she was in, she had quite deliberately chosen to say 'our'. She did not know where George was, and she was very worried, but for now she certainly was *not* going to behave as if he were dead.

She handed the phone back to Bill, and waited while he grilled the person on the other end. It gave her a distant sense of satisfaction to observe the relentlessness of his approach.

When he put the phone down, he said, 'I couldn't get much, but there's one thing that's come to light.' Clare stiffened. 'A piece of red and green striped material has been found floating nearby. They didn't know what it was, but apparently some of the men said that George usually carried it in his pocket.'

Clare's hand flew to her mouth. 'Emily gave that to him,' she choked out. 'He always carried it whenever he went away. You've got to phone back and tell them.' Tears flooded into her eyes. 'And tell them to keep it safe.' The desperation in her voice was all too starkly apparent.

Bill picked up the phone straight away, and he delivered a terse message before replacing it once more.

They sat quietly for several minutes.

'Please remember that you can phone us at any time of day or night,' Bill said gently.

'Thanks,' she replied. 'And Jane should arrive about lunchtime tomorrow. I'll phone her first thing to let her know what's going on.'

'I think you should phone her now,' said Bill firmly.

Clare's body sagged. 'Yes, of course. I'll do it as soon as I've let you out.'

Bill took her hand again for a moment as he was about to leave. She stood in the doorway and watched him as he went up the path. At his door he turned and waved to her, and then he was gone. She closed her own door slowly, and then stood in the hallway where she seemed to freeze.

Clare had no idea how long she stood there, but it must have been for quite a while because her legs felt strange – almost numb. Her watch showed that it was late – midnight. She went to pick up the phone, but hesitated. Then, remembering Bill's insistence about phoning Jane, she keyed in the number. She heard the sound of Jane's voice and began to cry.

Chapter Two

Jane slept badly that night. Clare's news had haunted her in her dreams, and whenever she dozed off, she soon jerked back into wakefulness, her mind full of worry and unanswered questions. Although Clare had sounded straightforwardly upset, Jane knew that underneath she was completely distraught. She wished that she could have gone to be with her and Emily straight away, but she had had to wait until the morning to catch her train.

Before she went to bed, Jane had phoned her friend, Eva, to let her know what had happened. Not only had she wanted to talk about it all to a trusted friend, but also she needed to let her know straight away, as the news might well affect their plans for the following weekend, when Eva was to spend some time at Jane's home.

Jane had known Eva for years. She cast her mind back to the start of their friendship, and despite her worry about George, Clare and Emily, she smiled. It had been almost accidental. She had hurt her ankle badly, and while she was resting, Eva had come with a friend, Ellen, who was visiting her at the time. As a qualified doctor who was also experienced in homeopathy, Eva had been a great source of support at the time. They had since become very good friends, and kept in contact regularly. In recent years, Eva had decided to involve herself in medical research, and had obtained employment in a relatively small, but very committed, team within a large research agency.

Jane rose early. She collected her things, and then secured the house. She slipped a note through her neighbour's door to explain that she might be away longer than the weekend she had already mentioned. In her heart she knew that she wanted to stay with her sister and her niece until they had more news of George. Her own struggles at the news were considerable. She could only guess at the magnitude of how Clare must be feeling, and what the impact all of this might be having on Emily. There was no way of predicting anything until they had more news. And what if no more news came? That was a possibility, but one upon which she did not want to dwell.

Emily and Clare were waiting at the station when her train pulled in. She could see them searching the windows for her. She waved, but they did not see her. She realised that she felt relieved to be here at last. Although it was less than twelve hours since Clare had phoned her, it seemed much longer than that.

It wasn't until she was on the platform with her suitcase and bag that they finally spotted her.

Emily ran down the platform. 'Daddy didn't come on his train, but you've come on yours,' she said. 'Auntie Jane, do *you* have any idea when Daddy might come? He promised he would come for my birthday, you know.'

Clare caught up with Emily and said gently, 'Neither of us know any more at the moment, love, but we promise to tell you as soon as we do. Don't we, Jane?'

Jane could see lines of worry etched on Clare's face. She gave her and Emily a hug, while saying, 'That's for certain, Emily.'

'I know,' replied Emily seriously.

Jane and Emily walked a few steps along the platform together, and Jane said, 'You'll remember that I had a long talk with Daddy about the present I'm going to give you tomorrow for your birthday.'

Emily stopped for a moment and stared at her solemnly. 'Yes,' she said. 'I remember.'

The three walked along in silence for a few minutes. Clare had taken one of Jane's bags, and Emily had insisted on carrying her aunt's handbag. Jane was left with her compact trolley suitcase, which she pulled along behind her.

'I managed to park quite near the front of the station,' said Clare, trying hard to find something ordinary to say. 'And Emily and I have got a plan for this afternoon. Haven't we, Emily?' she finished, touching her daughter's shoulder.

Emily bounced on one foot twice and said, 'Yes, Auntie Jane, David and his mum are coming round.'

'That's good,' said Jane. 'I'm so glad that they are close by. I haven't seen them for a while, but I often think of them.'

The afternoon passed unremarkably. It rained heavily, and the children spent their time engaging the others in choices of board games, followed by devising a simple recipe in the kitchen for some quick baking.

When Jane and Clare were alone later that evening, Jane said, 'I'm worried about that piece of material. It's been on my mind a lot. I think we should tell Emily about it.'

'Not until we have it here,' Clare replied adamantly.

'Why do you say that?'

'I want to be certain that it's the one. I don't think it's a good idea to tell Emily and then it turns out that it is something else.'

'You're right, of course. Listen, Clare, I've got to go up to bed now, but wake me any time in the night if you want me.'

The following morning, Emily woke early. At last, I'm eight! she thought happily. But at the same time she felt a heaviness in her chest, and she knew that it was because she wanted to see her daddy. He would have done everything he could to be here today. Of that she was certain. So where could he be? And not even Mummy knew. Then she remembered something very important. She got straight out of bed and went into Jane's room to wake her. She shook her aunt's shoulder gently until she stirred.

'Auntie Jane,' she said.

'Yes?' Jane replied sleepily.

'Auntie Jane, I dreamed about Daddy last night. He had lost that special material I gave him and he was very sad.'

Jane suddenly felt wide awake. 'I think that we should tell your mummy about that dream,' she said. 'I'll get up and we'll go and see if she's awake yet.'

Together they tiptoed into Clare's bedroom. She seemed to be asleep, and they were just creeping out again when she turned over and said, 'Hello, you two.'

Immediately Emily dived into bed with her, and Jane sat on the edge while Emily talked about her dream.

'You were right, Jane,' said Clare immediately, 'I should have told her.'

'Told me what, Mummy?'

'The man on the phone told Bill that a piece of material had been found in the water. It sounded like the one you gave to Daddy, but because I couldn't be absolutely sure, I didn't want to tell you.'

'Oh…' said Emily. Her mother could see that she was struggling with this information, and she put both arms round her as they lay together.

'Can we go and see it, Mummy?' asked Emily urgently.

Clare turned to Jane. 'Will you help me to arrange it?'

Jane nodded. 'Of course,' she said emphatically.

'Can we do it *now*?' asked Emily.

'I don't think that we'll be able to see it straight away,' said Jane, 'but maybe we could get them to photograph it and send a digital image to Bill's computer? What do you think, Clare?'

'I think we should try to fix that,' Clare replied.

Jane noticed that her sister sounded exhausted.

'Mummy, do you think that Daddy will never come back?' asked Emily suddenly.

'Emily, it's possible,' replied Clare gently, her arms still around her daughter.

'Might he be dead?'

'Yes, he might be dead.'

Emily cuddled close to her mother while she considered this. She had heard a lot about people dying at the hospital. She knew that David's dad did everything he could to help people to stay alive, but that there were many times when it didn't work. She remembered the little bird that they had rescued from a local cat. They had tried very hard to keep it alive, but had not succeeded, and had buried it in the garden. She didn't like to think about Daddy not being alive any more.

'When will we know?' she asked.

'There's no way of telling,' Clare replied.

Jane saw fragility in her sister's frame, a frame that had always appeared so sturdy and invincible, and she saw that Clare seemed to shrink inwards as she spoke.

Emily's birthday was spent quietly. She had been clear that now for her birthday all she wanted was to know what had happened to Daddy. Clare phoned the few friends that they had invited for the afternoon, and one by one, she explained the situation to them. Although she found this very hard, she also felt supported by the responses she had. Everyone offered their help, and said that instead of the small party that had been planned, they would call round during the late afternoon with Emily's presents, and stay only for a short time.

Emily was certain that if no one knew where her daddy was, the next best thing was to see the material that had been found. Clare made a number of phone calls about it, and eventually was able to tell Emily that they would have a photograph of the material by the end of the day.

Jane's present to Emily was the money for her and Daddy to go together to see a special place in Wales that demonstrated new ways of living, using less water and electricity. Whenever George had talked to Emily about his work, he had explained that it would not go on forever, because oil supplies would come to an end. He did not know when that would happen, but he knew it was coming, and young though she was, Emily and he used to talk together about how people might have to live.

In the middle of the afternoon, Bill came to the door carrying a large envelope. Clare let him in, and straight away he handed it to Emily saying, 'This is the picture you wanted, Emily.'

She took it and squatted on the floor, where she slipped the A4 print out of its cover and examined it carefully.

'It looks like it,' she said in a whisper, 'but I've got to be absolutely sure...'

Clare nodded to the others, and they waited for Emily to finish scrutinising it.

'Yes, here it is,' she confirmed. 'Look, Mummy, you can see the little flower that I stitched into the hem.'

Tears began to course down Clare's cheeks as she recalled the intense care and concentration with which Emily had completed that task. She had been only six years old at the time.

'Bill...' she began, with desperation in her voice.

He looked at Clare and waited patiently.

'What if George is never found? People who are lost at sea are sometimes never found.' She began to shake.

'We'll have to wait. It's too soon to be sure of anything,' Bill stated reasonably, although his own voice was not entirely steady.

Emily stood beside her mother and leaned up against her, saying nothing.

Jane began to speak. 'When we were waiting for the photo to come, I decided that I wasn't going to go home this evening. My train ticket will let me travel after ten in the morning. I'll phone my boss first thing and explain what's happened. I think I should be able to arrange some more time off at the end of the week, or next week at the latest.'

'You don't need to do that,' said Clare quickly. 'I'm sure we'll manage.'

'We should all be together at the moment,' said Jane firmly. 'And in any case, I want that.'

Clare's shoulders sagged. 'I want that too,' she admitted.

'So do I,' Emily's voice joined in.

Chapter Three

That week, Jane arranged that some of her remaining annual leave was allocated to Friday and Monday for the next three weeks. She felt a little easier once she had organised this, and set her mind to being able to return to Clare's straight after work on Thursday. She had had a long talk with Eva on the phone, and they had postponed their proposed weekend together, intending to rearrange it when it became feasible. Eva had impressed upon Jane that if there was anything she could do to help, to let her know.

As time passed, and the possibility of news of George became increasingly remote, everyone gradually began to accept that he must indeed have drowned in a freak accident that had taken place unobserved. A Fatal Accident Inquiry took place, during which nothing further came to light. None of the safety measures on the rig had been breached in any way, and what had happened remained a mystery.

Although it was normally the case that a missing person was not in law considered dead until seven years had passed, Clare was informed that if she applied to the Court, the circumstances of George's disappearance would be taken into account, and it would be highly likely that he would be pronounced dead – presumed drowned.

With the help of Eva and all Clare's friends, Jane supported Clare and Emily through this agonising process, and when at last it was complete, Clare and Emily had the task of considering their life without George.

Together the three organised a memorial service. It was very well attended, since although he spent much time away, he was also well known in the community in which they lived. Mercifully, he had taken out substantial life and sickness insurance when he began to work on the rigs, and both Clare and Emily were well provided for.

Jane continued to worry about her sister. She continued to arrange regular long weekends with her and Emily, and she was all too aware that although Clare had been able to carry on, as the months passed she continued to look pale and shocked.

The next blow came all too soon. One evening, during one of their frequent phone conversations, Clare fell silent for a moment. Then she said, 'Jane, I've got some news that might turn out to be not so good.'

Jane swallowed and replied, 'Just tell me what it is.'

'I've found a lump on my breast.'

'Have you been to see the doctor?'

'Not yet, but I've made an appointment for next week.'

'When did you find it?'

'I think I first noticed it about ten days ago.'

'Why on earth didn't you say straight away?'

'I don't know… I think I knew it was there but didn't know, both at the same time.'

Jane knew immediately that this was the ongoing effect of her shocked state, and she said sympathetically, 'I think I can understand that.' She paused for a moment, and then said determinedly, 'But we must be sure that you're seen as quickly as possible. Can you try to see your GP tomorrow? There's bound to be an emergency surgery.'

'I'll give it a try,' replied Clare without enthusiasm.

'And you're bound to be referred to the hospital,' said Jane, her mind racing on. 'I'll make sure I'm with you when you go for that appointment. Have you told Asma about it yet?'

'No, you're the first.'

'Will you give her a ring after we've finished talking? And please find out if she can go to the GP with you.'

'I really don't think that's necessary.'

'Trust me, Clare. You need someone with you,' said Jane emphatically.

'Okay,' Clare agreed reluctantly.

'We'll speak again tomorrow evening about it,' said Jane before she rang off.

The following evening the news was good. Clare had indeed spoken to Asma, the GP had seen her that day and had arranged to refer her to the hospital, and Asma had told Bill of the situation.

'It's a good thing you've caught it early like this,' said Jane confidently.

'Yes,' replied Clare.

Jane noticed that there was a kind of deadness in Clare's voice, and her confidence turned to anxiety. Trying to sound as normal as possible, she asked, 'Did your GP say how long it was likely to be before you would be seen?'

'About four weeks I think, but Asma has told me since that Bill has a colleague who can see me privately next week to hurry things along. They're pushing me to take this up because they are worried about me.'

'Quite right too,' said Jane. 'I think you should let yourself be guided by Bill in this.'

After the call, Jane felt a distinct sense of unease. Clare was still in the early stages of her reaction to the loss of George, as it was only eight months after his disappearance, and she was very vulnerable. Jane herself still felt in a state of shock, and she knew that Clare's situation was far more complex than hers. She had often read that the stress of bereavement could interfere with immune response. Although she knew that if this were breast cancer there was now a high rate of success in treatment, Clare's very stressed state might well prejudice the chances of a good outcome. She decided to phone Eva to discuss the whole situation, and it did not take long before the two were deep in conversation.

'Eva, have you got time to talk?'

'Yes, of course. How are you? And how are Clare and Emily?'

'Actually I'm phoning because I'm worried about Clare.'

'What is it?' asked Eva immediately. 'I know that you've been worried about how she's coping with the shock, but there's something else, isn't there?'

Jane went on to tell Eva about the lump on Clare's breast, and about how worried she was that Clare really did not have any reserves to cope with this on top of everything else.

'I'm very sorry to hear this,' said Eva when Jane had finished speaking. 'Of course, I hope that it won't come to anything much. After all, some lumps are completely benign. But if it *is* cancer, then I too would be worrying about the effect of her stress on her recovery.'

'It isn't just the stress,' said Jane worriedly. 'I've noticed another big change in her. She has always loved Emily dearly, and they have always had a very close relationship, but now at times it seems to me as if her thoughts are miles away.'

'They probably are,' reflected Eva. 'In a way, it would be surprising if they weren't at this stage. She still doesn't know what happened to George and where he is, and she probably never will.

This is likely to prey on her mind for a long time yet. And there must be many other things that she's thinking and wondering about. In fact, there will be things on her mind that she herself hasn't got hold of yet, and it will be impossible for her to talk about them until she does. You're right that this will mean she's more vulnerable. I'll certainly be thinking about all of this, and please will you let me know as soon as you have any more news.'

'What a relief it is to be able to phone you,' said Jane. 'I know that I can tell you everything, and it's a great help to me to have a friend like you who has got a medical background.'

'Well, I'm a bit limited because I don't have access to any notes, but I'll do my best. I have to say that I'm very glad that Clare has Bill helping her.'

In the event, Jane did not go with Clare to the hospital. Asma had insisted that she would go to this appointment and to any others, thus leaving Jane free to devote her days off work to spending long weekends with Clare and Emily.

A biopsy revealed that the lump on Clare's breast was indeed cancer, and a treatment programme was put in place immediately, including early removal of the lump. At first, Jane felt optimistic about the likely outcome. After all, the lump had been small, and it seemed that Clare had spotted it quite quickly.

At first, everything seemed to progress satisfactorily. Clare had given up her job to give herself the best chance of a full recovery, and she rested at home, occupying herself with looking after Emily, seeing friends, and developing some simple handcrafts. Months passed, and her health seemed stable. She began to think about what she might do when she recovered fully.

However, later tests revealed that the lymph nodes under her armpits had been affected, and further examination revealed that the cancer had spread to other sites. Having learned this, Jane became very worried. She could see that by this time her sister had no inner strength left with which to fight.

Jane had many long conversations with Eva about the whole situation, and together they thought of everything they could to try to support and encourage Clare through her illness.

Clare continued to care for Emily, but as time passed, Jane could see that she was struggling to manage. Jane did everything she could to help, but over the weeks, it became more and more clear that Clare was slowly fading, and would soon no longer be able to cope.

Jane moved fast in making arrangements. She handed in her notice at work, she arranged for a trustworthy agent to keep an eye on her house, and she moved in with Clare and Emily. She knew that the most important thing now was to be with her sister for however long they had together, and she wanted to provide security for Emily. She promised Emily from the outset that if her mummy did not get better, she would adopt her, and they could live together for as long as Emily needed and wanted.

'But what about your job?' Emily had asked.

Jane had replied that she would see about some work once she had a better idea of what was happening.

She watched Emily very carefully over the months of Clare's decline, and she constantly marvelled at Emily's apparent maturity and wisdom. But at bedtime she often cried herself to sleep in Jane's arms, and in the daytime she asked Jane many questions about Clare's illness when her mother became too unwell to reply.

When the hospital treatment was discontinued, Jane had a long talk with Asma and Bill and then with Eva about the best way to care for Clare. Emily was insistent that she wanted her mummy to be at home so that she could help to look after her, and Jane wanted this too, but she needed to feel confident that it was the right thing.

Throughout, Asma, Bill and David were a source of constant support to them.

Near the end, Emily asked many questions of Jane about what their future was to be, and Jane kept reiterating that they could talk about ideas, but that they would make decisions about it later. In her brighter moments, Clare loved to hear Emily talking about her ideas, and encouraged her as much as she could.

During Clare's final days, Emily stayed at home to be with her. Jane knew it would be wrong to encourage her to go to school, so she made no attempt to do so. She talked it over in her now daily phone calls with Eva, who was in full agreement.

Jane and Emily spent their days sitting at Clare's bedside. Sometimes they would talk to each other, sometimes they would read aloud, and sometimes they would sit quietly, holding Clare's hands. A nurse that Bill had found for them called in every day to help and advise them. If Jane needed to go out, Asma would always come to join Emily, and so would David on the occasions when he was not at school.

Clare died just two days before Emily's tenth birthday. It was at a moment when Emily and Jane were holding her hands and Bill and Asma had called round. Clare opened her eyes, and seemed to see them all there. She smiled with the kind of warm glow that had always been there, and then she slipped away.

Through her tears, Emily said, 'Mummy has gone to be with Daddy now. I think that's where she really wanted to be. I know that she didn't want to leave me, but she couldn't bear being without Daddy.'

'I think you're right,' said Jane through her tears. She felt relief that her sister's suffering was over, but she knew that she would miss her terribly. It was exactly two years since she heard that George was missing, she realised.

Chapter Four

Over the following months, Jane brought some of her possessions to Emily's house, and put most of the furniture in store, prior to letting her bungalow on a six-month lease. She was very grateful when the agent identified a pleasant couple to take it on. They had just retired from working abroad, and were very pleased with the bungalow and its situation. At first, Jane stacked her packing cases in the garage at the house which was now hers and Emily's, planning to sort through the contents at her leisure.

Emily was clearly a very bright child, and although she had missed many days of school over the last two years, with support from Jane and collaboration from the school, she had kept abreast of most of the necessary work.

As the months passed since Clare's death, and the formalities of the necessary paperwork had advanced, the two began to talk more and more about their future.

'This is your last year at primary school,' mused Jane as they sat together one evening.

'Yes, all my friends are talking about going up to High School.'

'What do you think about it?'

'Auntie Jane, I think I would like to live somewhere else.'

Jane sat bolt upright in her chair. It was as if Emily had spoken out her own thoughts.

'Are you sure?' she asked. 'I must admit that I'd been wondering about that myself, but I never said anything because I thought that you would want things to stay as much the same as possible, and for a long time.'

'I like my friends, but I've been asking about the High School, and it doesn't do anything but the usual subjects.'

'That's quite common.'

'But I'd like us to try to find out about other schools,' said Emily. 'And most of all, I want to live somewhere where we can grow things to eat,' she added passionately. 'Daddy and I used to talk about that a lot. He said that when he wasn't working away from home any more we could move to a place where we could grow some of our food.'

By this time, Jane had begun to see that separately they had each been thinking many of the same thoughts, and she put any caution on one side, and said, 'Let's just say anything that comes into our heads about what we think we might do. We don't *have* to go ahead with any of it, but we can if we want to, and can find a way.'

'Mummy told me that you had just finished studying for an Open University degree and that you were hoping to get a better job. Do you feel sad about not having a job?'

Jane was not surprised by Emily's directness. She had always been a thoughtful child, and as she had grown older and had suffered so much, Jane had observed that she had been able to apply this capacity to everything she had had to face.

In reply she said, 'I was completely sure that what I wanted to do with my life when Clare became ill was to give up my job and come to live with you both for as long as you needed.'

'I know,' said Emily seriously, 'but what about now?'

Jane looked straight into Emily's direct gaze and said, 'At some time I would like to have some work to do as well as being with you.'

Emily nodded.

Jane continued. 'As you know, Mummy took out insurance on her own life after your daddy went missing. We have enough money to keep us for a long time. We have the money from her insurance and you have your own money from your daddy's insurance. I have let out my bungalow, and after paying any expenses, that gives us some money as well.' She was quiet for a minute and then said, 'Emily, if we lived somewhere else, wouldn't you miss this house and your friends, and everything that you're used to?'

'I might,' Emily replied. She paused for only a moment before adding, 'But we have to find out what's right for us. I have to miss Mummy and Daddy every day, even in this house. I used to chat to Mummy about plans that I had, and she liked that. Maybe we will be doing some of what I thought.'

Jane was impressed by Emily's matter-of-fact description of the truth. 'Well,' she said, 'I've just had an idea…'

'What is it, Auntie Jane?' Emily asked eagerly.

'It's coming up for the Easter holidays. Why don't we make some daring plans to travel about a bit and talk to Estate Agents and people like that, and see what comes of it?'

Emily's face shone. 'I'd like that. I'd really like that.'

Jane continued. 'And we've got the whole of the summer holidays. We'll have to put your name down for the local High School, but that can be changed if we do move away from here. I like the idea of growing things to eat. If we stay on here we could try to get an allotment, but if we move, maybe we should think of going to a place that has a suitable garden.'

Emily nodded excitedly.

Jane could see that she was well pleased about the direction that this conversation was taking them. 'I'll start making some arrangements,' she said. Her mind rushed on and she added, 'I think that in the weeks from now until Easter I should make an effort to get on with finishing looking through those packing cases that are still stored in the garage. If we might be moving, I don't want to be taking any redundant clutter with me!'

Emily began to giggle.

Jane watched her with amusement and asked, 'Why are you laughing?'

'Auntie Jane, I do like your "redundant clutter"!' Emily gasped for breath, and tears came into her eyes. 'Look Auntie Jane, I'm crying… but it's because I'm happy.'

Jane gave her a hug and said, 'That's lovely.'

When Emily was able to speak again she said, 'I like looking through your things with you.'

'Oh, that's good. And I like the company.'

'Can we do some soon?' said Emily eagerly. She looked intently at her aunt and asked, 'Now?'

Jane was a little surprised at her enthusiasm. Emily had often been near at hand when she was sorting through things, but she had always thought that this might be to do with a feeling that she ought to help. Jane smiled warmly at her niece. 'Okay,' she said briskly, getting up from her chair. 'Let's go and choose a box.'

Out in the garage they counted the remaining containers.

'Twelve,' said Emily happily. 'How long is it until the Easter holidays?'

'About a month, I think.'

'That means we should do three boxes a week,' said Emily without hesitation.

Emily had always had an instinctive grasp of figures, and such simple calculations were a normal part of her conversation.

'You can choose the first box,' Jane suggested playfully.

Emily took an upright chair that stood at the back of the garage and placed it next to the boxes, which were stacked in pairs. She stood on the chair and leaned over them as far as she could, shut her eyes, and directed her palms downwards, moving them about as if somehow scanning the boxes.

Jane watched quietly. She felt puzzled, but was also fascinated. She said nothing, and did nothing to interfere with what Emily was doing.

Emily continued to concentrate intently upon her search. She seemed to be drawn to one pair of boxes in particular. However, she then moved her hands back near the others several times as if to check. Finally she pronounced triumphantly, 'It's definitely this one!' She pointed to the pair of the large containers to which she had been drawn.

'How do you know?' asked Jane in astonishment.

'I could feel,' Emily replied without hesitation.

Jane made no comment and instead put the two containers side by side. Then she turned to Emily and asked, 'Which one?'

Emily jumped from the chair, stood next to the boxes, shut her eyes and repeated her scanning motion.

'It's this one, Auntie Jane,' she said matter-of-factly.

'Okay,' said Jane in light tones. She thought it best not to question what was going on. Emily seemed so confident about what she was doing, and after all, she could see no harm in pursuing this. 'Right now,' she continued, 'can you give me a hand with it? It's quite heavy.' Jane spoke briskly, dismissing from her mind thoughts of any possible significance of what she had witnessed. Surely this was just a child's game?

Together, they slowly moved the container into the sitting room and removed the lid. The first layer revealed a number of ornaments, carefully wrapped in tissue paper and surrounded by bubble wrap. They took it in turns to free them, and placed them on the mantelshelf along with some that Clare had collected. Emily insisted that Jane told her the story of how she had come by each of them, and Jane took much pleasure in recounting their history. The next layer consisted of several items of clothing that Jane had placed there for further protection of the ornaments. She scrutinised them, and then pronounced confidently that their next trip to the charity shop should include them.

The final layer was the one that had made the container so heavy. There were many books, piled in heaps of five or six.

'Oh, Auntie Jane! Look at these books,' exclaimed Emily.

'You can have a look through them if you want to,' Jane encouraged her. 'There may be one or two that you would like for yourself.' She smiled. 'I'm sure that I can let you have any that you want especially, and if we both want one, we can share.'

'Can I really, Auntie Jane?' said Emily with barely-concealed excitement. She hesitated before picking up the first one, and said, 'But they're all yours really.'

'Never mind about that for now. Let's just see what there is.'

The following hour passed pleasantly as they examined the books, reading passages to each other from those that interested Emily.

They had almost exhausted the supply when Jane exclaimed, 'Oh goodness! Fancy that! It's that diary.' Then she fell silent and sat very still as her mind slipped back to the time when she used to write in it.

Emily stared at her intently, saying nothing, waiting, until her aunt began to move again. 'What is that diary?' she asked. 'Please tell me all about it.' Again she waited patiently.

Jane took a deep breath. 'There's a long story behind some of the contents of this diary,' she began. 'In fact, it's a very long story. But I'll gladly tell you about it.' Here she paused, and then laughed as she said, 'It's so long that I think I should tell it to you in chapters!'

Emily's face broke into a smile. 'Start now, Auntie Jane. Start now.'

Jane looked at her watch. 'I'm hungry,' she said, 'and so should you be. Let's make some supper, and then I'll tell you the first chapter. One thing I'll say straight away is that my friends Eva and Ellen both know all about this, too.'

'Oh, good!' said Emily. 'You *must* tell me all about it straight away.'

'Soon,' Jane promised. 'We must get our supper first.'

Emily screwed up her face, and then raced into the kitchen saying, 'I'll help, and then we'll be quick.'

As they worked together to prepare their meal, Emily asked, 'When is Eva coming to see us again?' And before Jane had time to reply, she rushed on. 'I hope it'll be soon.'

'I don't know,' Jane replied, 'But we could phone her and see.'

'And we could tell her about our plan for the holidays,' said Emily excitedly.

'Of course. She would be a good person to talk to about our ideas. At the very least, she's bound to have some interesting things to say.'

Their meal over, and the kitchen tidied, they sat down with the diary, and Jane began its story.

'I'm going to start by showing you some of the pages,' she said.

She turned the pages carefully until she found what she wanted, and then passed it across to Emily.

'Oh! What lovely spiral patterns!' she exclaimed. 'Auntie Jane, I didn't know you could draw like this.'

'Neither did I,' said Jane, 'and I haven't drawn anything like that since.'

'What do you mean?'

'I don't even know if I drew them, yet it must have been me, because I was the only one who was there when they appeared. By the way, turn over the pages and you'll see some more.'

Emily carefully turned a page and gasped at what she saw. 'They're amazing!' She stared and stared, as if drinking in the forms that were there. Eventually she turned one more page. 'And there's a kind of *double* one here,' she said incredulously. 'Auntie Jane, every one of these spirals is made up of tiny dots and dashes and curves. There are no proper lines at all. And some of the spirals even have little branches coming off them. It must have taken you *ages* to draw them.' She turned to her aunt. 'What do you mean you don't know if you drew them?' she demanded.

'Well, I'll tell you exactly what happened.'

Emily sat still on her chair, her face a study of intense anticipation.

Jane began. 'I'd been on my own for a couple of days. I don't think that there was any particular reason for this. It just happened to be a quiet weekend. I had gone to bed for the night and I was writing my diary. I must have dozed off, and when I woke, these spirals had appeared. I don't remember anything about drawing them. One minute I was writing about my day, and the next minute I was waking up, and I saw these spirals.'

Emily stared and stared at her aunt.

Jane continued. 'Yes, I know it might sound strange, but that's what happened.'

'I don't think it sounds strange,' said Emily emphatically. 'And I found where they were in the boxes, and that felt completely normal to me.'

'You're right,' said Jane apologetically. 'It's just that I can't find a way of understanding what happened. That's all.'

Emily jumped out of her seat and put her arm round her aunt. 'I know it's real, and that's what matters,' she said seriously.

They sat and looked at one another. Although Jane was familiar with Emily's wisdom, she was often surprised by her mature comments.

Emily began to speak again. 'Do you think it's weird that I found the box that they were in?'

'Of course not!' exclaimed Jane instantly. 'It was fascinating. I don't know how you knew how to look for them when you didn't even know they existed, but it certainly wasn't weird.' She stopped as she realised what she was saying. If she didn't think that Emily's choice of box was at all strange, then why should she question the appearance of the spirals in her diary?

Jane took Emily's hand and squeezed it affectionately before speaking again.

'There's one thing that might be important,' she said.

'What is it? Auntie Jane, tell me what it is.'

'I'd just been reading some of a book that affected me a lot.'

'Which book is it?' asked Emily eagerly. 'Is it here somewhere? Have we seen it today?'

'I haven't seen it in this container, but it should be around somewhere. I certainly wouldn't have thrown it out.'

'I want us to read it,' said Emily suddenly.

'Well, I can tell you a bit of what it was about, if you want.'

'Now?'

'Yes, of course.' Jane thought for a moment, trying to think of the best way of conveying the story to her niece. 'I'm just trying to remember the title. Ah, yes, I've got it now. It's "Communications" and it was written by someone called Frances Ianson.' She paused, gathered herself, and then began. 'It was about a mother and her son. The son couldn't communicate in words, and he was often extremely agitated. People didn't understand, and were sometimes frightened of him because of this. His mother struggled for a long time to find a way of communicating with him, and when she eventually succeeded, he became very calm and peaceful, and he started working to clear their garden.'

'That's really good,' said Emily. 'Did he grow anything?'

'Yes, he grew herbs and vegetables.'

'That's what we want to do.'

'Maybe I should tell you something about how he grew things,' mused Jane, half to herself.

'Yes, you *must*.'

'He arranged the plants in spiral patterns.'

'Spiral patterns! Like the ones in your diary, Auntie Jane?'

'I don't know. Unfortunately, there was no detailed information in the book about his layouts.'

Emily was clearly disappointed. 'But I wanted there to be,' she said with uncharacteristic impatience. 'How can we find out?'

'I don't think that there's any way.' Jane noticed that Emily looked quite withdrawn for a few minutes, and she let her have time to recover a little before she said, 'Actually, *I* was very disappointed about that, too.'

'I want to find out,' said Emily determinedly. 'I want to know about his spirals.'

'I can't think how,' replied Jane, 'but we won't forget that that's what we want.'

Emily nodded her head vigorously.

'Emily, there's more that I can tell you about the spirals in my diary.'

'I know. You said there would be quite a few chapters,' Emily reminded her. 'Can I have the next one now?'

'No, I think that's enough for today. It's not far off bedtime. We'll have some more tomorrow. Would you like to have a hot drink before you go for your bath?'

Half an hour later, Jane was saying goodnight to Emily, who was already looking very sleepy as she lay in her bed.

Jane woke suddenly in the middle of the night. She was quite certain that she could hear someone moving around in the house, and she felt very worried. Silently, she slipped out of bed and tiptoed to the landing. She could see that Emily's door was wide open, and the bed beyond was empty. The glow of the nightlight on the landing allowed her to make her way downstairs. Peering cautiously round the door of the sitting room, she could make out the shape of Emily, who was sitting in one of the chairs, leaning forward slightly over something that she had on her lap.

As her eyes adjusted, she could just make out that Emily's hands were positioned palm downwards, as they had been in the garage, and she seemed to be using them to scan whatever was on her lap.

Jane remained perfectly still and quiet. Instinctively, she knew that she should not disturb Emily. If she had been sleepwalking, it was important that there was no sudden movement or sound around her, and if she had come downstairs in full consciousness that night, Jane trusted that it must be for some important reason.

Eventually, she observed Emily making a movement as if shutting a book, and she stood up and put something on the low table before making her way towards the door. Jane stood to one side and watched her carefully as she slowly, but confidently, made her way upstairs and repositioned her door. She could hear a creak as Emily climbed back into bed.

Jane returned to the sitting room and put on the light. On the low table was her diary.

The following morning, Emily appeared downstairs looking bright and fresh. Over breakfast she reported cheerfully, 'I had a really interesting dream last night.'

'Oh,' said Jane carefully. 'Do you want to tell me about it?'

'Yes, of course I do, silly,' said Emily, patting Jane's hand affectionately.

'Go on, then. I'm all ears,' said Jane, laughing.

'I could see a girl. She was dressed in what looked like old sacks, and she had things tied round her feet that weren't proper shoes. I've never seen anyone dressed like that before.'

'How old do you think she was?'

'About as old as me.'

'Do you remember what she was doing?'

'I think there were some hens running around.' Emily shut her eyes and screwed up her face for a moment before saying, 'I think she might have been feeding them.'

'Do you remember anything else?' inquired Jane.

'There was more, but I can't remember what it was. I think there might have been sounds.'

'Sounds?'

'Yes, but I just can't remember what.'

'Well, be sure and tell me if you remember anything else about it.'

'Of course I will.'

'Maybe I should tell you what happened last night,' said Jane.

'Something else happened as well as my dream?'

Jane went on to tell Emily what she had witnessed.

'I came downstairs and looked in your diary?' said Emily, her eyes open very wide. 'But I don't even remember getting out of bed.'

'I certainly saw you, and I'm sure I was fully awake.'

Emily digested this information, and then said urgently, 'Did you see which pages?'

'No, I didn't. And of course you shut it before you put it down on the table.'

'Tomorrow's Monday, and I'm back at school,' said Emily. 'But I finish early on Wednesday. Can we choose another box to do on Wednesday?' Then she added suddenly, 'Maybe we'll find that special book.'

'Don't get too excited about it,' said Jane. 'But we can certainly do another box on Wednesday if you want. I'd like that.'

'And today you must tell me more about the story of the spirals.'

'I'll try,' said Jane.

'But you *promised.*'

'What I meant to say was that I'll try to remember as much as I can. Yes, we'll spend some time talking about them again after supper this evening.' Jane looked at her watch. 'Goodness!' she exclaimed. 'I'd almost forgotten about the swimming pool. We'd better get our things together. David and Asma will be here in a minute, and they'll be wondering what on earth's happened if we aren't ready on time.'

The children had always loved their trips to the pool, so Jane and Asma usually arranged to go together most weekends.

'All right, Auntie Jane. I'll be ready really quickly.' Emily jumped out of her seat and ran from room to room as she collected her things and put them in her swimming bag.

Soon the four were making their way down the road to catch the bus to the pool. The Sunday service was quite frequent, and the journey itself was only about fifteen minutes. Jane and Asma sat together on the seat behind David and Emily, who chattered away happily to each other.

'Here's the stop,' Emily reminded them as she jumped from her seat and pressed the bell. Jane smiled as she remembered the day when they had all been so deep in conversation that they had missed the stop and had to walk back to the pool.

Although it was quite busy, the pool was full of cheerful, friendly people, and the children made new friends as they played around in the shallow end. They both enjoyed swimming, but on busy days like this they preferred to play with the other children who had come, and on Sundays various animal-shaped floats were made available for them. The usual lifeguards were on duty, and had welcomed them cheerfully as they climbed into the pool. Jane and Asma swam up and down, sometimes stopping at the turns to have a chat.

After an hour, they all got changed and had a drink before they left, feeling relaxed and glowing.

On the way home, Asma told Jane that Bill was working all evening. 'How about coming to our house, and then we can make something to eat together?'

'That's a really nice idea,' said Jane. 'What do you think, Emily?'

David didn't give her time to answer, and said, 'Emily definitely wants to come. Don't you, Emily?' He nudged her, and the pair burst into laughter.

'Can David and I make something?' asked Emily.

'We can, can't we, Mummy,' said David. 'I'll get my cookbook out,' he added importantly.

'Have you got flapjack squares in yours?' asked Emily.

'Not sure, but it's got crispy crunchers,' replied David with an air of mystery.

'Crispy crunchers!' exclaimed Emily. What are those? I haven't had any before. Tell me what they are.'

'It's a secret,' said David, 'but when you come to my house, I'll let you see my book that tells you.'

Asma pulled at David's collar affectionately. She turned to Emily and said, 'Don't take any notice of his mysteries, it's all quite straightforward really.'

In the end the children were too tired to make anything, but spent a lot of time poring over David's cookbook, making plans for other occasions, while Jane and Asma made a rice dish from a recipe that Asma had recently discovered.

Back at home that evening, Jane and Emily sat down for the next 'chapter' of the story of the spirals.

'Are you sure you aren't too tired?' Jane teased Emily.

'Of course not,' Emily replied indignantly. Although she did feel tired, she wasn't going to admit it. 'You said Eva knows about them. What does she know?' She thought for a moment and added, 'And why has no one told me about them before?' She stared at her aunt accusingly, although she had a smile on her face. 'And when did the spirals come?'

'Questions, questions,' said her aunt. 'And you aren't giving me a chance to answer any of them before another one comes!'

'But there's so much I want to know,' Emily protested.

'I can see that. And I'd be just the same if this were about someone else's spirals. I've been trying to think about the date ever since we came across the diary. It must have been when you were very small... No... in fact... they came before you were born.'

'Before I was born! But that was *ages* ago.' Emily screwed up her face in intense concentration as she tried to think about her aunt's life then.

'And actually, I had the spirals for a while before anyone else saw them.'

Emily waited, as she could see that Jane was searching her memory.

At last her aunt continued. 'I first showed them to Ellen when you were only a baby, but I must have told her about them a little before that.'

Emily relaxed in her chair, her growing body had not yet reached the point where her legs fitted the soft seat exactly, but she was able to flop back. Her eyes grew dreamy. 'I like that,' she said contentedly. 'I like having the feeling that the spirals and I were born at the same time.'

'I don't think that they were born on the same day,' Jane corrected her, laughing. She suddenly became serious. 'How silly of me!' she exclaimed. 'I can't believe it!'

'What is it, Auntie Jane?'

'I've had the spirals in my diary all this time, and I've never really thought about the date when they came. Let's get it and have a look.'

She took it down from the shelves behind the sofa, where she had put it to keep it handy, and passed it across to Emily. 'I think it should be you who looks,' she said. 'After all, if it weren't for you, I wouldn't be thinking about the date.'

Emily looked pleased. She placed the diary across her knees and searched its pages carefully. 'November,' she said with a note of suppressed excitement.

Jane watched her. She could see that Emily was barely breathing in her concentration and sense of suspense. 'Here they are!' she exclaimed triumphantly. 'And it was on November 12th. That's just thirteen days before my birthday.'

'Are you sure?' asked Jane unnecessarily.

Emily looked at her, puzzled.

'Oh, I'm sorry. Of course, you're sure. It's just that I'm remembering what your mother told me.'

'What did she say?' asked Emily urgently. 'Tell me, Auntie Jane. Tell me.'

Jane noticed a note of mild panic in Emily's voice, and she took her hand, saying, 'We both miss her very much. I wish she were still here to talk to you herself, and I promise I'll always do my best to tell you everything she and your dad said to me.'

They sat together holding hands while Jane explained that Clare had told her that Emily had been due on the 12th, but that she had not given birth until nearly two weeks later.

'Does that happen to other people too?' asked Emily.

'As you know, I haven't had any children of my own,' Jane began. She started to say something else, hesitated, and then continued. 'Well... I have you... and you are very precious to me.' She stopped, and for a moment tears welled up in her eyes.

Emily didn't say anything, but she stroked her aunt's arm in the way that a daughter might stroke her mother's arm.

When Jane spoke again, she said gently, 'But, of course, I didn't give birth to you. In answer to your question, from what I've heard, I think it's not uncommon for a baby to be born a couple of weeks after the date it was due.'

Emily thought quietly about this, and Jane added, 'Another thing she told me was that she was certain about the date she had conceived, because your daddy was just home for a weekend.'

'I like that,' said Emily. A glow spread across her face. Her mother had often told her how they had longed for a baby, how happy they were when she was conceived, and how wonderful the pregnancy had felt. 'So,' she said slowly, 'the spirals were born on the day I was supposed to be born, but I waited for a while after that before I popped out.'

Jane smiled at Emily's graphic description. 'That's right.'

'And when did you tell Eva about them?'

'It was when Ellen brought her to visit me. I hadn't met her before. Ellen and Eva had been to a meeting that I should have been at, but I'd hurt my ankle and had to rest it. They came on afterwards to see me.'

'I like Eva,' Emily reflected.

'We were going to phone her, weren't we?' Jane remembered.

'Yes, and you must find out if she might come to see us soon.'

Jane thought again about how much she had valued Eva's quiet and staunch support throughout the time of their loss of George and Clare. And since Clare's death, Eva had spent a day or a weekend with them from time to time. She always took a great interest in Emily's schoolwork, and they both had an affinity for mathematical problems. Emily loved all of her studying with Eva, and Jane would watch them both at work, joined in intense concentration.

'I think we should give her a ring sometime soon. I hope she'll be able to come to see us before the Easter holidays,' said Jane.

'Why don't we phone her now?' asked Emily eagerly.

'Okay. Let's do that.'

Emily handed the phone across to Jane, who was soon telling Eva about unpacking her boxes, the finding of the diary, and the plans that they were making for the Easter break.

When she had finished the call she said, 'Emily, I'm afraid she's tied up until nearly Easter, and you'll be on holiday by then. But...' Here she paused dramatically.

'But what?' Emily climbed on Jane's knee, her legs dangling. 'What? What?' she persisted, gently digging her elbow into Jane's arm as if to nudge her into action.

'I was just about to tell you, but you won't keep quiet long enough,' said Jane, teasing. 'Eva has invited us to go and stay with her for a few days. Maybe even a week.'

Emily leaped off Jane's knee and bounced around the room. She loved Eva's house with the sofa bed in the living room and the quaint stairway that led up to the one bedroom.

Her bouncing stopped suddenly when another question occurred to her. 'Do you think she'll help us to look for somewhere else to live?'

'I'm sure she would if we asked her,' Jane assured her. 'And even if she wasn't actually looking at places with us, she would certainly talk to us about our plans.'

'Oh good, I thought so,' said Emily contentedly. 'And I'm glad you didn't say anything about me and the spirals. I want to save that up until we're staying with her.' She hugged herself, as if nourishing their shared secret.

'That's very interesting,' said Jane, half to herself, 'because a lot happened in her house that was to do with the spirals.'

Chapter Five

The weeks up to the Easter holidays seemed to pass quite quickly. Jane and Emily managed to sort through the rest of the boxes and containers in the garage. Emily was disappointed that they had not found the book that her aunt had been reading just before the spirals had appeared in her diary. However, Jane assured her that since both Eva and Ellen had had a copy, she would surely have a chance to see it sometime.

Jane had confided to Bill and Asma about her conversation with Emily on the subject of a possible house move. She was interested to find that they too had been thinking of researching about other secondary schools. They were in agreement that although the local one was adequate, David might benefit from a school with a larger range of options. Emily had been very pleased to hear about this, and she resolved that wherever she lived, she would keep in touch with him. She made Jane promise that if indeed they moved away, he could come and stay in the holidays whenever possible.

Emily packed her things several days in advance of their trip to Eva's. She was obviously very excited about the prospect of the holiday. They would travel by train, and Eva would collect them at the station. The good news was that Eva herself would be on holiday too, and she had planned to drive them to various locations in the vicinity of her home.

The journey went exactly according to plan, and soon Eva was loading their luggage into the boot of her car.

'It's lovely to have you both,' she said. 'Emily, you can use my bedroom while you're here. Jane and I will be downstairs on the sofa bed.'

'Oh, Eva! Can I? Can I really?'

Eva nodded. 'Yes, I remembered how much you liked it when you first saw it, and I thought you might like to try it out on this visit. Of course,' she teased, 'it also means that Jane and I can have secret chats once you're in bed.'

Emily smiled happily. She trusted them both, and she knew that her aunt would never keep anything important from her.

Late that evening, long after Emily was in bed and asleep, Jane and Eva were still deep in conversation.

'I've thought about this from every angle,' said Jane. 'There are so many unknowns that we're just going to have to feel our way slowly. There are two things we're both certain about. We want to be near enough to a good secondary school, and we want to grow some of our own food. And there's one more thing... I'd like to have the chance of some employment once Emily is settled in.'

'Have you gone into the finances yet?' asked Eva tentatively.

'As a matter of fact, I have. Just last week, I tried to get some idea of how much my bungalow and Clare's house are worth. Oh, I know the house belongs jointly to Emily and myself, but I still think of it as Clare's. The agent who lets my bungalow told me that recently the couple who are in it had asked him if I might consider selling it sometime in the future. He'd told them he would mention it to me, and they were happy with that. So it looks as though I might have a buyer without even putting it on the market.'

'If you do end up selling to them, you must make sure you don't accept less for it than you could get on the open market.'

'I realise that. But I must admit that when my agent first told me, I felt so grateful that I didn't consider that angle. Silly of me, I know.'

'Well, that's what trusted friends and agents are for – to remind you of essentials!'

'Do feel free to prompt me about anything. Actually, I did manage to get some idea of the value of both properties, and I had quite a surprise. Although Clare's house is a fairly standard modern villa, the fact that it's at the end of a quiet cul-de-sac, is part of a small development, and near the hospital, means that it should fetch considerably more than the valuation. And the present value of my bungalow is astonishing. I haven't got used to it yet.'

'Those pre-war bungalows are often much sought after these days,' Eva commented, 'especially where there is a lot of commercial development close at hand.'

'I'm sure that's what's done it.'

Eva continued. 'I'm not at all surprised that the people who are in it at the moment are interested in buying it. Its situation is excellent, it's solid, it has pleasant rooms, and it's near to everything. It should hold its value well.'

'So I now have figures in mind that should help us when we're looking around,' Jane concluded.

'You've said before that you both have an adequate income from the insurance policies that George and Clare took out.'

'That's right. Mine lasts until Emily is sixteen, and hers lasts until she finishes her education.'

'Thank goodness you were both provided for.'

'It has certainly meant that things have been less complicated, but I know I would have managed somehow.'

'Since you told me about your ideas, I've been thinking,' said Eva cautiously, uncertain about putting her own thoughts into the equation.

'Tell me what's in your mind,' said Jane eagerly.

Eva went on. 'I've been asking around and doing a bit of research myself. I had no idea what your budget would be, but I wanted to let you know that there are some places within about a ten mile radius of here that might interest you.'

'Go on,' Jane urged her friend. 'Tell me more.'

'I was thinking about you both wanting to grow some of your food. Most of the properties in the immediate vicinity that have big gardens are large expensive houses, and at the moment there are no allotment schemes available. However, I know that a bit further out, some of the larger farms have workers' cottages that have long fallen into disrepair. I began to wonder if any of these might come up for sale, and if so, perhaps there would be enough land attached.'

'That's a really interesting idea!' exclaimed Jane. 'We must talk to Emily in the morning and see how she reacts to it. I must admit that my mind has been pretty blank about the kind of property to look for, but your idea sounds good. I suppose that with all the mechanisation that has taken place on big farms over the years, the number of employees has fallen. Do you know where this kind of place is advertised?'

'No, but I could drive you round to look, and we could contact local agents,' Eva offered.

'That would be great. Are you sure?'

'Of course I am. I'd like to. I know that you aren't necessarily hoping to live near here, but it's a place where you can start to get some more shape round your ideas.'

'What about schools?' Jane asked, almost to herself.

'That's easy,' Eva replied briskly. 'I can get a list of local secondary schools from the Internet.' She jumped up and switched on her computer. She soon had details on her screen.

'That's good,' said Jane, relief showing in her voice. 'There's quite a description about each school. This could well give us more ideas. Presumably there will be something for all the schools in the country.'

'That's right. Do you want me to print some of this off?'

'Please. Then I think we should go to bed.'

The next morning, Jane and Eva woke to the smell of toast, and Emily appeared carrying a tray of tea for them.

'Breakfast in bed,' Eva commented. 'I don't know how long ago I last experienced this. What a treat.'

'I think I should really get up,' said Jane.

'I'm not going to let you get up until we've talked about the spirals,' said Emily determinedly. 'I wanted to talk about them last night, but I managed to wait till today.'

'Okay,' said Jane good-humouredly, 'but at least let me go to the bathroom first.'

When she returned, she found Eva and Emily deep in conversation.

'Where have you got up to?' she asked.

'I've told her about my dream,' said Emily, 'but you'd better tell her what you saw me doing with your diary.'

Jane explained.

'That's astonishing!' exclaimed Eva. 'It just puts me straight back to the time when we were all so affected by the spirals – you and me and Ellen, and later the others.'

'I promised Emily that we'd tell her all about it while we're here,' said Jane. 'So much took place in this very room.'

'In some ways I wish Ellen were here to help tell the tale,' said Eva.

'Me too,' agreed Jane.

'I'd like to see Ellen,' said Emily. 'I've sometimes said hello to her on the phone, but I've never met her.'

'I'll have to see if we can arrange it sometime,' said Jane slowly. 'Maybe there will be a chance in the summer holidays. She lives not far from Alnwick, which is several hours' drive north of here.'

'I don't suppose you've brought your diary with you,' said Eva slowly.

'No, and now I wish we had,' replied Jane.

Emily looked disappointed. 'We should have packed it, Auntie Jane.'

'I know,' said Jane. 'I feel really annoyed with myself.'

'Never mind,' said Eva suddenly, 'I think I've kept my copies of the spirals here somewhere. I'll have a look through my files and see.' She thought for a moment and then added, 'You know, it must be nearly ten years ago that it all happened.'

'That long?' said Jane. 'Oh, I'm being silly. I know it must be. Emily is more than ten now, and the spirals appeared in my diary on the date she had been due to be born.'

Eva stared at her. 'I never knew that before!' she exclaimed. 'Why on earth didn't you tell me?'

'As a matter of fact, I only realised it a few weeks ago – soon after Emily and I came across the diary. To be honest, it didn't cross my mind to tell you at the time. I don't know why, except that my head's full of moving house.'

Here Emily joined in. 'And I told Auntie Jane that she wasn't to talk to you about me and the spirals until we were here.'

'All right, I understand,' said Eva. Then she added, almost to herself, 'Our experience with those spirals was very far-reaching. It certainly changed the way I see and experience things in all kinds of different ways.'

'Let me help you to look for yours, Eva,' said Emily eagerly.

'That's a good idea. Tell you what. Jane and I will finish this breakfast. After that we'll tidy the room, and then we can pull out the table and search through the files in that bottom shelf over there.' She pointed to an assortment of ring-binders and box files that were crammed into the bottom section of her bookcase. 'If we have no luck there, we must go upstairs and look in the cupboards inside the eaves of your room, Emily. I have a lot of paperwork stored there.'

The search of the files in the living room revealed nothing, so Emily led the way up the stairs. There were three doors in the bedroom, each of which was about Emily's height.

'Which cupboard shall I try first?' she asked politely.

'Mm... I think we should start with the one nearest the window,' replied Eva. 'I wish I could remember where I put them. In fact, I feel rather silly that I can't lay my hands on them straight away.'

Together they worked through the contents of the first cupboard, while Jane prepared a picnic for their outing. They had explained to Emily what they had discussed the previous evening, and she had been very pleased at the prospect of an exploration so soon.

'Oh look, Eva!' Emily exclaimed suddenly, 'Something has slipped down the back of this shelf.' Emily was pointing to a large brown envelope.

'Oh, well done!' said Eva. 'I think that must be it.' Carefully she extracted the envelope from where it had lodged, stuck behind a low shelf in the cupboard, and pulled out its contents. 'Yes, this is definitely it.'

'Let's go downstairs and tell Auntie Jane,' said Emily eagerly.

They hurried down with their treasure.

'Ah, at last,' said Jane. 'I was beginning to think we'd have to give up. I've got the food ready. What shall we do?'

'I think we should go out now,' said Eva. 'We need to be out and about during office hours, so that we have the best chance of speaking to people. We can spend the evening with the spirals.'

'I want to look at the spirals *now*,' said Emily emphatically. Then she looked confused and said, 'But I want to go out too. Oh no! I want to do both at the same time.'

Jane laughed. 'I'm not surprised. So do I. Now that we're with Eva, and you two have found them, I just want to sit together and tell you everything we remember about them. But Eva's right, we really need to go out now. We don't want to miss the opportunity of making a start on our chance of looking at houses.'

'Okay,' said Emily. 'I'll carry the picnic to the car.'

Soon they had loaded everything that they needed, and they set off.

Driving along with the windows open, the three enjoyed the sounds and smells of spring permeating the air. As they approached Middleswell, the local town, they all admired the beautiful displays of crocuses that filled ornamental beds.

'Those must be maintained by the local council,' said Jane.

'Yes, that's right,' Eva replied. 'All the time I've been here, there's always a good display. I hear that they have a very good landscaping department.'

'I like the purple crocuses best,' said Emily.

The first stop was at an Estate Agent's. Eva found a parking space not too far away, and soon they were looking at the properties that were displayed in the window. Inside, they had a useful discussion with the woman at the desk, and then chose some sheets of particulars. Before they left, Jane gave the woman a note of her details so that other information could be sent to her over the following weeks. Emily was clutching the pile of sheets and holding them close to her chest.

As they walked back to the car, Emily, continuing to clutch the bundle, remarked, 'It seemed funny when you told the woman that your name was Jane Robson.'

'Why?' asked Jane, puzzled. 'That's always been my name.'

'But it's different from mine,' Emily said emphatically.

'Well, as you know, your mummy's name was Robson until she married your dad.'

'But now *we're* living together, and we have different names. When I was living with Mummy and Daddy, we all had the same name.' Emily's voice had started to rise.

Jane could see that Emily was clutching the sheets more and more tightly to her chest, and she began to realise that this conversation wasn't just about names. She changed her approach. 'Yes, that's right,' she repeated. 'You and your mummy and daddy had the same name, Foulds. And of course I've always liked that name. When Clare told me that she'd met George Foulds, I thought straight away what a nice name it was, and then when I met your daddy, I knew it wasn't just the name that was nice.'

Jane saw Emily's tight shoulders begin to relax a little. By this time she was standing by the car, while Eva was unlocking it.

'Jane,' asked Emily, 'do you think we should have the same name?'

'I think it's fine the way we are,' Jane replied, 'but we can think about it some more later if you want.'

Emily seemed satisfied with this, and asked tentatively, 'Can we go and look at one of these places this afternoon?'

'I hope so,' replied Jane. 'At the very least we'll be able to look at one or two from the outside. Let's choose one once we're back in the car, and perhaps we can plan a route that takes us to a picnic spot on the way.'

Closer study of the sheets revealed that none of the properties specially drew their attention, but they agreed to go and look at a small converted barn that stood about half a mile from the farm to which it had belonged, and was surrounded by garden on three sides. On the way there, they stopped in a quiet layby to eat their food.

As they sat finishing off the last of the fruit, Eva said, 'Of course, for the kind of thing you're thinking of, it's often the case that it never comes on to the open market. People hear by word of mouth, and some deals are made privately. What we need to do is try to find a way into a circle of people who are in the know.'

'Good thinking!' replied Jane.

Eva continued. 'So I've been wondering if I know anyone who might be able to help and advise, but I haven't come up with anything yet.'

They brushed the crumbs from their sandwiches out onto the road, and Emily was delighted to see that a confident chaffinch flew down and began to feed from them.

'Oh look!' she whispered quietly, tapping Eva and Jane on the shoulder from her position in the back of the car. She had their attention immediately, and she pointed to the bird. Another joined it. 'I wish we had some more crumbs,' she said sadly.

'I'm afraid that we've eaten everything,' said Jane in a low voice.

'Except my emergency supplies,' said Eva. 'I've got some oatcakes in the glove compartment. Jane, would you hand them to Emily?' She turned to Emily and said quietly, 'Just use as many as you like. I've plenty at home.'

By this time another bird had joined the first two, and there was obvious competition for the remaining specks of bread.

Emily crumbled an oatcake and threw the crumbs onto the ground near the birds. Instantly they flew up in a minor panic, but quickly returned to peck busily, and they took little notice when she threw more crumbs for them.

They lingered on while she fed the gathering of chaffinches and sparrows, but at last the oatcakes were finished, and they set off to find the barn. They found that it was in a pleasant location, but the layout of the garden, and indeed the layout of the house itself, was not the kind that attracted either Jane or Emily.

After they left, Jane said, 'Do you know, I think it helps a lot even to see places that aren't suitable.'

'Auntie Jane,' said Emily, 'how many rooms will we have?'

'It depends on how expensive the property is in any particular area, but maybe we should talk about how many rooms we would like to have, and then see if there's anything like that that we can afford. We'll need a bedroom each and a living room, kitchen and bathroom. If we have a place with a spare room, it would give us the option of having paying guests.'

Emily digested this information quietly, and she said very little on the way back to Eva's home.

Later that day, over a simple meal, Eva said, 'There's one person I can think of who might be able to help us.'

'Who's that?' asked Jane.

'Adam.'

'You mean Adam Thomas?'

'Who's Adam?' asked Emily curiously.

Jane explained. 'He's another of the people who knows about the spirals. We met him because of Ellen.'

Emily looked interested. 'Someone else who knows about the spirals? It feels funny that I didn't know about them until we unpacked your boxes, Auntie Jane.'

'There's quite a story about how Ellen first became friends with him,' Eva reflected. 'It all started on a train journey.'

'Does this mean you'll have to make some more chapters for me for the spirals story, Auntie Jane?' asked Emily eagerly.

'I think that's very likely,' replied Jane, smiling. She turned to Eva. 'Why do you think Adam might be able to help?'

'Don't you remember? His work was to do with agricultural advice, and he did projects all over the country. Of course, we don't know if he's working in that line any more, but it might be worth phoning Ellen to ask if she knows.'

'And if he is, he may have contacts,' said Jane. 'It's rather a long shot, though.'

'I know,' said Eva, 'but let's give it a try.'

She left a message on Ellen's callminder, and then the three cleared the table and turned their minds to the spirals.

'How about starting by spreading them out?' Jane suggested.

'Yes, why not?' replied Eva. 'After all, that's what I used to do years ago when you and Ellen and I were together here.' She looked at Emily. 'Shall we do this together?' she asked.

Emily looked very pleased. 'Oh, yes, please,' she said.

Eva handed the envelope to her, and Emily carefully slipped the sheets out. Jane's eyes filled with tears as she saw that she did this in exactly the same way as she had taken the photograph of George's material out of its envelope, more than two years previously.

Completely absorbed in her task, Emily arranged the spirals in a row down the middle of the table.

'I can't remember the order they came in the diary,' she said sadly.

'Never mind,' said Eva, 'there's something else to do instead. She pointed to the sheet that showed the double spiral. 'You see how there's a diagram on this sheet. Because the spirals here are on separate sheets, it means that you can actually arrange them as shown in that diagram,' she explained. 'I always followed it myself.'

Emily was very happy to learn this, and Jane watched, while Eva and Emily slowly arranged the spirals together.

Eva and Jane then told Emily the story of how Ellen met Adam, and Eva confirmed how it had come about that she had met Jane. And they told her the story of what had happened with the spirals.

It was Eva who began. 'Ellen had been a friend of mine for years and years. I knew that her mother had died when she was very small, and I remember how her father was killed in an accident when she was in her twenties.'

Emily sat on the edge of her chair. 'I didn't know about Ellen's mummy dying such a long time ago,' she said. 'Was she younger than I was when my mummy died?'

Eva looked across at Jane. 'I would say so,' she said, 'but what do you think?'

'Yes, I think it was before she started school.'

Emily digested this information quietly. Jane could see that it was having quite an impact on her, and she signalled to Eva to wait before continuing with the story.

Eva waited for a while, and then went on. 'When Ellen's father died I was worried about her. She has no brothers or sisters.'

'Like me,' Emily commented.

'That's right,' said Jane.

Eva continued. 'She just withdrew from everyone for a long time. Even when she started going out and about again, she seemed slightly detached from people. Well, one day, she was going to a meeting by train when a man came and sat next to her in the seat that he had booked, and somehow they had a conversation. Despite herself, Ellen found that this meeting had made an impression on her. The man was Adam, although she didn't know his name until later. I remember her telling me about it on the way to a gathering of people who were discussing projects about the environment.'

'You mean talking about the kind of things I used to talk about with Daddy?' said Emily seriously.

'Yes, that's right. She told me about the man on the train, and she told me about Jane and her spirals, and how she would ask Jane more about them after the meeting.'

Here Jane took over. 'But as you know, I'd hurt my ankle and couldn't be there. They were both so disappointed that they drove quite a long way specially to see me. Eva helped me with my ankle, and they stayed the night.'

'That's how you met my Auntie Jane, Eva,' said Emily dreamily. 'And it was because you wanted to know more about the spirals.'

'I remember that weekend so well,' said Eva. 'We were both worried when Ellen went into a strange state after she first saw the spirals. And we felt that we had to be so careful with her afterwards, because she seemed to remember nothing about what had happened to her.'

Here Jane added, 'If I remember correctly, she said that the last thing she remembered was studying the double spiral.'

'That one is extra special,' said Emily with conviction.

'How do you know that, Emily?' asked Jane gently.

'I just do,' replied Emily.

Jane gave Eva a meaningful glance, and Eva nodded before continuing with the story.

'I remember how I saw that Ellen's lips were moving as if she were speaking, but no sound came.'

'Yes,' said Jane, 'and after that we only looked at the spirals in this house – in this very room. It wasn't until much later that we heard Ellen speaking actual words when affected by them. Eva and I always prepared very carefully to be sure that Ellen would be all right.'

'Yes, it was all here,' said Eva, 'except for the last time, when everyone was at Ellen's.'

Emily listened to all of this with total absorption. 'Tell me about the last time,' she said, almost in a whisper.

Eva wavered for a minute. 'I thought perhaps we'd told you enough for now. After all, it's a very long story.'

'Please, Eva. *Please*.'

Eva looked at Jane, who said, 'I think you should.'

'It really is very complicated,' said Eva, a little worried. 'I'll make it as brief as I can for now. We can come back to it another time.' Then she continued. 'By that time there were several more people involved. It was truly amazing. Each one of us in the room was affected, each in a different way, but all of us closely and very deeply linked. My life has been affected by it ever since.' Here she paused before going on. 'There were things as well as the spirals that had led to us all coming together in that way. I can't pretend to understand it all, but I have certainly been a part of it, then and ever since.'

Emily was clearly transfixed by this information. She was leaning forward in her chair, staring at Eva, and looked as if she was straining her whole being in order to take in every word she uttered.

Jane stroked Emily's back and said, 'I think that's enough for tonight. We've had a busy day, and I for one am quite tired. I think we should start to think about bedtime.'

'But I want to know *everything*, Auntie Jane,' said Emily determinedly.

'I know you do, dear, but we did agree that it would be a chapter at a time,' Jane replied firmly. 'It's something that really can't be rushed. Eva and I promise that we'll tell you more soon.'

Emily seemed to relax. 'All right. Can we have a game of Happy Families before I go to bed? I've brought my cards in my bag.'

'Of course,' said Jane, smiling.

The following half hour was spent enjoying the game. It was obvious to Jane that Emily wanted it to go on forever, despite the fact that she was having trouble keeping her eyes open.

'Come on and clean your teeth. You're nearly asleep,' said Jane. 'You're too big for me to carry upstairs now, so we'll need to keep you awake until you're safely in bed.'

Before Emily finally agreed to go to bed, she asked suddenly, 'Can we leave the spirals out for the night?'

'I should be able to squeeze the table into one corner to make enough room for the sofa bed,' said Eva. 'Don't worry, I'll do my best.'

Although it was not much later that Jane went upstairs to say a final goodnight to Emily, she found her fast asleep.

In the morning, when Jane went to see Emily, she found that she was still asleep. She noted that her cheeks were a healthy pink colour and that she was breathing slowly and evenly. She heard the phone ring, and she crept downstairs again to find Eva deep in conversation.

'It's Ellen,' Eva explained. 'I think perhaps it would be best if you speak to her.'

Jane took the phone, and after a few pleasantries, spent the next minutes telling Ellen the beginnings of the plan that she and Emily were exploring. Ellen was only too keen to help, and promised to let Adam know, to see if he had any useful contacts.

'I think we should let Emily sleep on this morning,' Jane said as she finished the call.

'I agree. This idea of moving house is a big project, and there's a lot going on in all our minds. I think she needs her sleep, even if it means we don't go far today.'

It was nearly lunchtime when Emily eventually emerged. She looked a little disorientated, and Eva and Jane chuckled at her amazement as she noticed the time.

When she caught sight of the spirals again, she jumped.

'What is it, Emily?' asked Jane.

'I don't know... I feel a bit funny... and... Oh! I dreamed about that girl again.'

Jane and Eva waited.

'It was a bit different this time. I could see her in those clothes, but this time she was working in a kind of kitchen place. The room wasn't very big.'

'Was there anyone else around?' asked Eva.

'No, I don't think so.'

Chapter Six

The next couple of days passed pleasantly. Jane bought maps of the surrounding area, and Eva drove them to see a number of locations where property prices were realistic. Jane and Emily marked these on the maps, and whenever they visited a property, they would put a small coloured sticker on the map to show where they had been. Emily enjoyed this project greatly, and pursued her part in it enthusiastically. The weather had been favourable throughout. There was no rain or cloud, and the sun was warm, and pleasant for the time of year.

There had even been time to fit in a visit to the local swimming pool. In addition to this, Jane and Emily had accompanied Eva when she went to have her hair cut.

When they arrived back at Eva's house after the hair appointment, she examined her neat appearance in the mirror. 'I never know whether or not to start dyeing my hair,' she said with a note of uncertainty in her voice. 'Everyone else seems to be doing it these days, and I'm finding more and more grey hairs.'

'But you look fine,' said Jane, surprised. 'I must say that I don't give it any thought myself. And actually, I don't intend to,' she pronounced, with a note of rebellion in her voice. 'Anyway,' she added, 'wasn't it you who said that some hair dyes weren't safe to use?'

'You're right,' said Eva. 'How could I forget! Well I'll just put the silly notion out of my mind. I must have been affected by looking at all those posters of models that the hairdresser had up on the wall.' She felt annoyed with herself, but grateful that Jane had reminded her of the most important thing – her health.

'Why do people dye their hair, Auntie Jane?' asked Emily innocently.

'That's a very good question,' Jane replied. 'The easy answer to it is to say that people seem to want to look young all the time, but I don't think it's quite as simple as that.'

Just then the phone rang. Eva picked it up.

'Oh, hello, Ellen, it's good to hear you... You've got news? Great... Shall I hand you over to Jane, then?' She passed the phone across.

'Hello, Ellen... Oh, hang on a minute, I'll get something to write on.' Jane was about to put down the phone, but Eva handed her a notebook and pen, and she started to write. 'Harold Barber, Smithy Farm, Brookgate... Yes, I remember seeing Brookgate on the map. I'm sure we can find it okay. You've got his number? Excellent.' Jane wrote down the number and read it back to Ellen. 'Good, got it. I think we'll get on to that this evening.'

Emily tugged at Jane's sleeve.

'Hang on a minute, Ellen, Emily wants something.' She turned away from the phone and asked, 'Would you like a word with Ellen?'

Emily nodded, and Jane handed the phone to her.

'Hello, Ellen,' said Emily. 'I just wanted to tell you that Eva and Auntie Jane have been telling me quite a bit about the spirals.' She took a deep breath and added in a rush, 'Please can you come and see me and Auntie Jane some time?' Without waiting for a reply, she said hurriedly, 'I'll give you back to Auntie Jane now.'

Jane took the phone and said, 'Ellen, I'd like that too. I haven't seen you for years. Any time you're going to be travelling south, just let us know.'

When she put the phone down, she turned to the others and said, 'You've probably realised that she's managed to get hold of Adam, and he's given us a lead. I've got Harold Barber's details written here now. Apparently Adam's done a number of projects for Mr Barber over the past ten years or so, and knows him well. He's spoken to him about us, and Mr Barber is happy to help us as much as he can. He and his family have farmed Smithy Farm for several generations, so he's likely to be a good source of information.'

'It couldn't be better,' said Eva cheerfully. 'Let's see if we can fix something for tomorrow.'

A brief phone call resulted in an arrangement being made for the following afternoon, and once Emily had this news she could hardly sit still.

'It can't possibly be the answer to everything,' Jane warned her.

'I know, but it feels so nice that we've got more people to help us now,' said Emily.

Smithy farmhouse was set back from the road. Eva guessed that it had been built in the late nineteenth century. It was substantial, but was not in any way grand. Mr Barber was a pleasant man, probably in his sixties. He had the erect posture and broad stature of a farmer, and a welcoming but crushing handshake. His face was weatherbeaten, and the skin on his hands was rough and cracked.

'I've been looking forward all day to meeting you,' he said warmly. 'Adam Thomas' friends are always friends of mine. Please call me Harold.'

Eva, Jane and Emily introduced themselves, and he took them into the large kitchen. Emily noticed straight away that a corner of the room was barricaded off, and she went across to see why. Immediately two newborn lambs jumped to their feet and started making a lot of noise.

'It's nearly feeding time,' said Harold cheerfully. 'These are orphan lambs. Do you want to help, Emily?'

Emily's eyes shone. 'Oh, yes,' she said, breathless with excitement.

'I'll be back in a minute,' said Harold. He disappeared into a room off the kitchen, and soon returned carrying two feeding bottles of milk. 'Here you are,' he said, smiling. 'One for you and one for me.'

The lambs knew exactly what to do, and the milk quickly disappeared.

'That's got them settled,' Harold commented. 'Now we can get down to business.'

Jane glanced across at Eva. She felt mildly anxious in case Harold had received a different message from Adam than the one she had thought, but she saw that Eva looked completely relaxed, and her anxiety dissolved.

'You're looking for a bit of land,' Harold stated.

'Just enough for Emily and myself to grow some vegetables,' said Jane quickly.

He went on. 'And you want somewhere to live?'

'Yes, that's right, but we haven't decided where that might be,' Jane hurried to inform him. 'We're just toying with ideas at the moment, but we're very grateful that Eva's been taking us around this locality, and that Adam put us in touch with you. I'm hoping that the more we talk about the subject, the clearer we'll get about our ideas.'

'I can see that I might be jumping the gun, but I've got a proposition that could be of some interest to you.'

Jane stared at him.

'I've got some farm workers' houses about a mile from here. There are four of them – two pairs. I was trying to decide whether to knock them down or renovate them to let them out as holiday homes. I hadn't been thinking of selling them off, but I might consider it. At the moment, there's some fenced garden around them. Of course, it's completely overgrown, but that's easily fixed. I'm a single man, and when I'm gone my nephews will take over here, but I hope that'll be a long time ahead.'

'Er... I don't know quite what to say...' Jane stumbled.

'You don't have to say anything,' Harold reassured her. 'Why not just come and have a look?'

'Please, Auntie Jane,' said Emily determinedly. '*Please*,' she repeated insistently.

They all climbed into the Land Rover that was parked in the yard behind the house, and were soon standing outside a row of dilapidated buildings that were surrounded by flourishing patches of nettles, blackberry bushes and tree saplings.

Harold laughed. 'It's a bit of a mess, I know. But there's nothing that can't be fixed. All the outer walls are still intact, and the roof on this first pair is sound.'

Emily ran forward and disappeared through the door into the first house.

'Be careful!' Jane called after her.

'She'll be fine,' said Harold. 'Let her explore. I'll take you round the back and we can meet her inside. It'll give her a bit of excitement.'

Each house had a living room, kitchen and bathroom on the ground floor, together with a small bedroom. In each of the first two houses a precipitous staircase had been installed, leading up from behind the small lobby at the front door to two bedrooms in the roof space. Out at the back of each pair of houses was a row of outhouses that Jane guessed had been used for many different things over the years.

'I've got floor plans back at the house,' said Harold. 'You can take copies away with you if you want. Don't feel under any pressure or obligation. I'm not in any rush at this end.'

Emily, who had been very quiet for most of the visit to Harold's, didn't stop talking all the way back to Eva's house. By the time she was ready for bed, Jane and Eva both felt very tired. Emily had made only a token protest – complaining that they hadn't talked about the spirals that evening – but she did not have to be persuaded that after the excitement of the day, bed was the only option.

'I don't think I've ever seen her like this,' said Jane as she flopped down on the sofa bed, fully dressed.

Eva chuckled. 'It's been worth getting worn out for it. The visit was certainly a stunning success.'

'But what about her education if we move to a place like that?' said Jane worriedly. 'This morning I looked up the school for that catchment area, and it's no different from the one she'd be going to if we didn't move.'

'Mm, but not all education comes from schools,' Eva reminded her.

'That's right,' Jane acknowledged. 'Oh, dear, there are so many imponderables.'

'I know that I'm racing ahead,' said Eva, 'but I may as well tell you what's in my mind.'

'Go on.'

'If you were living so close to me, I'd love to do some studying with Emily.'

'Do you really mean that?' asked Jane.

'I wouldn't say it if I didn't mean it. I know she's a very bright and apt child. There are a number of subjects that she and I could explore quite deeply if I had regular contact with her.'

'I know she's very fond of you,' said Jane slowly, as she tried to take in the significance of what her friend was saying.

'And I noticed that Harold seemed to take to her.'

'I noticed that too.'

Eva yawned. 'Oh dear, I'm worn out,' she said. 'Why don't we sleep on it? We've got another couple of days before you leave, and there'll be plenty of time to talk about it all.'

Jane woke in the middle of the night, certain that she could hear a creaking sound. She froze, wondering whether or not to wake Eva. She looked at the bedside clock that Eva had placed on a small table, and could just make out from the luminous hands that it was 2 a.m.

She strained to see in the darkness, and it was then that she thought she could see a shape moving on the staircase.

Realising with some relief that it was Emily, she slipped out of bed to go and speak to her, but Emily made no sign to her, and instead walked straight to the table where the spirals were still laid out, and stood motionless beside it for a few moments. Jane stayed stock still, so as not to disturb her, and waited.

As she watched, she saw Emily lift her hands and hold them, palms downwards, over the spiral layout, in much the same way as she had held them over the diary weeks earlier.

Jane had no idea what to do. It was obvious to her that all of Emily's energy and concentration was focussed on what she was doing, and that what she was doing was entirely real to her. However, as yet, Jane had no way of understanding what this might be about. She wished that she had understood what had happened to Emily that had drawn her to the diary in the night. Maybe that would have given her some clues as to what was happening now. But it was no use thinking like this. The truth was that she simply didn't understand what was happening. And what about the scanning that Emily had done in the garage over the boxes? If only she had asked her more about that, rather than sidelining it in her mind as being some kind of game. After all, Emily had been fully awake at the time.

Jane began to feel cold. Her dressing gown was on the hook behind the kitchen door, and to reach it would have meant risking disturbing Emily. In any case, she knew that she could not stand still like this for much longer. She thought that one of the dining chairs must be quite close by, and began to edge her way towards where she thought it stood. She stubbed her toe on something very hard, and struggled to stifle a yell, as it was so painful. Her instinct was not to interrupt what Emily was doing, and to allow her the time that she needed with the spirals, but she realised that this could be difficult if she could not reduce her own discomfort.

At last she found the chair, and she slowly lowered herself onto it. Her bare feet encountered a heap of something soft on the floor, and she realised with relief that it was the cardigan that she had hung on a chair earlier. She did not take her eyes off Emily while she slowly lifted the cardigan and felt her way first into one sleeve and then the other. That felt better.

From her position on the chair she could still see the clock, and she saw that twenty minutes had passed already. She knew that from her new position she could last out for as long as was needed, and she began to think about the detailing of what she was observing.

At first, Emily had not seemed to be using any particular pattern of movement as she scanned the spirals, but as time passed this changed. It seemed to Jane that to begin with, she had been carrying out some general scanning movements that were quite slow, and mostly from one side to the other and back again. However, when she seemed to become more sure of what she was finding, her movements became quite detailed and specific. Whereas the original scanning had been done with both hands at the same height from the table, the movement of her hands now took place in several different planes, and the flow, speed and direction of the movements of each hand went through many changes.

It was nearly a quarter to three before Emily finished what she was doing. Jane saw her still the movement of her hands before reaching out and embracing something invisible above the spiral layout. After that she crossed her arms across her chest and bowed her head for a moment, before retracing her steps up the staircase. Jane waited until she heard the sound of Emily getting back into bed before she herself climbed in beside Eva and tried to sleep. But her feet were very cold, and her mind was crowded with questions about what she had just witnessed, and consequently she lay awake for a long time.

Chapter Seven

Eva woke at seven. She was surprised to find that she felt quite energetic, and she got up straight away. There was no sound from upstairs, and Jane was obviously in a very deep sleep, so she took her clothes into the bathroom and got dressed there, before tiptoeing back through the living room to the kitchen, and shutting herself in there to make porridge for her breakfast. She felt very hungry, and did not stint on the quantity. After this, she wrote a note to Jane and Emily to say that she had gone out for a walk, put on her coat and boots, and set off at a brisk pace. The air was cool and clear, and she felt invigorated.

It was a pity that they hadn't had time to talk about the spirals again last night, she thought as she strode along. Never mind, they could take some time this evening. And there was all the excitement about the visit to Harold's farm and seeing the cottages. 'I wonder what Jane will decide to do?' she murmured. It was good that Harold had made it clear that there was no rush to decide.

Eva turned left at the end of the road and began to climb the stile into the field.

'I wish I'd brought my stick,' she said aloud. Then she stopped with one leg over the stile. 'My stick!' she exclaimed. 'How silly of me. I must remember to get my special stick out and show it to Emily while she's here. It's all part of the story, and she's bound to be interested.'

The rest of the walk was spent looking at the bursting leaf buds of the trees, and thinking about how lovely it would be if Jane and Emily were living nearby. She could study so many subjects with Emily. The list was almost endless.

She arrived back at the house at about nine. Still there was no sign of movement from either Jane or Emily. The sun was shining by now, and was strong enough to warm the small porch that she had had made at the back door last summer. The porch was just big enough for a comfortable chair and a small table, as well as there being room for passage in and out of the back door of the house – a door that led from the kitchen. Quietly she selected a book from the shelves in the living room, and made herself comfortable in the porch. Soon she was engrossed in her reading.

It was eleven when she checked her watch. 'Goodness! How the time has flown,' she murmured.

Still there was no sound from the others. She began to wonder if she should wake them, but decided against it, and returned to her book.

At noon she made herself a drink. She thought again about waking the others, but it just didn't seem right to disturb them. After all, they were thinking about taking some big decisions in their life, and yesterday had put in front of them a pretty attractive possibility. Today should be a quiet day. There was no need to go anywhere.

She was just making herself some cold lunch, when Jane appeared in the kitchen wearing her nightclothes, with her cardigan on top with the buttons mismatched. Her hair was in a tangle, and she looked worn out.

'What time is it?' she asked, in a voice that was still thick with sleep.

'Half past one,' replied Eva, smiling.

'Half past one!' Jane repeated, astonished. She groaned. 'I've had quite a night.'

'Yes, you've had a long sleep,' said Eva.

'Yes, and no,' said Jane. 'I'll try to explain in a minute, but I feel a mess. I think I'll go and get tidied up first. Is there any sign of Emily?'

'No, I've not seen her, or heard anything.'

'I'm not surprised,' Jane commented as she headed for the bathroom.

Eva was puzzled, and waited patiently for Jane to return so that she could learn more. Jane's cryptic comments did not seem to make sense, but she was sure that there was some explanation.

'That's a bit better,' said Jane when she reappeared. She was now clothed, and she had sorted her hair out. She perched on the kitchen stool and said, 'Emily was up in the night for nearly an hour.'

'What was the matter?' asked Eva, concerned. 'Is she ill?'

'No, she seemed fine, but I don't know if she'll remember anything.'

'What do you mean?'

'She certainly didn't make any sign of seeing me when she came downstairs. And she spent the entire time focussing very intensely on the spirals.'

'Oh!' said Eva.

'Yes, exactly,' replied Jane. 'She stood there scanning the spirals the whole time. Look, I feel parched. Let me put the kettle on for a drink, and then I'll tell you everything I can remember.'

Eva sat listening quietly while Jane sipped her drink and tried her best to describe everything that she had witnessed.

When she was sure that Jane had finished, Eva said, 'It seems clear to me that Emily is relating to the spirals in a way that none of us ever achieved before.'

'I'd say that you're absolutely right there,' said Jane. 'In fact, I would go as far as to say that instead of being affected by them as we were years ago, she is connecting with them, and having some kind of interaction with them.'

'That could be right,' Eva agreed excitedly.

'Actually,' said Jane, 'I think the nearest I can get to describing what was happening is to say that Emily was in some way *reading* the spirals.'

'From what you've said, it certainly sounds as if she was interacting with them. And yes, part of it could be a kind of reading of them, but I've a gut feeling that there's even more to it than that.'

Jane and Eva sat in silence for a while, thinking about what they had said. If it were all true, then they were involved in something of potentially enormous import – something that could provide a giant leap forward into the unknown.

Eventually Jane broke the silence. 'Remember how we used to worry about keeping Ellen safe when she was affected by the spirals?'

'I could never forget that,' said Eva with feeling. 'Are you asking because you're worried about Emily?' she added hurriedly.

'No, definitely not. Curiously I feel no anxiety at all about her connection with the spirals. I began to speak about it because I wanted to say how differently I feel about Emily's situation. It's a huge contrast. Of course, it could just be to do with the fact that Emily and I live together, whereas Ellen lived alone.'

'That might be a part of it, but I don't think it's the main one,' Eva reflected.

'Ellen used to go pale and cold,' said Jane, 'and that isn't the kind of thing that happens to Emily. In fact, she seems to gather power and stature. Oh, I know it might sound an odd thing to say, but it's the nearest I can get to describing it.'

'Obviously you felt that Emily was okay afterwards, because you didn't feel the need to go upstairs to check that she was all right,' Eva observed. 'And I expect you'll remember as well as I do that as time went on, Ellen was less drained when affected by the spirals.'

'Oh... yes, she even seemed to glow.' Jane stopped for a moment, and then said, 'Eva, do you think that Emily could be starting from where Ellen left off?'

'I suppose it's possible,' said Eva slowly, 'but at this stage we have so very little to go on. It's best not to make any assumptions.'

'I agree entirely,' said Jane. She stood up and switched the kettle on again. 'I feel a bit cold. I think I'll have another hot drink.'

Eva looked at her sharply. The air temperature in the kitchen was comfortably warm, and could in no way be described as chilly. She reassured herself by thinking that maybe Jane was feeling cold because she was tired after being up in the night.

Just then there was a noise from the living room, and a moment later Emily appeared in the doorway, smiling broadly.

'Guess what time it is?' she said cheerfully. And before the others had time to reply she added, 'I've been asleep for ages and ages and ages!'

'I won't bother looking at my watch,' said Jane, 'because I know it must be about the middle of the afternoon by now.' She gave Emily a hug. 'It's good to see you,' she said, 'although...' Here she paused dramatically.

Emily was startled. 'What do you mean, Auntie Jane?'

Jane turned and winked at Eva, and then she looked straight into Emily's eyes and said, 'You were up for quite a while in the night.'

Emily protested. 'But I don't remember,' she said. Then she added, 'I suppose I didn't remember when I went downstairs that night at home to look at your diary...' She stopped and thought for a moment, and then asked, 'What was I doing?'

'You were looking at the spirals,' Jane explained. 'Look, you must be starving by now. Let's make some toast for you, and then I'll tell you what I saw. It'll take a little while because you were up for nearly an hour this time.'

Emily said nothing while Jane told her everything that she could remember. She just sat nibbling her way through her toast, taking in the whole picture.

When Jane had finished, Emily said, 'Thank you for sitting up with me, Auntie Jane.'

'You don't need to thank me,' said Jane. 'I just wanted to be with you.'

'I know, but if you hadn't, I wouldn't have known,' said Emily. She had a determined expression on her face as she tried to make her aunt understand the importance of what she was trying to convey.

'It's been a very big thing for us both,' Jane acknowledged.

Emily looked pleased. 'We didn't have time to talk about the spirals last night,' she said happily, 'but instead I got up and *talked to* the spirals!'

Jane smiled.

'It's going to be difficult to decide what to do this evening, isn't it?' said Eva. Then she added firmly, 'I think we should just wait and see.'

'How many more days have we got left?' asked Emily, a little anxiously.

'Don't worry,' said Eva reassuringly, 'I've got to go back to work in a couple of days' time, but if you want to stay on a bit longer, you're both welcome.'

Emily's eyes shone.

'Are you sure, Eva?' Jane asked.

'What do you think?' asked Eva, smiling. 'And now I've got a surprise for you.'

'A surprise?' said Emily, bouncing around the kitchen. 'Tell me what it is.'

'I've a friend who makes pottery, and when she heard that you were coming to stay, she told me to ask you if you'd like to make something with her. I could give her a ring to check that she's in, although I'm pretty sure that it will be okay to go across, because today is one of the days she suggested.

The phone call confirmed that it was indeed all right for them to go.

When Eva rang off, she said, 'It won't take us more than fifteen minutes to walk there. It's less than a mile away.'

A plump, round-faced woman, who seemed to be in her fifties, was waiting at her door to greet them, and she waved when she saw them coming along the road.

'Come on in,' she said. 'Now, you must be Emily... and you've brought your aunt with you. I'm Meg. Nice to meet you both. I've got some clay ready, and I've just put some cheese scones in the oven. I'm sure you'd all like a bit of fresh baking.'

Emily enjoyed the scones, and by the time she had finished making various shapes from clay, and had admired the bowls and jugs that Meg had made ready to go into the kiln, it was time to go home again.

'Now, you must take the rest of these scones back with you,' Meg insisted. She chuckled. 'If you leave them here, I'll only eat them, and there's a bit too much of me as it is. I can put your things in the kiln with mine, and when you come again you can see how they've turned out.'

'But...' Emily began. Meg silenced her. 'No buts,' she said firmly. 'I don't know when it'll be, but you'll be back. I'm sure of that.' Again she waved as they went back down the road, with Emily skipping most of the way.

At home they spent a quiet evening. Eva did some more reading, and Jane showed Emily how to do some string games – using a book that Eva had found in a charity shop.

When Emily was in bed, Eva suggested to Jane that the following day they could go and look at a few more properties.

'I'm open to that,' said Jane, 'but let's see how the night goes.'

'Yes, of course,' Eva replied. 'By the way, when I was out for a walk this morning, I thought of my carved stick, and wondered if Emily might like to see it. What do you think?'

'That's an idea, Eva,' said Jane. 'If we all have a good night, I'll make another picnic tomorrow. We can spend the day looking round, and then in the evening we can introduce Emily to your stick.'

Chapter Eight

The night passed uneventfully, and Jane felt refreshed when she woke to the sound of Eva moving things around in the kitchen. She jumped when she realised that someone was in bed with her.

'Surprise!' said Emily, who had been hiding under the covers, on the side of the bed that Eva had vacated.

'I think you must have had a good night,' Jane observed, smiling. 'That means that everything's right for another trip today.'

'I'll help to make the picnic,' said Emily eagerly.

'By the sound of things, Eva might already have made a start. Why not go and see, while I get myself ready.'

Emily jumped out of bed and disappeared into the kitchen. Jane could see that she was already dressed.

Eva appeared with a cup of tea in her hand. 'I'll put it on this table for you, Jane. Emily and I are busy planning our itinerary. By the way, do you mind if I put some breakfast into the picnic for you? It'll mean that we can leave sooner.'

By the time Jane had finished her drink, the others had loaded everything into the car and were ready to set off.

'I'm a lady of leisure this morning,' Jane commented with amusement.

'I think you deserve it,' said Eva.

'Oh, but I don't do all that much,' Jane protested. 'I just stay at home and look after Emily.'

Eva responded by looking hard at her and raising her eyebrows. 'I don't think I need to say anything about that,' she said. 'Now, Emily and I have decided that we're going to make our way to Overton. It's not easy to get to by public transport from here, but by car it's simple enough. The buses aren't all that frequent, and they take a rather circuitous route. There'll be an overlap between Overton and Middleswell in the properties being advertised, but I'm sure there'll be things we haven't come across yet.'

'That would be good,' said Jane. 'I haven't been to Overton yet. Whenever I've stayed with you before, we've always used the shops at Middleswell.'

Eva was about to drive off, when Jane stopped her. 'Could I just go back into the house and pick up the sheets about the secondary schools? I'd like to have them handy.'

'Good idea,' replied Eva. 'Don't worry, I'll go and get them. Wait a minute.'

She was soon back, carrying the information.

'I'd like to look,' said Emily. She took the pile of papers from Eva, put them on her knees, and began to sort through them carefully. Except for the rustle of moving paper, she was quiet for a long time, and Eva was nearing the next town before Emily spoke.

'There are four schools, and I've put them in order,' she pronounced. 'The one on top is the one I like best, and I wouldn't like to go to the one at the bottom at all.'

'That's really useful,' said Jane. 'We've been so busy, and I haven't studied them in any detail yet.' She peered over the back of the seat. 'Oh, I see that you've chosen the one that's in a very interesting building. I noticed it when I printed it off. What does it say?'

Emily read aloud from the page: ' "Seven hundred and fifty pupils." That's quite a lot, isn't it?'

'I know it sounds a lot, but secondary schools can be much bigger than that. The one you'll go to if we don't move has more than a thousand.'

'More than a thousand!' exclaimed Emily. 'But my school has nearly two hundred and fifty, and that's quite big.'

'And universities have many thousands of students,' said Jane.

Emily's eyes were open wide with astonishment as she absorbed this information.

'What else does it say, Emily?' asked Eva.

Emily returned to her sheet and read, ' "Co-educational. Small boarding house for overseas pupils." What does that mean, Auntie Jane?'

'It means that some pupils who usually live in another country can live at the school during term time.'

'Do they go home in the holidays?' Emily asked with a tinge of anxiety in her voice.

'Yes, usually. Although in the shorter holidays, they may stay with a friend or relative. Can you read out anything it says about choice of subjects?'

'That's what I'm excited about,' said Emily. '*And* it says there are lots of clubs at the school as well.'

Eva drew up in a car park, went off for a ticket, and stuck it to the windscreen.

'Have I missed anything?' she asked.

'No, we waited for you,' Emily reassured her. 'Look, Eva. Look at the long list of things here.'

She pointed to the second sheet about the school, and Eva exclaimed, 'Wow! No wonder you're interested in this one. Environmental studies, engineering, horticulture... I wonder how on earth they manage to arrange their timetable to include all of these. Let me see where it is.' Emily handed a sheet to her, and she peered at the small map. 'I hadn't known this school existed. It's a little off the beaten track, but not way out. Actually, I could work out how to drive past it later today if you want.'

'Let's see how the day works out,' said Jane sensibly. 'It's a good idea, but it might depend a bit on the location of the properties we might see today.'

A quick visit to each of the three estate agents produced particulars of six properties that could have been of interest, but on closer inspection did not appear to be suitable in one or more respects.

Again, Jane had left her details with each of the agents. 'Don't let's be put off,' she said energetically. 'Remember what I said before – even looking at places that aren't quite right can be helpful. Let's pick two and have a look.'

The first was a quaint bungalow that seemed to consist mainly of mismatching extensions, and it looked as if there wasn't much garden, although the particulars had implied that there was garden ground all round it.

'I wonder what it looked like before all this was done to it,' said Eva. 'And I wonder how they got planning permission for the extensions. What a mess.'

'The photo on the particulars was taken very cleverly,' Jane observed. 'You don't get a proper idea of the mess until you arrive!'

The journey to the next property was taken up by responding to Emily's endless questions about extensions and permissions. As was usually the case, she seemed to grasp the new information quickly, but there was a lot of it.

The next house was another surprise. It was a modern house – not unlike the one that Jane and Emily shared. What was so different about it was that it had a double garage set well to one side of it, and through the gap between they could see that there was a very large garden.

'The schedule says "extensive garden ground",' said Eva, 'but I had no idea that it would be as big as this.'

'Mm, it could be quite interesting,' said Jane. 'I wish now that we'd phoned to see if we could have a look round.'

'Never mind,' said Eva. 'Let's have a look at the immediate neighbourhood and see what we think about that. The house looks occupied, although I don't think anyone's in at the moment, and there's a private phone number on the schedule for arranging viewing. We could phone later if we're still interested. Come on, we'll leave the car here and have a good look round.'

They strolled together up and down the road. The neighbouring houses were a selection of designs, all of which were similar. By unobtrusively looking through gaps in vegetation and buildings, they eventually managed to make out that the garden of the property for sale was much longer than any others.

'How unusual,' mused Jane.

'I think we need to find a way of looking at it from the back,' said Eva decisively. 'Let's go and see.'

She marched briskly down the road to find the side road that she had noticed when she drove past. Jane, and even Emily, struggled to keep up with her.

'Wait for us!' called Emily breathlessly. 'I'm all floppy from sitting in the car for too long.'

Eva stopped and looked round. 'Sorry,' she said. 'I seem to be on a mission. I think I'll just have to get off it again.'

Emily was so convulsed with giggling that she couldn't walk at all for a minute or two.

While they were waiting for Emily to recover, Eva noticed a narrow footpath between the high fences of two houses.

'Look!' she said. 'There's a path here, and if Emily hadn't been giggling, I wouldn't have noticed it. I was so busy rushing off to find a road. Let's give it a try.'

The path took a sharp turn along the backs of the gardens of the houses that they had already passed, and led to a substantial brick wall at what seemed to be the side of the long garden.

'How very strange,' said Eva. 'I've never seen an arrangement like this before. Let's have another look at the particulars.' She pulled the sheets out of her bag and studied them. 'There's definitely nothing here about the path, so it can't be for access to the garden.'

The path followed the line of the wall. On its left they could see the bottoms of the gardens belonging to the houses on the side road that Eva had intended to follow. After a short distance, they could see the remains of what looked like the roof of an old-fashioned greenhouse attached to the garden side of the wall.

'That's interesting,' Jane remarked. 'It could be that these houses were built in the substantial grounds of an older house. Look at the size of this greenhouse. It extends quite a long way along the wall.'

'I think you're right,' said Eva. 'Let me think… the houses aren't more than forty years old, so I expect that we could find out fairly easily what was here before.'

By this time, the path was going downhill, and they could see that it led to a stretch of water surrounded by trees and undergrowth. As they neared it, they could see that signs had been posted around it. Emily ran on ahead to read one.

She soon came rushing back. 'It says "Save our Pond"!' she announced dramatically. 'Come and see.'

Eva and Jane hurried to see the sign. 'Oh dear,' they said together.

'What is it?' asked Emily insistently. 'What does "landfill" mean?'

'It means that if it goes ahead, there's no way that we would want to be living here,' said Jane flatly.

'Why not?' asked Emily innocently. 'Doesn't it just mean that someone is thinking of filling in the pond?'

'Well… yes,' said Jane slowly. 'But not only would the pond be lost, but the site would be used for dumping rubbish.'

'Dumping rubbish?' echoed Emily incredulously.

'I think that this would just be the access route,' mused Eva. 'They can't tip so close to the houses. Maybe there's an old quarry or something further on.'

Although they decided to abandon any further thoughts of the house, they walked round the pond, and could see straight away why the local people were trying their best to protect it. It was a lovely spot – full of wildlife interest.

'I wish them all the best of luck,' said Jane on the way back to the car.

Emily plied Jane and Eva with questions about landfill sites that stretched their knowledge to the full.

'So what Daddy told me is right,' Emily concluded. 'If everyone thought about how to use things over and over again, we wouldn't need so many of these places. Auntie Jane, we must try harder not to waste things!'

'We try pretty hard as it is,' Jane reminded her, 'but I'm more than willing to try even harder.'

Back at the car, Eva looked at the map. 'Give me a minute, and I'll see exactly where that school is.'

'Please can you tell me how far it is from your house and from Harold's farm?' asked Emily. She sounded very mature as she said this, and Jane understood straight away why she wanted to know.

'Well...' said Eva slowly. 'It's about four miles by road from here.' She studied the map again, and added, 'It's seven from my house and ten from Harold's farm.'

'If I came to live near you, Eva, how would I get to that school?'

'I'm not sure, Emily. We'd have to investigate, but it doesn't look straightforward.'

'That poses a problem,' said Jane. 'Emily and I rely on public transport, and there might not be a school bus that goes in the right direction.'

'Things can change,' said Eva, 'but I take your point. In any case, we may as well go past and have a look at it. It isn't much out of our way.'

Suddenly Emily said, 'Auntie Jane, I'm really, *really*, hungry. Can I have some of the picnic?'

Jane looked at her watch. 'No wonder,' she said, 'it's three thirty already! I think we should all have something straight away.'

By the time they reached the school, it was nearly five.

'I could drive in and see if the office is still open,' said Eva. 'We might be able to get more information that way.'

'Yes, let's,' said Emily from the back seat.

Eva turned the car through the imposing stone gateway that was clearly the remains of something far more grand. She drove along the curve of a drive that was lined with interesting shrubbery, and stopped in a parking area next to the main building. There was no one in sight, and the main door was closed, but Jane got out to check whether or not it was locked.

As she approached it, a man with a large bunch of keys was just securing it from inside, and she signalled to him that she had something to ask. He opened the door with an air of slight reluctance, and Jane quickly explained that she might be moving to the area and that she would like some details about the school. Gruffly, he asked her if she had looked at their website, and when she said that she had, he became more amenable, and he let her in while he unlocked the office and collected some more information.

'I'm sorry I can't be of any more help,' he said. 'I'm just the caretaker. Office hours in the holidays are mornings only. We don't have to look for pupils to come here,' he finished. He locked the door behind her.

Jane returned to the car.

'How did you get on?' asked Eva.

Jane explained. 'It was a bit mixed,' she said with a bemused expression on her face, 'but I do have some more information that we can look through. I got the impression that the school's pretty oversubscribed.'

'What does that mean?' asked Emily.

'It means that far more pupils want to come here than there are places for them.'

'Oh,' said Emily as she took this in. Then she turned her attention to the information that Jane had passed to her, and Eva headed in the direction of home.

Emily was very quiet in the back of the car, and from time to time Jane glanced behind her to see if she was all right. It seemed that she was determined to make as much sense as she could of what she was reading, without asking for help, and Jane did not intrude.

Over the evening meal, they discussed their day.

'It's strange, isn't it, how much you can take in during only one day, without realising it,' Jane reflected.

Emily began to look very tired, and Jane suggested that she went to bed early.

When she had tucked her in, she returned to the table where Eva sat reading about the school, and said, 'I know you didn't get a chance to show her your stick, but there's so much going on at the moment, I

71

didn't want to overload her.'

'Quite right,' Eva replied. 'I thought the same. That's why I didn't mention it.' She sighed. 'One more day, and then I'm back to work. I know it seems odd starting on a Friday, but it's just the way things have worked out. At least I'll be able to spend the weekend with you afterwards.'

'Yes, that'll be good,' Jane agreed. 'And I think that Emily and I should go home again on Monday morning at the latest.'

'I'd like you to stay until then,' said Eva warmly. 'If it would help, I could drop you off at the station early that morning.'

Jane looked thoughtful. 'I'd like that, but Emily's due to start school again on the Tuesday, and I think we need a couple of days at home before that. To be honest, I think we should leave here some time on Saturday, but we can speak to Emily tomorrow and decide finally what to do.'

The following morning, they decided that Emily and Jane would catch the midday train on Saturday.

'I don't want to go away and leave you, Eva,' said Emily. Her face had a serious expression. 'But I do have to get ready for school.' Then she burst out, 'Auntie Jane, I'm worried that we won't be able to do everything here before I go home.'

'Don't worry,' said Eva soothingly. 'You can come back in the summer holidays if you want. There'll be more time then. I might have to be at work, but I'll certainly be around in the evenings and at weekends.'

Emily relaxed visibly. 'And can I talk to you on the phone if anything important happens?'

'Of course you can, dear,' said Eva. She felt touched by the fact that Emily regarded her as being fully involved, and she felt quite tearful.

'What's the matter, Eva?' asked Emily, touching her arm.

At first, Eva felt at a loss as to what to say, but eventually managed to let Emily know that she would miss her. Inwardly she became very aware that she hoped that Emily and Jane would indeed come to live nearby, but she was determined that she would do nothing that would put pressure on them.

'There's something I want to show you, Emily,' she said. Then she faltered and turned to Jane. 'Is that all right, Jane?'

Jane could see that her everlastingly competent friend was struggling. She could see that she was feeling closer to Emily, and that this was having a profound effect on her – one that she could not yet put into words.

Jane turned to Emily and said, 'We'd planned to tell you about this before, but our time has been rather action-packed in a lot of ways, so we'd put it off.' She smiled across to Eva and asked, 'Where is it?'

By this time Eva had recovered her composure. 'Tell you what,' she said to Emily. 'Shut your eyes, and I'll be back in a minute. Don't open them until I say.'

'Okay,' Emily replied as she engaged with the drama.

Eva slipped off as quietly as she could, and returned with her stick, which she put on the table in front of Emily. 'You can open your eyes now,' she said.

Emily looked at the stick and said, 'It's a walking stick. It's the same colour as the one that Mummy used when she was very ill. But... it's got some carving on it.' She looked at Eva. 'Who did the carving?' she asked.

'I'm not sure,' Eva replied, 'but I've always assumed that it was the old man who gave it to me.'

'Will you tell me about him?' asked Emily instantly. She looked at Eva attentively and waited.

'I'll tell you what I can remember,' Eva replied. 'I was driving home from Scotland and I needed a rest, so I turned off the main road and stopped in a lane. It must have been autumn because the hedgerows were laden with blackberries.' She laughed. 'I couldn't resist them, and filled a small bag. Then I came across a cottage where an old couple lived, and they gave me a wonderful drink.'

Jane noticed that Eva's eyes looked dreamy as she remembered it.

'I've no idea what the drink was made of, but it tasted heavenly, and for a while afterwards I seemed to see things in a different kind of way.'

Emily made as if to ask something, but managed to hold back and let Eva continue.

'After that they showed me several sticks, and asked me to choose which one I wanted. I was certain that it was this one.'

Emily's finger traced the carving as if almost caressing it as she listened to Eva's story, and when Eva had finished she said, 'I think

73

this is two people trying to be very close about something important.'

'That's what we thought,' said Eva. 'There's one more thing I want to tell you. There have been times when this stick has helped me, and I believe that it helped a girl who used to come here.'

'Tell me about her, Eva,' Emily urged.

'The girl's name was Hannah, Hannah Greaves. She used to come here with her father. She was quite ill when I first knew her, but she gradually got better, especially once she'd found out what happened to her mother.'

Emily sat bolt upright in her seat. 'Something had happened to her mummy!' she exclaimed.

'Yes, her mummy had disappeared when she was quite small, and it wasn't until she and her daddy searched and found out exactly what had happened to her that she got properly better.'

Emily swayed a little in her seat, and Jane quickly pulled her chair next to her and put her arm round her.

'I'm sorry, Emily,' said Eva, gently, 'I hadn't thought that I'd end up talking so soon about Hannah.'

'It's all right, Eva,' Jane reassured her. 'Emily and I talk a lot about her mummy and daddy not being with us.'

'I know you do. I just think that Emily has had so much new information this holiday that I should have waited until another visit before I told her that part of the story.'

'No, I'm very glad you told me,' Emily interrupted emphatically. 'Where is Hannah now?'

'I'm afraid I don't know,' said Eva. She turned to Jane. 'How old do you think she must be by now?'

'I would guess she must be just about grown up. Possibly about twenty?'

'Had her mummy died?' asked Emily.

'Yes. It transpired that she gone away abroad, and that she got very ill and died,' Eva explained.

'We still don't know what happened to my daddy,' said Emily sadly. 'But we know everything that happened to Mummy.' She was quiet for a moment, and then sobbed out, 'I want to know what happened to my daddy!'

'I know, love,' her aunt comforted her. 'All of us want to know what happened to him, and I never give up hoping that one day we might know.'

'Do you really?' asked Emily, looking a little less distressed.

'Of course,' Jane confirmed. 'I know I don't say much about it, but it's on my mind nearly every day.'

Emily stared at her. 'You should have *said*.'

'I can see that now.'

They hugged each other tightly, and Jane said confidently, 'I promise I won't make that mistake again.'

Emily looked across at Eva and said, 'Thank you for showing your special stick to me.'

'That's all right,' Eva replied. 'I liked telling you about it.' She stood up. 'I think I'll put it away for now.' She picked it up, and as Emily did not object, she went to put it away in a cupboard. When she returned, she asked carefully, 'Do you still have that special material?'

It was Jane who replied. 'Yes,' she said. 'If you remember it took quite a while before we got it. Clare had to keep on at them before they sent it.'

Here Emily took over. 'Mummy and I chose a special frame to put it in, and we hung it on the wall in my bedroom. When we move house, I must carry it myself,' she added emphatically.

Jane took up Emily's cue and said to her. 'Since we've been here, it looks as if both of us have decided that moving is definitely on the cards now. I've been thinking quite a lot about what it's going to involve, and I know that's only a start. The main thing is that we mustn't rush at it. Not only is it a big change for both of us, but also it'll be rather expensive if we make a mistake about the house we buy. We've a lot to talk about over the next weeks.'

'I'd like to see Harold again before we go home,' said Emily. 'Can we, Auntie Jane?'

'I'd like to as well,' Jane replied. 'Eva, shall we give him a ring and see if there's a chance?'

Eva handed the phone across, and Jane keyed in the number. There was no reply, and she left a message.

Since this was so important to them, they decided to stay at home to see if he might phone back. Eva found some biscuit cutters in the back of a kitchen cupboard, and she and Emily spent most of the afternoon making a considerable quantity of spicy biscuits.

'They're really for Sunday because it's Easter,' Emily explained, 'but we can eat some now while we're still here.'

'I think you should take most of them home with you,' Eva suggested.

'No, Eva,' said Emily firmly. 'We'll share them out properly.'

They were just finishing the last of the tidying up when they heard the phone ring. It stopped quickly, and they assumed that Jane had picked it up.

'If that's Harold, we can leave it up to her,' said Eva.

A few minutes later the door opened and Jane said, 'That's Harold now. He says he can come and pick me and Emily up tomorrow afternoon and bring us back later. What do you think?'

Emily bounced up and down. 'Yes, yes and yes!' she said loudly, hoping that Harold would hear her.

Jane returned to the phone. 'I think you'll have heard that the decision has been made. Yes... we'll be ready around two.'

Chapter Nine

Eva left early for work the next morning, and Jane let Emily sleep on. She had been so excited about the plan to spend time with Harold that she had found it difficult to fall asleep that night, and Jane had had to read to her for a long time before she eventually slept. She woke her at eleven so that they could have some time together first.

'I want to feed the lambs again. I want to feed the lambs again,' Emily sang as she put on her clothes. She called down the stairs, 'Auntie Jane, can you hear me?'

'Yes, I hear you. We can ask him.'

'I know that,' said Emily almost dismissively. 'It's about something else.'

'What's that?'

'We haven't asked Eva about the book yet.'

'Which book?' said Jane in puzzled tones. At this precise moment her head was full of house valuations, buying and selling houses, and growing food.

'The one about the boy.'

'Which boy?' called Jane as she stirred porridge that Emily had requested.

Emily came running into the kitchen, half-dressed. 'Auntie Jane, you know the one I mean. It's the book where the boy grows things in the garden in spiral patterns.'

'Oh! I'm sorry. My head's full of so many other things. I'll write a reminder to myself and leave it on the table. We mustn't forget to ask her.'

Harold arrived early in his Land Rover.

'Couldn't wait to show you my lambs again,' he explained, smiling broadly as Emily climbed in beside him. Emily made herself as narrow as she could, and Jane climbed in next to her.

'Off we go,' said Harold cheerfully. 'And I've had some ideas I want to talk over with you. No obligation on either side.'

'What does that mean?' asked Emily politely.

'It means that we can all chat to each other about what's in our minds, and nobody has agree to anything,' Jane explained.

'We do a lot of that. Don't we, Auntie Jane?' said Emily confidently.

'Would you like a tour of the farm before we go up to the house?' asked Harold.

'Yes, *please*,' said Emily, not thinking of turning to her aunt for confirmation.

Jane smiled to herself. She loved to see Emily looking so happy, and being so spontaneous. This holiday had been good for them both.

'I'll start by showing you round all the fields,' said Harold. 'I'll tell you what I'm using them for this year, but don't worry if you don't remember any of it. I'll just enjoy your company while I check them.'

An hour later, he drew up at the farmhouse.

'Come on in,' Harold said expansively. 'I've been looking forward to this ever since I got your message.'

Emily went into the kitchen and gasped with surprise. The two lambs that had been there the last time now had several companions.

Harold laughed. 'Yes,' he said, 'it can be a busy time of year. I've got some orphans here, and one or two were born as triplets and the ewes couldn't manage.'

'I'm an orphan,' said Emily, looking up at Harold as she imparted this as a piece of factual information.

For a moment, Harold faltered, but he gathered himself and said, 'Yes, there are a lot of us about – lambs, and people, too. My mum and dad died when I was just about grown up, but I was still quite young. Although I was only eighteen, I took the farm on, and as you'll have seen, I made a go of it.'

It was difficult to hear over the noise of the lambs. They had jumped up as soon as they heard Harold's voice, and were making quite a din. He looked at his watch.

'Only half an hour to go. I think we'll feed them now,' he decided. 'Otherwise we'll get no peace.'

Jane watched Emily revel in the task. She got a mixture of milk and saliva all down her jeans, but it didn't bother her at all. In fact, she seemed to be quite proud of it, and compared the stains with the ones she could see on Harold's clothes.

Later, when they were seated round the large wooden table,

munching biscuits and drinking tea, Harold said, 'This table has been here from before I was born. I remember my mother rolling out the pastry on it. Of course, at that time we had quite a few staff, and they all would come in for something around ten each morning. She prided herself on having something substantial for them.' He paused only for a moment before saying decisively, 'Right, let's get down to brass tacks. I'll give you my thoughts, and then you can give me yours.

'As you know, I've got those houses that are in danger of falling down. Since I met you, I've been having ideas of doing them up. The first question is whether or not you'd be willing to advise me about décor. It's something I've never taken an interest in, so I wouldn't know where to start, and I don't want to ask some faceless person that I've never met.'

Jane opened her mouth to speak.

'No,' said Harold firmly. 'I haven't finished yet. If that plan went ahead, I'd pay you for the service, of course. Thought number two is that since you're thinking about moving, you might like to live in one yourselves, renting it from me, to see what it's like living somewhere else. That way, if it doesn't work out, you could just go home again. I'd have the garden cleared and turned over, so you could get on with growing the things you wanted. Thought number three is that you might like being there so much that you might want to buy from me. The answer to that is I think it would be possible.'

Jane was looking pink. She felt flustered and stressed, and didn't know what to say. Emily was looking at her expectantly, but no words came from her aunt.

'Sorry,' said Harold, 'I'm blunt, and I usually come straight to the point. Remember that there's no obligation, and definitely no rush to decide. I told you before, they've been lying empty for years, and I haven't bothered with them so far.' He paused, struggled a little, and then added, 'I just want you to know that I'd be happy for you to be there. I think we'd all get on fine together.'

Jane gathered herself and said, 'Thank you very much. I feel touched by your suggestions, but this is all so unexpected that I'll need a lot of time to think things through. Can I leave it that I'll get back to you within the month?'

'You can have longer than that if you want,' said Harold. 'Just take your time.'

'There's Emily's schooling to consider, for example.'

'Yes, I'd thought of that, and I've no idea what the schools around here are like now. It's a long time since I was at school, and I left at sixteen. As it worked out, it was a good job I did, because I was better prepared for taking over.'

'I like it here,' said Emily shyly. 'I'm not big enough yet to know everything about the money and things like that, but I know that Eva would love us to be near, and she's said that if I ever live near her she can give me extra lessons in lots of subjects. I'd like that,' she said, hugging herself. She added dreamily, 'And maybe David and Asma and Bill could come and stay for some holidays...'

'Let's leave the whole thing for now,' said Harold in his blunt way. 'I've got some old farming photos in albums upstairs. You might be interested to have a look through them. Collecting them has been a hobby of mine for the last few years.'

They made their way upstairs together, and Harold led them into what had been a large bedroom. 'This was my parents' room,' he said. 'I changed it into my office about thirty years ago. You can sit at my desk, and I'll hand the albums over to you.'

Jane and Emily settled themselves, and Harold passed album after album from the rough shelving that he had strapped to one of the walls.

'Stop, you're going too fast,' said Emily. 'I want to look at them all properly.'

'All right, I'll get on with some of this paperwork. Ask me anything you want as you go along. And don't worry if you don't get through it all. You're welcome to visit again when you come back to see your friend Eva. Any friends of Adam's are friends of mine. He's given me good advice over the years, and I'm mightily grateful to him for it.' Then he lapsed into silence as he worked through a pile of papers.

At length, he paused for a break.

'How are you doing?' he asked. But without waiting for a reply he said, 'You're good work companions. I've got plenty done. Thanks.' He looked at his watch. 'Nearly six. Better be going. Eva will be wondering where you are.'

'We've had a wonderful afternoon, Harold,' said Jane. 'Thank you so much.'

'That's all right,' he replied gruffly as he reached in his pocket for his keys. 'Come on then, the taxi's waiting.'

Emily nudged her aunt as they made their way down the stairs.

'What is it, Emily?' asked Jane in a low voice.

'Ask him if we can phone him from home if we've got any questions about what he said,' she whispered.

'All right, I'll ask him on the way back in the Land Rover.'

They were nearly at Eva's house when Jane spoke to him about it.

'I feel a bit hesitant about asking, but Emily and I wanted to know if we can phone to talk about your ideas if we need to.'

'Phone away whenever you want,' Harold replied. 'In any case, you can phone for a chat if you want, whether or not it's about houses. As far as I'm concerned, you're friends. We might move into doing some kind of business together, and we might not.'

He dropped them off at Eva's house and disappeared up the road.

There was no sign of Eva when they let themselves in.

'That's funny,' said Jane uneasily, 'I thought she'd be back by now. Let's make a start on the evening meal.'

'Yes, let's,' said Emily as she hung up her coat and went to wash her hands.

As they prepared the vegetables together, Jane said, 'We're going to have to get up early tomorrow morning, ready for Eva to drop us off at the station, so we mustn't stay up late.'

'I'll pack my things before I go to bed,' said Emily cheerfully. 'I don't want to leave Eva, but I do want to go home to see David. I've got lots and lots to tell him, and we've got to get ready to go back to school. We've only got one term left, and then it'll be summer, and after that it's a new school for both of us. I wonder where I'll be going?'

'That's one of the things we've got to put our minds to,' said Jane.

They had just set the pans ready on the cooker when Eva came in.

'I'm sorry I'm so late,' she said. 'There was a huge tailback on the main road. I think there'd been some kind of accident. There was certainly broken glass all over the place at one point.'

'Thank goodness you're all right,' said Jane. 'I had a feeling that something was wrong. What a relief you're back safely.' She gave her friend a close hug.

'We've got the food ready to cook, Eva,' said Emily. 'And we've got lots of news. Haven't we, Auntie Jane?'

Jane smiled. 'I'll turn the cooker on now, and soon we can tell Eva about our afternoon.'

As they ate their meal, they told her about what had happened, and Eva's reaction to their story was one of unconcealed delight.

'I know you've not decided anything yet,' she said, 'but this is such a good opportunity. Once you're back at home, you *must* keep me up to date about the direction your thoughts are taking. Of course, if there's anything you need to know about the general locality, all you have to do is ask me, and if I don't know, I'll find out for you.' Although she hadn't finished eating, she stood up and began to stride round the room energetically. 'Oh, my head's full of all the things that we'd be able to do together if you were close by.'

Jane watched her with open amusement.

Eva stopped her marching and demanded, 'What is it?'

'I've never seen you look like this before, Eva,' said Jane. 'You're always so calm and ordered. I've just not seen you showing your feelings like this.'

'I like it,' said Emily.

'So do I,' said Jane.

'Eva!' said Emily suddenly. 'I've got to ask you something important.'

Eva stopped in her tracks and waited.

'Auntie Jane said that you might have your copy of the special book that she had been reading just before the spirals came into her diary.'

'Of course I have. It'll be somewhere in the house, but exactly where I can't remember at the moment.'

'Can I look for it now?' asked Emily with some urgency. 'We're going to be leaving tomorrow, and if we don't find it now, I won't have seen it.' Her last words were rushed, and her face grew pale. She looked as if she were going to cry.

'Don't worry,' Eva hurried to reassure her. 'If we can't find it tonight, I'll keep on looking. But there's something else, isn't there?' she said astutely.

By this time Emily had pushed her dish away from her placemat, put her arms on the table and her head down on them. Jane got up and stood behind her, stroking her back.

'I think I want to go to bed, Auntie Jane,' Emily's muffled voice came from under her arms.

'I'll help you to get ready if you want,' Jane offered.

'Just come up when I'm in bed.' Emily slid off her chair and disappeared into the bathroom, leaving Jane and Eva staring after her in consternation.

'I think I'll just do as she asked,' said Jane. 'Perhaps something will come out when I'm with her upstairs.'

'Call down to me if there's anything you want,' said Eva. 'I'll tidy up a bit, but I won't be doing anything that I can't interrupt.'

Emily slipped out of the bathroom silently, like a shadow, and vanished up the stairs.

Jane and Eva waited for a few minutes, and then Jane followed, while Eva began to clear away the dishes. When Jane entered the bedroom, she couldn't see Emily at first, as she had burrowed down so far under the duvet that all that was visible was a bulge. She perched on a corner of the bed and waited.

At length, she felt movement in the bed, the top of Emily's head appeared and then Jane could see her eyes.

'Shall I guess, or shall I wait for you to tell me?' she asked.

Between them, this was already a well-established way of going about things, and Jane waited for her instructions.

'You start, and I'll join in,' said Emily in a wobbly voice.

Jane began. 'It's been extra special staying with Eva. We've had the time and energy to do a lot more things than we'd planned, and some really lovely things have come out of it, but we haven't had much time to talk about it all yet.'

The whole of Emily's head appeared, and she nodded vigorously.

'Harold has been very kind to us – just like a daddy might be.'

Emily's lip began to wobble, and tears sprang into her eyes.

'I've felt a bit like that about it too,' said Jane quietly. 'And another thing is that I think we've both seen a side of Eva that we haven't seen before.'

Emily nodded vigorously again, and then started to sob. 'I don't want to lose *her* as well,' she managed to choke out.

'Oh,' said Jane, light beginning to dawn, 'you were as worried as I was when she wasn't at home.'

Emily wiped her nose with a tissue. 'Yes.'

'And when she was striding round the room, she reminded me so much of how your mum used to walk when she was very determined about something.'

'Yes.'

'And she doesn't say how important we are to her because she doesn't want to feel that she's putting pressure on us to come and live near her.'

'Auntie Jane, shall we ask her to come up so we can tell her that we know?'

'I think that's a very good idea. I'll call for her.'

Soon Eva had joined them, and they sat and talked for a long time. When Emily eventually dozed off, Jane and Eva tiptoed downstairs.

'I'm very glad we had that talk,' said Eva sincerely. 'It isn't the kind of conversation that you can have on the phone.'

'Absolutely not,' Jane agreed. 'By the way, don't worry about looking for that book tonight. I'm certain that Emily's concern about it was more to do with our need to get together to talk than about having the book right now.'

'I agree, but I'll have a quick look before we get into bed, and if I don't come up with it, I'll see if I can get a copy on the Internet and have it sent to her.'

'Thanks, I'm sure she'd like that.'

Next morning, on the way to the station, Eva told Emily that she hadn't managed to find the book, but said to her that she would do her best to get a copy for her. Emily was well pleased with this arrangement, and when the train drew into the station, she gave Eva a hug, said that she would speak to her soon. She waved energetically from the train as it left the platform.

Chapter Ten

'Surprise!'

Emily woke to the sound of David's voice. But where was it coming from?

'Surprise!'

This time it was louder. What on earth was happening?

'Come on, Emily, I've got a surprise for you!'

It was definitely David's voice, but it wasn't coming from *inside* her house. Her window was already ajar, and she jumped out of bed, opened it wider and looked out. There was David, holding a tray. It obviously had something on it, but it was covered with a cloth, so that Emily couldn't see what it was.

'Hello,' she called. 'What've you got?'

'It's our breakfast.'

'Our breakfast? Hang on, I'll come down and let you in.' She ran downstairs and opened the front door, still in her pyjamas. 'Show me,' she demanded.

'I've got to put it down in the kitchen first. I don't want to drop anything,' he said anxiously. 'It's too important.'

By this time Jane had joined them. She was laughing, because Asma had told her the night before what was going to happen, and she had been sitting waiting for David to come.

David put the tray very carefully on the kitchen worktop, whipped off the tea towel that covered it, and revealed three painted eggs neatly placed in brightly-coloured eggcups.

'I did them,' he said proudly.

'Oh David, they're lovely!' exclaimed Emily. 'But they're too beautiful to eat.'

'Don't worry,' Jane reassured her, 'Asma took all the egg out before David decorated them. We can keep them as ornaments, and I've got some others we can have for breakfast.'

'We've got lots of news for you,' David informed them as Jane prepared the eggs.

'And we've got lots for you, too,' said Emily. 'Auntie Jane, can they all come round this afternoon and stay for tea?'

'That's a very good idea. I'll ask Asma as soon as we've finished breakfast.'

Emily and David chattered to each other as they ate their boiled eggs.

'This is my second breakfast,' he said, patting his stomach. 'I had a chocolate egg for my first one. Mum said I had to save it until later on, but I didn't take any notice.'

Jane smiled. She knew that David had reached the age when he was very likely to ignore much of what Asma said, but she also knew that he would do it in his inimitable impish way, which made him appear all the more endearing.

As he left, David said, 'By the way, I nearly forgot, Mum said to ask you round for tea.'

'Why didn't you say so when we were talking about tea?' asked Emily.

'Oh, I forgot,' he replied airily. 'Are you coming?'

'I think I'll come and have a word with your mum now,' said Jane firmly. 'Then I'll be certain of getting the right story.'

After a few words with Asma, an arrangement was made to share the preparation of their Easter meal, and eat it at Asma's house. Unusually, there was a good chance that Bill would not be called out that night.

'I'm looking forward to all your news,' Asma called after her as she returned to her house.

Over the meal it transpired that Bill and Asma had been following up their plan to research alternatives to the local high school for David, but thus far had not found anything better.

'At the moment, we don't want to think about moving,' said Asma. 'With Bill being settled at the hospital, it's good to live so near his work.'

'Yes,' said Bill, 'schooling for David is becoming a dilemma that we'll have to put a lot more thought into. The more we've looked at the local high school, the less happy we are about it. We've found out that since the new head took over last year, some problems have become very apparent. We don't know yet if it's to do with inherited problems becoming more obvious and whether or not he'll be able to pull things round, but it doesn't look good, and we're being open with

David about that.'

'I'll be asking around some more,' said Asma. 'You know how I joined a number of local interest groups over the winter? Well, in one way or another I've been able to make contact with quite a few of the existing parents, and I'm building on that.'

'Please keep me up to date about it all,' said Jane. 'Although Emily and I are pretty clear now that we want to move house, I don't know when that will be, and in any case, I'm having to think about secondary education a lot at the moment. Even information about bad schools can be useful. It'll help me to organise my thoughts and be clearer about questions I want to ask.'

Bill and Asma nodded.

Bill continued. 'One option we might follow is to let David start at the local school and see how things work out. Apparently the morale and enthusiasm in the first couple of years still seems to be good enough, but when the courses for external exams start, problems can arise.'

'That's interesting,' mused Jane. 'Maybe there's something amiss with the current exam system.'

'That may well be the case,' said Bill seriously, 'but nevertheless, from what Asma is telling me, my view is that it is exacerbated by failures and inadequacies within the school itself.'

'Apparently a number of the most senior staff retired when the previous head left,' said Asma.

'Mm,' said Jane. 'That in itself could have a lot to do with what's happening now.'

'We realise that,' said Bill, 'but we can't be sure, and we can't bank on the situation improving. In fact, there's a chance that it might go further downhill. The whole thing does leave us in a dilemma. We want the best for David, but my work is a big consideration.'

Throughout much of this conversation, David and Emily had been out of earshot. Their footsteps had at times been clearly audible in the room above that was David's bedroom. But now there was the sound of rushing on the stairs, and the two appeared, looking excited.

'We've worked out what to do,' David announced importantly.

'Yes,' said Emily. 'So you don't need to worry any more.' She turned to David. 'You start,' she instructed.

'Emily's been telling me all about her holiday, and how she might move house to be near Eva, and that Eva will help her to learn new things. If she moves there, I'm going to go and spend my holidays with her, and Eva will teach both of us.'

'Hang on a minute,' said his father gently.

'No!' said David, putting up his hand towards his father as if to stop him from moving. 'You've *got* to listen.' His face was flushed with the effort of what he was doing, but he didn't falter.

Bill looked at Jane and Asma. 'Will that be okay with you?'

Jane said firmly, 'I think it's a good thing if David and Emily tell us what they've been planning. We can all discuss it later.' She looked directly at David and said, 'Go on.'

'We can both start at the school here, if Emily hasn't moved by then. You said it isn't too bad at the beginning.'

Here Emily took over. 'And if I move, and if David's school gets bad later, he can come and live with us and go to my new school. Well... he could come for holidays and then decide.'

Jane didn't hesitate in her response. 'You two have got some very good ideas, and I certainly want to talk them through with Bill and Asma. As we all know, Emily and I have got a lot to do before we decide finally about a move, but we'll let you know as soon as anything is fixed.' She looked at her watch. 'I think that Emily and I should be going in a minute. It's getting late.'

When Emily was in bed, she asked Jane to sit and talk for a while.

'Do you think we really *really* could go and live near Eva?' she asked, staring intently at her aunt.

'I think we could,' Jane replied. 'There's a lot to look into, and I'll need to get the right kind of help to sell this house and mine, if that's what we decide to do.'

'I know,' said Emily. 'And I don't know how to help with that. But Harold said that we could go and try it out first. Would that mean we wouldn't have to sell anything straight away?'

'That's right. And it's something I've been considering. Now, let's get some sleep, and we can talk again in the morning.'

Chapter Eleven

It was Monday morning, and Harold had been up since five to do his rounds of the farm. He had returned to the house with another pair of orphan lambs that he had found wandering along the roadside verge. Somehow the mother had pushed her way through a weak part of the fence in a corner of the field, and had been knocked down on the road. Fortunately he had rescued the lambs before they had been killed as well.

'I wish drivers would at least have the courtesy to come and knock on my door,' he grumbled aloud. 'And that was one of my best ewes.' He put the lambs in the kitchen, and returned to the Land Rover to collect the ewe. He put her body in a shed ready to arrange for its disposal. 'A crying shame,' he muttered angrily.

This kind of thing is all too common nowadays, he reflected. People don't seem to realise any more that sheep provide food and clothing. They rush around the roads as if they were in some kind of fairground, and not real life.

He went upstairs and tried to settle to his paperwork for a couple of hours, but every time he tried to put pen to paper, all he could think of was the nice feeling he'd had when Jane and Emily were sitting looking at his picture albums.

Half an hour passed without any progress. He realised that he had been staring out of the window, but not taking in the view. Instead, he saw only his memories of when his parents had been alive, and the farm had been a place that was busy with hard-working, good-minded people. He pulled himself together and picked up his pen again, but it slowly fell out of his fingers.

'I could phone them,' he said to the picture of one of his prize ewes that was hanging on the wall. 'No, I couldn't... I don't have their number... but I've got Eva's. But I can't phone her. That wouldn't be right.' He had a vague sense that he didn't think it would be appropriate, but didn't know quite why. He felt irritated with himself. He knew he was usually clear-headed and decisive. That's how he had lived his life successfully, so why was he feeling so muddle-headed and lacking in confidence all of a sudden?

He stood up and paced around his desk a few times. 'Ah! Now I know what to do,' he proclaimed aloud. 'I'll phone Adam. Why didn't I think of that before?' He reached for the phone, but stopped with his arm outstretched. 'But what will I say?' he muttered. 'I haven't got any problems on the farm at the moment.' He sat down heavily in his chair and put his head in his hands. 'Why the heck is my head not working properly this morning?' he burst out. Then he realised that it had been working perfectly well until he had come up to work in his office, and that this was the first time he'd sat here since Jane and Emily had been there with him.

'I want them to come and try out living in the cottages,' he said decisively. 'And I'll make them an offer they can't refuse.' Then he stopped. 'But I can't. I've already told them there's no pressure from me. Come on Harold, get a grip!' He seized his pen, and stared at the sheet of paper in front of him.

After five minutes of struggling, he managed to see what it was about. He dealt with it and consigned it to the 'out' tray, before determinedly working through a considerable number of the outstanding things that had gathered on his desk.

Eva sat in her kitchen, sipping acorn coffee. A friend at work had given her a small quantity to try. 'Mm. This isn't bad,' she told the cup. 'And it's Easter Monday. I don't have to go into work... But I suppose I may as well.' She stared at the cup. It was one of her favourites, decorated with a delicate floral pattern that included a hovering butterfly. She made a mental note to grow some butterfly-friendly annuals in her small garden. 'Maybe I could walk down to the garden centre and see what they've got.'

She realised that she felt a little dejected. 'Not like you,' she said to her reflection in the shiny surface of the stainless steel pan that stood on the cooker, where Jane had left it after their last meal together.

'Oh no,' she murmured. 'I really miss them both. I don't want to go to work today. It's companionship that I want, not work.' A thought struck her. 'I know. I'll phone Meg and see if she's in. I could call in on my way to the garden centre.'

Half an hour later, she was sitting with Meg, sipping at one of her special brews.

'I won't even try to guess what this is,' she said, smiling.

Meg beamed, but said nothing.

Eva went on. 'I'm glad you're at home. To be honest, I'm missing Jane and Emily terribly.'

'I'm not surprised,' said Meg.

Eva felt as if the warmth of her friend's personality was enveloping her, and she began to relax.

'By the way,' Meg continued. 'You can let Emily know that I've fired her pots, and they've come out fine. And remind her that she's welcome to come and do some more any time.' She pointed to a large round container that stood on the table. 'Help yourself to some of my macaroons.'

By the time Eva was once again on the road, she felt restored. Her sadness that Jane and Emily were no longer staying with her hadn't gone away, but it didn't seem to affect her in the same way any more. She walked briskly to the garden centre, where she chose packets of seed mixes, and once home again, she planted them in seed trays and put them in the back porch.

'I must look for that book now,' she said aloud.

Although she searched the house high and low, she could find no sign of it.

'What on earth can have happened to it?' she asked her stick as it stood in the corner of the cupboard where she had left it on Friday. Just as she spoke, it clattered to the floor, and she jumped. 'What a fright you gave me,' she said as she picked it up. 'How on earth did that happen?'

Just then the doorbell rang, and she went to the door.

'Hello, Harold,' she said as she saw him standing there. 'This is a nice surprise. Come on in.'

Harold seemed rooted to the spot.

'Come on,' she urged. 'I'll put the kettle on.'

As he followed her into the kitchen, the image of a lost lamb came unbidden into her mind, but she didn't say anything about it. Instead, she turned on the tap and filled the kettle.

'Take a seat,' she said, motioning to one of the kitchen chairs. 'I'm glad you've called round. I'm missing Jane and Emily. I've a hunch that you might be, too,' she added bluntly.

Harold's strong frame began to relax a little. 'You're right. To tell you the truth, I nearly phoned you this morning to ask for their number.'

'I can easily give it to you,' said Eva, making towards the door to the living room.

'Don't!'

Eva looked at him in surprise. He seemed to be in a state of mild panic.

'Don't give it to me, because I might be tempted to phone Jane and press her to get on with a plan about my cottages, and I don't think that would be right,' he confessed. He looked very uncomfortable.

Eva laughed, and touched his arm lightly. 'That's what I want to do, too.'

Harold stared at her, and then his body started to shake with mirth.

'That's better,' Eva commented. 'What a relief. But we're both going to have to wait to see what happens.'

Harold had regained his normal self, and said decisively, 'I'm going to leave it for a month, and if I haven't heard anything by then, I'll get on to Jane.' He winked. 'And I might just plan some kind of attractive incentive, in case they need to be persuaded.'

After Harold left, Eva felt content. She knew that he wouldn't put undue pressure on Jane, but at the same time, he wouldn't let the project slip.

She returned to her thoughts about the book. 'I'll see if I can order another copy on the Internet, and then I'll try to find mine again,' she said aloud.

She tried a few websites without success, and she was beginning to think that she'd have to ask Ellen if she still had her copy, when a thought came into her head. It was as if she could hear a voice saying, 'slipped down.' 'Okay,' she murmured, 'the spirals had slipped down behind a shelf, and my stick slipped down today for no apparent reason, but where does that take me?'

Absentmindedly, she began to look under the cushions on the sofa bed, but found nothing. 'Slipped down'. The words persisted in her mind. Where else could she look?

She tried everywhere that she could think of, but found nothing. As a last attempt, she looked again through the various heaps of magazines that had gradually spread themselves across the bottom of the big cupboard that was accessed from her hallway. She had begun to stack them there years ago, and the piles had grown bigger and bigger, until they tended to slide across the floor.

This time, she even searched through each magazine. Her thoroughness was rewarded, because she found the book nestling inside a copy of one that was about cross-stitch. She could see how she had missed it before. The front page of the magazine advertised a free pack of embroidery threads, and she had assumed that this was the reason for the bulge.

'How on earth it got there, I'll never know,' she pronounced. She felt triumphant, and looked forward to being able to tell Emily that she had found it at last.

Emily and Jane had spent most of their day at home, apart from a walk that they had shared with David and Asma in the afternoon. Bill was back at the hospital again. There had been a pileup of vehicles on the motorway ten miles away, and ambulances were ferrying the casualties.

On the walk, there had been excitement when they caught sight of a kingfisher flashing past, up and down the river.

'I haven't seen one here before,' Jane told the others. 'It must mean that the river is clean enough for there to be enough fish for it.'

'That's a very encouraging sign,' said Asma.

They walked in pairs along the river path, while Jane and Asma turned over their thoughts about the future education of Emily and David, and the children tried unsuccessfully to spot fish.

When Emily went to bed that evening, Jane began a conversation about their future.

'Maybe it's not the best time to be saying this,' she said, 'but in the three days since we had that talk with Harold, I've thought of little else but your education and the idea of moving across.' She laughed. 'I feel as if I've been running around all over the place, and now I'm exhausted.'

Emily looked concerned. 'Don't run so fast, Auntie Jane, Harold said we had lots and lots of time to decide.'

'I know. But if we're going to go ahead, there's so much involved. For instance, I'd have to decide what time of year we'd go, and I haven't a clue how long it would take to do up one of those pairs of houses. It'll probably take months and months, and that can only start once tradesmen are lined up to do the work. And I don't have any contacts with builders. I'll have to find out about that, too. And we can't go ahead with any of that until we've decided whether or not we want to buy or rent. If we're renting, Harold will be in charge of all the renovation, although he'd want us to have a big say in it.'

Emily stared at her aunt with her eyes wide. 'I'm glad you told me, Auntie Jane. I hadn't thought about it like that.'

'I don't want to overburden you with details, dear.'

'But how can we decide if I don't know enough about what we are deciding about?' asked Emily. Her simplicity of thought could not be challenged.

Jane gave her a hug. 'You're right again, of course. Well, let's look at one bit of it, and then you must go to sleep so that you'll be fresh for school tomorrow.'

'Okay, Auntie Jane. You choose which bit,' said Emily as she snuggled under her duvet.

'Supposing we were going to move to Harold's, what time of year would we go?'

'I think it'd be best if I was there for the start of the new school.'

'I agree, but that's less than five months away.'

'Oh!' said Emily, with dawning realisation.

'So even if we told Harold straight away that we wanted to either rent or buy, we wouldn't have a house to live in at the start of term. And we haven't worked out yet which school you'd be going to.'

'Bring everything you got from Eva's computer,' said Emily urgently.

'No,' replied Jane firmly. 'It's too late for us to look through it tonight.'

'Please, Auntie Jane. *Please*,' said Emily, desperately trying to persuade her.

But Jane would not budge in her resolve. 'It's sleep for you, my girl,' she said determinedly. Then she softened a little. 'Tell you what... I could have a look myself tonight. At least I should be able to see which school serves the area where Harold's farm is, and then we can talk about it at teatime tomorrow.'

'Promise.'

'Yes, promise. Goodnight.' Jane gave Emily a quick kiss, and left.

Emily sighed contently, and was soon asleep.

Emily found it hard to concentrate on her work at school the next day. All she could think of was talking to Jane again. She told David as they left school together that afternoon, and they jogged home so that Emily would get there as quickly as possible.

Jane saw them coming down the cul-de-sac, and she guessed the reason for their haste. She opened the front door, and Emily charged in, throwing her schoolbag and coat in a heap in the hall.

'Hm,' said Jane. 'You'll have to put those away first, you know.'

Emily pulled a face, but picked them up and put them neatly in the hall cupboard.

Inwardly, Jane felt pleased to see Emily's carelessness. One thing that had concerned her for a long time was how Emily had tried so hard always to be good since she lost her parents. She had seemed a bit freer at Eva's and since they came back, and Jane felt that this was a change for the better.

'Why not go and get yourself a drink,' she suggested. 'I'll be all ready for you in the front room.'

Emily appeared, carefully carrying a saucepan in both her hands.

'Whatever are you doing?' asked Jane, astonished.

'I've brought a drink for you as well. But I'm so excited that I thought I might spill it.'

Jane chuckled. She took a glass out of the pan and said, 'I've never seen that done before. Very ingenious.' She waited until Emily was settled before continuing. 'Now, let's get down to business. I've got some interesting news for you. When I looked through these, I saw that Harold's farm is very near the boundary between two catchment areas, so if we went there, we'd straight away have two schools to choose from.'

'Tell me about them, Auntie Jane.'

'On the surface of it, they look much the same. Each has around a thousand pupils. One was built about ten years ago, and the other about fifteen. But there's something here that I know will interest you. The older one won an award for conservation two years ago. Part of their electricity is supplied by solar panels that seem to cover much of the roof area. And they have a system that collects rainwater for flushing the toilets. Some of the older pupils are working on environmentally-friendly projects, and there's a vegetable garden which is due to be enlarged soon.'

Emily's eyes were shining. 'Can we go and see it?'

'I think the first step would be for me to make some enquiries. I can contact the school to check whether or not you would definitely get a place, and see if there's any other information they can send us. But maybe you're right, and I should ask if we can visit.'

'But it might be ages before we could go. Can't we ask Eva if she would go and look?'

'We really do need as much information as we can get. Shall we give her a ring after tea?'

'Now!' said Emily emphatically.

'She won't be back from work yet.'

When they spoke to Eva, she was more than willing to do some research.

'Let me get the map out,' she said. 'I want to see exactly where it is, and how far it is from here, and from Harold's.'

Jane gave her details, and it didn't take her long to find it.

'How silly of me,' said Eva. 'I've driven past there many times. It must be set back from the road, though, because I don't have a picture in my mind of any buildings. I can visualise a sign, and to be honest I think I'd assumed it was a college, not a secondary school.' She took some quick measurements. 'It's about five miles from here, and three from Harold's. Give me the phone number. I'll ring them in the morning before I leave for work. There's likely to be someone in the office after eight. I'll speak to you again tomorrow evening, and let you know how I get on.'

'That's great,' said Jane. 'And I'll phone the school, too. I think I should make some direct contact. Bye for now.'

'Hang on a minute,' said Eva quickly. 'Put Emily on the phone.'

Jane handed it to Emily. 'Hello, Eva,' she said. 'I'm missing you.'

'And I'm missing you,' said Eva sincerely. 'And I think someone else is, too. Harold came round to see me yesterday, and I got the distinct impression that he's looking forward to your next visit, whenever that might be.' Eva thought it best not to be honest at this stage about the precise nature of their conversation. 'And now, here's the big news,' she announced dramatically.

'Tell me what it is!'

'I've found the book. I thought I wasn't going to find it anywhere, and I tried to order one on the Internet, but had no luck.

Then I looked again, and eventually found it inside a magazine in the hall cupboard, of all places. I'll parcel it up and put it in the post to you soon.'

'Hooray!' Emily shouted.

Jane jumped.

'It's all right, Auntie Jane,' said Emily. 'Eva has found the book, and she's going to send it.' She spoke to Eva again. 'But will it be safe?' she asked anxiously.

'Just to be sure, I'll send it by special delivery,' Eva promised. 'Don't worry. I'll make sure that good care is taken of it.'

'But I'm still worried,' said Emily.

'Do you want me to keep it here until you come again?'

Emily was silent as she thought about this.

'Are you still there, Emily?' Eva asked.

'Yes, I'm thinking. It's really difficult, because I want to see it now.'

'Don't worry. I'll keep it here until you decide. Bye for now. I'll phone again tomorrow evening.'

The next day Emily had the same difficulty in concentrating on her work at school. On the way there she had told David all the news, and again they ran home together after school.

Jane greeted her at the door. 'I've spoken to the school,' she said. 'If we were living at Harold's, there would be no question that you'd get a place. I said we'd looked at their website, and asked if there was anything else they could send. There isn't anything at the moment, so let's see what Eva can find out.'

The phone rang only an hour later, and Jane was surprised to find that it was Eva.

'But you're at work,' she began.

'No, I'm not. I phoned the school this morning as planned, and I arranged to go there straight after the end of the school day. I left work early, because I felt it was so important. There was nothing that I *had* to be there for, and I do put in a lot of extra hours at other times. They couldn't give me long, but one of the senior pupils offered to show me round. I must say that I'm very impressed with what they're doing.'

Jane started to say something, but stopped as Eva carried on.

'And I made sure that I arrived a bit early so that I could watch the pupils leave. I noticed straight away that there was an atmosphere of cheerful calm amongst most of them. Yes, some of them were quite boisterous, but I didn't see any who were agitated or aggressive.'

'That sounds promising,' said Jane.

Eva had to work hard to stop herself from trying to persuade Jane to make an instant decision, and instead said, 'I'll get off the phone now so that you and Emily can have a chat about it. Let me know if I can help with anything else.'

On Friday evening, Jane and Emily made a decision. They would phone Harold over the weekend, and say that they definitely wanted to go and live there, for a while at least.

'I'll need to have a long talk with him about the costs of renovation, and exactly what's feasible,' said Jane. 'After that we'll be able to decide whether we're going to rent from him or sell our houses and buy from him. I'll need a lot of figures in front of me before I'll know what to do.'

Emily could hardly suppress her excitement as Jane phoned Harold. He wasn't in, but Jane left a message, asking him to phone back so that they could begin to discuss a way forward.

He hadn't phoned back by the time Emily went to bed, and she was very disappointed. 'Do you think he's gone away?' she asked Jane as she tucked her in bed.

'No, I don't think he goes away. It must be something else.'

Later that evening, Jane was sitting knitting a cardigan for Emily when the phone rang. She was startled, but put her knitting down and picked it up.

'Hello,' she said.

'Hello.' Straight away she recognised Harold's voice. 'I'm sorry I couldn't get back to you any sooner. I was tied up, and I've only just listened to my phone messages. Is this too late?'

'Not at all.'

'You said in your message that you wanted to talk about a way forward. What have you got in mind?' Harold was struggling to keep his voice steady. He had felt deeply affected when he got Jane's message, and he had phoned straight away. He wasn't quite sure what he was feeling, but he thought it might be excitement. Yes, the kind of excitement that he remembered feeling when he was a boy, when his dad was just about to teach him something new about the farm.

'Emily and I have been keen to follow up the idea of living on your land, but we needed to look into her schooling. By chance, there's a very good school just three miles from where you are, and so we feel we want to push ahead with the move, but there's a lot that you and I need to discuss. You'll probably realise that if we move, it would be best if Emily started at the new school at the beginning of September. Obviously there wouldn't be time to get a house ready for then, so we'd have to make some other arrangement. What I'm trying to think about now is how to go about the renovations, and how long it might take.'

'You haven't said yet whether you're looking at renting or buying,' said Harold. 'If you're renting, I'll be in charge of the work. And once I've got people lined up, it shouldn't take more than a few months. But first I'd have to get plans drawn up and approved, and all that. I'd be very surprised if it wasn't ready by next Easter, but it'd probably be earlier – say Christmas. If you're thinking of buying, I can put you in touch with some good tradesmen.'

Jane found his blunt response comforting. 'I like to talk to you about both options, although I don't have enough figures to base our final decision on yet.'

'Tell you what,' said Harold, 'I'll get a surveyor round early next week, and that should set the ball rolling.'

When Jane told Emily over breakfast, she was ecstatic.

'It's *so* exciting!' she said as she bounced around the kitchen dropping crumbs everywhere.

'Come on,' her aunt chided. 'If you don't stop that, we'll have to spend the rest of the weekend cleaning.'

Emily froze to the spot in mock horror, before returning to her seat and finishing her breakfast with an apple. 'Auntie Jane,' she said suddenly. 'I think we should have David and his mum and dad round, so we can tell them everything. I told David about the school, but he doesn't know anything else yet.'

'I haven't seen much of Asma over the last few days,' Jane replied. 'But yes, of course, let's see if they can come round this afternoon, or maybe tomorrow.'

As it worked out, they spent most of Sunday afternoon together, and fortunately Bill could be with them.

'I'm very interested in that school,' he said thoughtfully when

Emily and Jane had told them all that they had found out. 'I'd like to have a look at it myself. Maybe I'll take a drive over there when I next have a weekday off. What do you think, Asma?'

'I'd like you to do that,' she agreed.

'Why don't you go with him?' Jane suggested. 'David could come in to us after school.'

'Thanks very much,' said Asma. 'I'll take you up on that.'

Jane turned to Bill. 'If you can get a couple of days off, David could stay overnight with us, and you'd get more time to yourselves.'

'I'll look at the staffing rotas for the next few weeks, and see if I can work something out,' said Bill enthusiastically.

'I'd very much like you to see the place and tell me what you think,' said Jane. 'As you know, Eva was certainly very impressed.'

'We'll let you know soon about dates,' said Asma as they left. 'And be sure and let me know when you've heard from Harold about the survey.'

Chapter Twelve

Jane and Emily were not left in suspense for long. Harold phoned midweek, when they were just about to do Emily's homework together. Emily sat very still while Jane spoke to him.

'The surveyor's been, and I've got a verbal report that'll be confirmed in writing. I had a full structural survey done,' Harold told Jane.

Jane realised that she was holding her breath as she waited for him to tell her the results.

'The news is interesting. The shell of the pair we looked at together is relatively sound. Of course, there's a lot that has to be done – floors and ceilings replaced, plumbing replaced and rewiring done. Some of the windows will have to be replaced too. But the other pair of houses is going to have to come down.'

'Why's that?' asked Jane.

'There's some kind of undermining. The foundations are very unstable, and unless money is no object, there's no point in trying to sort out the mess. I certainly wouldn't want to put any of my money into it, and I would advise you to think the same way. Actually, it makes the whole venture a lot simpler. Rent or buy, you'll have more ground to work with, and you won't have to think about who you want for neighbours.'

Jane suddenly snapped into a business-like mode, and surprised herself by asking confidently, 'I need to know what you would be looking for if I bought the plot from you as it is.'

'I'll have it for you by the end of the week,' Harold replied. 'There's just one more thing at this stage,' he added.

'What's that?' Jane asked tentatively.

'If we strike a deal on that basis, I'll throw something in free of charge.'

'I'm mystified. Please could you explain?'

'I'm inviting you and Emily to live in the farmhouse with me from the beginning of September until the work on your new home is completed. Actually, that offer stands, rent or buy.'

Jane was completely lost for words.

She heard Harold saying, 'Are you still there?'

She managed to stutter, 'Er… that's very generous of you.'

'Maybe I came in with that too soon,' he said. 'But I didn't want you to be worrying about the start of the school year. I know you might prefer to stay with Eva, but remember that here you'd be able to keep an eye on the work. Anyway, give it some thought. I'll be back to you in a couple of days with a price.' He laughed. Jane noticed that it was a deep rich sound. 'Then we can begin bargaining.'

He rang off before Jane had a chance to ask him what that meant.

She looked at Emily. 'Phew!' she exclaimed. 'I'm having to work hard here. Now, let me tell you what's been happening.'

Emily continued to sit quietly while Jane told her everything.

When she had finished, Emily wriggled in her seat and said, 'I can't wait for the next news.'

'But I need time to think about the finances,' said her aunt. 'If we bought from Harold, there would be the money for that, and then there would be all the money for the clearing of the dangerous pair of houses, and the renovations for the pair that we're taking over. Realistically, I think we'll be able to afford it, but I can't help feeling on edge until I have some figures in front of me, and the first step is to get the price from Harold.'

Emily stared at her solemnly and said nothing else. She could see that her aunt was preoccupied with things that she herself knew little about, and she decided that the best thing would be to get ready for bed.

Jane hardly noticed as Emily slipped out of the room, and when she eventually went to look for her, she found her asleep in bed. She glanced at her watch and found it wasn't yet ten, so she phoned next door to see if Bill was at home.

'He's just in,' said Asma. 'I'll hand the phone to him.'

'Hello, Bill,' said Jane. 'Have you got a few minutes? I'd like to run something past you.'

'Fire away.'

Jane told him the content of the phone call with Harold.

'So you're waiting for a price tag now.'

'That's right.'

'If I were in your shoes, I'd get my own survey done.'

'Why's that? I trust Harold completely.'

'In a transaction of this size it would be sensible, whatever the level of trust,' Bill assured her. 'Put it this way, if I were offering a building to you at a specific price, I'd advise you to at least get a valuation survey of your own done.'

'I see,' said Jane slowly.

Bill continued. 'Why not phone the local branch of Jones and Marsden in the morning? They'll be able to tell you if they have a branch not too far away from Harold's.'

'Thanks, Bill. I'll do that.'

'I'm glad to help. By the way, I wanted to tell you that I've booked Thursday and Friday off at the end of next week. Would it still be okay for you to have David?'

'Of course. Why not tell him to come in for breakfast on Thursday morning, and then you can get off as early as you want?'

At nine thirty the following morning, Jane found the number for Jones and Marsden and picked up the phone. Having ascertained that there was a branch at Overton, she took down the contact number. She was about to phone to make an arrangement when she realised that she should first contact Harold to let him know. She felt a little uncomfortable about the situation, but gathered herself and keyed in Harold's number.

She heard the sound of his now-familiar voice. 'Hello, Harold Barber speaking.'

'It's Jane here.'

'Good to hear you. It's too soon for more news, though.'

'I know. I was phoning about something else.' There was silence at the end of the phone, and Jane continued. 'My neighbour said that it would be best if I got an independent valuation survey done, and I wanted to say that I'd like to send someone from Jones and Marsden round.'

'Excellent advice. Give them a ring, and then get back to me about the timing. I'll be here for the next hour.'

Jane phoned the branch straight away, and found to her delight that one of their experienced staff was already travelling to a property in the vicinity that afternoon, and could do the work straight afterwards. She let Harold know, and he promised to be there.

She found it difficult to settle for the rest of the day. Her mind went over and over endless sets of fictitious figures, calculating and recalculating, but all the while she knew that there was nothing else she could do until she had some real figures in front of her.

She walked up the road to meet Emily coming home from school, and she explained what she could of her efforts. They walked back to the house slowly. Both felt at a loose end. Their thoughts were only with the waiting, and although they would have news within the next twenty-four hours, the waiting seemed endless.

At five thirty, the phone rang.

'I wonder who that can be,' said Jane as she went to pick it up.

She found to her surprise that it was the surveyor, who had just got back to the office and was about to leave for home.

'I'll arrange for the written report to be sent to you,' he said, 'but I thought you might find it helpful to have my figure straight away.'

'Thanks for phoning,' said Jane. She felt extremely grateful to this man for cutting their waiting time short.

'I'm putting a figure of a hundred and ten thousand on it. One of the buildings will need to come down, and the ground be cleared. The other building requires a considerable amount of repair. The outhouses for both buildings are sound.'

'Thank you for letting me know. I'll be able to advance my planning,' said Jane formally. She put the phone down, grabbed Emily and bounced round the kitchen with her. 'I think we're going to be able to afford it.'

'I don't want to go to school tomorrow,' said Emily. 'I want to wait here for when Harold phones.'

'But he might not phone until the evening.'

'I still don't want to go.'

'I think I'd feel the same in your shoes,' Jane acknowledged. 'Let's do a deal. If he phones before your lunchtime, I'll cycle up and see you in the playground. If he phones in the afternoon, I'll come and meet you at the school gate. Will that do?'

They both felt more relaxed that evening than for the last few days, and once again Emily opted to go to bed earlier than usual.

It was mid-morning when Harold phoned. Without any preliminaries, he got down to business.

'You'll have your verbal report?'

'Yes.'

'Here's my proposal. A hundred thousand. I'm going to arrange for the plot to be cleared, including the removal of the unsafe block. The offer that you can live in the farmhouse with me from September onwards rent-free still stands.'

'I want to say "done",' replied Jane, 'but I think I should speak to Emily first. After all, it's her money as well as mine that'll be going into the project.'

'I don't think she'll object,' said Harold, chuckling. 'There's one more thing. I've drawn up a list of good tradespeople that you might want to use. I'll put it in the post to you if you give me your address. It's entirely up to you what you decide. And there's the number of the best architect I can think of, but if you're not thinking of making any changes, you won't be needing one.'

'Will you send it anyway,' Jane requested. 'At this stage, everything's a bit up in the air.'

'I'd better be getting on, but I expect we'll speak again soon,' said Harold.

He put the phone down rather abruptly, leaving Jane staring at her handset, before replacing it and looking at her watch. 'I've just got half an hour before I must set off up to the school to see Emily,' she said aloud. 'Mm... I think I'll start getting a file ready to put everything in.'

She hunted in the cupboard, and came across a lever arch file that was full of old bills. She flicked through them and put them on one side, having decided that she would get Emily to help her to shred them that evening. Then she found the valuations that she had for Clare's house and her bungalow, and put them in the file.

After that she made a number of notes on a plain sheet of paper, and added that. One more thing, she thought. She collected the information about schools that she had brought back from the trip to Eva's, and put that in the file.

'That's a start,' she said aloud as she took her jacket and went to the garage to get her bike. Soon she was pedalling along the road in the direction of Emily's school.

She found Emily standing at the gate. When she told her the news, Emily was ecstatic.

'Auntie Jane, this is the best day of my life! I'll go and tell David. See you later.' She ran off.

Jane knocked on Asma's door when she arrived home, but no one was in, so she phoned Eva and left a message for her. She made a cup of herb tea, and sat in the kitchen to think.

If they were going ahead with this, the best thing would be to move fast. Her instinct was to put Clare's house on the market as quickly as possible. This time of year was usually a good time to sell, and she didn't want to risk leaving it until the summer, when there was a possibility of there being a lull in the housing market. She had been told to expect about two hundred thousand pounds for it. It seemed a huge amount of money for a relatively compact house, but she knew that there was pressure on local housing for people who worked at the hospital, and that this had kept the prices at a favourable level for sellers over the past few years. The sale would release the capital she needed for buying Harold's plot, and she would have money left over to advance the restoration of the block that was sound. At this stage, she had no idea how much that would cost in total. She would have to approach a builder and get some kind of estimate. The price and terms that Harold had quoted were very generously weighted in their favour. She felt a little nervous about this because she was uncomfortable about feeling indebted to him, but she also realised that he felt that he would gain from their presence as neighbours, and that he was therefore more than willing to make the deal attractive to them. She didn't want to think about selling her own bungalow at the moment. In January, the occupants had signed a lease for the year, so for now she could put off thinking about its sale. As far as she knew, they were still interested in buying it from her, but if they changed their minds, she felt certain that it would not be difficult to find another buyer.

She was still sitting at the table, lost in thought, when Emily burst through the door. Her cheeks were glowing. 'When do we start packing?' she demanded.

'Oh, we've a lot to do before then,' Jane explained gently. 'The first thing is to tell Harold that we're accepting his offer.'

Emily grabbed the phone and handed it to Jane.

'We'll phone him this evening,' said her aunt calmly. 'I know it's tempting to rush ahead with everything. Actually, I've been making some decisions while I've been waiting for you to come home, and the main one is to make this house look good so that we can put it on the market. There's plenty we can do this weekend about that, and the first thing is to help me to shred this big pile of old bills so that we can throw them out.'

'Why do we have to shred them like this?' asked Emily as she carefully tore several bills into strips. 'Can't we just screw them up?'

'I used to think that was all right, but then I went to a talk by the police. One of the things I learned there was never to throw anything away that thieves could use to get into my bank account.'

'That sounds *horrible*.'

'It *is* horrible,' Jane agreed. 'Apparently, some thieves can be very clever at using names, addresses and identification numbers of various kinds so that they can steal money. I don't know exactly how they do it, but they do.'

'I'll remember that,' said Emily determinedly, 'and I'll tell David about it.'

The pile grew smaller and smaller, and Emily asked, 'What do we have to do after this?'

'We don't have to do it all this weekend, but we've got to clean and tidy the house from top to bottom, and make sure that the windows are sparkling as well. After that we should start to think if there are any things that we don't need any more – things that we could give away. Remember that we're going to have to pack everything away for months and months until we get into our new place, so the less we have, the better. But the first step is to make everything here look good.'

They spoke to Harold after tea, and Jane and Harold agreed to organise the legal side of the transaction as soon as possible, and that Jane would transfer the money to him when Clare's house was sold.

Before he rang off, Harold said gruffly, 'You might want to put your furniture in store, but you're welcome to stack some of it here if you want.'

'Can we phone Eva now?' asked Emily. 'I want her to know everything.'

Eva was out, but Jane left a long message on her callminder, telling her the news.

'And we must tell Bill and Asma and David,' Emily insisted.

'I'm sure we'll see them sometime over the weekend,' Jane replied, 'and we can tell them then.'

Emily worked very hard that weekend. Apart from spending a little time with David and Asma to give them the news, Emily hardly ever stopped working. Jane marvelled at her stamina as she scrubbed and polished and tidied, hour after hour.

'Don't you want a break?' she asked half way through Sunday afternoon.

'There's nothing else I want to do,' Emily replied, with the simple logic of someone who was certain of her actions.

'I'll work on the garden tomorrow, when I've made contact with the estate agent again,' said Jane. She felt somewhat weary, but like Emily, she wanted to press on with the task in hand. 'I'm glad that Bill and Asma are going to look at your school this week.'

'And I'm glad that David is staying with us,' said Emily. 'He'll be able to help with the cleaning.'

The 'For Sale' sign was up at the front of the house by Tuesday evening, and on Thursday evening, the first viewing time, Jane, Emily and David sat, looking very neat, in the middle of an unnaturally tidy sitting room. Emily and David had been busy in Emily's bedroom since they came in from school, apart from emerging occasionally from time to time, and going from room to room whispering to each other. Although Jane had asked them what they had been doing, they had avoided answering her questions.

'I don't suppose anyone will come this evening,' said Jane a little nervously, 'but it's good to be ready just in case.'

'My dad's put up an advertisement for it on the hospital notice board,' said David. 'I helped him to make it,' he added proudly. 'He says there's a special bit for houses for sale or let.'

'That's really good,' said Jane. 'I knew he was going to, but I didn't think he'd have been able to do it so quickly.'

'I hope someone comes,' said Emily. 'I want to show my bedroom. I've made it look really good.'

By eight o'clock, David and Emily were wilting. Their rather stiff postures had long begun to sag, and Emily was beginning to wish that eight thirty would come, when she and David could have their supper and get ready for bed.

'I told you that you could have a game out to play with if you wanted,' Jane reminded them.

'No, no,' Emily and David said in chorus, 'everything's got to look tidy.'

Jane herself was feeling restless. The minutes seemed to drag past. She wished she could think of a word game to do with the children, but somehow she hadn't got the energy to put into it.

The clock said eight fifteen. 'Why don't we just give up for tonight,' she said with forced cheerfulness. 'I could go and put the kettle on.' She had a flash of inspiration. 'You two could keep watch at the window, and let me know if you see anyone coming.'

Emily and David sprang to their feet immediately, and stood like soldiers at the front window. Jane smiled, and went to the kitchen. But before she had time to reach for the kettle, Emily came dashing through.

'Come quickly! Someone's coming in a car,' she whispered loudly.

'They might not be coming here,' said Jane. But she rushed to the window to join David, and there she saw a man and a woman getting out of a car just up the road.

The woman pointed to the 'For Sale' sign, and she and the man started to walk towards the house. 'Okay,' she said. 'Sit down, and I'll open the door when they ring.'

'We're sorry to call so late,' said the man as Jane opened the door, 'Would it be possible to see round the house now, or can we come back some time tomorrow?'

Jane smiled. 'I'm sure the children won't mind staying up a little longer. Do come in.' She let them in and shut the door behind them. 'The door on the right leads into the sitting room.'

The couple went into the room, and Emily said very politely, 'Good evening. David and I will show you round upstairs.'

Jane was stunned. She knew that she could always count on Emily to behave appropriately in a variety of social situations, but this one was entirely new, and she was flawless.

'Yes, the children are keen to help,' she said, 'but don't hesitate to call me if there are any questions you want to ask. First I'll show you round the ground floor and the garden and garage. I'm afraid I don't have any schedules yet because it only went on the market this week.'

Their tour of the ground floor completed, the couple followed Emily and David upstairs. They returned about ten minutes later carrying two sheets of paper.

'Thank you very much for your help,' they said as they left.

When Jane closed the door behind them, she asked, 'Have you any idea what they were carrying?'

'Don't worry, Auntie Jane,' Emily replied. 'David and I drew some floor plans to give to people that came round. We measured everything with my school ruler when we came home. It took ages. You'd said the estate agent had measured everything, but I knew there couldn't have been time to have things to hand out for today.'

'That's amazing!' Jane exclaimed, hugging them both. 'Have you got some more so I can have a look?'

'Yes, we've got one lot left,' said David. He ran up the stairs and soon returned carrying two sheets of paper. 'I did these, and Emily did the others.'

'They're very good indeed,' said Jane with obvious admiration. 'Can you keep these somewhere safe until Sunday?'

'What happens on Sunday?' asked David.

'It's the next viewing day, silly,' explained Emily importantly.

'Can I come and help again?' he asked instantly.

Emily looked at Jane, and Jane said, 'It would be really good. I hope you can come. The viewing hours are during the afternoon. Two to four.' She looked thoughtful, and then added, 'I don't think that we'll have schedules by then either. It's unlikely that the estate agent will have them available before next week.'

'We can make some more,' said David and Emily together.

'I'm not sure how many we'll need,' said Jane slowly. 'Weekend viewing can turn out to be quite busy. There are people who are genuinely considering buying, but some people come just because they like looking inside houses. Would you mind if I borrow your last one and get some photocopies?'

Emily looked at David. They both nodded, and Jane found a large envelope that was stiffened with card, and slipped the two sheets inside.

'Will anyone come tomorrow?' asked Emily.

'It's unlikely, but not impossible,' Jane replied. 'If people see it advertised they'll know when the viewing times are, but if they just happen to see the board, they won't.'

'People don't usually come down our road unless they know someone here,' David observed.

'That's right,' said Jane, 'but I think that Emily and I will have the house tidy each evening, just in case. You never know.'

Jane could hear Emily and David chatting to each other in Emily's room until quite late. She decided not to intervene, as they were obviously excited, and needed time to settle. She put her head round the door on her way to bed, and found that David had become entangled in his duvet as he lay on the mattress on the floor beside Emily's bed. She tugged at it gently so as not to disturb him, and covered him properly.

Bill and Asma arrived home in the middle of the afternoon, and went straight round to see Jane. She was in the middle of sorting through more of her clothes, to see what she no longer needed. She was startled when she heard the doorbell, and felt disorientated, thinking that it must be people who wanted to view the house. She jumped up quickly and almost ran to the door. When she saw Bill and Asma, she sighed with relief.

'Thank goodness it's you,' she said.

'Is something wrong?' asked Asma, concerned.

Jane laughed. 'Not at all. I just thought that it might be people who wanted to view the house, and I'm not in the right state for that at the moment. Come in and let me have your news.' She let them into the sitting room, and as she sat down added, 'The children were a great help yesterday.'

'We've had a very interesting time, Jane,' said Bill. He glanced across at Asma and asked, 'Shall I start?'

'Of course. I can join in if I think you're in danger of missing something out.'

'I don't think Asma and I had time to tell you before we set off, but we'd booked a couple of appointments.'

Jane looked interested, and waited for Bill to explain.

'We'd made one to see one of the deputy heads at the school, and I'd also been in touch with the hospital at Overton.'

'Why the hospital, Bill?' Jane asked, surprised.

'I wanted to get an idea of the lie of the land,' he replied. 'As you know, Asma and I have been talking a lot about David's schooling. Although we think it would be okay for him to attend the local school for a couple of years, we're not enthusiastic about it. The more Asma has found out, the more we have thought about other options. Now that we know you and Emily are definitely moving, we began to wonder if we too might move.'

'But that's impossible,' said Jane. 'You can't do that.'

'Why not?' asked Bill quietly.

'But your life's work is in the hospital ...   And your input is invaluable.'

'No one is irreplaceable,' said Bill. 'Obviously we're not going to make any rushed decisions, and it may turn out that it's best if we stay here, for the time being at least. Anyway, let's get back to talking about what we've found out so far.'

'Sorry.'

'Don't feel that you have to apologise, Jane,' said Bill. 'Your reaction is understandable. By the way,' he added, 'we drove past your new home.'

'What did you think?' asked Jane. 'I'm so excited about it. There's so much to do, and the whole project can seem daunting, but I'm certain we'll be doing the right thing by going there.'

'So are we,' said Asma, smiling. 'We haven't met Harold, but the location is lovely, and you are very close to a wonderful school.'

'Jane,' said Bill. 'Asma and I were deeply impressed by the school. We can confirm everything that Eva told you, and more. You should have no hesitation in sending Emily there.'

'Tell her about the hospital, Bill,' Asma reminded him.

'Yes, do,' said Jane. 'There's obviously something here that I need to know.'

'The hospital at Overton is smaller than ours, but like ours, it's well run and the morale is good.'

He paused, and Jane thought that there was a definite hint of drama in his manner. She had rarely seen him like this. She had always assumed that the consistently measured way in which he spoke was a result of his long years in charge of emergency care, and had long ago come to expect it.

'Go on,' she encouraged him. 'There's obviously more to say.'

'It's being expanded,' he said bluntly. 'From what I learned, a range of jobs will become available at my level and above.'

'When will that be?' asked Jane.

'I've got to do some research,' Bill replied. 'It's a different health board, and I'll have to familiarise myself with how they go about things. Oh, I know that in theory there's supposed to be standardisation between health boards, but in practice it often doesn't work out. There's a lot of new housing in the surrounding area, and there seem to be plans of closing down an old cottage hospital some miles away. Apparently the building is in need of extensive repair, and it's been decided that the money would be better used by contributing to the expansion of Overton Hospital. I would guess it'll be another year or so before jobs are advertised.'

'Actually, Jane, we're both feeling quite excited,' said Asma. 'I know that there's nothing concrete yet, but we're definitely going to follow this up in as much detail as we can.'

'That's wonderful news,' said Jane, her mind racing ahead. 'So there's quite a chance that you'd be able to move to Overton in a couple of years' time.'

'I suppose there is,' said Bill. 'No promises, but it's not impossible.'

'The way things look at the moment,' said Asma, 'we'd have to look for property about half way between Overton and Middleswell to be in the catchment area for your school.'

Jane nodded, and added, 'I don't suppose you've had time to think about schools on the other side of Overton. There might be something even more attractive.'

'From what I've seen of the school that Emily will be going to, that's highly unlikely,' said Bill, 'but you're right that we should look into it.'

There was a long ring on the doorbell, and Jane went to let the children in.

David flung himself into his father's arms. 'You're back,' he said excitedly. 'Did you like the school and can I go there?' he asked without pausing for breath.

'Steady,' said Bill. 'One thing at a time. Perhaps the best thing would be if we go home for now, and then you can ask all your questions.'

Before they left, Bill reminded Jane that she should contact the school as soon as possible, to let them know that she would be moving into the area, and that Emily would need a place in September.

After they had gone, Jane spoke to Emily about Bill and Asma's visit to the school, but said nothing about the hospital, in case they weren't ready to talk to David about it.

Emily was happy with the news, and spent the evening helping Jane with her clothes. She loved Jane's stories of where she had found some of the items, and what had drawn her to them, and she often said, 'Are you *sure* you want to put this one out, Auntie Jane?' Jane's response was usually brisk, but at times she would falter and put an item into the 'save for now' heap.

Sunday afternoon viewing turned out to be quite busy, and Jane was thankful that she had the photocopies of the work that Emily and David had done. Whereas on Thursday she could easily have managed on her own, today she was very grateful for their assistance in escorting people up the stairs and round the bedrooms. Several people commented to her on their way out about how helpful the children had been. After she closed the front door behind the last couple, a father and daughter, she went into the sitting room and flopped down on the sofa.

'Oh,' she groaned, 'that's really hard work. I have to smile all the time, and I have to say all the same things in answer to the same questions, and look as if it's the first time I've been asked.'

'We did that too,' said Emily, 'but I liked it.'

'So did I,' said David. 'Can I come again on Thursday after tea?'

Jane stared at him. 'Would you really?' she asked. 'I'd be so grateful. To be honest, I'm finding this harder that I'd envisaged, and until today I hadn't let myself think how long this stage might go on for.'

'We can do the upstairs until it's sold, can't we?' said Emily to David.

'I'll tell Mum and Dad when I go home,' David replied, full of enthusiasm.

When David had gone, Emily said, 'I want it to be someone nice who buys our house. I didn't like some of the people who came today, and they weren't people that should be living next door to David.'

'I hadn't thought about that before,' said her aunt, 'but you're right. I'll keep it in mind. But when we get an offer for the house, I can't guarantee that I'll remember from just the name what the people were like when they came to view.'

The following two weeks were very busy. Keeping the house clean and tidy for most of the time was tiring in itself, but Jane found that the task of showing strangers round their home became very exhausting indeed, and she began to realise that without the cheerful support of David and Emily, she might have given up.

Meanwhile, they heard from Harold that he had set the wheels in motion for the demolition and clearing of the unsafe pair of houses.

'He's moving fast,' Jane told Emily.

'I'm glad,' said Emily. 'Auntie Jane, I'm moving fast too.'

Jane felt puzzled. She knew that her niece was quick in many ways, but she didn't know what she meant. 'Is there something I don't know about yet?' she asked.

Emily dashed off upstairs, and returned with some sheets of paper.

'Have you been drawing up more schedules?' asked Jane. 'That's good of you, but I don't think we need any more. If you remember, the estate agent sent us quite a pile of them last week, and he's got more if we need them.'

'No,' said Emily. 'Look.'

She handed the sheets to her aunt, who studied them. They appeared to be floor plans, but certainly not of this house.

'They're of our house,' Emily explained.

'Not this one.'

'Our *new* house.'

'Oh!' Jane was astonished. 'How on earth did you manage to do them?' she asked, bewildered.

'Put them on the table, Auntie Jane, and I'll show you the different rooms. I did my best, but I might not have got them quite right. I had to try and remember how big the rooms were.' She smiled. 'But I'd measured some with my trainers when we were there, and that helped.'

'Emily, I'm so impressed!' exclaimed Jane. She put the sheets on the table. 'Why not pretend that I've never been there, and you can give me a tour,' she suggested playfully.

When Emily had finished, she said, 'Auntie Jane, I want us to start talking about what we need to do to the house. I know we have to be careful with our money, and I think the houses are nice as they are. I don't want to change them, I just want us to mend them.'

'I was thinking about that in bed last night, and I agree,' said Jane. 'The only change that came into my mind was whether or not to make a door downstairs that means we can go between the two houses without going outside.'

'Oh, I like that idea,' said Emily excitedly. 'It could go through the wall at the bottom of the staircases. She made marks on one of her drawings, and then said, 'We won't need all that room to live in straight away, will we? There are two bedrooms in each house so we only really need one house.'

'I've been thinking about that, and I'm not sure yet quite what to do. We'll have to have all the necessary external work done to both houses at the same time. After all, they're each a part of one building. It's the internal work that I'm not sure about. Like you say, at first we need only one of the houses to be complete, but it might be sensible to have both done at the same time. After all, the tradesmen will be there anyway. I suppose we could have the work done, and then leave the other house unfurnished until we're sure what we're going to be doing. I think I'll have a chat with Bill and Asma about all of this sometime soon. It's going to need a lot of thought.'

The phone rang the following morning, soon after Emily had left for school, and Jane answered it to discover that the call was from the estate agents' office to say that a substantial sum had been offered for the house, conditional on it being available by the end of July, and that the buyer required a decision within forty-eight hours.

Jane was stunned. After she put down the phone, she wandered around the house in a kind of daze muttering 'two hundred and twenty thousand pounds'.

'What on earth am I going to do?' she whispered worriedly. 'We can live at Harold's from the beginning of September... But what about August? And it would be stupid to turn down this offer. In any case, I don't think that I can face much more of showing the house to people.' She took a firm hold of herself and said, 'We'll just have to find somewhere to cover the five weeks from when we leave here until we move into Harold's.'

She told Emily as soon as she came in from school, and they decided that they would phone Eva that evening.

'Do you know who it is that wants our house?' Emily asked.

'Hold on a minute,' Jane replied. 'I wrote it down, but I was in such a daze that I can't remember it.' She looked in the small notebook that was beside the phone. 'I think that there's some link with the hospital. I was told that the buyer had been looking for somewhere for a while, and a deal had just fallen through. And another thing, whoever-it-is is still abroad and hasn't viewed the house. Ah! Here's the name.'

'Does that mean we did all that hard work for nothing?' asked Emily, looking a little dejected.

'Not at all,' Jane assured her. 'Apparently, the buyer's agent came round last week. I do vaguely remember a single man in a rather smart suit.'

'Yes, I do too,' said Emily, screwing up her face in concentration. 'He didn't say much, but he looked in every cupboard, and asked to go up the ladder to look in the loft.'

'And I remember how he stood in the garage for ages, making notes.'

After an early evening meal, Jane phoned Eva and was glad to find that she was in. She told her the news, and Eva immediately suggested that they live with her until they moved into Harold's.

'That's really kind of you, Eva,' said Jane, 'but won't it be too much? A week is one thing, but five weeks is quite another proposition.'

'Yes, it is, isn't it?' said Eva cheerfully. 'A delightful proposition, as far as I'm concerned. And don't worry about all your things. We can ask Harold if he'll store them earlier than planned, and if not, there are bound to be local firms that will do storage.'

Jane tried again to raise her concern that it might be too much for Eva to have them staying for a long time, but Eva cut her off.

'Nonsense!' she said firmly. 'I'm not going to listen to another word on that front. And you must phone the estate agent in the morning and accept that offer.'

'Thanks, Eva. I'll tell Emily straight away.'

Jane put the phone down and turned to Emily. 'I expect you've already guessed what Eva said.'

'Are we going to stay with her?'

'Yes, it's all fixed. She told me to accept the offer, and we're going to move in with her at the end of July.'

'Hooray, hooray, hooray!' shouted Emily as she danced round the room. 'It's just what I wanted.'

'It's a good thing that term ends a few weeks before we leave,' Jane reflected. 'That means we can do most of the packing together.'

Chapter Thirteen

There was so much to attend to that the remaining weeks of term seemed to fly past. Emily and David made plans of how to keep in touch with each other, and Bill, Asma and Jane spoke more about the possibility of Bill's applying for a post at Overton Hospital. There was much discussion about David's schooling. In the end it was decided that he should spend the first year of his secondary education at the local school, but that they would keep thinking about whether or not to move him after that.

The buyer of the house was indeed to be employed at the hospital where Bill was working. He was from Germany, and had a contract that was initially for three years. His sister, who was a nurse, hoped to join him for two of the three years, and was in the process of trying to organise this.

Harold had long since cleared the ground around their new home, and at Jane's request had arranged for a local builder to begin the external work on their house. He was not able to accommodate their possessions any earlier than the end of August. Eva found a store not far from her home, and Jane booked space there.

The day of the removal came. Emily carefully packed the red and green material, still in its frame, by covering it with bubble wrap, and padding it further with some of the clothing that she was taking with her to Eva's. She and Jane said goodbye to the house, and set off with their luggage to take the train to Eva's, while Asma supervised the loading of their possessions into the removal van. She had promised Emily that if anything was accidentally left behind, she would keep it safe until she saw them again, and she and Bill had promised to drive across to bring David to see her one day in the holidays. Emily had been greatly reassured by this, and embarked confidently upon the first stage of her adventure.

It was one of the slow trains that stopped at every station on its way to Middleswell. Once again, Eva was waiting to meet them at the station. She had taken the day off work. Emily flung her arms round

Eva exuberantly, and Jane noticed how Eva looked tearful for a fraction of a second before beginning a cheerful conversation with Emily.

'I thought you'd like to use my bedroom again, so I've got it ready for you,' she said.

Emily skipped along the platform for a few yards, smiling broadly. Then she stopped suddenly and turned to Eva to ask, 'Can I have your special stick by the bed?'

'Of course you can,' Eva replied. 'I used to have it there, but it ended up in a cupboard downstairs. Yes, let's take it back up when we get home.'

Emily skipped along the platform a little further. Then she turned again and rushed back to Eva.

'Where's the envelope with the spirals in?'

'I think I put them back in that cupboard, but you can check when you take your things up,' Eva replied.

Emily seemed to have finished her questions for now, and she ran on ahead, leaving Jane and Eva to talk.

'It's been a stressful time,' said Jane, 'but I've never doubted our plan to move. And everyone's been so helpful. It made such a difference once I knew we'd be coming here first, and Harold has done far more than I'd envisaged, so we've got a head start. Do you know, he's even offered to do some renovation of the outhouses for us? It's on the basis that Emily will help next spring, by looking after lambs that he'll pen there. To be honest, I was happy to agree. There are so many positives in the idea.'

'I've been counting the days until you came,' Eva confided. 'I missed you both so much after Easter, and I was so happy when I knew you would be coming here for a few weeks. And after that you won't be very far away.'

'Yes, we'll be able to see plenty of each other.' Jane reached across and squeezed Eva's arm affectionately.

When Eva drew her car up in front of her house, she turned to the others and said, 'Welcome home. I've made a salad for our lunch. Come on in and get yourselves settled. By the way, Emily, Meg can't wait to see you again. She's got your pots for you.'

The kitchen was rather hot and stuffy, and Eva suggested that they took their food out into her small garden. They sat there relaxing for most of the afternoon, taking slices of poppy seed bread and piling them high with salad.

'What a relief,' said Jane, sighing. 'I seem to have done nothing but sort things out and pack things for weeks and weeks. Now that I'm here with just a change or two of clothes, I still have a feeling that I ought to be doing something urgent, but I'm absolutely certain that I can't.'

Eva chuckled. 'Yes, there's nothing you can do here except relax.'

Emily had grown more and more quiet. She was lying on the grass, and the straw sunhat that Eva had found for her in a cupboard had slipped over her face. Eva reached across and lifted it up gently to find that Emily had fallen asleep.

'I think we shouldn't disturb her,' she said. 'With all that work and excitement she must be exhausted.'

'Yes, we can play some games together this evening when she's recovered a bit and it's cooler,' said Jane. 'Actually, I think I could do with a nap myself. Do you mind if I go in and lie down for a bit?'

'Not at all. I'll stay out here with Emily and read some of my book.'

Jane went into the living room and lay down on the sofa, which Eva had not yet pulled out to make the bed. She welcomed the relative coolness of the room, and soon started to doze. She was grateful to be in the familiar surroundings of Eva's house, and she could feel the tension that had stored up inside her over the last weeks begin to leave her body. One by one, images focussed in her mind, and then dispersed. Her bedroom at her bungalow... George... Clare... spiral patterns... For a moment she started into full consciousness, then she reassured herself that there was nothing important to think about after all, and fell asleep.

When she woke, she could not at first work out where she was. Then she became aware of voices that she recognised as being Emily's and Eva's. The door creaked open, and Emily crept in.

'It's all right, Emily. I'm awake.'

'Oh, good. I've kept coming to look. You've been asleep for ages. Eva said we could play some games this evening, and I've been waiting. Can we play Scrabble?'

'I'll get up and help Eva make something to eat,' said Jane, swinging her feet down on to the floor.'

'It's all right,' said Emily proudly, 'we've got it all ready. Come into the kitchen and you'll get a surprise.'

Over their meal, Emily addressed Eva with a serious expression on her face.

'Eva, please can I look at that book in bed tonight?'

Eva smiled. 'I thought you might want to, so I put it on the shelf near where your head will be.'

Emily beamed happily, and quietly finished her meal.

No one wanted to draw the Scrabble evening to a close, and it was nearly eleven when Emily eventually put the game away, said goodnight, and made her way upstairs. When Eva and Jane had tidied the kitchen and made up their bed, Jane found that she had no difficulty in falling asleep again, even though she had slept for so long in the afternoon.

She woke in the night with a start, but had no idea why. She felt a stab of anxiety, but then told herself firmly that everything was fine, and that she should go back to sleep again. But sleep eluded her, and she rapidly became restless. She tried her best to keep still because she did not want to risk waking Eva, but as time went on, it became more and more difficult.

What was that? She strained to hear. There was nothing. But then she thought that she could hear a rustling sound. Was it a mouse? No, it was the wrong kind of sound. A mouse would make a scratching, scraping sound, and this was definitely a rustle. She was barely breathing as she struggled to identify the source of the sound. Nothing. It must have been an illusion. But there it was again, and this time she was fairly certain that it was coming from upstairs.

She slipped out of bed and made her way silently up the stairs. She peered through the half-open door of Emily's room, and by the light of the moon coming through the thin curtains, she could see Emily carefully taking sheets of paper out of a large brown envelope and laying them on the floor beside her. She was completely absorbed in what she was doing, and showed no awareness of Jane's presence.

Jane stood motionless for a few minutes, trying to decide what to do. As far as she was aware, no harm could come to Emily, and if she missed a lot of sleep it didn't matter, because they had nothing that they had to do over the next few days. Silently, she reversed her steps and returned to her place beside Eva. It was not long before she was asleep once more.

In the morning, Emily was up quite early, bright and full of energy.

'Can we go swimming today?' she asked eagerly.

'I'll have to go in to work for a few hours,' replied Eva, 'but I could drop you two off on my way.'

'We can share a towel,' said Jane.

'Don't worry about that. I've got plenty, and it's easy to dry things in weather like this,' Eva assured her.

'Emily, I think we should wait and have our breakfast when we get back,' Jane suggested.

'Okay,' said Emily, and she dashed off to look in her bag for her costume.

It was while they were trying to practise back crawl that Jane suddenly remembered what she had seen in the night. As they rested, holding on to the side of the pool, she decided to say something to Emily about it, but she thought carefully before beginning.

'Did you sleep okay?' she asked.

'Yes, Auntie Jane. I love Eva's bedroom. The bed is so comfy, and I like having all her things around me. I saw where she'd put that book, but I didn't read any of it last night.'

'Maybe you'll read some tonight.'

Emily looked uncertain. 'Actually, I think I'd like you to read it to me.'

Jane felt pleased by the prospect and said, 'I'd very much like to do that. Let's be sure that we make an early start, and then I can read a chapter or two.'

Emily's eyes had a faraway look. 'I had a lovely dream last night,' she confided.

'What was that?'

'I can't really remember it all now, but I remember the wonderful feelings.'

Jane waited to see if Emily would say anything more. But she was silent, and with the same dreamy look in her eyes, she swirled her body slowly in the water, still holding on to the side of the pool. Jane decided that for now she would say no more. Although she did intend to tell Emily sometime what she had seen, she knew that it was not the right time yet.

Back at Eva's, they had their lunch and were just tidying away when there was a ring at the door. Jane grabbed the tea towel to dry her hands and went to open the door. She found Harold standing there, beaming from ear to ear.

Jane had no reason to conceal her delight. 'Harold! How nice to see you.'

'Nice to see you, too,' he replied. 'I was just passing, and I thought I'd see if you were in.'

'Come on in. Emily and I will make you a mug of something.'

Harold took his boots off. 'They're filthy,' he commented.

'Bring them through and we can stand them in the porch,' said Jane. 'I was going to phone you this evening to let you know that the money for our plot will be transferred to you tomorrow. Oh, I know that our solicitors are dealing with it, but I wanted to tell you anyway.'

Emily had recognised Harold's voice, and had already put the kettle on by the time he appeared in the kitchen. Her manner exuded barely-suppressed excitement, and she burst out, 'When can we come and see you? I want us all to go and look at our new house.'

'As a matter of fact, I've got a couple of hours free now,' Harold replied, smiling. 'Just give me a glass of water, and we can get off straight away.'

Emily carefully chose a glass with a handle, and filled it from the tap. She watched in amazement as Harold gulped it down with considerable speed.

'I can't do that,' she told him.

'And you don't need to learn how, either,' he replied. 'Come on, then. Let's get off. You'll see quite a difference when we get there.'

Not long afterwards, Harold drew the Land Rover up in the lane outside their house.

Emily gasped. 'It's all changed!'

'Yes, it looks quite a bit different now I've got everything cleared away that's not wanted.'

'And you've put a new fence all round the plot,' said Jane.

'I thought you'd need that,' he said with a smile. 'If I put any animals in the field and you're growing vegetables, they might take a fancy to something, and they would have flattened that old fence.'

'I hadn't thought about that,' said Jane. 'But in any case, it's very good of you to do this, you know.'

'Just sensible,' said Harold bluntly. 'I don't want to have to come running down here every five minutes to rescue your garden.' He laughed heartily.

Jane knew that there was more to it than that, but decided not to press the point. Harold was showing considerable generosity towards them, and it was clear that he was deriving pleasure from doing so. She felt that it would be wrong to challenge him on this. However, she made a decision that if he continued to heap kindness upon them, she would have to ensure that they talked about what they could do in return. He had let them have the plot at a price that was favourable to them, and in addition he had insisted that he didn't want the money for it until Clare's house was sold. He had convinced her that it made sense for him to get the external work on the house started for her straight away. His clearing of the land was part of the original deal, as was his invitation to stay at the farmhouse with him once term began. His refurbishing of the outhouses was on condition that Emily would help look after lambs that he would house there, so there was some give and take in that. Certainly the fencing had needed some repair, but a brand new fence was definitely on the generous side, even if he tried to pass it off as being in his best interests. Yes, if he tried to give them anything else, she must insist on a full discussion of what they could do in exchange.

Harold was showing Emily the progress that was being made to the house.

'Look up there,' he said. 'That's where they're working on the roof. There are some rafters inside that will have to be replaced. Come on in, and you'll see a bit of a change already.'

Jane waited at the gate. She sensed that it was a good thing to let Harold show Emily round. The sun was pleasantly warm as she leaned on one of the stone gateposts. At times, she could hear Emily's voice as she chattered to Harold, and sometimes she could make out the deeper sound of his.

When Emily reappeared, her face was flushed with happiness.

'It's so exciting, Auntie Jane. All the rubbish has gone. There are some stairs missing, and there's a big hole through the wall at the bottom of the stairs where the new door's going to be. The kitchen's completely empty and the floor's disappeared!'

'Yes,' said Harold, 'part of the staircase and the whole of the kitchen floor were rotten. Not surprising really. The roof over the kitchen was full of holes, and had been leaking like a sieve for a long time. I know I should never have let it get into such a state, but I...' Here he struggled to speak, but no words came out.

Jane wondered what was happening. To her, Harold looked

upset, but Emily was so taken up with the progress of their new home, that she didn't seem to notice. Instead she chattered on. 'I'm very glad you didn't mend the house before. Someone else might have been living in it, and then we wouldn't have been able to buy it.'

Emily's logic seemed to pull Harold out of whatever was affecting him, and he said, 'No one's been working here today, but there's often something going on. The tradesmen are going between several jobs, and this is just one of them.' He turned to Emily. 'As you can see, there's plenty for you and Jane to organise. It's all up to you now, apart from the outhouses, and I'll make sure a start is made on them soonish. Don't hesitate to get in touch with me if there's anything you want to talk over. I can't say that I'll have all the answers, but I'll probably have something useful to say.'

Emily giggled. 'It would be a terrible mess if we didn't get it right, wouldn't it?'

'Yes, terrible,' Harold agreed. 'Now, I think we'd better show Jane round, hadn't we?' He winked across at Jane.

Emily immediately sprang into action. 'I'll be the guide.'

Jane was very impressed by the progress that had already been made.

'We're most grateful to you for everything you've done,' she said. 'It's been extremely helpful to get the external work off the ground for us. It looks to me as if we might be in by the end of the year.' She felt a little uncertain, but did not show it. 'What do you think, Harold?'

'There's a good chance,' he agreed. 'Yes, unless something unexpected gets in the way, you'll be in before Christmas.'

'Hooray!' shouted Emily, jumping up as high as she could.

'It's good you've got a lot of spare energy, Emily,' said Jane. 'Even when all the tradesmen's work is finished we'll have a lot to do. There'll be plenty of cleaning for a start.'

'I got some practice when we sold our house,' Emily reminded her.

'Yes, you worked very hard.' Jane looked at her watch and turned to Harold. 'We should get back now. I think we've used up your spare time.'

They went back to the Land Rover and climbed in.

Emily was thoughtful during the journey, and Jane had a conversation with Harold about the options for the heating system for the house.

'I've been putting a bit of thought into it,' Jane began, 'and I'd like to go down the route of investigating whether or not we could install a ground source heat pump.'

'Funny you should say that,' said Harold. 'I've been wondering whether to mention that option. The initial outlay is greater than with a standard heating system, but the running costs should be a lot less, and of course, the system is environmentally friendly.'

Here, Emily joined in. 'I know that. My daddy told me.'

Harold looked very surprised, but said nothing. Inwardly he was astonished that this child should have remembered what to him was quite a complex concept. But maybe Jane had been talking to her about it recently. That would explain it.

Jane continued. 'I've printed some information off the Internet, together with names of firms who will supply and install. The other thing I've been looking into is fitting a very high specification of insulation throughout the whole of the house. That way, we won't need much supplementary heating, if any.'

Harold dropped them at Eva's house, and with a cheery wave disappeared up the road.

'I want a heat pump very much, Auntie Jane,' said Emily gravely.

Although she spoke calmly, Jane noticed that her face was tense.

Emily continued. 'Please can we have one? If my daddy was going to live here, I'm sure it's what he would do.'

'I'd very much like us to use some of George's money for that,' said Jane sincerely. 'I'll do my best to research the whole thing properly and push ahead with it, I promise.' Her voice faltered a little as she said, 'I wish George and Clare were here with us now.'

Emily's eyes filled with tears, and they held hands as they unlocked Eva's front door and went in. They sat together quietly on the sofa for a while, each lost in memories of life before George's death.

The silence was eventually broken by Emily, who asked, 'Can we talk about colours for all the rooms, Auntie Jane?'

Jane smiled. 'There's a long way to go before we get to the painting stage. But why not?'

The next hour passed pleasantly as Jane and Emily imagined painting, and sometimes repainting, the walls of various rooms in their home-to-be.

They were still absorbed in their task when Eva arrived home. She was carrying a plastic bag that was bulging with food.

'Emily, would you give me a hand to bring in the rest of the bags?' she called. 'Phew, it was a bit of a struggle getting round the supermarket. It isn't usually as busy as that at this time of day.'

'You should have had us with you to help,' said Jane. 'I feel bad thinking about you doing that on your own.'

'Don't worry,' said Eva. 'It was on my way. Now... what shall we have this evening?'

As they prepared a meal together, Eva said, 'I wish I could take more holiday, but there are things that are pressing now at work.'

Jane laughed. 'I think that Emily and I would like a nice long holiday, but we've got something to do that's even better.'

'Yes, Eva, we've got a lot of work to do for our house,' said Emily seriously.

'Eva, do you mind if I use your computer and your phone while you're at work tomorrow?' asked Jane.

'Help yourself, and I'll look forward to coming home and finding out what you two have been up to in my absence!'

After the meal, Emily reminded Jane about the book. 'I'll go up and get it,' she said.

While she was upstairs, Jane said, 'I think she's keen that we all read it together.'

'What a nice idea,' replied Eva. She spoke to Emily who was now coming back down the stairs. 'I'm going to enjoy this. It's ages since I last looked through it, and I'm sure there'll be things that I've forgotten.'

Emily handed the book to Jane. 'Please will you read the first chapter?'

'Of course.'

They settled themselves, and Jane began to read aloud. Soon they were so engrossed that it was only when Jane had nearly reached the end of the chapter that they noticed that Emily had fallen asleep.

'What a shame,' said Jane. 'Never mind, tomorrow evening we can go over it again.'

Emily was so sound asleep that they decided to pull out the sofa bed and help her into it. Eva would sleep upstairs for the night.

Although at times she was aware that Emily was restless, Jane slept well. When Emily woke, she was intrigued to hear how she had ended up in the bed with Jane.

'I remember Eva reading about the boy and his mummy,' she said, 'and I remember wondering where his daddy was, and after that I must have fallen asleep.'

'We can start again from the beginning tomorrow evening,' Jane reassured her.

The day seemed to fly past. There were many phone conversations about their proposed heat pump. It was obvious to Jane that they would need to advance this soon, as it would involve work in the garden as well as in the house. By lunchtime, she had made an arrangement with a specialist firm to view the site and the house at the beginning of the following week.

After that, they made a list of tradespeople to phone. Jane worked her way through it methodically, arranging provisional dates for different parts of the work on the house. First she made contact with the builder and the joiner who were already working there. After that she phoned a plasterer, a plumber and an electrician. She was glad to find that all the people she phoned knew the others quite well, and were used to working with them. This was a big load off her mind, as she knew that getting jobs to follow one after the other in an orderly sequence could be quite tricky. She and Emily made notes after each phone call, and secured them in the file.

There was only a little time left at the end of the day, and they decided to stroll down the road for half an hour until Eva was due back.

'Eva,' said Jane excitedly as soon as she appeared through the door, 'we've got the ball rolling, although I know that there'll be plenty of hitches along the way.'

'That's good news,' replied Eva.

Jane went on. 'I'm really pleased that there's not going to be a problem about the extra insulation – walls, windows and ceilings. We're going to be offered some choices, and I'm determined to go for the most effective ones. I don't want to cut corners with something so important.'

'And a man's coming about the heat pump next week,' said Emily, smiling contentedly.

Emily was wide awake that evening, during the second reading of the first chapter of Eva's book. She insisted that they read another chapter before she went to bed, and she took the book with her.

'Don't stay awake too long,' Jane warned her. 'We've had a big day, and there'll be plenty more evenings for reading while we're here.'

'All right, Auntie Jane,' Emily called over her shoulder as she disappeared up the stairs.

Chapter Fourteen

Jane spent much of the next morning doing some cleaning and tidying. Eva had left for work quite early, and Emily was still asleep.

When Jane later decided to stop for a drink, she was surprised to find that it was already eleven fifteen. Thinking that she should perhaps check to see if Emily was all right, she went quietly up the stairs and peered round the door to find her wide awake.

'Hello, Auntie Jane. I had a lovely dream, and I can remember it this time.'

Jane sat on the edge of the bed. 'I'd like to hear all about it,' she said. 'And there's something I meant to tell you about the night you had that other dream, but I can save it up.'

'No, tell me now,' Emily insisted.

'I woke in the night and could hear a rustling sound. After a while, I thought it was coming from up here, so I came to see.'

'Did you find anything?' asked Emily curiously.

'Yes, I saw that you were out of bed and on the floor. It was quite dark, but I could see that you were taking some sheets out of an envelope. I decided not to disturb you, and I went back to bed.'

Emily was excited. 'Did you really, really see me doing that?'

'I wouldn't have said so otherwise,' Jane assured her. 'And I was very interested when you told me at the pool that you'd had a dream that had left you with a lovely feeling. Now, tell me what you dreamed last night.'

'I dreamed about the spirals, of course,' said Emily in a matter-of-fact way.

'Why the "of course"?' asked Jane, puzzled.

'When you told me about them at first, you said that they came in your diary after you'd been reading the special book.'

'I see what you mean. We sat together reading the book last night, and then you came upstairs,' said Jane as she turned the situation over in her thoughts. Then she asked, 'Did you read any more before you went to sleep?'

'Just a few pages. After that I must have gone to sleep, because when I woke up this morning I found it had fallen onto the floor. I was worried in case it had got bent, but it was all right, and I put it up on the shelf to be safe.'

'And now you must tell me about your dream.'

'I laid the spirals out like I did with Eva when we stayed here at Easter. When I was sure they were all in the right place, I stood back and looked at them. I was feeling just right. It wasn't only the spirals that felt right, everything felt right. It was such a wonderful feeling.' Emily paused and clasped her hands beneath her chin, as she remembered.

It was clear to Jane that Emily was experiencing a very intense connection to whatever had happened in the dream, so she said nothing and waited quietly for her to be ready to continue.

'There seemed to be a glow coming from somewhere. I don't know if it was coming from the spirals or somewhere else or even from me, but it was definitely there.'

Jane felt a surge of excitement run through her as Emily said this. That glow was something that had been associated with her spirals before, but not through Emily.

Emily was so immersed in the memory of her experience that she did not seem to notice Jane's reaction.

'Then the palms of my hands felt strange. I've never felt anything like that before. It was very strong – a sort of rushing feeling – and I had to hold my hands over the spirals, just like I held them over your boxes, Auntie Jane. But after that it was different.'

'How do you mean?'

'My hands were going up and down and backwards and forwards and curving inwards, all at different times. They were sort of flowing.'

'Were both your hands doing the same thing?'

'No. Oh… it's so hard to explain.'

'Why not just show me?'

'That's a good idea. I'll try.'

Emily sat up in bed, then put her hands out in front of her with her palms downwards and shut her eyes. At first she was very still, but then she started to move her hands slowly, and Jane began to see what she had tried to describe. It was fascinating to watch, but she had no idea what it meant.

'I don't think I can do it any more at the moment, Auntie Jane,' said Emily. 'When I was doing it in the dream I could have done it forever, but this time I feel very tired.'

'Just lie down again,' Jane advised. 'You've given me a very good idea of what happened, and that's enough. Do you know, Emily, this reminds me very much of when we stayed here at Easter.'

'You mean when you saw me come down the stairs in the night?'

'Yes. I would say that the way you were using your hands above the spirals then was almost exactly how you've shown me just now, from your dream.'

'I'm so glad,' whispered Emily.

'At Easter I had felt that you were in some way reading the spirals.'

'Stop, Auntie Jane, there's more dream,' said Emily passionately. 'And I *must* tell you about it.'

'That's all right. Carry on.'

'Words were coming in through my hands.'

'I'm not sure I understand what you mean.'

'I couldn't hear words and I couldn't see words, but there were words coming from the spirals. They came through my hands and up my arms and into my head.'

Jane was stunned. She was completely lost for what to say.

'And it was very hard for me because I didn't understand any of the words.' Suddenly Emily changed from appearing serene to looking upset, and Jane put her hand on her shoulder to steady her. 'They were beautiful words and I wanted to understand them, but I couldn't. Don't worry about me, Auntie Jane, this is nice upset and not horrible upset.'

Jane smiled at Emily, and kept her hand on her shoulder.

Emily went on. 'I don't know why, but I thought that some of it meant "go to the".'

'That's interesting,' said Jane calmly. Her mind was racing. What was this? She wished that Eva were here and not at work. In fact, she wished that Ellen were here, too.

As if she had read her thoughts, Emily asked, 'What time is Eva coming home?'

'I can't say exactly. I expect it'll be around the same time as usual. But we could send her an e-mail if you want.'

Emily nodded. 'I'd like that. Can we do it straight away?'

'I'll go and boot up the computer, if you get yourself dressed.'

Jane had just switched on the power when the phone began to ring.

'Drat,' she said. She thought of ignoring it, but decided that it could be something important, and picked it up. 'Hello,' she said, in a voice that would deter any opportunist salesman.

'Hello, is that Eva? This is Ellen. I thought you'd be at work, and I was going to leave a message.'

'Ellen! It's Jane. Emily and I are staying here for a few weeks. I'm *so* glad to hear you. I was just thinking about you. What message were you going to leave?'

'A few weeks?'

'It's a long story. I'll bring you up to date once you've given me your message.'

'I was phoning to let Eva know I'll be travelling through next week and wondered if I could stay overnight.'

'Oh! We'd love to see you. There's so much to talk about.'

'But I won't be able to stay, because there won't be enough room. I'll book somewhere nearby.'

'No, don't do that. I'm sure we'll find a way of squeezing everyone in.'

By this time Emily was standing next to Jane and asked, 'Is she going to come and see us soon?'

'Yes, very soon,' Jane replied. 'Next week.' Jane spoke to Ellen again. 'I'll let Eva know as soon as she comes in. We'll phone back this evening and get everything fixed. Bye for now.'

She put the phone down and said to Emily, 'This is just what we want, isn't it?'

Emily nodded vigorously, and then murmured, 'She *has* to come. It's the right time.'

Inwardly, Jane agreed that it was the right time, but she made no comment upon what Emily had said, as she felt that there was more to it than she realised. In fact, it had come across more as a kind of prediction than an observation. She began to write the e-mail message to Eva, and Emily joined her.

When they had sent off the message, they spent some time looking at booksellers' websites to see if there were any copies of the book. Jane was not surprised to draw a blank, as she knew that Eva herself was good at tracking things down, and had had no luck.

'I wish I knew where my own copy has got to,' she said irritably.

'I'd hoped that it would finally turn up when we were packing, but there was no sign of it.'

'Never mind,' said Emily, trying to comfort her.

'Actually, I feel quite upset about it,' Jane admitted.

'Are you sure you brought it to my house when you moved?' asked Emily.

Jane pondered for a moment. 'Do you know, I can't be certain that I did.' She fell silent again, and then said, 'If I didn't, then either it's gone forever, or it's still at my bungalow. It's all very strange, because I would have thought that I'd packed it next to my diary when I moved. I think I'll write to the tenants. I don't suppose anything will come of it, but I should give it a try.'

Emily found Eva's pad of writing paper, and Jane wrote a brief letter. She added a postscript to say that she would want to reimburse any postage if indeed they had the book. After that they checked the messages to find that there was already a reply from Eva.

'Oh good,' said Jane. She opened it to discover that Eva would be back around six, and that she was delighted to hear the news of Ellen.

Emily was hopping from one foot to the other and back again. 'Can I post the letter *now*?' she asked urgently.

Jane smiled. 'Thanks,' she said. She put a stamp on the letter and handed it to Emily, who dashed off out of the front door at speed.

That evening, there was much to discuss.

'Eva, do you have a blow-up mattress?' asked Emily.

'Yes, it's in one of the cupboards upstairs.'

'Good. When Ellen comes she can sleep upstairs in the bed, and I'll sleep on the mattress on the floor.'

'Are you sure?' asked Eva. 'There isn't all that much room.'

'I'll put my head at the window end,' said Emily. 'Then if Ellen gets out of bed, she'll only step on my feet.'

Emily's practical approach made Jane and Eva laugh.

'Let's ring her now, and see if your idea will suit her,' Eva suggested. She picked up the phone and was soon speaking to Ellen. Jane could hear her chuckling as Eva explained Emily's plan. There was further conversation about dates and times, after which Eva replaced the phone.

'That's it fixed,' she said. She turned to Emily and said, 'And now I want to know all about your dream.'

After Emily and Jane had finished telling her, Eva said, 'I think that if Ellen weren't just about to come, I'd phone to tell her that she had to.'

On the day before Ellen was due to arrive, the doorbell rang while Emily and Jane were eating breakfast. Emily dashed to open it, with Jane following close behind. It was the postman.

'It's a packet for you,' he said. 'Special Delivery. You'll have to sign.' While Jane was signing a sheet that was clipped onto a small board, he handed the packet to Emily.

'It's addressed to you,' said Emily as Jane closed the door.

'Me? I thought it would be for Eva. I wonder what it is.'

They returned to the kitchen, where Jane took scissors from the drawer and carefully snipped open the packet.

'Oh, look, Emily!' she exclaimed. 'It's my copy of the book. The people in the bungalow did have it after all.'

'Where did they find it?'

'I don't know, it doesn't say. Oh, hang on a minute, there's a note pushed in between the pages.' She took it out and read it. 'I can hardly believe this.'

'What is it, Auntie Jane?'

'It says that when they moved in, they found I'd left it on the bedside table, as if inviting them to read it. How very strange...'

Ellen was looking forward to seeing her friends again, and to be meeting Emily at last. Through her earlier contact with Jane and Eva, she had known much about her young life, and had always taken an interest in it.

She decided to set off early and break the journey around half way. She packed her things, and set the alarm for six. When she woke, she had no difficulty in getting up, and she left just before seven. As she drove along, she enjoyed the fact that the morning air was pleasantly warm. The forecast had predicted a very hot day, and with luck, she should avoid being on the road in the worst of it.

She took a short break around nine, and phoned Jane to give her some idea of when she would arrive.

'Don't worry,' said Jane as they ended the call. 'I'll wait in for you. Whatever you do, don't hurry. The important thing is that you

135

get here safely.'

Emily was so excited that she could hardly sit still.

'Why don't we bake some biscuits while we're waiting?' Jane suggested. 'Then they'll be ready for when she arrives.'

Emily agreed, but insisted that they look for a new recipe amongst Eva's books and magazine cuttings. She was eventually drawn to one that used cinnamon and oats in the ingredients, and was soon engrossed in her task.

Ellen arrived when Jane was just in the process of lifting the biscuits out of the oven, so Emily went to let her in.

'I've been so excited about you coming,' Emily burst out as she took Ellen to the kitchen. She hesitated, and then added, 'But now you're here, I can't think of anything to say.'

'I'm feeling much the same,' said Ellen cheerfully, and she could see Emily relax. 'It's a pity I'm only here for a night. I wish we had more time to spend together, because I think we've got a lot to talk about.'

'We surely have,' said Jane with obvious feeling. 'I didn't tell you on the phone because the whole thing was so new and seems complicated, but Emily had a really big dream the other night about the spirals.'

Ellen looked startled, but to Jane's surprise, she said calmly, 'Ah, yes... the spirals. Emily, although this is a big surprise to me, in some way it's not, and I'm very glad indeed to be here.'

'In fact,' said Jane, 'you phoned to speak to Eva just after Emily and I had been talking about her dream. I was in the middle of trying to take it all in.' She broke off. 'Ellen, I haven't even asked you yet how your journey went.'

'Never mind about that, it was completely uneventful. Jane, I could do with something to drink, but after that I'd like to hear all about what's been happening.'

Emily served out drinks and her biscuits, and Ellen made appreciative noises as she sampled hers.

'I like your long hair, Ellen,' said Emily as she gently fingered the thick plait at the back of Ellen's head.

Ellen smiled. 'Thank you, Emily. I've always had my hair like that. I've never felt like being adventurous with it. Of course, it isn't quite the colour that it used to be.'

'That's what Eva says about hers,' said Emily, 'and we told her not to put any dye in it.'

'Yes,' said Jane, 'we like her best just as she is.'

'Ellen,' said Emily, 'I think you're a bit taller that Eva, but you'll still fit in her bed.'

'I expect so,' Ellen replied, laughing. She looked at Jane and said in a very direct way, 'Before we begin, tell me exactly how much Emily knows about the spirals.'

'Quite a lot,' Jane replied. 'We came across my diary together some months ago, when I was trying to clear some of my boxes out of the garage at Clare's.'

'Yes, I remember you telling me about that one day when I phoned.'

'Of course. What else have I told you?'

'I can't remember anything else, except that you described how Emily had seemed to sense with her hands that there was something important in that box.'

'Mm, well, quite a lot has happened since then.' Jane turned to Emily. 'Shall I tell her, or do you want to?'

'You tell her about the things you saw me doing when I was walking about in my sleep, and I'll tell her about my dreams.'

'Okay. Here goes...'

Ellen asked very little, while they took it in turns to explain everything.

When they had finished she said, 'Emily, how much did Eva and Jane tell you of how I reacted to the spirals years ago?'

'They said they had to watch you carefully because they were worried about you.'

Jane broke in. 'Eva and I told her quite a bit of what we remembered.'

'Yes, we talked about the spirals in chapters,' Emily added cheerfully.

Ellen looked puzzled.

'What Emily means is that there was so much to tell that we split it up into a number of evenings. It was a good thing, because that way we all had time to think. We told Emily something of how you could change so quickly when the spirals were laid out.'

'It sounds to me as if what has been happening to Emily has some similarity,' said Ellen, 'but I never got to the point where my hands felt as if they were *reading* the spirals.'

137

'I wish it would happen when I am awake,' said Emily with a tinge of sadness in her voice.

'It's early days,' said Ellen wisely. 'If my experience is anything to go by, other things may well happen. I'm fascinated to learn that the spirals appeared on the day that you were supposed to be born. None of us knew that at the time when we were working with them.'

'That had a big impact on me, too,' said Jane. 'And if Emily hadn't insisted on looking at the date in my diary, I might not have made the connection even yet.'

'Emily, I don't want to lose sight of the dreams you had about the poorly-dressed girl,' said Ellen determinedly. 'And please will you both remember to let me know if anything else happens. I'm here for just one night, but I'm only a phone call away.'

Jane and Emily gave her an assurance that they would keep in touch, and then Ellen said, 'I think I could do with a stroll. We must talk again about all of this later, when Eva comes home.'

They all agreed to walk by the river, taking with them some sandwiches and a drink. Despite the heat, it was pleasant. They eventually arrived back at the house just after Eva, who had been able to leave work a little early.

The evening passed all too quickly, and when Emily began to yawn, Jane helped her upstairs to bed, and then she, Jane and Ellen decided to follow suit. The arrangement upstairs worked well, with Ellen finding it easy to step over Emily's feet and make herself comfortable in the bed.

The next day breakfast was something of a rush, because Eva had to leave by eight and Ellen by nine, but there was time for some conversation with her after Eva had left.

'Thanks for letting me use the bed, Emily,' said Ellen. 'Were you okay on the floor?'

'Yes, but I don't remember you coming to bed.'

Ellen chuckled. 'Then you must have fallen asleep straight away, because I came up not long after you.' Suddenly she swayed a little in her seat, and took hold of the table.

Jane put her hand on her arm. 'What is it, Ellen?' she asked.

'It isn't anything.'

'No,' said Jane firmly, 'something's amiss.'

Emily brought a glass of water and handed it to Ellen, who took a few sips, before shaking her head slightly as if to clear it. 'Sometimes one of my ears blocks for a second or two, and it makes me feel disorientated. It's fine now.'

Jane scrutinised her face, but Ellen looked her normal self, so she said nothing more.

However, Ellen herself said, 'Wait a minute. There is something... When I woke up this morning, there was something in my mind, but I pushed it on one side in the rush of getting up to say goodbye to Eva.'

'What was it?' asked Emily. 'Was it something about me?'

'I don't think so,' Ellen replied slowly. She was about to turn her mind to her impending journey when she remembered something. 'This must sound silly,' she said, 'but the word "barn" seems to be something to do with it.'

'It doesn't sound silly to me,' Jane assured her. 'I know it was years ago now, but there were words you said then that turned out to be important.'

Ellen nodded. 'You're right,' she replied. 'I'll certainly let you know if anything else comes to me.'

As Jane and Emily waved her off at nine, Emily called out, 'I wish you could come back this way and see us again soon.'

'I wish I could, too, and I'm sorry I can't,' Ellen called back. 'It's been so lovely to see you.'

Chapter Fifteen

The rest of Jane and Emily's stay at Eva's passed very quickly. They bought school uniform for Emily, ready for the beginning of term, and they moved to Harold's the weekend before term started. The farmhouse seemed huge compared with Eva's compact dwelling, and at first Emily felt a little lost as she wandered from room to room. She and Jane decided to share a bedroom, at least until she had settled in, and Eva promised to come and see them soon. Jane decided that she would leave their main possessions in store meantime.

Now that they were only just up the road from their new home, they walked down to see it every day. Already the necessary trenches for the heat pump had been prepared. Most of the external work on the house itself had been completed, and the internal work was advancing, although there was still much to do.

Emily settled at school after the first day. She was excited about the list of subjects she was to study, and she phoned Eva about it so that they could work out when to begin their sessions together. It was agreed that after the half-term break would be the best time, thus making good use of the long dark evenings.

Now completely confident that they had made the right choice, Jane threw her energies into overseeing the work on their house, and helping Harold with some of the paperwork for the farm. She found that she enjoyed these challenges greatly, and her confidence increased by leaps and bounds.

She realised with a shock that since she had given up her job to care for Emily, she had slowly and imperceptibly come to doubt her ability to be in full-time employment. The process had been so gradual that she had not noticed it happening. Not only was she shocked by the realisation, but also she was puzzled. After all, she had worked for many years before George's death, and indeed she had studied for her OU degree. Why should she doubt her capacities now? As she pondered this question, she began to realise that this must be something to do with the effect of Clare's death upon her. The more she thought about it, the more it made sense. She had lost her only sister, and underneath she had been so afraid of losing Emily, too, that she had given up everything to be there for her. And giving up everything had included giving up any thought of her own future. Yes, this was how her confidence had slipped. Once they were established in their new home, she would have to put her mind to remedying this situation, she told herself firmly.

In between her main tasks, Jane would sometimes fill Harold's kitchen with baking. The room certainly lent itself to the preparation of large quantities of food, and she was pleased to feel that she was giving Harold something in return for all his kindness. The years seemed to fall away from him when he came in to the smell of baking, and he appeared almost boyish at such times. After the half term break, a pattern soon emerged in which Eva would often come and eat with them on her way home from work, and then stay on to tutor Emily.

They kept in touch with Bill, Asma and David, and planned together that David would come and stay as soon as he could after they were settled in. They learned that the new neighbours were pleasant and hardworking.

Harold was greatly impressed with their house as it progressed.

'You'll be nice and snug in here,' he said one day as he and Jane inspected it. 'It's nothing like my draughty old place with the high ceilings and nothing much to pad it. Maybe when I retire I'll build myself something warm.' He laughed loudly. 'But that's a good few years away,' he added hurriedly. However, Jane could see that he had started to think ahead, beyond the next year or two.

Emily was clearly growing to be very fond of Harold. Sometimes he brushed her attentions to one side, but this never deterred her.

'He just needs practice,' she explained to her aunt.

Jane observed that a particular kind of relationship was developing between the two. It wasn't that of a father and daughter, or of an uncle and niece, or indeed a grandfather and granddaughter, but it was certainly a relationship that could be found within families, and it was close.

Harold would talk to Jane about how Emily was getting on at school, and he obviously had in his mind thoughts about her future. It was clear that he wanted things to work out well for her.

Emily's eleventh birthday passed fairly quietly. Whenever Jane had asked her what she wanted for a present, she always replied 'our house', and would not be swayed from that. Things looked promising for their being able to move in during the Christmas holidays. The kitchen and bathroom were being installed in one side of the house, and the painters were working at weekends to finish the interior of that side. As time had passed, Jane had decided to leave the finishing touches to the other side of the house until the better weather. That way, she and Emily could do some of the work themselves, which they were both keen to do.

Harold was determined that whatever the outcome, Christmas would be in the farmhouse, with Eva as a guest. As it turned out, Jane moved their possessions from storage into their house the week before Christmas, and Harold had promised to help them to place the furniture and put the beds together once Christmas was past.

On the day that they officially moved in, Emily was ecstatic.

'But we're not leaving you,' she told Harold. 'We're just down the road, and we'll be coming up to see you lots.'

Harold felt warmed by her assurance. He had been dreading the day when his house would no longer be filled with the sound of her cheerful chatter. Jane had noticed that he had been a bit off-hand recently, and had guessed accurately the reason for this. She had already let him know that she would like to continue to help with the paperwork until they had cleared the backlog, and she had told him that she hoped that he would come and eat with them at least one evening a week. He had tried to brush off her offer of shared meals, but she surprised herself by being not just firm, but forceful, about it.

'You haven't got any choice,' she said determinedly. 'We've been living as a family for four months. You can't possibly put that on one side.'

He glared at her, and opened his mouth to say something grumpy and off-putting, but shut it again, swallowed hard, and said, 'Thanks.' He swallowed again, gathered himself, put his hand in his pocket, and took out a key. 'Here's your own key to the farmhouse. I'm giving up on the hiding place for keys. I've heard of too many burglaries of late.'

Jane was about to protest, but he stared at her belligerently, and said with a triumphant air, 'You'll need it to get into the office when I'm not in.'

She decided to accede, and she took the key saying, 'Thank you.

That's helpful.'

Right from the first night, Emily loved her own room. She had all her familiar things there now, and because the room was larger than the one she had before, Jane had bought her a desk and some bookshelves, so that she could study there if she wanted. She and Jane worked hard on the other side of the house whenever they could. The second bathroom was eventually installed there, and they decided to use the room that had been the kitchen for a utility room. They did most of the painting work themselves, and when it was all finished, they bought some simple furniture and invited Bill, Asma and David to stay at Easter.

Emily and David spent many happy hours roaming round the countryside in the immediate locality, in places where Harold had taught her that it was safe to go. They were tempted to collect some of the prolific frogspawn that they saw in the ditches, but remembered that it was better to watch it where it belonged. The black centre of each slippery globe was beginning to look comma-like in shape, and Emily looked forward to seeing baby frogs later on, and sending news of them to David.

As things worked out, this visit moved forward their plans about the future. Bill became certain that David should attend the same secondary school as Emily. He felt that although it was not necessary to go to the same school to keep in touch with each other, it certainly was important to give David a chance of better schooling.

Bill, Asma and David listened intently to everything Emily was telling them about her school life, and despite the fact that it was the Easter holidays, Bill resolved to push things forward. He contacted the school, and found that the deputy head was willing to see them straight away. This time, he and Asma took David with them, and after this, he was determined to find a way to make it possible for David to attend.

Chapter Sixteen

Over her years at secondary school, Emily grew into a graceful young woman. She loved helping Harold with tasks on the farm, and her wiry physical strength increased as she grew and matured. She became a little taller than Jane, but only by about an inch or so.

She excelled in her studies. Not only was she bright and intelligent in her school work, but also she broadened her academic skills under Eva's inspiring tuition. Jane could see that she now had an almost insatiable hunger for learning – particularly in subjects that led on from what George, her father, had taught her. Emily herself would comment on the fact that although she still missed her father very much, she felt close to him.

Emily had maintained her friendship with David during the years that he attended her school. Bill had at last fulfilled his ambition to obtain a senior position at Overton Hospital, and had become the head of a rapidly-expanding unit, so within two years of Emily's move, David had joined her at her school. Bill and Asma had bought a house on the Middleswell side of Overton, but despite this, his journey to school was time-consuming. However, studying on the bus soon became a habit of his, and so he used the travelling time well. He later gained a place at medical school, as he was determined to follow in his father's footsteps. Once again, he and Emily pledged to keep in touch with each other and to meet up in the holidays whenever they could.

With Emily at school and the house completed, Jane continued to help Harold, but also joined a temping agency, and worked an increasing number of hours as a secretary when local firms were in need of help. As time went on, her name was passed round as someone who was very reliable and competent, who could pick up the threads of a new situation with ease. At first she would only take on work that would allow her to be at home when Emily came in from school, but as Emily grew older, that became less of a necessity, and on the days when Jane would be late home, Emily liked to cook something for her.

To his surprise and relief, Harold had adapted quickly to joining in with Jane and Emily's household. In addition to finding excuses to call in or leave things on the doorstep, he usually ate with them at least once a week, and in the dark evenings they often sat up late – talking, or playing a few simple board games. On such evenings, Emily was more than happy to finish her studies early in order to have time with him.

Throughout these years, Emily never lost her awareness of the spirals. She thought about them in some way nearly every day. Mostly, her sense of them was as a strand of life that was quietly running alongside her studies and her daily interests and concerns. She knew that they had a continuing importance in her life, but she had no obvious clues as to what that might be. Sometimes they would present quite strongly in her mind, and at such times, she and Jane would sit and talk again about how they had appeared in Jane's diary, about the book that Jane had been reading, and about the experiences that Jane, Eva, Ellen and the others had shared because of them. They would always finish by going over what Emily's own experience of them had been. Although Emily sometimes found that she learned another detail of their effect on the others, their conversations never resulted in her feeling that any steps forward were being taken in the understanding of them, and of her part in that.

Whenever Jane and Eva spoke to each other about the whole subject, they pondered about why nothing more had happened regarding the spirals. They wondered if now that Emily was so passionately engaged in studies that were a constant reminder of her connection with her father, it might be that her openness to the effect of the spirals was lessened, but this was merely surmise, and they could in no way feel certain.

When the time came, Emily needed no encouragement to apply for a place at university, and she was accepted at the one of her choice, where she would be studying environmental engineering. Jane was very proud of Emily's achievements.

As the time drew closer to the day when Emily would leave home for her first term, Jane had no doubts about how much she would miss her niece. She realised that she must use this time to establish herself in an occupation that would not only absorb her energies, but would also stimulate her deeper interests.

On the day that Emily left, Jane and Harold took her to the station and waved her off. Tears were streaming down Jane's cheeks as she and Harold left the station together. She could hardly see where she was going, and was about to walk past the Land Rover, when Harold grabbed her hand roughly and pulled her back.

'Come on! And wipe your eyes,' he commanded.

Jane was taken aback. She felt that the sudden change in his behaviour was uncharacteristically harsh, until she looked at his face and saw that he too was obviously distressed.

'She'll be fine,' he said, 'and it's up to us to sort ourselves out. I've got something I want to talk over with you. Will you come in for a while when we get back?'

'Of course.'

The journey took place in silence, each of them lost in their own thoughts.

Back in his kitchen, Harold filled two mugs with tea, and sat with Jane at the table.

'I'm not getting any younger,' he stated baldly.

'You're pretty fit, though.'

'That doesn't mean I'm not getting older, and I've been starting to wonder when to hand the farm over to my nephews. But the more I think about it all, the more I know that I'll need to have something to be getting on with.'

'That sounds sensible to me.'

'And,' he said shrewdly, 'I wouldn't be surprised if you're thinking you'll need to be taking on something a bit more than before.'

Jane looked directly at him and asked, 'Exactly what have you got in mind, Harold?'

'Nothing concrete yet, but I've been wondering if we could set up a business together – something that wasn't as heavy work as I've been doing, but something that's a bit of a challenge. What do you think?'

Jane felt a spark of interest inside her and said, 'Perhaps we could think about it. Neither of us needs to be in a rush, though.'

Harold nodded. A seed had been planted. They could wait and see what grew from it. He shook her hand. 'Here's to the unknown.'

Jane was astonished. Harold had never spoken like this before.

As if reading her thoughts, he said, 'I didn't want any big changes while Emily was at home. I didn't want to unsettle her. She's had enough in her young life, and I wanted to help to give her something stable.'

Jane stared at him, reflecting on thefact that behind that often gruff exterior was a man of sensitivity and integrity. 'Perhaps we could sit down again like this in a week or two,' she suggested.

'Done,' he replied, and went to rinse his mug under the tap.

'I'll walk back down the road,' said Jane, picking up her bag.

Harold made no move.

Chapter Seventeen

Emily settled into university life with the same kind of ease as she had shown at secondary school. As with the change of school, this step constituted a complete change of location and of companions, but it did not in any way disturb her focus on her studies. She made a number of new friends, throwing herself into the kind of social life that she enjoyed, and trying out some new activities. She soon became known to the staff as a reliable student who gained good grades, and known to her peers as a pleasant companion who was always helpful.

She missed Jane and all the life that was based around her home, but not in a way that dragged at her energies. The holidays were full of talks about what she had been learning and about how things had changed in her absence, and she always made opportunities to keep in touch with David.

It was not long after Emily had returned to begin her final year at university that she first encountered him – a young man who was entirely new to her. The effect of this upon her was one that she could not recognise, as she knew that she had never felt like this before about anyone.

She had volunteered to go back a couple of days early, to help to familiarise the new entrants with the department. She was allocated to a group of three – two males and one female – and her attention was drawn immediately to one of the males. Although she had never seen him before and she did not know his name, she felt that she recognised him instantly. But what was it about him that had that effect? She guessed that he must be about six feet tall. He had ordinary-looking short brown hair, and he dressed in a nondescript way – with the usual kind of tee-shirt and denim jeans that one would expect – and noticed that he seemed a little detached.

So what was it that drew her so strongly? Puzzled, she listened carefully to the way he spoke, but there was no obvious clue there. His voice was lower than tenor, but not as deep as bass, and the accent that he had was almost indiscernible. Having got no further, she decided to sideline the dilemma for now, and think about the whole thing later. After all, there was no urgency.

When she had shown the group round, and answered their questions as best she could, she asked cheerfully, 'Anyone for coffee?'

By this time she had ascertained that the girl's name was Rose, and that the other male was called Joe, but still *he* was nameless.

She addressed him. 'Sorry, I didn't catch your name.'

'Barnaby,' he told her, with a guileless smile.

She nodded in acknowledgement. 'Follow me,' she said to the group. 'I know somewhere that's okay.'

From then on, Emily felt attached to him – yes, attached. Curiously, it did not occur to her to consider whether or not he knew this, or indeed if he too felt something.

At first she did not catch sight of him all that often, but when she did, she would always go to speak to him, even if only to pass the time of day. Her constant awareness of him did not trouble her, whether he was there or not. On the few occasions when she stopped to think about it, she was still unable to identify any other connection with a person that felt the same. But she did not spend time puzzling about this. She just accepted it. It was almost as if that connection had always been there. But how could that be, if she had met him only so recently? She hardly ever felt ruffled or disturbed about it, but if she did, she reminded herself of her connection with the spirals. After all, before she had conscious knowledge of their existence, she had been able to sense that there was something important in one of Jane's boxes, and this had led to her formal introduction to the spirals and everything that had since emerged about her connection with them. Could it be that, somewhere in her unconscious self, she had already known that she would encounter Barnaby? She felt that this was certainly something to consider, but perhaps only later. For now, she was content to leave that question, and focus solely upon her academic work.

As this was her final year, Emily was deeply engrossed in her studies. Barnaby's existence in her life did not in any way interfere with this, or indeed enhance it. She had no time or wish to seek him out, and she certainly had no need. And all the while, it seemed that he was there, somewhere inside her.

It wasn't until the latter part of the first term that anything of note took place between them, and it was something entirely practical. She came out of a lecture, and found him waiting for her outside.

'Excuse me,' he said politely. 'I wonder if you'd mind helping me with some of my work.'

'I will if I can,' she replied. She smiled and added, 'But if it's not my subject, I don't think I'll be much use.'

'One of my tutors told me you might be able to help,' he explained.

'Who's that?'

'Ben Cook.'

'Ben? So it's maths, then.'

'Is it your subject?'

'It is and it isn't. Have you got it with you?'

'As a matter of fact, I have.'

'Shall we go up to one of the open areas outside the library, and I'll have a look?'

'Thanks.'

They said very little as they made their way through throngs of students moving to diverse destinations. When they arrived, they found an empty table, and sat down.

'I like this space,' said Barnaby.

'Yes, we're lucky to have it. I think it was suggested by the Union about ten years ago, and everyone was really surprised when the idea was taken up.'

Barnaby began to take some papers out of the file that he had been carrying.

'Look, I should say that I haven't got much time today,' said Emily quickly, 'but if I get some idea of what it's about and I think I can help, we can fix another time.'

'Okay.'

Barnaby pushed the papers along the table, and Emily concentrated on them for a few minutes before taking her diary out of her bag.

'What time are you free on Friday?' she asked.

'Any time in the afternoon.'

'See you here at three?'

'Thanks very much. That would be fine for me.'

Emily wrote in the space for Friday 12th November. 'Library.

Barnaby. Three.'

Then she turned to him and said, 'I'll see you then.'

He nodded in a slightly formal manner, and they went their separate ways.

On Thursday evening, Emily worked on until late. This was not unusual. She loved the peace of the late evening, and the feeling of there being nothing that would disrupt her flow of thought, and so she often chose this time for her most concentrated study.

But when she eventually went to bed, instead of the near-instant deep slumber that she expected, her sleep was very disturbed. She tossed and turned, sometimes sleeping, sometimes dozing, and sometimes wide awake.

Morning came at last, and she was surprised to find that she didn't feel tired. She washed and dressed, ate some breakfast, and set off for her lectures. She was soon engrossed in the first.

Yet, over lunch with friends, she realised that she felt distracted. At first she put it down to the effects of her restless night, but later, on her way to meet Barnaby, she began to wonder if there was more to it, although she could not grasp what that might be.

As they sat together, she began by telling him of Eva, and the sessions they had had together over the years when she was at secondary school.

She finished by saying, 'She really was quite an extraordinary kind of tutor. Of course, I had known her a bit before then, because she was a close friend of my Aunt Jane.' She stopped and swallowed, and then said. 'My parents died before I went to secondary school, and Jane looked after me until I left home.' She looked down at Barnaby's file.

Barnaby had listened quietly and intently to everything she told him about Eva, and when she referred to her parent's death, his general demeanour changed very little, but his gaze showed compassion. 'Thank you for telling me,' he said.

Although Emily continued to look at Barnaby's file, she sensed the warmth of his response. She gave no reply, and instead looked at her watch. 'I think we should get on,' she said. 'I don't have all that long – about an hour.'

They worked side by side until after four, when Emily glanced at her watch and said, 'That's all for today. Let me know if you need any more help later.' She stood up and bent to pick up her bag.

'Thanks very much. I'm hugely grateful. I...' his voice trailed off. 'I mean, would you be willing to do some more next week? It's... fascinating.'

Emily consulted her diary. 'Same time, same place?'

'Thanks,' he called after her as she walked away briskly.

And that had been the beginning of their spending time together.

As she lay awake in bed that night, Emily thought of the abacus that Jane had bought for her when she was small – that, and the magical set of bricks. Those bricks... Jane had given her the first ones, and then her dad had added to them. She had always kept these very precious things in her bedroom, long after she had finished using them, and they were in her bedroom at home now, safely packed away. When she was there, she would sometimes take the bricks out and handle them, remembering watching her father's strong hands working with them as they sat together, playing. Then she thought of Harold, and all that she had learned from him. After that, she thought of Eva's rather quaint house, and the time that she had lived there with Aunt Jane. And, of course, the spiral patterns...

November. November 12th. 'This is the date on which I should have been born,' she murmured, 'and the day when the spirals appeared in Jane's diary.'

Her body felt warm and deeply relaxed as she drifted off to sleep. And when she woke the following morning, it was as if the double spiral had imprinted itself in her mind.

Emily had been looking forward to going home for the Christmas break. Jane and Eva had planned to meet her at the station. When she had told Jane, during one of their twice-weekly phone calls, what her time of arrival would be, Jane had insisted that she and Eva would be there. Emily had pointed out that this had long since ceased to be necessary, but Jane was adamant.

In the event, as the train drew alongside the platform, it was Jane and Harold who were waiting for her. Harold took her bag as she stepped onto the platform, and she and Jane hugged each other tightly.

'Eva couldn't come after all,' Jane explained. 'She had to go to the dentist. Something painful started up in one of her teeth. She was disappointed not to be here.'

'Poor Eva!' said Emily. 'I'll give her a ring this evening, and I'll see her soon. Now, tell me how you two are getting on with your plans.'

'First, let's load ourselves into my Land Rover,' said Harold.

As he led the way to the car park, Emily remembered back to the day, almost two years ago, when Jane had announced that Harold was about to retire, and that he and she were going to set up a small business together. It had been a surprise to her at the time, although looking back, she realised that it shouldn't have been. Until then, she had retained her childlike view of Harold as being indestructible, and it had never crossed her mind that he would ever do anything other than run his farm. Since then, he had converted some of the farm's outbuildings into a cosy home for himself, and his nephews had taken over much of the farm, having split the farmhouse into two flats for themselves. One was an electrician and the other was a plumber, and each continued to work part time in their trade, while working the farm together. Both had shown no inclination to settle down as family men, but as they were in their late thirties, Emily supposed that there was still time. Harold had retained a piece of land and some of the other outbuildings, and he and Jane had set up a small garden centre, which had flourished and expanded. Their current project was to add a section that would sell locally-produced foodstuffs, such as bottled fruits and preserves.

When they reached the Land Rover, Emily patted it affectionately.

Harold laughed at this, saying, 'Yes, it's done me good service for a very long time, and I'll be sorry to part with it.' He noticed a fleeting look of upset pass across Emily's face, and so he added, 'But I would think it's got a few years to go yet.'

When they were settled, Jane began to update Emily about their new project.

'We've been doing some research in the local communities,' she explained. 'We've already got a list of thirty potential suppliers, and there are more to add.'

'There's no doubt that there's a growing demand for this kind of thing,' said Harold.

'But we plan to build it up slowly,' said Jane. 'We want to concentrate exclusively on high-quality produce.'

'We've had some samples in, and I'm the taster,' said Harold, patting his increased girth and laughing heartily.

153

Jane slapped his arm playfully. 'Come on, now.' She turned to Emily and said, 'We've saved quite few for the Christmas meal, because we'd like your opinion, too.'

'How many can come this year?' asked Emily.

'It's a surprise,' said Jane.

'No, tell me.'

'I was just teasing. There'll be you and me, and Harold and Eva. The surprise is that this year Bill definitely doesn't have to work on Christmas Day, and the three of them will be able to come.'

'That's wonderful!' exclaimed Emily. It had been so rare for Bill to be able to be with them on Christmas Day, and even when he thought he would be, there were times when he was called away.

Harold dropped them at their house with a cheery 'see you later', and drove off.

Emily unpacked her things, and then she and Jane sat down with hot drinks to catch up on more of the news. Despite their regular phone calls, they felt that there were things that never really got talked about properly until Emily was back home. As she grew older, these special times became increasingly less frequent, and all the more precious.

'I love the long dark evenings here at this time of year,' said Emily as she sipped from her steaming mug. She looked straight at her aunt and said, 'I'm very glad to hear about your business ventures with Harold. You two make a good partnership for that.' She looked thoughtful for a moment, and then said, 'Actually, I think that when I went away at first I was quite worried about you being here on your own.'

'I think I sensed that, and I was all the more determined to find something that would absorb my time and energies, and it had to be in the right way. I had my doubts about how Harold and I would get on. I was used to helping him out, but not to being a business partner. However, it's worked out well. Oh, I know he sometimes comes across as being a bit overbearing, but it's just his manner. He's not really like that.'

'I know,' said Emily. 'And I've noticed that he tends to do it when something's bothering him that he can't put into words.'

'You're absolutely right,' Jane agreed.

'I really love your specialist foods venture,' said Emily.

'It's a pity we haven't got further with it by now,' said Jane. 'In the run up to Christmas, I think that kind of product would sell very quickly.'

'Is there anything we could do about it?' asked Emily eagerly. 'Getting stuck into something like that for a week or so would suit me very well. I've got work to do, but I'd like a bit of a break first, and doing that kind of thing would be perfect.'

'I think we should speak to Harold about it,' mused Jane. 'Maybe he would agree to taking on a single consignment of each of a few lines for you to get your teeth into.'

Emily giggled, and Jane looked at her quizzically. For a moment Emily looked like the child that she used to be when they first moved there together.

'I like it when you laugh like that,' said Jane, 'but what's so funny? Oh, it's the teeth bit, isn't it? These days, I'm so busy being the businesswoman that I don't always spot the humour!'

Having recovered a little, Emily said, 'I think we should speak to him this evening.' She rubbed her hands together. 'I'll get him to agree to a list of a few suppliers, and see how far I get.'

Later that evening, they strolled up the road to Harold's new house, and sat round the kitchen table. Emily soon put her plan forward.

When she had finished, Harold said, 'I don't want to sound like a wet blanket, but I think that a lot of these suppliers will already be under pressure to deliver in the run up to Christmas, so they're unlikely to have spare stock.'

'You *are* sounding like a wet blanket, Harold,' Emily chided him. 'Don't concentrate on the ones that can't deliver, let's concentrate on the ones that might have stocks.'

Harold looked at her with a twinkle in his eye. 'I wouldn't do it for anyone else, but since it's you, I will. Come back up here first thing in the morning, and we'll get on to it.'

Jane smiled inwardly. She had been trying without success to get him to agree to something like this for weeks. Maybe somewhere inside he had been waiting for Emily to come home.

The following day brought a considerable measure of success for the project. Emily rose early, and was banging on Harold's door before he had finished his breakfast. Together they went through his list of likely products and their suppliers, and earmarked ten different lines, with a further five in reserve. A number of phone calls later, they had a list of seven destinations to visit that day.

'Come on, Harold,' said Emily. 'We can't afford to waste any time. Shall I take your Land Rover myself, or do you want to come?'

Harold had taught Emily how to drive when she was seventeen, and he knew that she was making no idle threat. He grabbed his coat and struggled into his boots, and soon they were driving to the first address.

Twenty minutes later, they were on the road again.

'Chutneys and pickles from home-grown ingredients, made to recipes from the eighteenth century,' said Emily triumphantly. 'Six cases. I think we could have done with more, but it's all they had to spare.'

'Look, this is just to be a small experiment,' Harold grumbled good-naturedly.

Emily ignored him, and read out the address of their next destination.

Half an hour later they had added four cases of crab apple jelly to their load, together with two cases of cranberry sauce, made to an old recipe.

'I must design some posters to go with these,' Emily pronounced energetically. 'I'm certain that customers will be more interested if they can see the list of ingredients, and have some idea of the origin of the constituents and the recipes.'

'Good idea,' said Harold warming to the suggestion. 'Why not come in when we get back, and we'll work on it together?'

By the time they were ready to return home, the back of the Land Rover was stacked high, as was the seat between Emily and Harold. Visibility was reduced, and Harold had to curtail his speed considerably to ensure their safety.

They produced some posters, and then set up the stand for Emily in a niche near the front of the garden centre. By that time there was only another hour until closing, but the stand drew quite a number of customers, and Emily made several sales before they shut the centre.

She and Jane spent the evening in their sitting room with their feet up.

'As you'll have noticed, I got Harold activated,' said Emily mischievously.

Jane chuckled. 'I was astonished. I admire your approach and its success.'

'I think he really wanted to do it, but he needed me to come back and badger him.'

'I thought that, too. It's no good if I try to push him. He just digs his heels in.'

'Maybe it's because he's had to push himself for a very long time,' Emily reflected.

'I don't mind going along with his bits of stubbornness. It's the least I can do after all the kindness he's shown to us.'

'He still is very kind.'

'You're right, and he wants the best for you and your future.'

They sat quietly for a while, and then Emily said, 'Auntie Jane, I've met someone interesting.'

'You mean a boyfriend?'

'No... Well, he's male, but not a boyfriend.'

'Tell me more.'

'I'm giving him some maths tutoring at the moment.'

'Oh...' said Jane, puzzled. She paused, and then asked, 'How are you finding it?'

'We get on well with it together. It's a bit like me and Eva, only it's Barnaby and me.'

Jane noted the name, but made no comment.

Emily continued. 'I first met him during Freshers' Week. He was in a group that I was showing round. The curious thing is that although I had never met him before, I felt as if I somehow recognised him straight away. Oh, I know that sounds odd, but it's how it was. It was as if something fell into place, and after that he always seemed to be there in my mind. And that felt right. It was never an intrusive or disturbing thing. For weeks I didn't see much of him, and would just pass the time of day if I saw him. It was early November when he was told by one of his tutors, a friend of mine, to come and see if I could help him with his maths.'

'Why didn't you tell me before?'

'I couldn't tell you about this on the phone because it's too important, although in what way, I don't yet know. And I should tell you that we first met to look at his work on the afternoon of November 12th.'

Jane looked very attentive.

'And when I woke the next morning, a very strong image of the double spiral came into my mind, so strong that it seemed to imprint itself in my brain. Since then we've met for an hour every week to look at his work together.'

'I can see now why you didn't try to talk to me about it on the phone,' said Jane. 'What's he like?'

'I don't really know. He's studious and earnest, and we just talk about maths. It doesn't occur to me to do anything else. It's as if we're together for that, and that alone, for the time being at least.'

'Obviously we can't really draw any conclusions at the moment,' mused Jane, 'but it might be possible that there's a link between your contact with him and the meaning of the spirals.'

'Surely not,' said Emily. 'It wouldn't be surprising for me to think about the spirals on their "birthday", whether or not Barnaby was in my life.'

'Have you thought about the spirals like that, and on that date, before?'

'Er... no.'

'That day was the first time you'd had a proper conversation with him, albeit about his maths?'

'Yes.'

'What else can I say? I've already said that neither of us is in a position to draw any conclusions, but it looks to me as if there could be something very interesting going on.'

Emily fell silent for a few minutes. Then she said, 'Well, at least now we've spoken about it, I think I'll be able to keep in touch with you about anything else that happens, or springs to mind, and not have to wait until I'm back home.' Here she paused, and Jane waited. 'Jane,' she said suddenly, 'I've just realised something.'

'What is it?'

'I think you could be right in what you said. I've just remembered that after I first met him, it went through my mind that the way I was drawn to him was a bit like how I felt drawn to the box with your diary in it.'

The sales of the specialist lines went smoothly, and by lunchtime on Christmas Eve, Emily had no stock left at all.

'It's a good job that I kept some of the cranberry sauce on one side,' she told Jane that evening, as they began to prepare the stuffing for the turkey.

'That was certainly good thinking,' replied Jane.

Christmas Day itself was wonderful. Everyone arrived around midmorning as arranged, and they stayed together until late into the evening. The day passed in a non-pressured way, with plenty of time for exchange of news and plans for the future, as well as time to eat, sing carols and play some games together.

Emily spent the remaining two weeks of her holiday between helping to establish the food side of the garden centre, working on her own studies, and spending some relaxed time with Jane and Harold. She also visited Eva and went across to see David, Bill and Asma again. By the time she was due to return to university, she was eager to grasp the challenge of further study.

Chapter Eighteen

Emily and Barnaby resumed their sessions soon after their return from the Christmas break, although the timing had to be changed until later on Friday afternoons. They spoke of little except their task, so that it was a surprise to Emily when, after a meeting at the beginning of February, Barnaby said, 'My folks are passing through this weekend.'

'I hope you have a good time with them,' said Emily cheerfully as she collected her things together.

'I told them at Christmas about how you're helping me.'

'Oh.' Emily didn't know what to say. She hadn't perceived herself as helping Barnaby. As far as she was concerned, they were just interested in something together.

'Are you going to be around?' asked Barnaby.

'I think so.'

'They'd like to say hello to you.'

Emily felt uncertain, and hesitated before responding. She had plans of her own for the weekend, and did not want to commit herself to anything that might get in the way.

'If that's going to fit in for you, of course,' Barnaby hurried to add.

Emily smiled. 'Sorry, I didn't mean to seem unfriendly. It's just that I've got things on. When are they arriving?'

'Saturday morning. Around eleven.'

'I'll see you outside here at half past?'

'Sounds good.'

Emily walked back to her room to change. She was going out with a group of friends that evening, and it was an early start. She was glad that she had, after all, agreed to meet Barnaby's parents, because now she had a feeling of rightness about it. At first, she had felt taken by surprise, but now she almost looked forward to it. Fleetingly, she thought of David. In some ways, Barnaby reminded her of David, but in many other ways he did not. Both were stolid and unpretentious, but there the similarity ceased. Barnaby was quietly studious. David had always been more outgoing, and had joined as many of the activities at his university as he could fit into his timetable.

Late that evening, she phoned Jane to tell her of how she had agreed to meet Barnaby's parents the following day.

When she woke on Saturday morning, once again she had the distinct sense of the double spiral in her mind, as if it had been imprinted there. As it faded, she began to think about the impending meeting with Barnaby and his parents. It shouldn't take long, and then she could catch the bus and rendezvous with her friends at the river. This year, she had joined the canoeing club, and the weekend practice sessions had continued, despite the cold weather.

She dressed warmly, put her things in her backpack, and set off in plenty of time to be outside the library by eleven thirty. She caught sight of Barnaby and his parents from a distance, waiting at the arranged spot. She waved and called Barnaby's name to attract his attention.

He introduced his father first. 'Emily, this is Paul, my dad.'

Emily noticed that Paul's handshake was warm and sincere, as were his words. 'Emily, I'm very glad to meet you.'

Emily had already noticed that Barnaby looked not unlike his father in height, although Paul's frame was a little broader. Their hair colour was the same, apart from a few grey hairs intruding into Paul's, and their features were surprisingly similar. He was dressed in a pair of smart dark-coloured trousers, and wore a thick substantial country jacket to protect him from the cold.

Then Emily turned to Barnaby's mother, who did not wait to be introduced and said, 'I'm Diana. We weren't sure if you would have any free time, and we're very pleased that you did.' She too shook Emily's hand warmly, and Emily could see that she was smiling with her eyes as well as her mouth. Although she was Barnaby's mother, she did not look in any way as if she were ageing. Emily judged that she must be the same height as herself. Her hair appeared to be its natural colour, fair. It was cut in a style that allowed it to fall onto her shoulders, and the wave in it made it bounce as she moved. She wore strong flat shoes, as if she were ready to set off for some rough walking, although her clothes were those of someone who was out for a day of socialising.

'Shall we find somewhere to sit down?' asked Paul. 'Our car

isn't far away, and Diana and I found a cosy café on the way here.'

'Thanks,' Emily replied. 'I'd like that.'

Later, when they were seated, she asked, 'Are you here for the weekend?'

'No,' replied Diana. 'We're on our way to see some old friends of ours, so we'll have to leave by the end of the afternoon.'

Paul ordered some hot drinks, and Emily found that the conversation flowed well, given the fact that, to her, they were complete strangers.

After initial pleasantries, Paul cleared his throat slightly and said, 'Diana and I wanted to have a chance to thank you for all the help you've been giving to Barnaby.'

Barnaby smiled. 'When they told me they wanted to, I decided that I'd let them. Over the Christmas holidays, I couldn't stop talking about how amazing it was to work with you like that.'

Emily felt embarrassed, and she felt her cheeks flush a little. Determined to represent her own view of their shared study, she said, 'I was very lucky to have had my friend Eva as a kind of tutor during my years at secondary school. All I've been doing is working with Barnaby as she used to with me.'

'Nevertheless, you're giving up your time, and it's your final year so you must be quite stretched at the moment,' Diana pointed out.

'Studying never feels stressful,' said Emily, 'and the study that I do with Barnaby is a welcome part of that.' She glanced at her watch. 'I'm afraid I don't have long. I must go in a few minutes.'

There was some general conversation about the university, and then Emily prepared to leave.

'Thank you for your time,' said Paul.

'Yes, thank you,' Diana added.

'It was good to meet you,' Emily replied. 'See you at the usual time on Friday, Barnie.'

Barnaby looked as if he were about to say something, but thought better of it, and instead raised his hand in assent. Inwardly, he had noted her use of 'Barnie' and was puzzled by it, because she had never called him this before. In fact, no one but his grandmother had called him by that version of his name since before he started school.

Emily walked towards the door of the café, turning her head and waving briefly to the three at the table. They smiled, and then continued their own conversation. But by the time she reached the door, she began to falter. 'Go back.' She heard the words in her head as clearly as if they had been spoken. She stood there as if rooted to the spot. 'Go back,' said the voice, which by now she was sure was in her head. She made herself walk through the door and out into the street, but her legs felt as if they were made of lead, very heavy indeed, and as if they did not belong to her at all. She leaned against a lamppost a few paces along the pavement and took stock of her situation.

Whatever was happening to her was a mystery – a mystery without any clues at all. She did not remember ever feeling like this before. As she mulled over her position, the fact that this state had come upon her straight after meeting Paul and Diana was indisputable, but whether it was connected could be in doubt. Except... Perhaps the instruction in her head meant that she should speak to them again.

'I'll give it a try,' she murmured uncertainly.

She turned back towards the café, and immediately felt lightness in her step. How very strange. The lightness continued as she went through the door and walked towards the table where Barnaby and his parents were deep in conversation.

As if she sensed someone coming, Diana looked up, and when she saw her, she asked, 'Have you left something behind?'

'I'm not sure,' Emily replied. She looked under the table, but there was nothing there except the expected cluster of legs and shoes. 'No, there's nothing. But I'm glad I came back to look,' she added. 'It's given me the chance to say that I'd like to see you again sometime. Let me know if you'll be coming back anytime.'

'Of course,' said Diana and Paul together.

As Emily left the café, there was no return of her former symptoms, and she jogged along the road to the bus stop.

The afternoon was short because of the time of year, but the canoeing group still had time to enjoy some strenuous activity. Emily was keenly aware that there was no sign at all of the symptoms that she had experienced earlier that day. In fact, her body functioned very well, so much so that some of her friends cheered her on a particular stretch of water. The group ate together afterwards, and lingered on into the evening, by which time Emily was healthily tired and went straight to bed.

The following day was spent with friends who attended a local

163

church, where she joined in with the many social activities. So it was Sunday evening before she could phone Jane for a long chat.

'Jane,' she began, 'I think we should get in touch with Ellen very soon.'

'Of course we can, but why now? Shouldn't we wait until you're back here for Easter?'

'No,' said Emily urgently, 'it's got to be now. More has happened that I must tell you about. I'll tell you everything, and then you'll understand.'

She went on to say how she had been aware of the double spiral again, and she described her experience when she had tried to leave her brief meeting with Barnaby's parents.

'You're right,' said Jane when Emily had finished speaking. 'Now I see what you mean. Actually, I think we should have contacted Ellen already, to tell her about your first meeting with Barnaby.'

'Yes, we should have been in touch at Christmas. I think I would have thought of it, had I not been trying to push forward the new part of your business.'

'Me too,' Jane agreed. 'We both got pretty wrapped up in it. The whole venture's gone very well, but it was at the expense of other things we could have done.'

'Never mind. I wasn't too convinced of a connection between Barnaby and the spirals then.'

'I'll give her a ring tomorrow evening,' Jane promised, 'and I'll let you know her reaction. Or you can phone her yourself if you'd prefer.'

'I'd rather you did it. After all, you and she were together almost from the beginning about the effects of the spirals. If when you speak to her she thinks it would be useful, I could phone her later.'

Jane found it difficult to wait until the next evening to phone Ellen. It had been too late to ring her after she had said goodbye to Emily. She had been tempted to try to speak to Eva, and her hand had hovered over the phone for several minutes while she stood next to it, undecided. However in the end, she made herself go to bed. But then she lay awake for several hours, from time to time peering at the luminous hands on the bedside clock.

The following afternoon, she phoned Ellen as soon as she had finished work, but was disappointed to find that there was no reply. She left a message and put the phone down, only to pick it up again as it rang.

'Jane,' said Ellen's voice. 'I just missed your call. I was in the kitchen with my hands covered in pastry.'

'I've got some very interesting news of Emily to tell you. Have you got time now, or shall we speak later this evening?'

'Can I phone you back in about an hour? I've got to get this flan in the oven, ready for my neighbour to take to the church for the bring-and-buy sale.'

'That's fine.'

Jane put the phone down and paced round her living room restlessly. Then she walked into the hall, through the door to the other side of the house, up the stairs and down again. She picked up the newspaper and turned its pages, but could not connect with anything she saw there. It was then that she realised that the level of disturbance she was experiencing was considerably more than she might expect while waiting for a phone conversation with a friend, and she sat down to think about it.

She slowly repeated aloud what Emily had told her the night before, and found herself ending up by saying, 'the *double* spiral'. The double spiral was surely the centre of it, but what 'it' was, she didn't know. Then her mind filled with the memory of the Easter holiday that she and Emily had had at Eva's, when Emily was ten. She closed her eyes, and it was as if she were again sitting watching Emily leaning over the spiral layout on Eva's table, 'reading' the spirals with the palms of her hands. And she remembered how, during their stay there that summer, Emily had dreamed about the spirals.

'The movements of her hands that she showed to me after that dream were so like what I had seen her doing in the Easter holiday,' Jane murmured. 'But that second time, she thought that words were coming from the spirals and up through her hands.'

She then thought about how it had been as if Emily had been stroking, touching and gently moving something invisible that was above the spiral layout. Maybe the spiral layout is a two-dimensional representation of something that is really three-dimensional, she wondered suddenly. She shut her eyes and imagined the spiral layout, and then put her hands out in front of her and tried to think about an invisible three-dimensional version there. After that she slowly began to move her hands as Emily had moved hers. At first her movements felt contrived, but she did not give up, and as the minutes passed, she realised that there were fragments of some kind of particular flow in her movements, and they felt as if they had a distinct meaning, although what that might be she could not guess.

'It'll be good to talk to the others about this,' she continued softly. 'When I feel connected to this I sense neither words nor music, yet in some strange way, I feel I am experiencing an amalgam of both.'

It was then that Ellen rang back. Jane jumped. She was startled by the sound, but quickly realising what it was, she went to the phone and picked it up.

'Hello, Ellen,' she said. 'I'm so glad to hear you.'

Ellen could sense relief in Jane's voice. 'Is something wrong?' she asked.

'No... Well...' Jane took a deep breath to gather herself, and then said, 'There's quite a bit to tell, and I'm not sure where to begin.'

'Don't worry about that,' Ellen reassured her. 'Just make a start anywhere.'

First, Jane told her of Emily's experiences. Ellen listened without saying a word, but as soon as Jane had finished, she asked urgently, 'Don't you remember?'

'I'm sorry, but I can't follow what you're trying to say.'

'Don't you remember what happened to me after that night Emily and I slept in Eva's bedroom?'

Jane cast her mind back. 'Oh, yes, you had a funny turn at breakfast... Oh! Now I remember. Of course, you had that single word in your mind, "barn". I'm sorry to be so slow, but I'd always associated it with a place to store bales or farm machinery. Actually, I've sometimes wondered if you'd predicted that Harold would eventually convert a barn to live in, but now I can see it's quite possible that it was something to do with this person that Emily has met at uni. In fact, that seems far more likely.'

'Jane, I'm really excited. I'm sure that there must a link between Barnaby and the double spiral. Can you give me Emily's number so that I can give her a ring sometime over the next few days?'

Jane could hear a slight breathlessness in Ellen's voice, as if she were trying to contain an urgency that she was feeling. 'There's no problem about that,' she said, 'she did say to let her know if you wanted to speak to her direct, so I'm sure she'd be pleased if you phoned her.'

She slowly dictated the number, and waited while Ellen wrote it down. Then she went on to tell Ellen what she herself had been thinking about the spiral layout.

'It sounds to me as if you're on to something important,' said Ellen excitedly. She paused before continuing. 'Jane, there's a lot to think about here. Shall we speak again soon?'

'Oh, please. I'm pretty busy for the rest of this week, but Saturday evening should be okay, or any time on Sunday. How are you fixed yourself?'

'Let's make a definite arrangement for Saturday evening. With luck, I'll have spoken to Emily by then.'

'It's a date,' said Jane decisively.

When Jane put the phone down, she went to get her mobile. She sent a text to Emily to let her know that Ellen would be in touch, and to remind her of Ellen's reference to 'barn', all those years ago.

Chapter Nineteen

Nothing further emerged from the phone conversations that followed between Jane, Ellen, Emily and also Eva, except that they agreed to keep in close contact, should anything else arise.

Jane made no attempt to discuss any of this with Harold. When she had tried, years ago, to interest him in it, she had felt offended when he had said 'stuff and nonsense' and walked off. She had wished that even if it were for Emily's sake, he would make the effort to show some interest, but had reluctantly accepted that it was very unlikely. He was so involved in their lives that it could feel as if there was an unwanted hole in their otherwise close relationship that could not be filled. Emily had always had a different attitude to his apparent indifference, and had merely accepted that he wasn't ready to be interested yet. Jane held the view that he never would be, but she kept it to herself.

The business was going from strength to strength, and the food side had never diminished after the start that Emily had made on it before Christmas. Already, a number of producers were approaching them to ask if they would act as an outlet. However, they stuck to their original plan of being selective about what they decided to stock, and were very careful about what they took on. Their general theme emerged more clearly as promoting only local produce. If the product was some kind of preserve, they usually selected only those for which the recipe had a long and interesting history. Before making a final decision, Harold and Jane would invite people round and would try out samples.

After one such occasion, Jane said, 'I think I'd like to put this in our promotional material.'

'What do you mean?' asked Harold, surprised.

'That we have a panel of food tasters who have vetted all the products we sell.'

'Do you know, I think you were born a businesswoman!' he exclaimed, slapping her on the back.

'Ow! Be careful, Harold,' she said, annoyance showing in her voice. 'You've still got a strong arm, and you nearly knocked me off my chair.'

Harold went on expansively, as if oblivious of her discomfort. 'I always thought you were good at paperwork when you used to help me with mine, but since we've started our business together, I've seen a side of you that I didn't know before. You seem to be full of new ideas, large and small, and all of them are good.'

Jane had decided not to make an issue of his overexuberance, and she said, 'I'm certainly enjoying myself. I love talking to producers and customers, and I find the paperwork perfectly straightforward.'

'I've noticed. There's nothing holding you back. I must admit I feel a bit like a spare part at times.'

'Oh, Harold! Don't say that. This is something that we do together. It wouldn't be the same for me if I were doing it alone.'

'Yes, I know I'm a good spare pair of hands. I'm still up to heaving things around and all that.'

Jane stared at him in astonishment. She had been so confident about the development of their joint venture that she hadn't realised that Harold had been feeling like this. He had appeared to be his usual good-hearted self, and had given no sign of his discomfort.

'Is there anything I've been doing to make you feel like this?' she asked, concerned.

'Now, don't stop anything you're doing, mistakenly thinking that I'll feel better, because I won't. Everything you do is right. That's just the point. It's a joy to see you flourish, but it just rubs it in that I'm only an old blunderer by comparison.'

Jane gaped at him. 'Old blunderer?'

'And don't try to convince me differently,' said Harold stubbornly. 'Let's face it, I'm not getting any younger, and I've got to hand things over to the next generation. I've done that with most of the farm, and now it's time to accept that I'm a helper and not a front runner in our business.'

'Harold, that's a lot of nonsense, and well you know it,' said Jane, wagging her finger at him. 'I'm not having you talking like that.'

'Well, it's the truth.' Harold got up from his chair and made for the hallway to grab his coat, but Jane got there before him and stood in his way.

'Sit down!' she commanded.

Harold was so surprised that he meekly went back to his chair, where he sat down heavily. He had never seen Jane behave like this before, and he felt lost.

'Look,' said Jane, gently, 'could we just put all of that on one side for a few minutes while I tell you what's been coming into my mind over the last couple of weeks?'

Harold nodded mutely.

'Rare breeds.'

'Rare breeds?'

'Yes, rare breeds. I know you've been using your remaining land for various things. It's something we don't really talk about, because it's not up to me what you do with it, but recently I've been wondering if you'd consider using at least some of it for rearing some old breeds of pigs, sheep or goats.' Her voice carried energy and vitality as she went on. 'Just think how it could work out for our business. We could be selling our own home-grown meat – meat with a history to it. It would all be up to you, of course, because I'm no expert in animal husbandry. What do you think?'

Harold sat up straight. He felt lifted out of his belief that he was useless. In fact, he felt transported, and into something that could be his passion.

'I've always thought how narrow-minded it was to stick to a few breeds,' he mused aloud, 'but until now I've never felt the urge to do something about it. I suppose it was always the cash flows that I was looking at, and not experimentation and diversification.'

Jane noticed the latter terms, but made no comment. It seemed to her as if underneath Harold had been preparing for something different. He had just needed her to name it, and he recognised it as his straight away. This was borne out by what he said next.

He stood up, collected his coat, and came back to speak to her. 'Sorry about the gloom and doom. Let's say no more about it. I'm off home now to look through some magazines I've kept in case I wanted to look at them again. I'm sure there are some contact details in some of them.'

Harold strode off into the night looking ten years younger, and Jane went to bed feeling cheerful and relaxed. In fact, when she tried to clean her teeth, she found that she couldn't, because she was still singing a happy song that had come into her head soon after he left. She laughed heartily, cleaned her teeth, and fell into bed, looking forward to telling Emily the news when they next spoke.

When Jane went to open up the garden centre the following day, she got a nasty shock. The lock on the main door was broken. She glanced up at the external part of the alarm system, and saw straight away that it had been well-nigh destroyed. Without pausing to wonder how this could have been accomplished without the alarm being activated, she went inside to assess how much damage had been done. She and Harold had been only too aware of the rising crime rate in the locality, and had done everything they could to protect the building, but obviously some skilled criminals had thought that it could be worth their while to target it.

'How strange,' she murmured. 'Our takings are relatively modest, and we don't leave any money here overnight. Surely burglars with this kind of skill wouldn't bother with us?'

She took her mobile from her bag, first phoning Harold and then the police. She had been about to check through everything, but decided not to in case it interfered with what the police had to do.

Harold arrived first.

'Lousy blighters!' he said through gritted teeth. Despite the situation, he looked well and in fighting spirit. 'What's the damage?'

'I haven't looked. I thought we should wait for the police to come.'

'Good thinking.'

Jane thought how fortunate it was that she had come to work very early that morning. Enthused by what had arisen from their talk of the night before, she had woken early, and decided to do a couple of hours' work before opening time. This meant that there were no customers or deliveries expected for a while.

'Let's hope the police can come soon,' she commented as she peered around the tills and the stands for signs of damage.

Her mobile started ringing, and she answered it to find that a police car was on its way and would be with them in about fifteen minutes.

'That's good,' said Harold as she told him. 'I've heard they can be hours for something like this, if there are priority calls. Let's keep having a good look round without touching anything, so we can tell them what's been disturbed.'

Soon they were giving details to two officers, who then examined the damage, while Harold and Jane sat watching.

'We've drawn a blank on the front of things missing or damaged,'

Jane told them. 'I think we've been very lucky.'

'Yes,' replied one of the officers, 'either they've been disturbed, or else they're practising.'

'Practising?' asked Jane, astonished.

'Yes. We've had enough cases like this recently to make us think that there's something bigger afoot.'

'Tell us more,' said Harold.

'They're picking on relatively small, out-of-the-way places, but ones that have modern alarm systems.'

'I follow your meaning now,' said Harold. 'We put ours in last year. There wasn't any point before. And we chose a good system.'

'We'll see if we can pick anything up,' said the officer, 'but I doubt it. They make sure they leave no traces behind.'

'It won't take long,' said the other. 'We'll soon be out of your way.'

'Thanks for coming so promptly,' said Jane. 'It looks as if we won't have to delay opening this morning. I'll call the locksmith now, if that's okay with you.'

'Yes, go ahead.'

After the officers had gone, Jane turned to Harold and said, 'In some ways, we've been lucky. They could have caused a lot of mess and damage if they'd wanted to.'

Harold clapped his hand on her shoulder. 'Always look on the bright side. That should be your motto.'

Jane looked at him with a glint in her eye, and said meaningfully, 'You can adopt it too, you know.'

'I did last night. I sat up with my magazines, and I've sent some e-mails off already. So here's to our new adventures!' He gave Jane a hug.

Jane was stunned, and she could hardly breathe. It was like being in the clutch of a friendly bear. But it wasn't a bear, it was Harold, and he had never behaved towards her like this before, or towards anyone else for that matter, at least as far as she knew.

He let her go as suddenly as he had taken hold of her, and she took a deep breath.

As if reading her thoughts, he said, 'I was on a survival treadmill for well over forty years, and I couldn't get used to the idea of semi-retirement. It felt like being on the rubbish heap.'

Jane opened her mouth to speak, but he put his hand over it. 'We don't have to go over last night again. Just take it that now I've got a different kind of job, I know I'll be fine.' He looked at his watch. 'I ought to stay here with you until the locksmith comes, but I've got things to do,' he said briskly. 'Do you mind if I go? I'll keep my mobile with me.'

Jane agreed without difficulty. But her mind was whirling. Harold, carrying his mobile? Whatever next? She had persuaded him to buy one nearly two years ago, but he had hated it from the beginning and professed to 'forget' to carry it, but she had always suspected that his 'forgetting' was a more deliberate act than he would ever admit.

She was relieved to find that no customers came until it was nearly ten. By that time she felt less agitated about the break-in, and had settled into her work. The locksmith phoned her to say that he had been delayed, but that he would come around five. She settled for that, particularly as he had added that he had some new, more secure options that he could offer.

Chapter Twenty

When the Easter break came, Emily opted to spend most of it in the library at university, deep in study for her finals. She had given up her sessions with Barnaby a few weeks previously, because now she needed all her time for herself. She went home only for the Easter weekend to see Jane and Harold, and even then she carried several files of notes. On Easter Sunday they shared a meal with Eva, but apart from that she saw little of anyone. Jane and Harold were absorbed in their business, and the Easter break had brought with it throngs of visitors. Already they were planning to extend their premises.

Barnaby sat his first year exams, and Emily sat her finals. The academic year finished with its usual array of celebrations. Emily got a good degree, which she had certainly earned. She preferred not to attend the graduation ceremony, and although Jane felt rather disappointed about this, with Eva's help she accepted Emily's decision.

Emily decided to work with Harold and Jane for a few weeks, but she was also planning her future. She had long felt drawn to finding work abroad for a while, helping in a disadvantaged country, but she felt even more strongly that she wanted to put something back into her own country first. Repeatedly she found herself thinking of obtaining work in youth schemes in inner city projects. However, she wanted time to think, and she had wanted to see what her exam results were before making any firm decisions. Both Harold and Jane were adamant that there was a place for her with them for as long as she needed it, and that it was important not to make any rushed decisions.

'You could spend a year with us,' Jane suggested one evening. 'At the very least you would build up your knowledge of running a business, and in this day and age, that includes some very useful skills.'

'I feel torn between all the different options,' said Emily. 'I know it might sound as if I'm avoiding taking responsibility for my life, but

I have a sense that I'm waiting for some kind of sign.'

'It doesn't sound like avoidance to me,' Jane replied stoutly. 'And you've got work here for as long as you want it.'

'Thanks, Auntie Jane. That certainly makes it easier for me. That way I can choose to wait, but be doing something useful at the same time.'

'If I didn't have your help at the moment, I'd certainly have to employ someone from outside,' said Jane. 'More and more, I find I need someone to take over the day-to-day running at a moment's notice, while I research new products that are being offered to us. But at this stage I don't want to hand anything over to someone new, and it leaves me having to work long hours, often feeling overstretched.'

'I can see that, and in some ways it makes me want to take a positive decision to work here until the winter, but in my heart I want to stay flexible, so that if I feel I'm directed elsewhere, I can follow that, without feeling I've let you down.'

'I understand perfectly,' said Jane sincerely.

'I'm really glad about that,' said Emily with relief.

Jane thought for a while, and then said, 'Do you think you might be able to do the next two or three months?'

'There'd be no problem about that at all,' said Emily eagerly. And she noticed that the lingering sense of indefinable oppression that she had felt lifted instantly.

Jane became very businesslike. 'Now that's settled, can I give you a list of duties to start from tomorrow? You've been a great help on the tills and the arrangement of stands, but I think you're being under-stretched.'

Emily began to laugh. She laughed until tears rolled down her face and her cheeks hurt.

Jane looked a little offended. 'What is it?' she asked irritably.

'You suddenly changed from my Auntie Jane into a competent businesswoman,' Emily managed to say. 'And you didn't just sound like another person, you *looked* like another person, too.'

At this, Jane began to see the funny side, and she too began to laugh. And the sight of Emily clutching her sore cheeks made her laugh even more.

Just then there was a knock at the door, and Harold came to join them.

'What's all the hilarity?' he asked, beaming at them. 'Can I be let into the secret?'

'In a minute,' Jane gasped as her laughter threatened to engulf her once more. She went to the sink for a glass of cold water, and having calmed herself, she explained what she and Emily had agreed.

'But what's so funny about that?' he asked, mystified.

'Nothing,' said Emily. 'It's just that Jane looked so...' Here she started to laugh again.

'Don't bother trying to explain, Emily,' Jane advised. 'Otherwise, we'll keep on like this forever.'

'Well, whatever it is, let's have a drink on it,' said Harold dramatically.

Until now, he had kept his coat on, and it was buttoned up. Added to this, Jane had thought that he was sitting rather awkwardly.

Now, he slid a bottle out from under his coat and said, 'Surprise!'

'What is it?' asked Jane curiously. 'Let me see.'

She reached across to take it from him, but he clutched it to his chest and said, 'Get some glasses. You've got to taste this and tell me what you think.'

'Another product?' asked Emily.

'I don't know,' he replied. 'We haven't done any drinks so far, but this one came my way, and I was so impressed by the story behind it that I wanted us to consider it.'

Jane went to a cupboard, and returned with some small crystal glasses.

'From what you say, we ought to do it justice with some good-quality glassware,' she commented.

Harold took the cork out of the top of the bottle, and poured a little of the pale brown liquid into each glass. Then each of them carefully took their first sip.

'This is amazing!' said Emily, her face a picture of astonishment and delight.

'You're right,' agreed Jane. 'I can't describe the taste at all, but it's truly amazing.'

Harold said nothing, but sipped again from his glass. Then he grinned from ear to ear.

'Where did you get this from?' Jane demanded.

'I'm not telling you,' Harold replied, looking smug. 'And I took the precaution of removing the label from the bottle in case you tried to read it.'

Jane tried to glare at him with mock annoyance, but she found that her face could only take up the shape of a smile. She sniffed at the liquid in her glass. 'Mm... There's definitely no alcohol in it,' she pronounced.

'There wouldn't be, would there?' said Harold. 'We agreed from the outset that whatever happened we'd stay alcohol-free.' His face took on a serious expression. 'I feel very excited about this find. It came to light when I visited one of the farms I'd contacted about rare pigs. The owner, Mrs Mace, had some very old cookery books that had been handed down through her family. The oldest ones were handwritten notebooks. She found the recipe for this drink in one of the notebooks, and recently tried it out. She was amazed at the result. She was keen to tell me all about it, but she was anxious that I kept it more or less secret for now. I said that I would tell you two, and no one else. She agreed to that, and I told her I'd get back to her once we had a chance to sample it, and then take it from there. For now, she's reluctant to think in terms of marketing it, but you never know. Her stance suits us at the moment, because after all, we're not into drinks yet.'

'Yes, herb tea mixes and bottles of plain water in our "tea" corner seemed fine for now,' Jane agreed.

Emily had said very little so far, and Jane turned to her to ask for her view. However, she could see straight away that something was happening to her.

'What is it, Emily?' she asked, standing up quickly to go to her.

'It's all right, Auntie Jane,' Emily replied in a distant voice. 'I think I should lie down, though.'

Emily stood up slowly, and made her way towards the stairs.

Jane watched her carefully, but when she saw that Emily was quite steady on her feet, she relaxed, and continued her conversation with Harold.

'I feel very keen for you to stay in touch with that woman, Harold.'

'No problem about that. I'm going to order some piglets from her soon.'

He looked at his watch and got up as if to leave.

Jane delayed him by asking, 'Harold, is there any more to the story of the drink?'

'I believe there is. Mrs Mace didn't seem keen to give me the details, so I didn't press her.'

'Maybe she'd be willing to tell us later,' said Jane thoughtfully. 'I'd certainly want to ask her if we ever got to the stage of marketing it, but as that's pretty unlikely in the short term, there's no rush.'

She let Harold out, and bolted the door behind him. Ever since the break-in at the garden centre, she had taken this simple precaution.

Then she went upstairs to check that Emily was all right. She had no real concern about her, but thought that it would be best to look in on her.

She tapped on Emily's door, and hearing no response, pushed it ajar to find Emily fast asleep in bed, looking deeply relaxed. She crept out of the room and pulled the door to, before getting ready for bed herself.

When she woke the next morning, she found Emily in bed beside her, wide awake.

'I was waiting for you to wake up,' Emily explained, 'because I've got something important to tell you.'

It was so many years since Jane and Emily had last shared a bed that Jane could not remember when it had been. She decided that this was irrelevant, and she asked Emily to tell her what was on her mind.

'Do you remember those dreams I had when I was young? The ones about the girl in sackcloth?'

'Yes, I do.'

'Well, I had another one last night.'

Jane, who had been feeling rather dopey from her night's sleep, suddenly felt very alert.

'You must tell me everything you can remember about it,' she said.

'I'm afraid I can't remember much at all. I just know that the girl was there. She was in the kitchen place again. She was stirring the contents of something like a cauldron. It was hanging over the fire.'

'Maybe you were seeing the first person who made that drink years and years ago,' Jane suggested lightly.

'That might not be far wrong,' said Emily seriously. 'When I woke up I had the sense of the imprint of the double spiral in my mind again. I knew that something was happening to me yesterday evening, but I didn't want to say anything while Harold was still there. You know what he used to be like with this kind of thing.'

Jane nodded. 'And I've not tried to say anything to him since then, so I don't know if he's any different.'

'Well,' said Emily decisively, 'perhaps now's the time to try again.'

'Are you sure?' asked Jane. 'Don't you remember, he could be quite unpleasant.'

'That isn't going to put me off trying,' Emily assured her. 'I'll tell him what happened last night. That would be a good start, because even he might see that there could be a link to the drink. After all, he saw how I had to go up to bed. It must have been obvious that I'd been affected by it.'

Just then the phone rang, and Jane picked up the extension at her bedside.

'Harold? We were just talking about you... Yes... Emily's here in bed with me. You want to speak to her? I'll hand the phone across.'

Emily heard Harold's strong voice. 'You seemed a bit overcome last night, and I wanted to check that you were all right,' he said, carefully trying to cover up any anxiety that threatened to leak into his tone.

'I'm fine, thanks,' Emily replied. 'I was just telling Jane how I dreamed last night about the girl dressed in sacks – the one that I used to dream about when I was young.'

'Stuff and...' Here Harold's voice trailed off. 'Did you say "a girl in sacks"?'

'Yes.'

'Er... I think Mrs Mace mentioned some such story. I didn't take much notice at the time, because I put it down to fabricated nonsense. Now,' he said decisively, 'I'm going to put on my clothes, and come down to see you both before we start work.'

He arrived at the door ten minutes later, looking rather dishevelled. His thinning hair was sticking out at all angles, and the way that he had buttoned his coat was entirely askew.

Emily wanted to tease him about it, but thought better of it, since he was clearly agitated, and he had made his phone call out of concern for her.

'Sit down,' she invited. 'The water in the kettle's hot.'

'Hot water? That'll be fine for me,' he said. Then he muttered under his breath, 'Not sure it's safe to be drinking anything else around here these days.'

Jane heard what he said, but ignored it. She did not want to get into an argument when there were important things to discuss.

Harold took a gulp from the steaming mug that Emily handed to him, and then instantly regretted it, as it was far too hot. Silently, Emily put a glass of cold water in front of him, and he swallowed most of it. Although still feeling agitated, his concerns about Emily were fading rapidly, and he wondered what to say next. He was tempted to make some excuse about work and leave, but he knew now that he could no longer avoid the subject that he had previously always managed to sideline or ignore.

'There's not enough time to talk now,' he began, 'but can we get together this evening? I've a lot to learn about dreams and suchlike things.'

Before Jane and Emily had time to reply, he stood up and left abruptly.

The two women smiled at one another, and Emily said, 'I think he might be ready now.'

The garden centre was fairly quiet during the morning, and Emily had time to think about her new position there and do some preparation. At lunchtime, Harold appeared unexpectedly. He was carrying a large book, which he put down on the desk in front of Emily. It was then that she could see it was an old photograph album, and she realised that she recognised it from her early times at Harold's farmhouse.

She looked at him inquiringly. He nodded towards the album and waited. She opened it at the first page and found that it was full of pictures of paintings of breeds of farm animals from bygone days.

'I've been doing a bit of rearranging,' Harold explained gruffly. 'Thought these pictures might come in useful. There's another couple of pages. Have a look and see what you think.' He didn't look at Emily as he said this, and she could tell that he was trying to hide the fact that he felt rather exposed.

Fleetingly she felt puzzled, but then it dawned on her what he was getting at. 'You mean, if we go ahead with produce from rare breeds, we might use some of these pictures alongside photos of your stock in our promotions?'

Harold looked straight at her. 'Correct.'

'Sounds good to me. I'll get Jane. I'm sure she'd like to have a look.'

Emily was soon back, with Jane at her side.

'I see there's quite a history to all this,' Jane mused as she studied the pictures. 'Mm... Gloucester Old Spot pigs. I like these.' She paused, and then turned to Harold and said, 'I want to learn more about what you're doing, but I don't want to risk treading on your toes.'

'No danger of that. I've been feeling out on a limb, thinking you weren't all that interested,' he admitted.

Jane registered that he was saying how he was feeling instead of being irritable with her, and she thought that this boded well for their impending, potentially tricky, discussion that evening. But she made no comment, and said cheerfully, 'Let's get together about it soon.'

'I'd like to have a go at making larger versions of these pictures,' said Emily enthusiastically. 'I think they'd have a better effect.'

Harold appeared satisfied. He picked up his album and left, saying half over his shoulder, 'See you at eight. I'll have something to eat before I come down.'

Jane took this to mean that he was feeling somewhat vulnerable, and didn't want to feel indebted to her by eating something that she had cooked, just before their talk. And also she suspected that he was happy to meet at their house so that he could leave whenever he wanted. She was content with this, as she knew it would give him the best chance of listening to what they had to tell him. She sighed. Yes, that evening would show them whether or not Harold was indeed ready to take a step forward in his thinking.

He arrived at the door of Jane's house at eight exactly, and let himself in.

'I think we should sit in the comfortable chairs,' said Jane.

But Harold would have none of it. 'Kitchen table or nothing,' he said determinedly, and Jane decided not to argue. She winked covertly at Emily, and they cleared it and sat down.

'I've been back to see Mrs Mace,' Harold said bluntly. Then he looked secretive. 'I might tell you about that later.' He turned to Emily, and asked in a softer tone, 'Will you tell me exactly what you dreamed about that girl?'

'I'll have to tell you some of the background,' Emily said calmly.

Jane noticed the deliberate way that she had paced her words, and she waited to see how Harold would respond.

He looked thunderous. 'I just…' he bellowed. But he stopped in mid-flow as his eyes engaged fully with Emily's. For a moment, he seemed suspended. Then he gathered himself and said, 'I'll probably find it very difficult.'

'I realise that,' said Emily with kindness in her voice. 'I can take it as slowly as you need.'

Harold nodded. His face was set, but as Jane watched him, she began to think that this was not to do with resistance, but was an indication of his determination to listen.

Emily began. 'The first time happened in the last weeks of term before the Easter when we first met you – when Jane and I came to stay with Eva,' she explained.

Harold swallowed hard, and then said, 'Go on.'

It was Jane who continued. 'I had some boxes in the garage that I'd brought with me when I moved across to Clare's, and I'd never got round to unpacking them. When I told Emily that I ought to sort through what was in them, she was keen to help.'

'Yes, I remember how much I wanted to,' said Emily. 'And when we went into the garage, I just knew I had to work out which one to unpack first. Without thinking about how to do it, I found myself using my hands, palms down, in a kind of scanning motion, until I knew which one. It seemed a completely natural thing to do.'

'Now, wait a minute,' said Harold, his voice rising as he spoke.

'Can you just accept it for now?' asked Emily, putting her hand on his arm.

For a moment, she thought that he was going to tug it away, but he did not, and instead it seemed to turn to stone under her touch.

'We found one of my old diaries in the box,' said Jane, 'and Emily saw the spiral patterns that had appeared in it just before she was born.'

'Appeared in it!' roared Harold. 'What non…' He tried to jump to his feet, but Emily increased the pressure of her hand on his arm. He managed to stay seated, but shouted, 'What has all this to do with the ragged girl?'

'We're coming to that quite soon, Harold,' Emily said calmly, trying to soothe him.

Jane continued. 'That night, Emily was sleepwalking, and I found her sitting downstairs. In the dim light, I could see her making scanning movements with her hands over a book. I later found that it had been my diary.'

Emily gripped Harold's arm tightly and said, 'When I woke in the morning, I'd dreamed about the girl. She was dressed in what looked like old sacking. She didn't have any shoes, but her feet were tied up in some funny-looking things. I thought that there'd been hens running round, and that she was feeding them.'

'Well, that bit sounds all right,' Harold remarked grudgingly. 'Why didn't you tell me that at the beginning.'

Emily looked straight into his eyes again and said, slowly and deliberately, 'Because I don't think I'd have had that dream if Jane and I hadn't found the spirals.'

Harold groaned. 'It's all too much for me.'

'No it isn't, Harold,' said Jane firmly. 'You just need a bit of time to get used to it.'

'Yes, that's right,' said Emily. 'And now I'm going to tell you about the other dream.' Without waiting for his permission, she began. 'It was when Jane and I were staying at Eva's that week at Easter.'

Here Harold broke in. 'Was it before I met you, or after?'

'Just before,' said Jane.

Emily took up her story again. 'We'd been talking to Eva about the spirals.'

'You mean *she's* all tied up with this as well?'

'Very much so,' said Jane. 'She was one of the first people who saw them in my diary.'

'We'd been talking to Eva about the spirals,' said Emily, 'and of course Jane and I had been thinking a lot about moving house, although at that stage we hadn't a clue where to go. I went to bed, and slept for a very long time. When I woke up, I realised I'd dreamed about the girl again. She was in the same kind of clothes, but this time she was in a kitchen, which, as far as I can remember, was a fairly small room.'

'Okay,' said Harold, a little unsteadily. 'I think I've just about got the gist of things, so now tell me what happened with the drink the other night.'

'I sampled the drink, and soon afterwards I felt strangely calm and relaxed. Then I thought I could see the girl again, but as you know, I went up to bed without saying anything about it.'

'That was because you knew I wouldn't take kindly to it,' said Harold bluntly.

Emily nodded, and then continued her story.

'I dreamed of her in the same kitchen as before, stirring the contents of a cauldron-like thing that was hanging over the fire. And when I woke, I could again see the double spiral.'

'Double what?' Harold looked thunderous.

Emily and Jane looked at each other meaningfully, and then said together, 'There's quite a lot more, Harold.'

'I think you should stick with it,' Jane advised him. She was surprised by how confident she felt. Until this evening, she had always felt silenced by Harold's reactions to any mention of this part of her life, but now she knew that however he reacted, she was not going to let it deflect her. It was time that he knew everything.

Harold was reassured by Jane's approach, and he said, 'Okay, okay. I'll do my best, but it's not easy.'

'I appreciate that, Harold,' said Jane. 'I would have told you some of this before, but I got the impression that you found it far too difficult.'

'Too right,' Harold muttered to himself, almost nastily.

Then Jane had an inspiration. 'It may help you to know that Adam was involved with the spirals at one time,' she said.

'Adam? So he's mad too?' Harold sneered.

Jane began to think that her idea had not been such a good one after all, but Harold pulled himself up, and said, 'I'm very sorry I said that. Adam's a good man, and I'll stand by anything he's been involved in. Tell me more.'

'The people who were involved with the spirals at the beginning guessed that the double spiral was an important indicator of something, but they couldn't get further than that,' said Jane.

Emily carried on. 'Somehow I knew, without being told, that the double spiral was important. And in my last year at uni, a very clear image of it came into my mind unbidden, several times, and each time was related to Barnaby in some way.'

'A boyfriend?' Harold questioned with a hint of aggression. 'What's his family like? Look, Emily, I don't want any nonsense going on round you.'

'He's not a boyfriend,' Emily assured him. 'I've helped him with his maths, just like Eva used to help me. And I met his parents briefly one day. They seemed nice people.'

Harold relaxed.

Jane reflected upon how hard she found some of his reactions. However, on the subject of boyfriends, she had to admit to herself that she was grateful to have a male presence who cared about Emily's future in that respect.

She was jerked from her thoughts when she heard Harold saying to Emily, 'Well, if he's not a boyfriend, he must be important in some other way, but we don't know what that is yet.'

It was so uncharacteristic of the Harold that she knew to speak like this, that for a moment she thought she must have dozed off and dreamed it. But then he said, 'And I'm sure you're both waiting to hear what I learned from Mrs Mace today, because that's important.' She knew then that she had not been mistaken.

Harold took time to rearrange himself in his seat. Jane thought that he was deliberately increasing the suspense, but again she said nothing. After what he had just managed to listen to, she decided that he deserved to have the chance to create some drama of his own.

Then he began. 'She showed me the notebook where the recipe was written down. It was very old indeed, and inside the front cover it said that the recipes had been handed down from mother to daughter for several generations, so goodness knows how old they are.'

'There's probably no way of finding out,' Jane commented.

'Anyway, there's a particular story attached to the recipe for the drink we had. She said it's written out in the back of the book. She wouldn't let me touch it because it's so old and crumbly, but she showed it to me. Are you ready?'

'Of course, we are,' said Jane and Emily together.

Harold took a deep breath, and then paused, successfully creating an intense atmosphere of suspense.

Emily struggled hard to contain her rising impatience, but she succeeded, and eventually Harold began.

'There was a problem with one of the generations,' he said, clearly revelling in the fact that he now had full control of the conversation. 'Apparently, a well-heeled gentleman managed to lead astray the wife of another, and a girl child was born. Her mother named her Morna. At first her husband didn't know. For a long time, she concealed her pregnancy by careful choice of the clothes that she wore, and by chance he had to go away for several weeks just before the baby was born.

'As soon as he knew he had a daughter, Morna's father had a special piece of jewellery made for her. It was a brooch that he got a local craftsman to make, and the mother used to fasten her baby's shawl with it. When her husband came home and found out what had happened, he was furious, and insisted that she could not keep her baby. Instead, the child was reared by a childless couple, who took her in as their own, and renamed her. Her new name was Charity. The couple did not have much money, but they fed her well, although she was always poorly dressed. At times, her adoptive mother made ends meet by making clothes for her out of emptied grain sacks, and her father bound her feet with strips of sacking.

'The adoptive mother was known locally as someone who could treat a number of ailments. This woman taught Charity all she knew from what had been passed down to her from her ancestors, and Charity would work hard in the kitchen, making up the recipes. As she grew older, Charity began to add ingredients of her own choice to the recipes, and in time it was demonstrated that the final effect was enhanced. The adoptive mother was very proud of her daughter.

'When Charity grew up, she secured a post as a maid to a local dignitary. Very sadly, she died in a terrible accident when a tunnel under the large house collapsed on her. But one of her recipes lived on. Mrs Mace has it, and that's the drink we tried.'

After Harold had finished speaking, there was a long silence.

Eventually Jane spoke. 'I don't know what to say,' she said softly. She was looking intently at Emily, and could see that her eyes were focussing on something that wasn't there.

'My head's full of the story, but it's full of my dreams of the girl, and the spirals as well. Actually... I feel really strange,' said Emily. 'I think I'd better go upstairs and lie down.'

'Do you want me to come?' asked Jane.

'No, I think I'm better on my own for now.'

Jane and Harold were left staring at each other in the kitchen.

'Can we just talk about work for a while?' asked Jane weakly.

'I've brought some of my rare breed plans to go through with you. Will that do?' said Harold.

'Perfect,' Jane replied.

Emily lay on her bed upstairs. The evening air was balmy, and she let her thoughts wander. She was grateful for the fact that neither

Jane nor Harold had tried to insist on coming with her. She knew that she had to be alone. She could hear the sound of their distant voices floating up the stairs, and this was adequate companionship.

She was very glad indeed that Harold was no longer resistant to this part of her life. It had been touch and go this evening, but the connection that he had made with Mrs Mace had meant that he had his own particular information to share, and that must have tipped the balance.

It seemed not unlikely that the girl in her dreams was Charity, and she wanted time to absorb this new information. But what was the link between Charity and the double spiral? And for that matter, what was the link between Barnaby and the double spiral? Of course, it was possible that the appearance of the double spiral in her mind was solely an indicator of important significance, but she had to consider the possibility that it might be more than that, and if it were, then there was a link between Barnaby and Charity. How strange... Emily closed her eyes and drifted into a kind of waking slumber.

Downstairs, Jane and Harold had finished talking about Harold's plans, and had returned to the subject of the drink.

'I'm not going to push Mrs Mace,' said Harold. 'I don't have to find an excuse to see her again because we're talking pigs, so I'll wait and see how things go.'

'I think that's the right approach for now,' Jane replied.

Harold noticed that Jane was looking a bit uncomfortable, and he said, 'Come on now. Spit it out. What is it?'

'It's actually something about Eva,' Jane began. 'You see...' Her voice trailed off.

Harold made himself wait.

'I think you should speak to her yourself,' said Jane firmly. 'Ask her how she came by her special stick. I think you should know about that.'

'You can tell me now,' Harold pressed her.

But Jane would not be shifted.

'Then at least tell me if Emily knows about this,' he said.

'Yes.'

Here Harold gave up, but planned to see Eva as soon as he could.

'I'm just going to check that Emily's okay,' said Jane.

She ran upstairs to find Emily at the top, about to come down again. Jane could see that she looked tired but otherwise fine, and she relaxed.

'Jane,' said Emily, 'I'm going down to say goodnight to Harold, and then I'll go to bed.'

Chapter Twenty-one

Emily applied herself to her position at the garden centre with much energy and concentration. She loved the work, and in some ways she wished she could stay here and join Harold and Jane on a permanent basis. There was so much that was of interest in the foods side of the business, and she was enjoying it immensely.

She was fascinated with Harold's project. Already he had picked up some Gloucester Old Spot piglets from Mrs Mace, and was caring for them tenderly in a pen that he had constructed behind his house especially for the purpose. He liked to watch them from his sitting room window. He had been trying to find a source of Norfolk Horn sheep for sale, but thus far he had drawn a blank. Those who had them were not selling. His initially modest ideas were evolving rapidly, and now he was talking about reclaiming a piece of rough waste land, and getting together a small breeding flock of Soay sheep to graze there. First he would have to buy the land, but he seemed sure that would not be a problem. Already he had contractors lined up to move in as soon as he had acquired it. The small, sure-footed Soay sheep could tolerate sparse surroundings, and at the same time create no damage to vulnerable substrates. He had ideas of putting a thin layer of topsoil wherever he could, and seed it with resilient grass species.

Yet despite all of this, Emily knew that somehow there was a restlessness in her, and although she was happy, and felt fulfilled, this was never very far from the surface. And she knew that one day this restlessness would find a focus that she would have to follow.

It was about a month later that a letter arrived, bearing familiar handwriting. At first Emily could not remember where she had seen it before. It was so familiar, yet at the same time it was strangely unfamiliar.

She opened the envelope, and read the name at the bottom of the letter that she found inside.

'Barnaby!' she said aloud. 'No wonder I didn't realise straight away. I'm only used to seeing figures and symbols written by him.'

She called to Jane, who was upstairs collecting her bag ready to take to work.

'What is it, dear?' Jane replied.

'I've had a letter from Barnaby.'

'I'll be down in a minute.'

When Jane appeared, Emily said, 'I hadn't expected that he would write. In fact, if you'd asked me, I wouldn't have thought he had our address.'

'What's he saying?'

Emily read from the sheet of paper:

Dear Emily,

I hope you don't mind my writing to you. I looked up your address in the 192 directory. It was easy to find because I remembered you told my parents that you lived at Brookgate. They were sorry not to have seen you again. You just missed them because I think you left a few days before me at the end of term.

I'm not at home because I'm working for nearly all of the summer for close friends of my parents. Actually, they're more like an aunt and uncle than friends. They are opticians, and their receptionist is off on maternity leave, so I'm filling in for as long as I can. Their practice is in Overton, but they live on the side that's furthest from Brookgate.

You might think it's a bit of a cheek, but I wanted to ask if there was any chance of doing some more maths together. I don't even know if you're at home yourself, of course, but if you are, would you be willing to meet from time to time?

The work here's quite interesting. In between my receptionist duties, I'm learning a bit about optics. I've always got a textbook handy for any slack times, and Peter and Helen, whose business it is, are happy to talk to me quite a lot about their work.

Regards,
Barnaby

Emily showed Jane the address.

'Mm... That can't be all that far from Bill and Asma,' mused Jane. 'Is David around?'

'Definitely not. He's got work for the summer as a relief porter at the teaching hospital. He left last week.'

'Silly of me to forget,' Jane commented. 'Back to Barnaby. It'll be a bit of a trek for him to get by bus to Overton and then to here, but it's not impossible. But do you want to see him?'

'Oh yes,' said Emily with great certainty. And now that feeling of indefinable restlessness that had been ever-present in the background was no longer there. She knew that she must see Barnaby. But it wasn't exactly Barnaby himself that was the issue, it was what Barnaby *meant* that was important to her. 'Jane, do you mind if I'm a few minutes late for work this morning?' she asked.

'That should be all right.'

'I'd like to write a quick reply and get it in the post.'

'I'll go on up,' said Jane, and left to walk along the road.

Emily thought for a few minutes, and then penned a quick note:

Dear Barnaby,
Good to hear from you. I'm working at my aunt's garden centre. Weekends are busy. Can you manage an evening?

Let me know,
Emily

She added her mobile number to the bottom of her letter, addressed an envelope, and was soon jogging along the road, past the garden centre, past the farm and on to the small post office in Brookgate. Having posted her letter, she retraced her steps to the garden centre, and found no difficulty in concentrating on her work.

At lunchtime the following day she received a text from Barnaby that said he could come on Wednesday because it was half day.

She went to look for Jane, and found her munching a sandwich with one hand and trying to sort out a pile of papers with the other.

'Not good for the digestion,' she chided.

Jane looked up. 'Thanks for interrupting me. I needed it.'

'I've got a text from Barnaby. He's got a half day on Wednesdays. I was wondering if I could finish early next Wednesday.'

Jane thought for a moment. 'Yes, that should be okay,' she said.

'You could finish at two.' She laughed. 'Although it might not look like it from what I'm doing, we're fairly well up to date. And apart from anything else, you've been working very hard and you deserve a break.'

'Sounds good,' said Emily. 'I'll text him now and let him know.'

Chapter Twenty-two

When Emily arrived home just before two the following Wednesday, she found Barnaby sitting on the doorstep reading a book. He looked up at the sound of her step.

'How did you get here so quickly?' she asked, surprised.

'The practice is near the bus station in Overton, and there's a small bus that leaves from there at twelve thirty and comes through Brookgate and on to Middleswell.' He laughed. 'On the way, it seems to stop at just about every cluster of four or more houses, and diverts at will. Maybe that's a slight exaggeration, but it took well over an hour to get to Brookgate. I jogged along from there because I didn't want to be late.'

A smile had spread across Emily's face, and it stayed there.

'Come on in,' she said. 'I'll get you some lunch.'

'It's okay. I brought something with me, and I had it on the bus.'

'Well, do you mind if I get mine?'

A few minutes later, they were sitting at the kitchen table.

'My aunt's at work,' Emily explained. 'She won't be in until after six.'

'I probably won't see her, because the last bus leaves Middleswell at six, and I've to be at Brookgate by a quarter past to pick it up.'

Emily made a mental note of the timing.

Barnaby misunderstood her silence, and added quickly, 'I can leave earlier if you're busy.'

'No, it'll be fine. I'll walk up with you, and I can go into the garden centre on the way back to make sure that Jane doesn't work late.'

'I haven't brought any work with me,' said Barnaby uncertainly. 'I wasn't sure if you'd be willing to look at anything today.'

'Oh, sorry, I suppose I should have said, but I assumed that you would have brought some. By the way, what book were you reading?'

'It's something that I picked up in a charity shop. It's quite entertaining. It's all about clockwork mechanisms.'

That seemed to suit Barnaby's character well, thought Emily.

'Actually, there are a few bits of ancient optical equipment that relied on clockwork,' he added. 'They didn't get very far, but it's an interesting piece of history.'

'I can't say that I know anything about that subject at all,' Emily admitted.

'You don't have to. It's just a hobby of mine.' Barnaby studied his fingers for a minute or two, and then said, 'I'm fascinated by spring devices. Metal fashioned into spiral forms has had so many uses, and still has.'

Emily was about to put her last piece of apple into her mouth, but when she heard the words 'spiral forms' she put it back on her plate.

Don't be silly, she told herself inwardly, Barnaby is just telling me about his new hobby. Aloud she said, 'Well, it all sounds very interesting. In these days of electronic equipment, mechanical things are so often sidelined.'

'Yes, that's something that worries me. If, as predicted, power supplies in the future become uncertain, we'll need things that are activated by direct human input. Resources should be put into developing this area rather than consigning it to history.'

'I think they are, but not enough,' said Emily. 'For example, I always use a wind-up radio. That's something that was developed in the last decade or so, largely for the benefit of Third World countries, but I think that we should use them as well.'

The time passed pleasantly, and when Emily looked at her watch, it was already half past four.

'I've an idea,' she said.

'What's that?'

'I could phone Harold and see if he's at home. I'm sure he'd like to meet you.'

'Who is he?'

'Oh, haven't I told you about him before?'

'No, you've only mentioned your aunt and your friend, Eva.'

'We bought this house and the piece of land around it from Harold. He used to have quite a large farm, but now he's older, he's handed the farmhouse and some of the land over to his nephews. He made a smaller house for himself by converting farm buildings. We've stayed friends, and in some ways he's been a kind of older uncle to me. My aunt and he own the garden centre. I'll give him a ring.'

As it happened, Harold was indeed at home. Having just learned that he had acquired the piece of waste land that he had been after, he was mulling over his final plans to transform it, but was demonstrably keen to have them call round.

'Come in, come in,' he called expansively as he heard them at the door.

As soon as he saw Barnaby, he stared at him, gimlet-like, for a second, as if trying to look inside him.

Barnaby held out his hand. 'Glad to meet you,' he said politely.

Harold was disarmed enough to give him a warm handshake, and he gestured towards one of the few empty chairs. 'Sit down, if you can squeeze yourself in here. As you can see, I'm in the middle of something.'

'We hadn't intended to interrupt you, sir,' said Barnaby.

'No, no, I need a break.'

Emily looked around the room. It was a long time since she had seen it like this. Documents, plans and maps were draped everywhere.

She grinned. 'I like seeing you like this.'

'I can't be long,' Harold said bluntly, 'but I'm glad you could call in.' He addressed Barnaby. 'So you're the maths fanatic.'

'I can hardly call myself a fanatic,' Barnaby replied, smiling, 'but the subject's certainly more than a passing interest to me.'

Harold looked at Emily and asked, 'Would you both like something to drink?'

'We're fine, thanks,' she replied.

He turned to Barnaby. 'Tell me what you're busy with these days, Barnaby.'

Barnaby spent some time explaining how he was spending his summer.

Harold made no comment, except to say, 'I'm glad to hear that you're a hardworking young man with useful interests.'

As they left, Harold told Barnaby that if he was anywhere nearby again, he should call in.

While they were ambling slowly along the road to Brookgate, Emily said, 'Harold took to you.'

'What makes you say that?'

'I promise you that he wouldn't have invited you to call round again if he didn't think you were okay. He hasn't got time for what he calls "wasters", and his definition of a waster is quite wide-ranging.'

By the time they reached the bus stop, there was still half and hour to spare, so they sat on the bridge, swinging their legs over the water, talking.

'Shall we meet again so that we can do some work together?' asked Emily.

'It would be excellent to carry on what we started,' said Barnaby eagerly.

'The trouble is that I'm not sure when I'm free again. I'll have to speak to Jane.'

'Don't worry. We don't have to decide anything yet. You know I've got Wednesday afternoons free, and I've got the bus times now.'

Satisfied with this arrangement, they fell silent until the bus arrived. Emily waved briefly, and then turned back down the road as the bus drove off.

When she arrived at the garden centre to collect Jane, she found Harold there.

'I thought I'd catch you,' he said amiably. 'I wanted to say that if you'd like to go to Overton one evening, you can ask me for the Land Rover.'

'But...' Emily felt touched by his offer, but for some reason she also felt flustered. Harold's thoughtfulness had affected her... but there was something else.

Harold went on. 'I know I'm making an offer that you might not want to take up. But it's there if you want it.' He turned away abruptly, picked up a sheaf of papers, and left.

'Harold likes Barnaby,' said Jane unnecessarily. 'And last week he had a long talk with Eva about the drink she was given just before she chose her special stick. He even asked to see the stick, and when he handled it, he told her that it felt different from any other stick he'd handled. Things are definitely changing.'

'Mm...' said Emily. 'I think that's why I felt so affected by his offer. It isn't just a kindness. He's really involved in the part of our lives that he used to shun.'

As it happened, Emily's next contact with Barnaby was when he phoned to tell her that Helen and Peter had invited her to come one evening.

'I know you might not be able to get here,' he said, 'but the invitation's open. Think about it.'

'I don't need to think about it. After you'd left, Harold told me that I could borrow his Land Rover if I ever wanted to see you at Overton. I think I'll take him up on it. I'll check what evenings it's likely to be free. Or maybe… maybe we could make a provisional date, and I'll get back to you to confirm it.'

'How about next Wednesday?'

When Emily drew up outside Helen and Peter's house, she found that it was a fairly compact, unpretentious, detached house. She could see Barnaby standing at the front window, and as soon as he saw her, he came to the front door and welcomed her in. He introduced her to Helen and Peter who had joined him in the hall, and they directed her into the sitting room. Her feeling was that they seemed to be very pleasant people, and not unlike Barnaby's parents. However, her mind was distracted by the impact of a very large frame that she had seen in the hall that was packed with pictures of people of all ages, arranged in a kind of collage.

She found it hard to concentrate on the initial pleasantries, and she was relieved when she heard Helen say, 'I expect you'll want to get on. I've told Barnaby that you can use the study, and I'll cook something to be ready around eight.'

'Oh… thank you very much,' Emily replied. 'It's very kind of you. I hadn't expected to be offered a meal.'

'I was looking forward to eating together,' said Helen. 'Your contact with Barnaby has meant a lot to him and his studies, and so it means a lot to us.' Here she included Peter, who inclined his head to show his agreement.

'Any friend of Barnaby's is a friend of ours,' Peter affirmed. 'By the way, don't worry if you have to move anything off the desk. I'm sure I'll be able to find it again.'

The study was part of a large extension at the back of the house that had not been visible from the road, and Emily could see that there was a long garden beyond. She tried to settle to their work, but found that she was still so distracted by thoughts of the collage, that she decided to ask Barnaby about it.

'I hope you don't mind my asking,' she began, 'but what's that huge picture in the hall? I can't stop thinking about it for some reason.'

'You noticed it, then.'

'How couldn't I?

'Helen and Peter told me that not many people seem to.'

'I can't imagine how that could be. Perhaps they're more polite than I am, and they don't ask.'

'It's got photos of most of the children and families that Helen and Peter have been involved with over the years of their marriage.'

'How do you mean?' asked Emily, intrigued.

'Helen and Peter wanted to have a big family, but they found that they couldn't have children of their own.'

'I'm sorry to hear that.'

'At first they were very unhappy, and felt cheated of their future.'

'I can understand that.'

'But it wasn't long before they realised that there were plenty of other ways of having a family, and since then, they've never stopped. That collage of photos shows most of their family.'

'You'll have to explain.'

Barnaby would not be drawn. All he said was, 'Ask them at dinner. I'm sure they'll tell you.'

Curiously, Emily felt satisfied with this, and was at last able to concentrate on their work, so much so that she jumped when there was a knock at the door, and Helen's head appeared round it to inform them that dinner was ready.

During the meal, Barnaby made no move to help her to open up the subject of the collage, so eventually Emily asked, 'I couldn't help noticing the huge collage of photos in the hall. Barnaby said I could ask you about it.'

Helen and Peter smiled at one another across the table, and Peter said, 'That's our family.'

'Yes,' said Helen, 'we found that we couldn't have children of our own, so we went ahead and made other arrangements.'

Then Peter took over. 'We've both had some good ideas about what to do instead, and over the years we've activated a number of them.'

'When we've finished eating, we could bring it through and introduce you to some of them,' said Helen. 'That is, if you'd like that.'

'I'd like it very much,' Emily replied sincerely.

Helen continued. 'When we built the extension on the back of the house, we designed part of it to accommodate people with special needs. Our plan was that we could take a child or an adult for weekend breaks, so that the parents or relatives could have a rest. It worked very well, and we've met so many lovely people. We have links with the social work department, but we've also heard of people through our patients at the practice.'

'Sometimes we've had overseas students staying who are undergoing training at Overton Hospital,' said Peter. 'We don't make a charge, and this means that students can benefit who otherwise would not have been able to afford to come to study here. You see, as opticians we've always earned a good salary, so we can do this,' he added modestly.

Then Helen spoke again. 'Yes,' she said, 'we've taken several who then return to help in villages in Africa that are full of AIDS orphans and ageing grandparents. Sometimes we've had two students at the same time. They've been perfectly happy to share, even though there's not a huge amount of room.'

Emily began to wonder what contact they themselves had with the hospital, and she said, 'When I was young, my aunt and I lived next door to Bill and Asma, a couple who moved across here when Bill got a job at Overton Hospital. We've kept in touch with them and their son, David, who's my age.'

'Bill? Do you mean Bill Blane who works in the infectious diseases unit?' asked Peter.

'Yes, that's right. They moved to this side of Overton when David left secondary school.'

'We don't know him well, but our recent students have spoken very highly of him.'

By now, Emily was beginning to grasp what 'family' meant to this couple. She was deeply impressed, and instinctively she felt that these were people with whom she could discuss her own plans to be of help to others.

After explaining how far her thinking had evolved, she said, 'I'm completely undecided at the moment. That's why I'm working at the garden centre for now. I don't want to get involved in anything else until I'm sure it's the right thing.'

'My mum's done quite a bit of youth work near her home in

recent years,' Helen reflected. 'She gave up two or three years ago because she's well into her seventies now.'

Peter chuckled and said, 'but she's got plenty of other things she does instead.'

Helen continued. 'I don't know if it'll be of any interest to you, but I could give you her number, and you can ring her if you want.'

'Thanks,' Emily replied. 'I'd like that.'

Peter passed a pen and a pad across to Helen, and she wrote her mother's name together with her phone number, and then handed it to Emily.

'Fay Bowden,' Emily said slowly. The name seemed strangely familiar, but she discounted the feeling since there was no reason why she could have known this person before.

'You'll like her,' said Barnaby. 'She's a sort of extra gran to me.' Emily did not feel the need to ask what he meant, but he went on to explain. 'She used to look after Helen and my mum together a lot when they were small.' He turned to Helen and said, 'That's right, isn't it?'

'Yes, she said that at one time she used to think of us as twins.'

By this time the meal was long over.

'Can I help with the washing up?' asked Emily.

'Yes,' said Barnaby briskly. 'We'll clear away, Helen.' And he set to work before she had time to protest.

When they returned to the sitting room some time later, Emily found that the collage had been lifted through and propped up against the sofa. She knelt on the floor to study it more closely.

'I'm assuming that the couple right in the middle must be you,' she said.

'Yes, that's Peter and me on our wedding day,' said Helen.

'You aren't wearing a dress,' Emily commented. 'It looks more like a jacket and trousers.'

'That's right... And the jacket has quite a story behind it,' Helen added quietly, almost to herself.

Emily heard what Helen had said, but since she did not continue, she assumed that the story was not one for sharing, at least not for now.

The rest of the evening was spent talking about many of the other photos in the collage. Emily found their stories fascinating and inspiring.

She left later than she had intended, carrying with her an open invitation to return whenever she felt she could.

Jane was asleep in bed by the time she arrived home, but she had left a note for her on the kitchen table to say that she hoped she had had a good time and that she would see her in the morning.

That night Emily slept very soundly, but when she woke in the morning she was aware that her dreams had been full of spiral patterns – spiral patterns that seemed to flow and merge, and then separate out again.

The next few days at work were very busy, and Jane and Emily would collapse, exhausted, on the sofa each evening to chat. The concept of meals had been temporarily suspended in favour of a number of nutritious snacks spaced throughout the day. There was always plenty to choose from in the ever-expanding range of foodstuffs that they now stocked.

Emily had told Jane all about her evening with Barnaby, Helen and Peter, and Jane had been very encouraging of the idea of phoning Fay some time over the next few weeks.

'For some reason I want to get used to the idea for a bit longer before I phone,' Emily confided one evening. 'And I don't want it to be at the end of a busy day.'

'Just take your time,' said Jane. 'If the contact is going to be right for you, it isn't going to be one that disappears overnight.'

'I've just remembered something,' said Emily, sitting upright for a moment before flopping back again. 'I don't know if I ever said to you, but when I first saw the name, it seemed familiar.'

'No, you haven't mentioned that before,' Jane confirmed. 'I haven't any associations with it myself, except that it isn't a common name.'

'Now this has come back to me, I'm sure there's something...' said Emily, screwing up her face in concentration. 'When I felt it at Helen and Peter's that night, I discounted the feeling, but now I know it's important.'

'I can't really be of any help,' said Jane, 'except to say that I'd like to know if anything particular comes to you about it. By the way, Harold's been talking about taking us over to meet Mrs Mace. I must admit I was quite surprised. Until now he's been giving off all the signs of keeping her to himself.'

'I wonder if he's told her about my dreams?' said Emily suddenly. 'I must ask him. If she doesn't know about them, I'd certainly like to tell her.'

'Even if he has told her, she may well be interested to talk to you directly about them,' Jane pointed out. 'I think he was saying he'll be going there at lunchtime tomorrow. I expect it's for another of his conversations about pigs. Apparently she's very knowledgeable about old-fashioned feeding practices, and he wants to learn everything she can tell him. Why don't you ask him if you can go along? I won't be able to come because there's no one to cover for me.'

'I think I'd like to go, if you're sure you don't mind,' said Emily.

'In that case, you should give him a ring now, and see if you can get it fixed.'

At twelve the following day, Emily picked up her bag and walked round to the yard, where Harold was waiting for her in his Land Rover.

'Jump in,' he called cheerfully through his window, as he saw her coming.

'I ought to be back at two,' said Emily as he set off. 'Jane's just heard that a couple of potential suppliers of rare poultry meat want to drop in, and it's best if I'm there to cover everything else while they're there.'

'But that's my territory,' snapped Harold, scowling.

'Now, don't get in a stew, Harold,' Emily directed. 'They phoned only this morning, and seemed very insistent. Apparently our reputation is beginning to spread, and they wanted to see our place on their way to some other meeting. Jane agreed to it only on the understanding that if they want to do any business, they'll have to arrange it through you.'

'All right, then,' said Harold, somewhat begrudgingly.

He took a direct route that led through quiet back lanes, rather than connecting with the main road, which would have meant a slightly longer and much less pleasant journey.

'How much have you told her about my dreams?' asked Emily as they neared their destination.

'I said you'd had some that might interest her – nothing more.'

They passed the rest of the journey in relative silence, and it was not long before Harold turned down a short drive and drew up outside a cottage.

A small, energetic woman appeared, whom Emily guessed must be Mrs Mace. It was difficult to tell her age, but Emily thought that she was likely to be in her sixties. It transpired that she ran her business from her cottage, which was the centre of a substantial smallholding.

'Been 'ere all me life,' she said, when Harold introduced her to Emily. 'Pigs are me speshulty, and were ma father's afore me.'

She showed them round her stock, and then invited them in for a cup of tea.

'So you've come to tell me about yuh dreams,' she said to Emily, with a directness that surprised her.

'I could certainly tell you what I remember, if that would be of interest,' Emily replied politely.

'I'll show yuh something before y'start.' Beth put the mugs of tea on the table, and rummaged around in a drawer in the dresser. ''ere it is,' she said triumphantly, as she put a small piece of metal on the table in front of Emily. 'What d'yuh think that is?'

Emily leaned forward to peer at it in the limited light. Outside had been bright sunshine, but in this room, with its small windows, she struggled at first to see.

'It's a coin,' she said, as soon as she could make it out.

'Aye,' said Beth. 'What kind?'

'I'm afraid I don't know.'

'Found it when I wus diggin',' said Beth proudly. 'Jammed atween some stones, in a dry bit.'

'I could take some details and try to find out for you if you want,' Emily offered.

'Thought you might. 'Ere.' Beth gave Emily a pen and a jotter, and then jabbered to Harold about pigs.

Emily made no effort to follow what we being said, and concentrated solely on her task.

Suddenly she became aware that Beth was addressing her again. 'I'm not 'andin' it in, and you 'aven't seen it. Right?'

'Okay.'

'Now tell me the dreams.'

Emily spent the next fifteen minutes telling her dreams to Beth and trying to answer her questions.

When this was finished, Beth said, 'Thanks. And I 'ear 'arold's told about the story of the girl that made ma drink.'

'Yes.'

'Maybe they're one and the same, and maybe not. You can come again sometime, but off you go now, I've got to get on.' Beth ushered them out of her cottage, and went off to pursue a task in the outbuildings.

Harold was silent on the way back home. When he let Emily out of the Land Rover at the door of the garden centre, he said, 'I'll see you about that coin later.'

In the evening, Emily told Jane about the visit.

'That coin sounds as if it might be a groat,' said Jane. 'We can have a look on the Internet to see if there are any details and pictures that might help.'

'First I want to phone Fay,' Emily announced.

'You sound quite different from when you first mentioned it,' Jane commented.

'I know. I feel convinced that this is the right time. Don't ask me why, though.'

She picked up the phone and keyed in the number.

The voice that replied was that of a man. 'Hello, Don Bowden speaking.'

'Could I speak to Fay, please. My name's Emily Foulds. I'm a friend of Barnaby.'

'Barnaby? Of course. I'll hand you across.'

'Hello, this is Fay. If you're Emily, then you must be the girl who's been doing some study with Barnaby. Helen phoned me to say you'd been across to see them, and that she'd given you my number. I'll help in any way I can, but I'm not doing youth work any more. I use what energy I have to raise funds for various charities.'

'I'd like to hear sometime about the youth work you did,' said Emily.

'I can certainly tell you about that, and if you're ever across this way, I might be able to introduce you to people in the schemes I used to work with.'

'Thanks. That's good of you,' said Emily. She was aware that already she felt completely comfortable speaking to Fay. 'I'm working for my aunt and an old friend for the summer, and we're very busy at the moment, but can I get in touch with you again when I can get a couple of days away?'

'Of course you can. Just give me a ring. We aren't away very often ourselves at the moment. And you're welcome to stay here when you come.'

When Emily put the phone down, she turned to Jane and said, 'This feels very good.'

'When do you think you'll go and see her?'

'Do you think I could get time off at the beginning of September?'

'I don't see why not. And in any case, it's a priority.'

'She said I could stay there when I go.'

'That sounds good.'

'I feel easier now I've spoken to her,' mused Emily.

'Good. And talking about this reminds me that we'll have to sit down sometime soon, to discuss how long you might be with us. Once I know when you're going off for a while, I'll have to think about engaging someone to do your work.'

'Okay,' said Emily. 'Now let's look to see if we can find something about that coin.'

An Internet search provided some clear illustrationsof small coins, together with information that the word 'groat' had been used for a number of different coins over a long period of history. A picture of an early Victorian fourpenny piece seemed to fit Emily's memory and notes of the coin she had seen.

'This says the date is 1840,' she said. 'I couldn't make out the full date on Beth's coin, but it certainly had 184 on it. I'll look forward to seeing Beth again and telling her what we've found.'

Chapter Twenty-three

A few days later, Harold surprised Emily by suggesting that she invite Barnaby over for the weekend.

'But that's a very busy time for us, and there's no bus on Saturday evening,' she said.

'I've thought about all of that. When he arrives, he can help me until you're free. After that he can stay the night at my place, and I'll give him a run back home around lunchtime on Sunday.'

Emily felt pleased with this plan. 'Okay,' she said, 'I'll send him a text and see what he says.'

She smiled to herself. It seemed to her that Harold was not satisfied with her assurance that Barnaby was not a boyfriend, and he was intent on putting him under some close scrutiny. But in any case, it would be good to have him across.

When she told Jane of her suspicions about Harold's suggestion, Jane proposed a slightly different interpretation.

'It could be that he likes him enough to want to involve him in what he's doing. If he spends some time with him, it gives him a chance to get to know him better, and also to keep an eye on your life.' There was a twinkle in Jane's eyes as she said this.

Barnaby was keen to come, and readily agreed to Harold's plan, so it was soon fixed that he would come across that weekend, arriving on the Saturday lunchtime bus.

That Saturday, Harold further surprised Emily by appearing at the garden centre just before closing time, and announcing that he and Barnaby would be cooking a meal for the four of them that evening.

'We'll need to get washed and changed,' said Jane firmly. 'I for one feel in a mess.'

'I agree,' said Emily. 'I certainly need a shower.'

'Barnaby and I will expect you any time after seven,' said Harold loftily, and disappeared in the direction of his house.

By the time Jane and Emily were ready, it was after seven. They were about to leave the house when the phone rang.

'Where have you two got to?' Harold asked with mock severity. 'The soup's waiting.'

'We'll be with you in five minutes,' said Jane. 'We were just leaving.' She put the phone down, and they walked briskly up the road.

When they arrived, Harold was waiting outside the front door for them. He hurried them inside.

'What's happened to your living room?' exclaimed Jane incredulously. 'There's no clutter *and* no dust.'

'We've been busy,' Harold replied evasively. 'We've been out and about, and we've been in the kitchen.'

'Hi, Barnaby,' said Emily.

'Hi,' he replied, beaming from ear to ear.

'It looks as if Jane and I are about to have a treat,' Emily remarked.

'I hope so,' Barnaby replied. 'Would you take a seat, ladies, and the soup will be served.' Expertly, he helped them to sit down.

'Hey, where did you learn how to do that, Barnie?' asked Emily.

Again, Barnaby noticed the use of the diminutive of his name, but he made no comment, and merely replied to her question. 'I used to earn some money at a local hotel when I was in sixth year. We had to practise how to push the chair in when someone was about to sit down.' He chuckled. 'We had some good fun with each other.' He disappeared into the kitchen, and reappeared bearing soup bowls containing thick pale-coloured soup. 'Parsnip,' he said as he went back to get some for himself and Harold.

'This is excellent,' said Jane, after her first spoonful.

When the meal was finished, Jane and Emily thanked the others for their hard work, and offered to do the clearing up.

'Not a bit of it,' said Harold determinedly. 'We've got a lot to discuss. You two ladies must wait in the sitting room, and we'll join you in a minute.'

Jane and Emily did as they were told. When the others joined them, Harold looked at them with a meaningful glint in his eye. 'I'm interested to know what Barnaby thinks of all the goings-on.'

Barnaby looked puzzled, and said nothing.

'I don't think Barnaby knows anything much,' said Emily. She felt perplexed by the way that Harold was behaving. There had been no need so far for her to talk to Barnaby about the spirals, or about her dreams of the ragged girl. Why, then, was Harold making an issue of it?

There was an uncomfortable silence, which was broken when Barnaby said, 'I'm intrigued. Please can someone explain?'

Emily could see that Harold was looking extremely self-satisfied. She thought quickly, and then said, 'Since you raised the subject, Harold, perhaps you'd like to begin?'

Harold looked uncomfortable, but then rose to the challenge, and to her surprise, he was soon telling Barnaby how he'd found this area of their lives so difficult that at first he'd coped by blanking it out.

'I've known others react like that,' said Barnaby calmly. 'However, my family and Helen and Peter's family have always talked openly about this kind of thing.'

Jane and Emily could see that Harold was looking at him with a fixed stare.

Barnaby continued. 'Yes, Fay, my extra-gran, went through a time when unexplained things were happening to her just about every week. That was before I was born. Mum was pregnant with me. But I've heard a lot about it.' He looked around them all and asked, 'Can you give me some specific examples of what's been happening in your lives?'

Completely disarmed by Barnaby's attitude to the subject, Harold relaxed back in his chair and said, 'From what I've heard so far from Jane and Emily, there's a story about spiral patterns that appeared in Jane's diary years ago. It's fascinating. I think it's best that you hear it from them, and not me.'

'Maybe we should wait until Barnaby's at our house again,' said Jane uncertainly, 'then I could show him my diary.' She addressed Barnaby. 'It's rather a long story. It started just before Emily was born, when the spirals appeared in my diary one night.' She hesitated, wondering how much more to say. Then she went on. 'You see, at that time I used to write something in a diary nearly every day, and this meant that I used a substantial hard-backed A5 notebook for the purpose. One night I dozed off when I was writing, and then when I woke up again, I found that several pages of my diary had been filled by spiral patterns of amazingly intricate design. I told my friend Ellen about them, and she and her friend Eva came across to see me. I'd hurt my ankle around that time, and was housebound for a few days.'

'Is that the Eva who's been your tutor, Emily?' asked Barnaby.

Emily nodded, and Jane continued. 'We all looked at the spirals, and Ellen went into a very strange state. That was the start of a long and complex series of events that unravelled. The whole thing involved quite a few people, and in the end they all came together in an amazing way.'

'Yes,' said Harold with a studiedly casual tone, 'and one of those people turned out to be a person I knew well as an agricultural advisor. His name is Adam Thomas. He's helped me a lot over the years.'

'Jane first told me the whole story when I was about ten,' said Emily. 'It's so long that it took several evenings. I remember how I used to call the evenings "chapters".'

'Wow! I can see that this is likely to be as complicated as the story I was told about Fay,' said Barnaby. 'There weren't any spirals, but as the story evolved, a very significant brooch came into it. My extra-gran still has her modern copy, and guards it carefully. Peter had it made for her, and she wore it at Helen and Peter's wedding.' He paused, and then added, 'As a matter of fact, I was born on their wedding day. My mother went into labour during the reception.'

'That's astonishing!' exclaimed Emily.

'This is highly intriguing,' Jane remarked. 'And I'm sure you'll be interested to know that when I first told Emily the story of the spirals, she wanted to know the date when they appeared, and when we looked, I suddenly realised that they appeared on the day that was supposed to be her birthday.'

'Supposed to be?' said Barnaby, looking mystified.

'Yes,' said Emily. 'You see, my dad was working away from home for years, and was only home on certain weekends, so my mum knew exactly when I was conceived. I was born nearly two weeks late.'

'Perhaps Jane's right, and I should see her diary before I hear the rest of the story,' said Barnaby slowly. 'And from what you've said, I guess there's a lot to it.'

Jane and Emily looked at each other.

'What do you think, Emily?' asked Jane.

At first Emily looked uncertain, but then she said confidently, 'I'm sure that we should leave it until later.'

Jane noticed that she seemed startled by what she had said.

'What is it, Emily?' she asked.

Emily looked bemused. 'I didn't know I was going to say that,' she explained. 'I thought I was going to say I wasn't sure.' She shook her head slightly, and then asked Barnaby, 'Is there something else you wanted to say?'

'Thanks for asking. Yes, there is.' He turned to Harold. 'Could you tell me more about Beth Mace's story? You mentioned it earlier today, and then said you'd leave it until this evening, when Jane and Emily would be with us.'

'There was a reason for that,' Harold explained. 'There could be a link between the story Beth told me and some dreams that Emily had years ago, not long before I first met her.'

'I could start by telling Barnaby my dreams,' Emily suggested, 'and then you can tell the whole of Beth's story.'

It did not take long for her to describe the two dreams she had had as a child, and she finished by telling Barnaby how she had 'seen' the girl again, not long after sampling Beth's drink.

Harold cleared his throat, and began to recount the story that Beth had told him about the origin of the drink. 'I have to say that drink is an extraordinary beverage,' he said as he began the tale.

He had just got to the place in the story where the baby was born and was given the name Morna by her mother and a special brooch by her father, when he noticed Barnaby looking a little strange.

'Are you all right?' he asked.

'I'm fine,' Barnaby replied. 'There's quite a lot this evening to take in all at once, but do continue.'

Emily felt that Barnaby seemed slightly evasive, but as she could not imagine why, she put the thought to one side.

Harold told how the baby had been given away and renamed, and how she had adapted her adoptive mother's recipe to produce the drink. He finished by telling of her untimely death in the tunnel.

When he came to the end of the story, there was a long silence. Jane and Emily were aware of waiting to hear Barnaby's reaction, but he said nothing at all. Instead, the colour started to drain from his cheeks. He tried to stand, but his legs would not support him.

Emily went to sit beside him, and Jane went to get a glass of water. She held it to his lips.

Harold was looking alarmed. 'I'm sorry, lad. I didn't mean to upset you,' he said.

'No upset...' Barnaby managed to gasp.

By now he was leaning very heavily on Emily.

'Try to sip this water,' Jane instructed.

Apart from struggling with the near dead-weight of Barnaby pressing against her, Emily found that she was wrestling with words that were coming into her mind. 'Tell him. Tell him,' they insisted. Tell him what? she wondered frantically. Then her mind cleared, and she said slowly and precisely, 'Barnaby, listen carefully. The day I first met you, I knew that something important would happen, but I didn't know what, how, or why. The day we first worked together was the anniversary of the appearance of the spirals in Jane's diary, and I "saw" one of the forms – the central one – when I woke up the following morning. And on the Saturday when I met your parents, I had woken into the same experience.'

Her words had an effect as if a switch had been thrown back into place, and Barnaby returned to normal almost instantly.

He took a few deep breaths, and then said, 'Whew! That was pretty difficult.'

'What was happening to you?' asked Emily.

'It was as if an enormous weight were pressing down on me. I didn't know if I would survive.'

'That's amazing!' exclaimed Emily. 'It sounds like a much more extreme version of what happened to me the day I met your parents. Actually, it's what made me come back to the café.'

'But I thought you were looking for something.'

'I pretended I was, but the truth was that I'd felt so heavy outside that I could barely move. I seemed to be directed to go back to you all again. Then the heavy feeling disappeared completely.'

'Look, everyone,' said Barnaby with an urgency in his voice that was new to Emily, 'I've got something extremely important to tell you. I can't tell you very much of it now, but I'll give you some idea of it.'

Harold opened his mouth as if to say something, but shut it again and remained silent.

'Just take your time, Barnaby,' Jane advised.

They all waited quietly, and he began. 'Fay suffered from a mysterious and lengthy illness before I was born. During the course of it, it became clear that she was sometimes remembering the death of someone from a long time ago. The name of that person was Morna.'

'Morna?' Emily burst out, unable to stop herself from interrupting. She looked at Harold, and could see that he had clamped his hands over his mouth. He looked so funny that she had a strong urge to laugh, but she managed to contain it.

She heard Barnaby reply, 'Yes, Morna.'

'I see now why you felt you had to tell us this,' said Jane. 'Please do go on.'

'As time went on, she and Don found in a local museum a catalogue cabinet that had recently been gifted by a stately home. Fay began to sift through the filing cards in the drawers, and came across one that bore a picture of a brooch of an unusual design. Instantly, she felt drawn to it. She turned the card over, and on the back she could see written, "Morna's brooch". Fay was desperate to have a copy of the picture, and the museum agreed to provide one. Peter subsequently found someone to copy the brooch from the picture, and Fay wore it at Peter and Helen's wedding, the day that I was born.'

There was a stunned silence.

Emily felt that her mind should be flooding with questions, but it was full of the impact of this stunning revelation, and none came to her. She could see that Jane was staring at Harold, and she wondered if she was worried about how he might react, but he looked surprisingly relaxed. In fact, to her astonishment, he appeared as if he was sitting talking about one of his favourite subjects.

It was Barnaby who finally broke the silence by saying, 'There's a lot more to Fay's story, but I've told you the part that's the most important for now.'

Then Emily spoke. 'There are so many things that could be linked together. There's me, the spirals, Fay, the drink, you... the list seems endless.'

After this, Harold spoke. He leaned forward in his seat and said, 'I promise you, I'll stick with you all in this maze until we find what's at the centre of it. And I'll bet my bottom dollar there's an answer somewhere in those spiral patterns, if only we could decode them.'

Emily stared across the room at the man who had sheltered and supported her for so many years, a man who was no blood relation of hers, but who had faced some of his worst anxieties and fears in order to stay close to her. She could see that Harold was transformed. He had accepted fully that there was something beyond his own well-founded view of life, and now he was ready and willing to grasp the impossible, the invisible and the indefinable.

Although her vision was clear, her thoughts were not. There was now too much filling her mind for any coherent discussion, and her brain seemed to be in a kind of haze.

She saw Harold stand up, and heard him announce, 'I think it's best if I take charge here.' No one made a move to object, and he went on. 'I think we should all get some sleep. Jane and Emily have got work in the morning at the centre, and Barnaby and I have plans we'd agreed to follow up before I take him back to Helen and Peter's. Jane and Emily, I'm going to run you down the road. It's well after dark, and the state you're in, you might end up walking off into the night. I'm not going to run the risk of that.' He went to collect his keys, and returned to chink them in front of Jane and Emily. 'Come on, you two.'

They stood up and followed him obediently. When Jane looked back on the scene from the safety and comfort of her bed, she thought that she must have looked much like a newly-hatched duckling following its mother. She was immensely grateful for the entirely matter-of-fact approach that Harold had taken. Goodness only knows what he himself had been struggling with, but he had managed to keep it away from everything that was coming out of him in words and gestures, and she felt in awe of his achievement. Over a only a short period of time, he had allowed himself to open into an unprecedented kind of culture shock that would have rattled any ordinary man to the core. Yet he was not only rising to it, but also he seemed to be maturing beyond it, and gathering energy as each challenge presented itself to him. He had always kept his age a secret from them, but if, as she had guessed, he had been in his early sixties when they first moved here, he would be at least seventy-five now. Yes, he had always been a very fit man, but that kind of physical fitness did not ensure long-term emotional stability, especially under stresses of unknown size and origin.

Neither Jane nor Emily had spoken on the way home, or indeed as they went upstairs to bed, except to bid each other goodnight.

Once back in her own room, Emily sat on her bed for a while. She had no concept of how much time passed before she slowly began to make herself ready for bed. She knew that something momentous was about to take place, or perhaps more correctly, had begun to take place, and she knew also that none of them had any real idea of what it was. All they had at the moment were signs and indications. And the signs themselves were so amazing that it would be all too easy to take any one of them as an endpoint in its own right. However, such interpretation would provide only a narrow and limiting view, and it was fortunately one which none of them appeared to be tempted to take. It had been revealed to her now that she and Barnaby had each been born into particular situations that had already known the presence of signs that defied everyday explanations. Now she and he were being exposed to signs that they themselves could see – signs that had clear links to those which had appeared to the generation before them.

At first she had sensed that Barnaby's presence in her life was important in some particular way, and she was now certain that the imprint of the double spiral appearing in her mind had been confirmation of this. Later, it had been his determination to seek her out that had brought them together again. Now it was the beginning of their coming together in the knowledge of what had affected them from their ancestry. Emily felt both startled and grounded by these words, as they appeared in her mind, unbidden. Whatever they meant, or would mean in the future, was as yet a mystery – one into which she longed to be able to see.

While Harold was taking Emily and Jane back home, Barnaby quickly tidied away the remaining things. He said goodnight to Harold when he came in, and then went to his room. When he came here, Harold had given him the choice of either of his two spare rooms, and Barnaby had been drawn to this one. Its cell-like simplicity had attracted him, whereas the piles of memorabilia in the other room brought discomfort to his orderly mind. The room was just big enough for its single bed and empty chest of drawers. There was a coat hook at the back of the door, and a simple lamp beside the bed on a small table. The walls were painted pale green, and the curtains were a darker green. He knew that there was no possibility of sifting through everything he had begun to learn that evening. That would take several days at least. He looked forward to being able to discuss it all with Helen and Peter, and most of all he wanted to phone Fay. But not yet. Instinctively he knew that the time was not right. There was still the next morning to experience, and even after that there was no need for urgency. He took a notebook out of his bag, and jotted down a few cryptic headings, before changing into his pyjamas and getting into bed.

Harold sat up for a long time. He had dropped Jane and Emily off at their door at exactly midnight. Now he needed some time to himself. He usually went to bed at this hour, but he rarely slept for more than five hours. Tonight he would sit up, because if he went to bed, he knew that he would just lie there, staring at the ceiling. If he went to bed at two, that would be soon enough. He put on his coat, and walked around outside for a while. He knew that he had to be out in the open air. If his nephews happened to be up, and caught sight of him, they would not be bothered, as he often inspected the buildings late at night, albeit not usually this late. He was grateful for the fact that the inexorable march of modern housing had not reached so far towards their land that the attendant lighting did not contaminate the night sky. He looked up and studied the stars, as the night was clear enough for him to follow many of the familiar single stars and constellations. He knew that he did not need to dwell on the details of what he had heard from Barnaby that night, and that he did not need to guess what else he would hear over the weeks to come. But he certainly needed to think about the impact that all of this was having on him.

How could he ever have known that his long and fruitful association with Adam about the running of his farm could have led to this? Without his contact with Adam, he would never have met Jane and Emily. Adam had never spoken to him of his friends, and certainly not of the spirals, but it had been through Adam's friends that Jane and Emily had come into his life. His intuition, or whatever anyone wanted to call it, had insisted that he did everything he could to encourage them to take over those derelict houses. It had been so strange. The only intuition that he had ever had before had been to do with his stock and his crops. Never before had it been to do with people. And it had come as a shock – one that had been hard to deal with on his own. Yes, very hard. He remembered how he had felt the day after Jane and Emily had gone home from their week at Eva's, and how he had contacted Eva, and found that she too was missing them.

A lot of water had gone under the bridge since then. At times he had wished fervently that he were twenty years younger, and at times he had even thought how, if that were the case, perhaps he and Jane could have talked about getting together. But he had had to shut any such thoughts out of his mind very firmly, and accept that the bachelor existence he had chosen for himself after the death of his parents would remain. Nevertheless, his inner attitude towards Emily was not that of merely an involved neighbour. In his very private moments, he practised the roles of uncle, grandfather, and even parent, but in all his interactions with her, he aspired to hold the position of an older friend. He knew that at times the mask that concealed his deeper feelings would slip, and that he would become irritable and say things that he regretted, but he was confident that by and large he had steered the course that he intended. He had worried about the lack of an obvious male figure in her life. He had asked careful questions about the staff at her school, and had been reassured to learn that she had some good male teachers. But that did not really fill the gap that the death of her father had left. He knew that Jane's position certainly went a long way to providing the mothering that she needed, and that Eva was also a central figure, but the male side was lacking, and at times he agonised about how best to fill it. He knew of her early association with Bill Blane, and having met him, he could see how valuable this had been, and still was. Yes, there was much for her in that relationship. But Bill did not live close by, and he had a demanding job at the hospital that more than filled his hours. In the first years after she moved here, there had been many times when he wrestled with impulses of wanting to scoop her up and care for her like a father would. He had even had fantasies of adopting her. But he had kept all of this to himself, and had been rewarded by being able to watch her flourish under the care of Jane, and the inspiring context that the school and Eva provided.

He thought about his lack of academic prowess. Yet realistically he knew that she did not need, and had never needed, any academic input from him. Relying on his boyhood memories, he knew that he had been able to give her a love and an understanding of the ways of the countryside, and that, together with his male presence and the weather-eye he kept open for her, had to be enough.

And now he was having to face his feelings about Barnaby. His early questions about him to Emily had partly put his mind at rest, but he had to be certain. One could not be too careful with such things. Although she had assured him that Barnaby was not a boyfriend, you could never be sure of what might happen in the future, and it was best to be informed and prepared. In this capacity at least, he could allow himself to think and act as if he were her father. And he had devised his plan. It had been a masterly move to suggest that Barnaby came at a weekend. That had forced a situation where he had more contact with him, as it was obvious that he could not stay overnight at Jane's. Oh, yes, there were spare rooms in the other side of their house, but it would have been improper for him to stay there. 'I might be old-fashioned,' he told the night sky, 'but I don't care. There's plenty of sense in avoiding grief and wagging tongues.'

The plan had gone well. He and Barnaby had worked together, and he had found him an apt and pleasant pupil. Then the cooking... Any real man should know how to cook a good meal. He snorted when he thought of those who invariably sat waiting for a woman to put food in front of them. He had been impressed with Barnaby's ability to prepare a meal, and the lad had had some good ideas about the flavouring for the soup. By the time Emily and Jane had arrived in the evening, most of his remaining anxieties about Barnaby being closer to Emily had dispersed.

There had been one remaining area in which he had needed to test them all. He had needed to know if Emily and Jane were willing to reveal to Barnaby what they had already revealed to him, and he had needed to know how Barnaby would react. He had to admit that he had had a rough time over the years with this stuff. Here he pulled himself up and corrected himself mentally, and put in the place of 'this stuff' the words 'these things'. But now that he was taking it all on board, he knew how very important it was, and he was not having anyone around who was not able to accept that. From his own struggles, he knew only too well that it could be touch and go as to whether or not the mind could open to accommodate the total experience, and expand with it into whatever was to be revealed. He had wanted to know if Barnaby was up to it.

But Barnaby had proved without any shadow of a doubt that not only was he up to it, but also that he was an integral part of it.

This had been an astounding revelation to Harold, and he was sure that it had been to them all. It was this revelation that he had to reflect upon, and somehow incorporate. He had been glad that the others had acceded to his directions, and had not attempted to talk about what had taken place between them. He could see straight away that it was far too big for that, and that they each needed time away from the gathering to think through what they had learned.

He welcomed the warmth and quiet of the night that allowed him the time he needed to mull these things over. On impulse, he directed his steps out on to the road, and made his way through the dim light to the house where Jane and Emily were sleeping. For a long time he gazed upwards, first at Jane's room and then Emily's, before silently retracing his steps back to the farm.

When he put his head round the kitchen door, he could see by the clock on the cooker that it was already well past two. He decided then to call it a day and go to bed. He felt ready now to make best use of whatever time he had left with Barnaby that day. The last thought he remembered before falling asleep was that he would contact Adam very soon. Yes, he could invite him to see the rare breeds project, and then, when he had him here, they could talk about the spirals...

When he awoke, he could only hear noises from the farmyard, where his nephews had begun their day's work. The house seemed completely still. But when he got up, he found that Barnaby was in the kitchen, quietly preparing a pan full of porridge.

'Hello, there,' he greeted Barnaby.

'Good morning. I hope I didn't wake you.'

'Certainly not, you were so quiet I didn't think you were up.'

'Would you like some porridge? I've done enough for two.'

'As a matter if fact, I would. But where did you get the oats? I don't usually keep any here.'

'I got them from the garden centre yesterday afternoon,' said Barnaby, as he served the porridge out into two bowls. 'I called in when you came back here to do some phoning. There's certainly an excellent array of good quality foods.'

'We pride ourselves on selecting and stocking only the best,' Harold replied proudly. He took a spoonful of porridge and sampled it. 'Delicious,' he pronounced.

'I'm glad you like it,' said Barnaby modestly. 'By the way, I was fascinated by the posters and information cards. It was most interesting to read about the history of the products.'

'That's another of our specialities,' said Harold, trying hard to contain a desire to puff out his chest. 'As well as providing nourishing food, we aim to educate our customers.'

'I didn't have time to read through everything, so I'm looking forward to finding time to go back.'

'I'm not sure there'll be time this morning,' said Harold. 'You and I should go for a stroll, and after that I should take you back to Overton.'

Barnaby knew that Harold had things to say to him, and did not want to be deflected, so he said, 'That sounds fine to me. Where shall we head for?'

'If we take the road past Jane's house, there's a quiet track off to the left not much further along. It'll give us a few miles of enough peace. It's reasonable underfoot.'

Soon they were strolling along together. At first, neither of them showed any inclination to speak. They had covered a mile or so before Harold asked abruptly, 'Have you thought much about last night?'

'Yes, I've thought about it a great deal. And you?'

'I went out after you went to bed. Don't need much sleep these days. Had a lot on my mind,' he said cryptically.

'We'll all need quite some time to get used to what we learned,' said Barnaby. 'In my view it was the beginning of a long process of bringing the two stories together – two stories that had emerged quite separately. Where the merged version will take us, I can't begin to guess. All I want to concentrate on at the moment is how the two stories fit together.'

'That'll do for me now, too. My old brain's creaking a bit at the size of it all, but I've got every intention of bringing it up to speed.'

'I'm looking forward to talking to Helen and Peter when I get back. I want to phone Fay, but I think it's important that I talk to the others first.'

Harold was reassured by the fact that Barnaby seemed to have such a clear grasp of how to proceed with his side of things, and he said, 'I'm glad to hear that you've got a plan of action. I'm in the middle of trying to work mine out.'

'Don't worry too much about it,' Barnaby replied. 'I'm sure that it'll come to you in time. Mine's pretty obvious when you think about it.'

'I've a gut feeling that the next step would be to get Eva across one evening,' said Harold suddenly. 'Actually, there are a lot of things I'm tempted to try to push forward, but that would be through impatience rather than good sense.' He laughed, and slapped Barnaby across the back. 'I want you to know that you're a man after my own heart.'

Although Barnaby had nearly been knocked off balance by Harold's action, his words affected him greatly. It was important to him to hear that Harold accepted and respected him.

On their way back past the garden centre, they could see that the car park was not only full, but overflowing.

'I'll have to consider extending it at this rate,' Harold commented jovially. 'Shall I say goodbye for you to the others?'

Barnaby agreed, and together they decided that now was the time for Harold to drive him back to Overton.

Chapter Twenty-four

Barnaby let himself into Helen and Peter's house. He was not surprised to find them out, as on Sundays they often engaged in activities that were attached to the local church. He made himself a sandwich, and chewed at it meditatively. It might be late in the evening by the time they returned. Would that be too late to talk to them about the events of yesterday evening? He thought it might. He wondered again about phoning Fay, but, as before, decided against it for now.

He settled down to read one of the books from the study. He had previously found it interesting, but to his surprise he could not concentrate on it at all.

He thought of contacting his parents, but he knew that they were still away in Kuwait, visiting Helen's uncle Martin. Since this was a subject that he only wanted to raise with them when they were at home, he would have to wait.

Then he thought of his mother's parents. Yes, Joan and Jim, he could certainly phone them. In some ways they would be ideal people to speak to, since they had both been deeply involved in helping Fay through her strange illness.

He took out his mobile, and found their number. It was Joan who answered.

'Hello, Gran,' he said. 'It's Barnaby.'

'Hello, Barnie. It's nice to hear from you. How are you doing?' Gran was the only person who still called him by that version of his name. Except... yes, except those times when Emily had slipped into using it.

'Fine. I'm learning a lot from being with Helen and Peter.'

'How are they?'

'They're very well, thanks. Busy of course. They're out at the moment, and I'm just back from visiting Emily. You know, the friend I told you about from university.'

'You're phoning for more than a social chat, aren't you?' said Joan perceptively.

'You're right as usual, Gran.'

'Is it me you want, or do you want Jim?'

'You'll do fine, Gran. I've got news. I'm pretty certain I've got some information about Morna.'

'What? After all these years. Are you sure?'

'The person is certainly someone who died a long time ago in a tunnel under a large house, and her name is definitely Morna.'

Fay struggled for words. Then she said, 'Hold on a minute, I'm going to get Jim.'

Barnaby heard her put the phone down and call out, 'Jim! Jim, come here! Barnie's got news of Morna... Yes, *Morna*.' Then she picked it up again and said, 'Tell me everything.'

'It seems that Emily once had some dreams about a girl dressed in sacking, and, recently, one of their long-standing friends who is a neighbour and a business partner met a woman who has a very old handwritten book of recipes. There's a story written in it about a particular recipe for a drink.' He then went on to recount in precise detail exactly what he had been told.

'I can hardly take it in,' said Joan breathlessly. 'From everything you've told me, it looks as if Emily had been dreaming about that girl who made the drink, and that the girl was Morna. Wait, while I tell Jim.'

Barnaby could hear her rapidly transmitting the information, and then her voice came back on the phone. 'No wonder Fay was so distressed when she was in touch with what Morna had been. We always thought that she was remembering Morna's death, and of course that was quite enough in itself to account for her distress, but now it looks as if she could have been remembering Morna being separated from her mother when she was only a tiny baby. And the bit about the brooch... That all fits now. No wonder she felt she had to have it when she saw the picture in the museum! And when Peter had one made for her, it had such an effect on her. And, of course... It all makes sense... I remember that dress she wore to Helen and Peter's wedding – the day you were born. It was linen, which is really a very smart version of sackcloth. And she was so determined to wear the brooch that day.'

'Barnaby, have you phoned her yet?'

'No, I wanted to speak to Helen and Peter first.'

'Quite right. That's very sensible of you.' Joan fell silent, and then said, 'Can you wait again? I want to speak to Jim for a minute.'

When she spoke to him again, she said, 'I'm going to hand you over to Jim now. He thinks you've got a lot more to tell us.'

'He's right,' replied Barnaby.

'Hello, Barnaby,' said Jim.

'It's good to hear you, Grandad.'

'Tell me the rest.'

'Okay,' said Barnaby, 'here goes... Some complex spiral patterns appeared in Emily's aunt's diary on the day that Emily was due to be born. Emily has some kind of connection with these spiral forms that allows her to sense things of a particular significance. And from what little I've heard so far, it sounds as if the story of these spirals and their effects may be just as complicated as the story of what you all found out through Fay's illness. Perhaps even more.'

'That's saying something,' Jim said with considerable feeling. 'How much do you know so far?'

'I know very little, but Emily and her aunt, Jane, have said that when we've got the time, they'll tell me all about it.'

'Look, Barnaby. I think I'll ring off so that Joan and I can talk this over. We'll get back to you in ten minutes or so.'

'That's fine,' said Barnaby. 'I'll get on with my book.' He rang off, and tried again to concentrate. This time he had more success.

When the phone rang, it was Joan again. 'Barnaby, we've had a chat, but I'm pretty lost for words. Of course, like you, I'm tempted to phone Fay straight away, but we've got to wait until Helen and Peter know. After seeing what Fay went through all those years ago, I've a very healthy respect for going about things very carefully. Jim and I have never forgotten how there were times when we had to watch her like a hawk, and even then she could slip into some kind of altered state very quickly. At those times she needed a lot of help, and we had to act fast, using a lot of guesswork. But you know all this. I'm talking about it now because I feel stirred up by your news.'

'I thought it might have that effect on you, Gran,' said Barnaby, 'but I knew you'd want to know.'

'There's no doubt about that. And you must ring again as soon as you know more. Promise.'

'Yes, and I'll stick to it.'

'I'll talk to Jim again now. And don't you worry about me, under these circumstances, this stirring up can only be a good thing.'

'Okay. Bye for now.'

Barnaby put the phone down. He wandered around the house for a few minutes, and then picked up his book once more. This time he had no difficulty in focussing on it, and was soon completely engrossed.

It was nearly ten by the time Helen and Peter returned. They had been to a talk on Third World debt, and had gone back to a friend's house afterwards.

'We're later than we intended,' Peter said to Barnaby when he saw him. 'Sorry we didn't phone.'

'It wasn't necessary,' said Barnaby.

'I know,' said Helen, 'but I prefer to keep in touch. How was your visit to Brookgate?'

'Very fruitful,' he replied.

Helen felt surprised. This was the kind of reply that she had least expected, and she could not make sense of the expression on his face. She said, 'I'm intrigued. What happened?'

'There's a lot to tell you both, but you might prefer to wait until tomorrow evening.'

'There's something important here,' said Peter immediately. 'I'll have to turn in by eleven, but let's make a start at least.' He took his shoes off, and led the way into the sitting room.

Barnaby began. 'My stay with Harold was very interesting in that I learned quite a lot about his rare breeds project.'

'Rare breeds?' said Peter.

'Tell us about the project, Barnaby,' said Helen.

'I can tell you about that later. For now, I'd better concentrate on the rest.' He hesitated only for a moment before stating baldly, 'I've learned something new about Morna.'

'Morna!' gasped Helen. 'How on earth did that come about? What's been happening? Have you phoned Fay?'

Peter put his hand on her knee and said gently, 'Give him time, Helen.'

Barnaby continued. 'No, I haven't phoned Fay. I thought I should wait until I'd talked it over with you. I did phone Gran, though, and I spoke to Grandad, too.'

'What did your gran say?' asked Helen urgently.

'She agreed with me that it was best not to speak to Fay yet.'

Helen relaxed back in her chair, but then sat forward on the edge saying, 'Barnaby, you *must* tell us everything.'

'Give him a chance,' Peter chided. 'Don't let that old impatience get the better of you, Helen. He'll tell us in his own time. I'm eager to know, too.'

Barnaby could see that Helen looked crestfallen, and for a moment she looked more like a teenager than a professional woman in her fifties. He had always felt amused by Helen's bouts of impatience, although they had never bothered him. But he could see that Peter had needed to comment.

Helen and Peter listened quietly, while Barnaby recounted what he had learned about Morna, and what he was beginning to discover about the spirals, and their presence in Emily's life.

When he had finished, Helen said nothing, and waited for Peter to speak.

'If I'm to be completely frank,' he began, 'I have to say that if I'd not already met Emily, I might be having a rather different reaction to what you're telling us. However, the combination of having met her and hearing the story of Morna that came from Harold's contact, Mrs Mace, allows me to accept fully that there seems to be some kind of link between Emily and Morna. This is clear from Emily's dreams and the effect on her of the spiral patterns.'

Barnaby nodded. He could see that Helen's cheeks were looking pink, and that she seemed to be struggling.

Peter continued. 'I...'

But here Helen could not prevent herself from interrupting. 'What do you mean "if I'd not already met Emily"? I think that's quite out of order,' she said crossly. 'Do you mean that you wouldn't believe what Barnaby was saying?'

Peter looked across at her and said, 'I can't say how I would have been. I just think that I might well have reacted differently. In what way, I don't know.'

Helen apologised instantly. 'I'm so sorry, Peter. The whole thing's so huge, and I think I'm a bit on edge.'

'Me too,' he added wryly. 'And remember, I've had a considerable weight of responsibility for you and Fay in the past. Maybe something could come from this that requires me to take that on again.'

Helen's hand flew to her mouth, and she said nothing more.

Peter turned back to Barnaby and said, 'So the next step is for you to learn more about the history of the spirals?'

'That's right.'

'I must say that I'm particularly struck by the fact that it seems they appeared on the day that Emily was due to be born. I know that could have been some kind of coincidence...'

Here Helen could not help but interrupt again. 'Peter,' she said. 'Don't you remember Barnaby saying that they know exactly when Emily was conceived?'

'Yes, I do, and I was about to refer to that when you got there first,' he said.

'I think I'm having a whole lot of feelings and reactions of the kind I used to get more than twenty years ago,' said Helen.

Peter squeezed her hand, and then went on. 'It strikes me as being significant that the spirals appeared on that day and...'

Uncharacteristically Barnaby interrupted at this point. 'I feel that there's a strong link between that and the fact that I was born on your wedding day,' he pronounced firmly. 'And now that I know Emily had a feeling of connection with me from when she first saw me, and that this somehow links with her experience of the spirals, I'm...' Here he stopped, took off his glasses, wiped them, put them back on again and finished, 'To be truthful, I feel... blown away.'

Barnaby's invariably calm and matter-of-fact presentation of himself had temporarily been punctured, and Peter could see that he looked very vulnerable, as if he were standing at a signpost that had too many arms, and none of them showed the right way.

Peter realised that this was not too distant from the way he himself was feeling, and he said, 'I think we've just got to accept that we all feel rather at sea at the moment. It's stunning even to hear the story of Morna's early life. I'm looking forward to letting Fay know about that. But that's straightforward compared with the rest of what we're learning.'

At this point, he looked at the clock on the mantelshelf. It was already well after eleven, and he said, 'I must go to bed now.'

Barnaby stood up, 'See you in the morning, Peter.'

'My first appointment's at ten,' said Helen, 'but I'd better come up now, too.' She smiled. 'I guess I'll have to count every animal in several herds of sheep so that I can get to sleep.'

At lunchtime the next day, Barnaby received a text from Emily to say that she had a book she wanted him to read, and that Harold would deliver it later that day.

When he returned to the house that evening, there was a small packet on the mat that had been hand-delivered. His name was on the front. He opened it to find a book. He looked at the title. '*Communications.*' Inside was a handwritten letter from Emily.

Please take great care of this book, as we can't get other copies. Jane and I had a long talk last night about the best way of telling you more about the spirals. We decided that the first step was to lend you this book to read. Jane had been reading it in bed just before the spirals appeared in her diary. She'd just finished the third chapter. I don't know if you've had a chance to speak to Helen and Peter yet. If they want to read the book, that's fine by us. E

Barnaby went straight into the study and sat down at the desk. He began to read, and soon became completely absorbed.

Later, when Helen and Peter opened the front door, the house was completely silent.

'I wonder where Barnaby is?' Helen commented. 'He's usually doing something in the kitchen about this time.'

Throughout his stay, Barnaby had insisted on contributing to the preparation of most of the evening meals, and thus Helen and Peter had been introduced to several variations on traditional dishes.

'I expect he'll be in soon,' said Peter.

They were finishing their meal when Barnaby appeared.

'Had a good time?' Peter asked.

'I didn't hear the front door,' said Helen cheerfully. 'Have you been somewhere interesting?'

'Actually, I was in the study, reading this book.'

'Oh! I'm sorry,' said Helen instantly. 'I would have called you if I'd known.'

'I probably wouldn't have heard you,' said Barnaby. 'Emily sent this book across. I had a text from her to say that Harold would deliver it. I didn't think he would be able to come across so soon, but it was waiting for me when I got in. Once I'd started reading it, I couldn't put it down. I had to finish it.'

'Let me get you something to eat,' said Helen.

'I'd rather wait. I don't feel hungry at the moment.'

'Can I have a look at the book?' asked Peter.

Barnaby handed it across to him, and Peter read from the cover: '*Communications.* It's by someone called Frances Ianson. What is it about?'

'The first thing I should tell you is that Jane had been reading some of it just before the spirals appeared in her diary.'

'That makes sense of why Emily wanted you to read it,' Peter reflected.

'I feel very affected by the content of it,' said Barnaby.

'Do you think she would mind if we read it as well?' asked Helen eagerly.

'No, she won't mind at all. She put a note in with it to say that you could if you wanted. To be honest, I think that would be the best thing. In fact, I was going to ask you both if you would read it, and then we could discuss it.'

Peter was already engrossed in the book. He nodded absentmindedly without looking up from it, and Barnaby went into the kitchen to get himself something to eat. Peter continued reading, and Helen watched him for a while, before quietly clearing the table. He was so absorbed in the book that he did not notice.

In the kitchen with Barnaby, she asked, 'Could you tell me a bit about it? Peter's disappeared into it.'

'I'm not surprised,' said Barnaby. 'It's very compelling. It's about a woman and her son. The son can't speak, and he has some behavioural difficulties that alarm people. The mother is certain that people are misunderstanding him, and that it's the reason why he gets angry and upset. She sticks with him until she makes a real connection with him. It takes a long time, and a lot of determination and ingenuity, but in the end she makes that connection. After that he becomes very calm, and later he takes charge of their overgrown garden, and grows vegetables and herbs in it, and he hangs things in the trees that the wind sings through.'

Helen felt tears spring into her eyes as she thought about the dedication of the mother to her son, and for a moment she lost track of what Barnaby was saying.

'Could you say that again?' she asked.

'I was just saying that, significantly, he grew the plants in spiral patterns.'

'Spiral patterns?' asked Helen, astonished.

'Yes.'

'I'm sorry, my mind was so taken up with the rest of the story that I thought I might have misheard you. I *must* read that book as soon as Peter has finished.'

It was after ten when Peter closed the book. He rubbed his eyes, stood up, and went to look for Helen.

'Sorry, I couldn't put it down,' he said when he found her. 'It's riveting. It's the story of how one woman on her own achieved something in relationship that one might have thought impossible, and the fruits of her dedication were astounding. In itself it's something that's worth anyone's while studying, and especially for us, if we're thinking of expanding our special family further. But the fact that this has some connection with the spirals, and therefore with Emily and Barnaby, makes it all the more important for us to study it.'

'I don't think I can wait to read it,' said Helen. 'Tomorrow morning I was going to catch up on some of my CPD, as I don't have patients until after lunch, but I think I'll stay up tonight and read it, and then sleep on in the morning. Do you mind?'

'No, love. Not at all,' Peter replied. 'I'll say goodnight now.'

Helen sat up until two in order to finish the book. There were times when she felt herself sliding into sleep, but she stood up and paced round the room for a few minutes to refresh herself so that she could read on. She felt deeply humbled by what she read, and when she climbed into bed next to Peter, she felt intensely grateful that she and he had always had each other in their responsibilities. She had never before tried to imagine what it must be like to feel entirely alone in the kind of situation about which she had just read.

At the end of the next day, Helen, Peter and Barnaby left work promptly, ate early, and sat down together for a serious discussion.

'I want to phone Mum,' said Helen bluntly. 'I don't think we should wait any longer before we involve her. It's not fair.'

'Remember what happened before,' Peter cautioned her.

'Of course I do. How could I ever forget? But that's a long time ago now, and we shouldn't behave as if Mum needs to be looked after.'

'What if it turns out that she does?' asked Peter. 'At the very least it's best for us all to be alert to the possibility.'

'Do you think that we ought to wait until Paul and Diana are back from Kuwait?' asked Helen.

'No, that would mean waiting another two weeks.'

'There's one thing you might be forgetting,' said Barnaby. 'I was always told that Don was often away during the time when Fay was so affected. It seems to me that's the thing that made it the most difficult. If there'd been someone with her most of the time, there would have been less of a problem.'

'You're right,' said Helen. 'And getting her to face the seriousness of her situation, and to agree to having people with her, was very difficult. In fact, sometimes I felt that was the worst bit, worrying about whether or not we could persuade her.'

'I think we've got to the nub of it now,' said Peter. 'I think we should phone her, tell her that there's something big, and tell her that we can't talk to her about it unless she agrees to have someone with her night and day for a few weeks afterwards.'

'What if she doesn't agree?' asked Helen worriedly.

'Then I for one won't be telling her,' said Peter determinedly.

'That's hardly fair,' Helen objected.

'Look, love, it wouldn't be fair on us if we didn't know that she was going to be safe. And look at the responsibility I'd be shouldering if I told her without her giving me that assurance.'

Barnaby had said nothing throughout this exchange, but now he joined in. 'I think Peter's right, and if I know my extra-gran as well as I think I do, I think she would agree with everything that Peter's said.'

'Then I'm going to go ahead and phone her right now,' said Helen decisively.

Peter made no move to restrain her, and she picked up the phone.

It was Don who replied.

'Hello, Dad,' said Helen. 'Good to hear you. I've really phoned to speak to Mum about something this evening, but now that you're on the line, I'd better say that it's something that might affect her a lot.'

'I knew something big was in the wind,' Don replied. 'Joan phoned briefly yesterday. She didn't feel free to tell me exactly what it was about, though.'

Helen could hear her mother's voice ask, 'What's all this, Don? Something's going on, and no one's telling me what it is.'

Don spoke again to Helen. 'I'll hand the phone to Fay now, but if neither of you have any objections, I'll pick up the extension in the hall.'

'That's a very good idea, Dad.'

'Hello, dear,' said Fay as she took the phone. 'What is it? You have to tell me, you know. Don't hold anything back.'

'First you've got to make a promise.'

'That sounds even more mysterious,' said Fay. 'Can't you tell me what it's about?'

'No,' said Helen flatly. 'I've agreed with Peter that I won't tell you until you've promised. If you need any more persuading, I've got Barnaby sitting here. I could get him to speak to you. He's sure that when you know what it is, you'll know you had to promise.'

'All right, I give in,' said Fay good-naturedly. 'What must I promise?'

'That you will never be alone, night or day, for at least four weeks.'

Fay stared at the phone speechlessly. Then she heard Don's voice say, 'I can assure you, Fay, from the little that Joan told me, it's absolutely necessary.'

'If it's as important as that, then you have my solemn promise. And now you must tell me.'

'You spoke to Emily?'

'Yes, and she might come for a visit. But what's that to do with my not being alone for a whole month?'

'Be patient, Mum. You'll understand in a minute.'

Fay said nothing more, and Helen continued. 'Barnaby stayed overnight at the weekend with the farmer who's been a close friend of Emily and her aunt since they moved there a number of years ago. When they were sitting together that evening, he learned that the farmer, Harold, has a contact who recently told him the story of Morna's birth.'

Fay dropped the phone and clutched at her chest, clawing at her jumper. Don was instantly at her side.

'My brooch, my brooch,' she gasped. 'Where is it?'

'It's all right,' said Don soothingly, 'Do you want me to fetch your replica of Morna's brooch?'

'Get me my brooch, Don,' Fay said desperately, trying her best not to shout. 'Please get it for me. It's in the drawer…'

'Don't worry, Fay, I know exactly where it is,' called Don as he went quickly up the stairs.

'Mum, are you all right?' asked Helen anxiously.

Fay picked up the phone again. 'Just give me a minute, dear.'

Don returned with the brooch, and helped Fay to pin it on the front of her jumper.

Fay spoke to Helen again. 'That's it, dear. I'm fine now. Don's brought me my brooch, and I've got it on. I feel more myself again.'

Helen took in what her mother had said, and she knew, without any shadow of a doubt, that Peter had been right in insisting on Fay not being left alone after this. She heard Fay's voice say insistently, 'I've made my promise, so you *must* tell me the rest of why you phoned.'

'I was just telling you how a friend of Emily's had been told the story of Morna's birth.'

'Yes, yes, of course. Carry on.'

Don could see that Fay was fingering her brooch lovingly, and that she appeared to be perfectly calm, so he returned to the phone in the hall.

Fay listened intently while Helen recounted the story, and as she listened, she herself became aware that she was tracing the intricate design of her brooch with her finger. It was a pattern that she knew so well, yet she never ceased to find pleasure in tracing its complex knot whenever she wore it.

When Helen paused, Fay said, 'Thank you so much for letting me know.'

'Actually, there's more,' said Helen.

'You must tell me,' said Fay emphatically.

Helen told her what she knew about the appearance of the spirals, the link that Emily had with them, and how Emily had dreamed about the girl who had been Morna. She finished by telling her about how Emily had, in some indefinable way, recognised Barnaby right from when she first saw him, and that this connection had been affirmed by her link with the spirals.'

'Ah, yes,' said Fay. 'I sensed from when I first heard about Emily that something would happen. I had no clues as to what it would be, and I didn't want to try to find out, because I was certain that it would be revealed to us.'

Helen knew now that Fay was going to be all right. Her voice sounded strong, confident, and completely balanced. It was certainly a good thing to follow the precautions that they had laid down in her promise. She felt sure that Fay would not only be fine, but that she would be a central part of whatever emerged.

'There's one more thing, Mum,' she said. 'Get a pen, and I'll give you the details of the book that Jane was reading just before the spirals appeared in her diary.'

'I've got one here,' replied Fay. She wrote down the details as Helen dictated them.

'You'll probably find it difficult to get a copy,' said Helen. 'But please keep trying, because you *must* read it.'

'Ah!' said Don's voice from the extension phone. 'You know how I like a good challenge. Nothing will stop me until I have at least one copy. Can you give me the name of the publisher?'

'Hang on. I'll ask Barnaby to get it.' Helen turned to Barnaby, but he was already on his way to the study. He returned quickly, and handed it to her. 'Here it is,' she said, 'Aspen Press.'

'What a lovely name!' exclaimed Fay. 'Aspens are amongst my favourite trees.'

'I'll get on to it as soon as I can,' said Don energetically. 'Now, is there anything else we should be saying, or shall we ring off, and Fay and I can have a long chat about everything?'

'Only if you promise to phone us if anything comes up,' said Helen.

'Another promise?' said Fay mischievously.

'Now, Mum. This is a serious matter,' said Helen. 'Oh! I'm beginning to sound like Peter, but maybe that's a good thing, because he's usually right.'

Then she said goodbye and put the phone down.

'That went really well,' she reported to Peter and Barnaby. 'There was a sticky moment at first, and Mum suddenly needed her brooch very quickly. But once Dad had got it and helped her to put it on, she was not only fine, but completely with us. In fact, in one respect she's been ahead.'

'In what way?' asked Peter.

'She knew from the outset that something big would emerge out of the connection between Emily and you, Barnaby.'

'My extra-gran doesn't just have a sixth sense,' he remarked. 'I think she has several more after that. I hope that Don manages to get a copy of *Communications*. I want to see what she makes of it.'

'He'll certainly try his best,' said Helen, 'and I'll be surprised if he fails. He's very resourceful with that kind of thing. I would guess that he'll get Joan and Jim on to it as well.' She laughed. 'It could end up as a competition between them as to who gets the book first.'

'There's a lot in that book that I'd like to discuss,' said Peter.

'Me too,' Helen agreed. 'But the thing that's most on my mind at the moment is the question of how it relates to the appearance of the spirals. We know for certain that Jane had been reading the earlier part of the book just before they appeared, but apart from that, we know nothing.'

'Maybe we will never know,' said Peter seriously. 'However, the mother shows a number of specific qualities that I feel are relevant, and it's relatively uncommon to find all of them in one person. For example, persistence, in the face of considerable adverse pressures, is an important one.'

'Determination, intelligence, creative approaches...' Helen added.

'Real love for her son,' said Barnaby. 'Commitment to reaching for authentic union between herself and her son.'

'Yes, all of that,' Peter agreed.

Helen noticed that his voice carried intense emotion. She could see that he looked tearful, and she was only too aware that his relationship with his own mother had fallen far short of any real closeness.

He went on. 'The thing that affected me the most is what happened once the mother made the decision to trust that her son was trying to communicate. After that, the book documents her unfailing dedication to the search for the right means to establish the connection between them. And finally, there is a sense of communion between them.' He took out his handkerchief and wiped his eyes.

'That's certainly the essence of it,' said Helen softly. 'You put it very well, Peter. Thank you.'

'I agree that's the core of the message the book conveys,' said Barnaby meditatively. 'I must keep that in mind for when I learn more about the spirals. It might be that applying that principle to them could be of use.'

Peter gathered himself, and said, 'It's impossible to say at this stage, when we know so little about them, but yes, let's bear that in mind.'

'From what I remember of the way Jane spoke about the spirals, she and her friends have always assumed that the book enabled, or facilitated, the manifestation of them in some way,' said Barnaby. 'But I can see now that it's equally possible that the book constitutes some kind of "instruction manual". I must put this to Jane and Emily and their friend Eva, if they haven't already thought of it.'

Chapter Twenty-five

Don sat up late that night, working at his computer. He first phoned Jim to tell him what had been happening, and to let him know about the book. As Helen had guessed, the search for the book was then immediately converted into a friendly competition.

'What's the prize going to be?' asked Don, laughing.

'The book, of course,' Jim replied.

But although both men searched and searched again, they drew a blank.

'I'm not beaten yet,' Don muttered determinedly, as he concentrated instead upon trying to find information about the publisher. A search quickly revealed that Aspen Press no longer existed, and he turned his mind to trying to find out when it had been in operation.

He eventually went to bed, but was up early in the morning reconnecting to the Internet. Aspen Press. He tried a number of searches, still without success, but he came upon a website that was devoted to the history of small publishers.

'Ah, this looks interesting,' he said aloud, as he logged on to it. The homepage gave him the following information:

Before the advent of digital printing systems, very few small publishing houses were set up, and many failed. Those that survived tended to publish only specialist books for subjects that had a large following. In time, many of these were taken over as imprints by larger publishing houses. Thus the name persisted, but the publisher did not.

He looked for a 'contact us' button, but could not see one. There were three other buttons, none of which looked helpful, but he tried them all the same, in case they revealed useful clues. However, they led nowhere. The website was obviously still under construction.

'Drat!' he said irritably. 'I thought there was a chance this might have got me somewhere.'

He scrolled the page down, and right at the bottom, in print that was far too small, was what looked like an address. He went to get his best reading glasses, and found it was indeed an address. He copied it carefully onto a sheet of paper, and closed the page.

'That's it,' he pronounced to the screen. 'I'm going to write to them and see what happens.'

Quickly he drafted a letter, and having checked through it, printed it off.

Dear Sirs,

I visited your website and found the above address.

I am interested in obtaining information about a publisher called Aspen Press. It no longer exists, but it published a book called 'Communications' by Frances Ianson, thirty years ago at the very least. If you can give me information about the publisher, or indeed direct me to a source of copies of the book, I would be extremely grateful.

Yours faithfully,
Don Bowden

He addressed an envelope, and was about to sign the letter, when he realised that he should have asked Helen for the exact publication date, and to check the address of the publisher that should appear on the back of the title page. He looked at the clock on the computer. Seven thirty. Yes, there was time to give her a quick call.

It was Barnaby who replied. 'Oh hello, Don,' he said. 'Yes, she's still here... The book... Yes, of course.' He put the phone down for a minute and went to get it. 'I have it here. It was published in 1963. As for an address, there's only a London PO Box number. I'll read it out to you.'

Don copied down the information and rang off. He amended his letter to include the publication date, added his e-mail address, put a fresh copy in the envelope, and sealed it. He was about to set off to the post box, when he remembered that he had promised not to leave Fay alone. He went upstairs to speak to her, but found that she was still asleep.

'I'll only be five minutes,' he murmured as he took the front door key off the shelf. Then he stopped in his tracks. 'Oh no, you don't,' he said aloud. 'I must wait until Fay's up and about, and then we can *both* go.' His mind flooded with memories of over twenty years ago, when she had been so vulnerable, and he knew that he had made the right decision. 'Better to be safe than very sorry,' he said as he picked up an old newspaper and idly thumbed through the pages.

Fay appeared about half an hour later, looking rested.

'Oh, Don,' she said. 'I had such a nice dream last night. I dreamed that I wore my special brooch all night, and I woke up feeling so very relaxed.'

Don smiled inwardly as he realised the significance of this, but he made no comment, except to acknowledge what she had said. He knew that when she was ready she would be able to make the connection for herself. Instead he said, 'I stayed up last night to try to track down a copy of that book. No luck yet, but I've written to the address I found on a rather minimal website about the history of small publishers. It's a bit of a long shot, but at least it might turn up something about Aspen Press.'

'Can't you just contact the publisher?'

'I'm afraid not. It's not operating any more, and the address in the book is only a PO Box number.'

'How frustrating,' said Fay. 'We'll see if Jim's found anything, but maybe your letter will bear some fruit.'

'Would you mind walking down the road with me soon, so that we'll be sure to catch the eleven o'clock collection?'

Fay smiled. 'Ah, so my watcher needs to go out,' she teased. 'Of course, I'll come with you. I'm as interested in that letter as you are.'

Chapter Twenty-six

Harold had decided that it was time to call a meeting with Emily, Jane and Eva. He raised the idea first with Jane one morning in her small office at the centre, and to his surprise she agreed with alacrity.

'I thought you might have wanted to put it off,' he commented.

'I know I'm an overworked businesswoman,' she joked, 'but this is too important to delay. Anyway, I'm taking your lead.'

'What exactly do you mean?'

'You've got plenty to do with your time, so a meeting is no idle suggestion on your part. And it didn't escape my attention that you rushed off to deliver the book as soon as Emily had got it ready. Barnaby has obviously passed the test of your scrutiny with flying colours. I wasn't going to suggest anything until they'd all had a chance to look at the book.'

'I think we need to do some preparation,' said Harold decisively.

'You mean before we start to explain more about the spirals to Barnaby?'

'Not exactly. We could go ahead with that whenever he can come again. It's not that that bothers me.'

'What is it, then?' asked Jane.

'I think that the way things are going, Emily's going to want to go and see Fay sooner than September.'

'Mm, I hadn't thought about that,' mused Jane. 'You may well be right, but I don't think there's anything we need to do about it at the moment.'

'Jane, I've told you before that you're a very bright woman, but sometimes you're dense, and at times I feel like shaking you.'

Jane was taken aback.

'Don't look like that at me,' said Harold. 'I wouldn't lay a finger on you, and you know it.'

'Will you please explain what I'm being dense about?'

'I think we all know that this thing is much bigger than any of us can see. We can't just wade into a situation where you're sitting talking to Barnaby about the spirals, Emily's rushing off to see Fay,

239

and whatever else might happen, without first having a meeting to discuss all the different angles. That way we've a chance of seeing at least some of the things that we can't see yet.'

Jane sat down suddenly.

Harold continued. 'It's called preparation. When we thought of setting up our business, we didn't just convert the building and fill it up with things. A lot of planning went into it. But there were people that we could consult for advice, and we used to have regular discussions. Here we are now, involved right up to the neck in things we don't understand. We've got no one to ask for help, and we've got responsibility for the safety of two young people. We must act responsibly.'

Jane's mind was whirling. In fact, she felt quite dizzy, and she clutched her desk. She had never imagined that Harold would reach this stage in his involvement, and the change in him had happened so quickly. Until only very recently he had been grumpy and dismissive about any of 'this kind of thing'. Then it had all turned around, and not only did she feel he was well on board, but also that his involvement had a life of its own, and it was invaluable.

'Harold, you're absolutely right,' she said sincerely. 'Thanks for pulling me up. When Ellen and Eva were first involved with me with the spirals, we soon found that we had to watch Ellen very carefully. We used to have regular discussions, make notes, and plan in advance. At the time, the whole thing seemed huge and complicated, but compared with what we're facing now, it was relatively simple.' Her shoulders sagged.

'Will you let me take charge, at least for now?' he asked gently.

At this, Jane began to cry, and her tears increased until her body was convulsed with sobs. Harold pulled the door open a slit, and adjusted the sign on its outer side to say 'Engaged'. He pulled a clean handkerchief out of his jacket pocket, and laid it on the desk. Then he put a chair up against the door, and sat on it and waited. He recognised only too well the state that Jane was in, and he knew that it was important not to risk cutting it short. The phone rang, and he reached out and switched off its ringing. The call diverted to the voicemail. 'It's nothing that can't wait,' he said quietly.

Nearly half an hour later, Jane's sobs subsided, and her body gradually became still.

'There's no need for any explanations,' said Harold. 'You've had to wait a long time for that to come. I did mine in my mid-thirties. I had cattle at the time, and my best cow had just died, despite the vet's best attempts. I couldn't stop crying. The vet stayed with me. He didn't say anything, but we both knew fine that it was really about my mother and father.'

'Harold,' said Jane, 'I'd really appreciate it if you took the helm for a while. I don't want to duck out on any of my responsibilities, but I do think that for now, your mind is working more clearly than mine.'

'Done,' said Harold. 'I'll fix a meeting at my house, and I'll tell you the day and time.' Then he stood up and left.

He went straight home, and left a phone message for Eva.

He was pleased when she rang him as soon as she arrived back from work.

'I'm free tomorrow evening,' she said. 'Or is that too soon?'

'That's absolutely fine,' said Harold. 'I'll tell the others. It'll be here, at my house. Come in on your way home from work, and I'll give you something to eat. Any time after six. I'll be ready for you.'

As it happened, Jane, Emily and Eva converged on Harold's doorstep. He opened the door with a flourish.

'Come in, ladies,' he commanded. He was wearing an apron, and had a white cloth over his shoulder. He ushered them into the living room, where the table was set. 'I haven't got many courses, but I've got something special,' he said with an air of mystery. He disappeared off in the direction of the kitchen.

When he came back, he was carrying a dish of steaming baked potatoes. 'My own,' he said, before disappearing again. The next appearance brought with it two dishes of green vegetables.

After that he was away a little longer, and Jane was beginning to wonder whether or not to go and give him a hand, when he appeared in the doorway carrying hot meat on a platter.

'I'm not going to tell you exactly what this is,' he said, 'but it's pork from a named rare breed, from a named producer. I want you to tell me what you think, as I'm wondering about buying in some stock from there.' As he served it out, he added, 'Sorry there's not a lot here, but it's from animals reared only with kindness and good feed, so it's real quality.'

'There's more than enough for me,' said Jane. 'In fact, your potatoes and vegetables are a meal in their own right. Your peas are delicious.'

When the meal was finished, Harold showed them into the sitting room.

When they were settled, he said, 'First I want to see what you all think about inviting Barnaby over again soon.'

'I think we should go ahead with that as soon as we can,' said Jane without hesitation.

'I've been speaking to him on the phone,' said Emily. 'He and Helen and Peter have read the book, and they've had quite a long conversation with Fay. I haven't got the whole story yet, but it's gone well, and Fay's husband, Don, and their friends, Joan and Jim, are trying to get copies of the book for themselves.'

'They won't have much luck,' said Eva. 'I've tried again, and as you know I'm pretty resourceful.'

'It sounded to me as if Don is quite tenacious with this kind of thing,' said Emily, 'and of course he has the advantage of being retired, so he's got more time.'

'I still think they're going to be disappointed,' Eva replied.

Harold continued in a businesslike way. 'How about arranging this coming weekend for Barnaby to come across? Any objections?'

Jane and Eva shook their heads, and Emily said, 'For all sorts of reasons, I think we should invite Helen and Peter across as well.'

'I don't think I could put them all up,' said Harold doubtfully.

'I don't mean that,' Emily explained. 'Barnaby could stay, as before, and perhaps Helen and Peter could come over for the evening.'

'In some ways, I think it would be a good thing if they spent some time with us soon,' said Harold, slowly. Then he pronounced, 'I've been worried about Barnaby.'

Emily showed instant surprise. 'Barnaby's fine,' she assured him.

'We've got some powerful things going on, and I feel I have some responsibility towards him if I'm inviting him to stay in my house. And from what I've heard so far from Eva about what happened in her house with the spirals and Ellen and Jane, I've got to be careful. I've got to be prepared in case anything like that starts up here. We've planned that you'll begin to tell Barnaby the full story of the spirals and their effects when he comes again, and if everything works out as we have planned, that means this weekend.'

'I see now what you mean,' Emily agreed.

'Harold's absolutely right,' said Eva emphatically. 'The more I think about how much Ellen was affected by the spirals in the early days, the more I want to plan things carefully if we're starting to involve other people. One minute I'd be laying out the spiral patterns, and the next Ellen would be unaware of us, in a state that we had no way of understanding until much later. I found it very worrying, and quite alarming.'

'Yes, that's how I felt too,' agreed Jane. 'We both put a good face on it and worked out the best thing to do. I'll never regret any of it, because it opened something to us that was beyond anything we could have dreamed of, but it was very, very hard.'

'Ellen should really be here with us now,' said Emily quietly.

The others looked at her. It was so obvious. Of course she should be with them.

Emily continued sadly. 'I so wish she was here.'

'For that matter, I wish Adam was here,' said Harold. 'I haven't told you yet, but I had it in mind to invite him across to see my rare breeds project. And...'

Emily finished his sentence for him. 'And when he came, you were going to talk to him about the spirals.'

'I wonder what would be the best thing to do,' said Eva uncertainly. 'Things have been happening so fast that it's hard to keep everything in mind at once.'

'We must phone Ellen,' said Jane decisively. 'I should have been keeping her up to date with everything.'

'We should get in touch with Adam, too,' said Eva. 'Have you any idea where he is at the moment, Harold?'

'He's often away from home,' Harold replied, 'but I've got a mobile number and an e-mail address.'

'I think I should phone Ellen now,' said Eva.

'Help yourself,' said Harold, gesturing towards the phone. 'And after you've done that I'll try to get hold of Adam.'

Eva rang Ellen's number, but there was no answer. She left a message to let her know that there was a lot to talk about, and that she would phone again before she went to bed that evening.

To his surprise, Harold heard Adam's voice when he rang the mobile number, and to the amusement of the others, he was soon deep in conversation with him about rare breeds. After a few minutes, Emily tapped him on the arm.

'Adam, I've got something else to run past you,' said Harold. 'I'm with Eva, Jane and Emily at the moment. There's a lot going on here, and we wondered if there was any chance that you might be able to come for a visit sometime soon. You could stay here with me if you want.' Harold listened to Adam's response, and then said steadily, 'You must try to find time to come. It's not just about rare breeds, it's about spirals.'

The others could hear a loud exclamation from Adam. This was followed by a quick exchange, in which Harold explained a little about what was happening. When he put the phone down, he said, 'He's promised to ring me tomorrow, and we can decide what to do. He's going to try to free up some time to come.'

'I feel easier now we've made a start about putting Ellen and Adam in the picture,' said Eva, relief showing clearly in her voice. 'Perhaps now we can get on with talking about this weekend.'

'I've been thinking,' said Harold. 'The only downside I can see is that I haven't met Helen and Peter before. But I'll just have to face that. I think it's far better to have them than not.'

'I've been wondering about bringing along my copies of the spirals, so that we can lay them out if we want,' said Eva.

Harold considered this, and then said. 'A good idea, but I think it might be a bit soon. I've a gut feeling that we need discussion, and time to think through things afterwards, before we risk moving into doing anything like that.'

'I think you're right,' Eva replied.

'And there's something else,' he said.

'What's that, Harold?' asked Jane.

'I've a hunch that it would be best if everyone concerned had read that book before we get into anything deeper, and it's my turn next. I'll ask Barnaby to bring it across with him at the weekend.'

'I brought mine with me,' said Eva. 'I went home to drop my files off, and on an impulse I put it in my bag. I can leave it with you if you want.'

'Good,' Harold replied. 'I'll take good care of it, I promise you.'

Eva handed it to him. He took it straight to his bedroom and put it on the bedside table. 'I'll look at it when you've all gone,' he said as he sat down again.

'That leaves Fay,' said Emily.

'Why should she read it now?' asked Harold.

'I... I don't know.' For a moment Emily looked quite withdrawn.

Harold waited, and Emily's state passed.

'It just seems obvious to me,' she said confidently, 'but I can't give a particular reason.'

'I agree that it would be interesting to see what she makes of it,' said Jane slowly, 'but I hadn't thought there was any urgency about it.'

'I want her to read it before I go to see her,' said Emily flatly.

'That I can understand,' said Jane. 'I'm sure there'll be a way of arranging it.'

'And that brings me on to next thing,' said Harold. 'Emily, you were thinking about seeing her some time in September.'

'That's right. But since last weekend, I've started wondering about going sooner.'

'I guessed you might,' said Harold, 'and I wouldn't be trying to stop you.'

Emily looked at him in surprise. She had fully expected him to try to deter her, and even delay her plan of going in September.

'What's in your mind when you say that?' she asked.

'I don't know how much longer we'll have Barnaby,' Harold replied. 'I don't know if he's going home for a while before he goes back to university. In any case, after he's studying again, it'll be quite different from having him just down the road.'

'The other side of Overton isn't just down the road,' Jane observed, 'but I take your point. Once he's left there, we probably won't be able to see him at all for weeks – maybe not until Christmas.'

Harold looked thoughtful. 'I think he said that his parents had decided to stay out in Kuwait for a few extra days, and that they are due back in a couple of weeks' time. It's the middle of August now, so at this rate Barnaby might go home at the beginning of September.'

'It's something we should ask him about,' said Eva. 'The timing of things over the next few weeks could be crucial. We've discussed Emily's visit to Fay, but I think there are many more things we need to think about and put into the right sequence.'

'Right again,' said Harold. 'I think we should think very

carefully indeed about this. First, I'd like to phone Barnaby. I want to check if he can come at the weekend, and whether or not Helen and Peter can join us for the Saturday evening.'

He picked up the phone, and was soon speaking to Barnaby. Helen was out, but Peter confirmed that he and Helen would be free that Saturday evening, and Barnaby arranged that he would arrive at Brookgate on the lunchtime bus.

'Now that's fixed,' said Harold, 'it clears the way for us to draw up a plan for the next few weeks.'

'Sounds good,' said Eva. 'And we can see what the others think on Saturday.' She turned to Emily. 'When you go to see Fay, I'm coming with you,' she said bluntly.

Emily looked uncomfortable.

'Oh, I know that sounds dictatorial,' said Eva, 'although it wasn't meant that way. I think you might need someone with you, and I want to be that person.'

'But Eva,' Emily protested, 'I've travelled around on my own for years.'

'That's not what I mean. I'll remind you again of the fact that I've witnessed some very intense reactions to the spirals,' said Eva.

Emily listened quietly, while Eva continued.

'When you and Fay get together, it won't just be two women meeting each other – Emily in her early twenties and Fay in her seventies. It could represent the coming together of two parts of a woman who had a difficult beginning followed by a short life that ended in a traumatic way. We don't know yet why Morna has been making herself known to Fay, and showing herself to you. We don't know what led Harold to meet Beth Mace, and why she decided to confide in him about the story in her notebook. Apparently, she'd never told anyone else before.' Here Eva paused before continuing. 'For a long time, I've had a growing respect for energies that are from those who have departed, and I can never be entirely sure why and how they manifest. In the case of Morna, it's something that we yet have to discover.'

'Oh, Eva, I'd been so fixed on the idea of meeting Fay, that I hadn't put any thought into what it might involve in a deeper way,' said Emily. 'Thank you so much.'

'That's the value of us all getting together,' said Jane. 'I remember time and time again how each of Ellen, Eva and I would have a slightly different view on things, and the same thing happened when Adam and others joined us.'

'This kind of talking is essential,' said Harold. 'I was right when I said we should get together this evening.'

'Yes,' said Jane wryly, 'and I remember how you had to work to persuade me.'

'That's water under the bridge now,' he said. 'We're in the middle of talking about Emily's visit to Fay. Eva, I agree that you should go with her. If you can't get the time, then I'll go, but I don't think I'd be the best person for it. I'm doing my best to get up to speed, but you're far more experienced with the kind of thing we're facing than I am.'

'Harold, I might be more experienced,' said Eva, 'but it's taking my breath away how quickly you're grasping things, and you can be ahead of me.'

Jane nodded. 'Yes, Harold, you're transformed.'

Harold tried not to look pleased, but he could not conceal his reaction, and Emily said, 'It's all right to feel good about it, Harold. In fact, this is something that you're going to have to learn about next.'

'What?'

'How to accept appreciation.'

Harold's face turned a deep red colour, and he whipped out his handkerchief and buried his nose in it, hoping to conceal his discomfort.

Emily decided to say no more. She was satisfied that she had made her point, and that it had struck home. She was sure that when he was on his own, it would be one of the many things that he would be thinking about.

'Right,' she said decisively, 'now back to my trip to see Fay.'

'If Fay can see us at a weekend, I won't have to book any time off work,' said Eva. 'The next few weekends are pretty clear for me. I've got plenty to get on with, but I've got nothing I'm committed to. By the way, I've already checked the map. The journey shouldn't take more than about two-and-half hours. We can do it as a day trip, but I'd rather have an overnight stay. I think we'd achieve more that way. I checked the public transport too, but it's so complicated and would take much longer, and we wouldn't be able to get back on Sunday.'

'That's such a shame,' said Emily. 'I'm looking forward to a time when public transport works for most journeys.'

'So am I,' said Eva. 'I hate having to use the car for work, but as things stand at the moment, I'd have to move house if I wanted to get to work by bus, and I'm not prepared to do that.'

'I wish I'd remembered to ask Barnaby about his plans for the rest of the summer,' said Harold irritably. 'That wasn't very efficient of me, was it? But we'll have a chance to talk to him about it this weekend.'

'That'll be soon enough,' said Jane.

'Yes,' said Emily. 'I think what we should do now is decide when Eva and I might go to see Fay. When we've spoken to Barnaby, we can phone Fay and check with her.'

'Let's aim for the weekend after this one,' said Eva decisively. 'And I think we should phone Fay now, to see if it's convenient for her. We can always change it if necessary, once we've spoken to Barnaby.'

'It's nine now,' said Harold slowly. 'That shouldn't be too late. How about it, Emily?'

Emily agreed with alacrity, and was soon speaking to Fay. The call was quite brief. Fay consulted Don, and after only a few minutes it was agreed that if Emily and Eva did indeed come that weekend, arriving around lunchtime, they could both stay the night.

'That's it fixed as far as we can,' said Emily as she put the phone down. 'I feel much clearer now that we've made a date. There was a kind of tension lurking around in me that's gone away now.'

Eva was making a note in her diary. 'I'm hardly likely to forget,' she said, 'but I always like to have things written down.'

When Fay put the phone down, she felt calm and relaxed. She realised that since she had first spoken to Emily, she had been waiting. It was not exactly that she was waiting for Emily to come. She realised now that she had been waiting for something to unfold, and she felt sure that knowing Emily would be coming soon was a step towards it.

'We'll put Emily in our "library",' she said to Don, 'and Eva can have the spare room.'

Don smiled. 'I'll have to do a bit of tidying. I've got things spread about as usual.'

The 'library' was their name for the small bedroom, which long ago they had lined with bookshelves, but there was still room in it for the narrow single bed.

'Fay...' Don began.

'What is it?' asked Fay.

'I've something I want to talk to you about before they come.'

'If you're thinking about the subject of Morna,' replied Fay, 'don't hold back. I think there's a lot we should cover before they come.'

Don relaxed inwardly, and smiled at her. 'Yes,' he said, 'we need to get on with that. But there's that book as well. I'm not any further with it, and neither is Jim.' He stood up and paced around the room. 'Let's make a start on Morna, but first I'll check my e-mails in case something's come.'

Fay agreed and closed her eyes, while Don went to the computer. She thought about her illness of all those years ago, and how, through it, she had learned about Morna's death by *experiencing* it. She had not known at first that it was Morna, nor had she known what was happening to her, but as time went on, it was as if she had *become* Morna. It had been so important to her when she found the picture of Morna's brooch, and Peter had found someone who would make a copy for her. That brooch – she had always treasured it...

'Here's something,' said Don, his voice full of suppressed excitement.

Fay was temporarily startled out of her reverie.

'Oh, no, it's just some clever spam,' said Don, annoyed. 'They get more and more ingenious every day.'

He made no move to leave the computer, and Fay closed her eyes again. Her thoughts ran on. And now Emily had come into their lives. Emily, dear Barnaby's friend. Emily and her dreams... and the spiral patterns, whatever they meant. Her dreams, and the story of the girl and the recipe, surely sounded like Morna. She patted her chest, and her finger traced the pattern of her brooch, although she was not wearing it. Morna's birth. How amazing! She sincerely hoped that the story were true. This would mean that at last Morna had a chance of the long-awaited transformation that she deserved. How old would Emily be now? she wondered. Barnaby would be twenty quite soon, and she must be about two years older than that. Yes, he would be twenty on the 21st of September, and Emily must be twenty-two in

November.

Fay began to feel a crushing weight bearing down on her. No, not now… She opened her eyes and saw the familiar frame of Don's back as he worked at the computer.

It was then she realised that Emily must now be about the age that Morna was when she was killed.

'Don, Don,' she said urgently.

He turned towards her instantly. 'What is it?' he asked anxiously.

'Oh, it's all right,' Fay reassured him. 'I'll tell you later. Have you found anything?'

'It's disappointing,' said Don. 'I'm not getting anywhere. I'll check my e-mails one last time, and then I'll close the computer down, and we'll have a chat.' He clicked on 'send and receive'. 'Wait a minute,' he said. 'This looks like something interesting.' His voice was tight with anticipation. 'Yes.'

'Read it out, Don.'

'It's very brief.' Don read:

Thank you for your letter.
Aspen Press. 1961-1963. Only three publications recorded, of which your book is one.
We would be pleased to make a search for you. Our time is limited and valuable, so we make a charge of £30 per hour.

Phillip and Lynne Thorne

Don clicked the 'reply' button.

Please go ahead. I authorise payment of up to two hours' work. If more time is needed, please contact me immediately.

Don Bowden

Don sent the message off, and then leaped from his seat, pulled Fay out of her chair, and tried to dance around the room with her.

'Hold on a minute, Don,' she protested. 'This doesn't mean we're going to get a copy.'

'I know, but we're more than one step closer to it.' Then he stubbed his toe hard on a leg of the coffee table. 'Ow!' He grabbed his foot, and hopped dramatically round the room.

'Come and sit down, Don. We've important things to discuss,' said Fay firmly. 'I'm worried that Emily might be in some kind of danger.'

'What do you mean?'

'I've been thinking through things while I was waiting for you to finish at the computer, and I think that Emily might well be the age that Morna was when she was killed.'

'Fay, what would I do without you? It's stupid of me not to have thought about that myself.'

'I don't think you're ever stupid, Don,' Fay said seriously. 'We've just got such a lot to think about, and it's difficult to hold it all in our minds at once.'

'I've been more worried about you than about Emily,' said Don.

'I can appreciate that, after what we all went through years ago. But I think the danger to me has passed, or at least is minimal. Listen carefully, Don. I've got something important to say. Don't interrupt. I don't know if I'm right, but I want to tell you what's been forming in my mind.'

Don closed down the computer, and sat beside her.

'I think that Morna's trying to transform,' said Fay. 'I used to think that when I'd somehow merged with her about her death, that was enough, but I don't believe that any more – not since we've heard about Emily's dreams and about Beth Mace's story. While you were on the computer, I was casting my mind back to when I was ill, and I'm beginning to see now that I've been clinging on to Morna through that brooch of mine. Oh, maybe those aren't quite the right words to describe it, but in any case, I think I've been holding her back from her destiny. Now that we know about her birth, about how her brooch was made, and about how she lost contact with both her parents, I feel that everything's falling into place, and I can see that I've been blocking her. I've been using my brooch for comfort, instead of facing whatever I have to face, and so allowing her to come together as herself. Then at last she will be able to transform, possibly into a realm that we know nothing of, and maybe never will. Morna was the embodiment of a wrongdoing. Her birth, her life and her death were consequences of a wrongdoing. Now that I know the circumstances of her creation, I must not continue to do wrong to her by preventing her progress towards completion. Now that I know about her beginning, I am starting to understand what has to happen. I am already separating out from her life essence. I shall always treasure my brooch, but it will become a reminder, rather than a symbol to which I cling. We must work together to further the separation, so that by the time Emily arrives, I am as ready as I can be to meet her truly. She and I will potentiate the transformation of Morna – and the distillation of the meaning of her creation, life and death can be free to work where it must. It must no longer be hampered by my old blindnesses. When I cried out to you earlier this evening, I felt again that I was dying in the tunnel, and I so wanted you to fetch my brooch for me. But I managed to pull myself back, and remember who I really was. That was the beginning of the separation.'

Don stared at her in stunned silence for a full five minutes. When he spoke, he said very little.

'Everything you say sounds so right, so very right.'

He took her hand and held it in his, and they sat together without saying a word, calmly sifting through the meaning of what Fay had spoken.

At length, Fay said, 'We must think very carefully indeed about Emily's safety. I'm glad that her friend will be travelling with her and staying here.'

'From what you've said, it's really Morna's safety that's at stake,' said Don thoughtfully, 'but any danger might well manifest through Emily at this time.'

'Yes, it's far less likely to come through me now,' said Fay.

Chapter Twenty-seven

Barnaby boarded the bus for Brookgate. In his bag he had the book to return to Jane and Emily. He knew that this weekend would be even less of a social weekend than the last had been, and he welcomed this. He was looking forward to spending time with Harold again, and Peter and Helen had promised to join them around eight that evening. When that meeting had first been arranged, Helen had phoned Fay and Don to let them know about it, and had promised to contact them afterwards to tell them everything that transpired.

When the bus drew into Brookgate, Harold was standing waiting for him.

'Thought I'd take a walk down to meet you, lad,' he said conversationally, as they strolled in the direction of Smithy Farm.

'It's good to see you, Harold,' said Barnaby. 'I've been looking forward to learning more about what you're doing.'

'I'll be glad to show you,' said Harold pleasantly. 'There's just one thing I need to get straight in my mind first.'

'What's that?'

'When are you thinking of leaving Overton?'

'I don't quite know. Mum and Dad'll be back the week after next, and I'd like to see them for a few days before I go back to uni. They usually like to see me some time around the date of my birthday. That's the twenty-first of September, which is of course Helen and Peter's wedding anniversary, too. I think if they're happy with it, I'd like to stay on until the middle of September.'

'That gives us about four weeks,' said Harold, relief showing in his voice. 'We need to have you here for long enough, and four weeks should do.'

'Long enough?'

'Enough time for us to get some of this sorted out. I've got a hunch that we need to have you and Emily more or less in one place until some things get a bit clearer. By the way, Emily's fixed to go to see Fay next weekend,' he added abruptly.

'That's good,' said Barnaby. 'Fay will be very pleased to meet her. Is she staying overnight?'

'Yes, and Eva's going with her.'

Barnaby fell silent while he digested this information. He was aware that had he had the opportunity, he would have jumped at the chance of taking Emily to see his extra-gran.

'Have you any objections?' asked Harold.

'No.' Barnaby said nothing more.

Harold sensed that something was amiss, but did not press him. By this time they had reached the farm, and he said, 'Come into my office. I've got plenty that'll interest you. After that, I'll show you how my reclamation scheme is coming on.'

At a quarter past seven, Harold was busy counting the seats in his sitting room. 'Six,' he said. 'That means we need one more. I'll get my office chair. It's comfortable enough.'

There was a knock on the front door.

'I'll get it,' said Barnaby. He opened the door to find Helen and Peter standing there.

'I think we're a little early,' Peter apologised.

'Come in. It'll be fine,' said Barnaby. He introduced them to Harold, who was returning from transferring his chair.

'Come and sit down,' said Harold, pointing towards the sitting room.

There was another knock, and Eva, Jane and Emily appeared. Eva was carrying a large brown envelope.

Harold pointed to it and said, 'So you brought them after all. We can lay them out in the living room, if we get that far.'

When everyone was settled, he said, 'I think we should just get started. The practical things are that Emily and Eva are travelling to meet Fay next weekend, and Barnaby has told me that he'll be around for about another four weeks.'

Barnaby turned to Peter. 'Is that okay?' he asked.

'That's excellent,' Peter replied. 'I thought you might not be with us for much longer. I'm very pleased.'

Harold continued. 'As you know, we're here this evening mainly to tell Barnaby about the spirals. I think that I'll be learning along the way, as I can't claim to know all that much about them. Helen and Peter, I'm very glad to have you both here. It feels better knowing that Barnaby has your support.' He turned to Jane, 'Over to you.'

Jane began. 'Since Helen and Peter know almost nothing about the spirals, I'll start at the beginning. The spiral patterns appeared in my diary on the day that Emily had been due to be born – November 12th. I had gone to bed early, and I'd read another chapter of the book, *Communications*. I began to write in my diary, but I must have dozed off, and when I woke, the spiral forms were there on the pages in front of me. They are unique in my experience, and the complexity of their construction has never ceased to amaze me. I have my diary here.' She took it out of her bag, and searched until she found the first spiral patterns. Then she passed it to Peter, who was sitting next to Helen and Barnaby on the sofa.

They studied the pages carefully for several minutes before handing the diary back to her.

'Harold, would you like to see this?' asked Jane.

'I'll look at it later,' he replied. 'I've seen Eva's copies a few times now.'

Jane looked surprised, but said nothing. Obviously, Harold had been doing some research while she had been tied up at the centre.

'I told my friend Ellen about them, and she later came to see me when I'd hurt my ankle. She brought Eva with her.'

'That's how I first met Jane,' said Eva.

'We looked at the spirals together, and Ellen was so profoundly affected that she went into a changed state. At the time, we couldn't understand what was happening to her. When she came out of it, she had no conscious knowledge of having been in it. That was the start. We had several meetings at Eva's house, and each time, Ellen was far more affected than either of us. With successive exposures to the spirals, under the supervision of myself and Eva, she started speaking when affected. At first we couldn't make out what she was saying, but some words did eventually become clear. Looking back on it, she was already being greatly affected by some kind of unconscious link that she had with Adam, whom she had met by chance on a train.'

'Oh!' said Eva suddenly, 'I should have said that I've got a message for us all from Ellen. I spoke to her recently on the phone about what has been happening. She says she hopes to travel down to see us some time over the next few weeks, and she's looking forward to hearing how this evening goes.'

Emily looked very pleased. She turned to Barnaby, and said, 'You'll be able to meet her.'

'That's good,' Barnaby replied.

'Adam's a sound man,' said Harold. 'He gave me a lot of excellent advice when I was running the farm. And it was through him that Jane and Emily were put in touch with me, when they were thinking of moving.'

'Yes,' said Eva. 'They were staying with me at the time, and I contacted Ellen, who in turn phoned Adam for advice about possible farm cottages.'

'I hope it won't be long before he can pay us a visit,' said Harold. 'I'm waiting to hear back from him about possible dates.'

'Shall I go on now?' asked Jane.

'Of course,' said Harold.

Jane continued. 'As Adam, and later his friend, Boris, entered Ellen's life and then the lives of the three of us, a couple of older men joined us. One was a professor, Edmund Barnes, who had an enormous fund of knowledge about historical artefacts. What happened when we all got together with the spirals was quite extraordinary, and really defies description. All I can say is that we seemed to be transported into a state of bliss that was beyond the world as we had known it, and that the effect of that has never left us.'

Barnaby had been looking increasingly agitated, and he burst out, 'What did Ellen say?'

The others made no comment about his interruption, since Barnaby never normally spoke out of turn.

It was Eva who replied. 'We were never completely sure, but "song of light" or "sound of light" were fairly distinct. There was also the mention of "grief" or "greaves". It's difficult to be sure about what this meant, since not only had there been much loss in the lives of Ellen and of Adam, but also I had been trying to help a young girl and her father, both of whom had suffered a profound loss, and whose name was Greaves.'

'That must have been Hannah,' said Emily. 'You told me about her when you showed me your special stick.'

'Yes, that's right.'

'It was very important for me at that time,' Emily reflected. 'You told me that Hannah's mother had died, and that Ellen's mother had died when she was young. After that, I no longer felt so alone and different.' She turned to Jane. 'You had done everything you could to help me, and more, and I'm eternally grateful. Added to that, you

256

had to cope with the fact that you had lost your sister. I don't know how you managed.'

'Barnaby told us that your parents had died when you were young,' said Helen, 'but we don't know what happened.'

'My father was lost off an oil rig, and my mother died of cancer not long afterwards,' Emily explained. 'Jane is my mother's sister. When Mum became ill, she gave up her job to look after us. And when Mum died, she moved in with me. We've been together ever since, until I went to uni.'

'Thanks for explaining,' said Helen. 'I'm so sorry. As you know, I've been lucky enough to have both my parents alive right up until now, but Peter's father died when he was about to leave home.'

Harold allowed time for thought before saying, 'Although we hadn't intended to display the spiral layout this evening, Eva has brought her copies of the spirals. She could lay them out on the table next door, if we want. Apparently, the effect of seeing them like that is different from seeing them on the pages in Jane's diary.'

Here Peter spoke. 'When I looked at Jane's diary, I saw what I took to be a layout diagram. Am I right in thinking that?'

'Yes,' said Eva. 'Well, we've always taken it to be that, and I've followed it each time I've laid them out.'

'I think that Jane and I have given you a reasonable overview of the story,' said Eva, 'but there's a considerable amount of detail that we haven't mentioned yet.'

'Of course,' said Peter.

'Would you like some time to think about what you've heard, rather than viewing the spiral layout?' asked Harold. 'Remember that this layout has affected several people very profoundly in the past, and there are four of us in this room who have never seen it before.'

'Harold, you're very wise to raise this,' said Peter. 'To be perfectly frank, I think that you, Helen and myself shouldn't attempt to view the layout this evening. It's enough for now to have seen the spirals in Jane's diary.'

Helen nudged him, 'Speak for yourself,' she said crossly, and then quickly put her hand over her mouth. When she spoke again she said, 'Peter, I'm terribly sorry. I do apologise.'

'It's all right, love,' he said, putting his hand on her knee. 'I understand.' He turned to Emily. 'I would like you to be the one to show Barnaby.'

'That's how it must be,' said Emily gravely.

'I'll go and lay them out, and then come to get you,' said Eva. She disappeared, and the others waited quietly.

When she returned, she said, 'Jane and I will come in with you.'

Emily took Barnaby's hand, and led him into the well-lit living room. There were the spirals arranged very precisely, in accordance with the diagram. Jane and Eva followed close behind.

'Auntie Jane,' said Emily urgently. 'Something's happening to me, and I'm not ready.'

Jane linked her arm through Emily's, and walked her briskly back out of the room and into the bathroom, where she ran a cloth under the tap and patted Emily's face with it.

Although Emily was shaking with the effort of controlling herself, she did not appear to lose track of what was happening to her. Her teeth began to chatter.

'Are you cold now?' asked Jane matter-of-factly.

'No,' said Emily in between bouts, 'I think it's just a release of some kind of tension.'

Meanwhile, Eva had stayed in the room with Barnaby, who was fascinated by the spiral layout.

'The visual impact is very intense,' he said, 'but the overall effect is far greater than purely visual.'

'We can stay here for another minute or two,' Eva advised him, 'but after that, I'll take you back to the others, and then I'll clear the layout away.'

When she went with him to the sitting room, Emily was talking to the others.

'This time, as soon as I saw them laid out, I felt sucked towards them as if by a giant magnet. No, that's not right. It was that I wanted to immerse myself in them. I wanted to dive into them and become enveloped in them. Oh... none of that's quite right, but it's the nearest I can get. I wanted to let go into the feeling and let my body take me there, but then I heard a voice in my head saying "not yet, not yet". Auntie Jane, do you remember years ago – when it seemed as if I was reading the spirals with my hands?'

'Yes, I remember very well,' said Jane.

'Well, this was as if I was going to read them with the whole of my body. I was filled with an intense feeling of pure joy, and that was all I was aware of until I heard the voice. It was a kind, compassionate, but strong voice, and I was in no doubt that I had to hold back. It was then I turned to you for help.'

'I'm glad you did.'

'You did the right thing,' said Helen, who had listened intently to everything that Emily was saying. She turned to Peter. 'Peter, you were so, so right,' she said. 'I'm so grateful for your wisdom and caution.'

'And I love your spontaneity,' he said warmly. 'It's just that sometimes it tries to get out of hand.'

'Emily,' said Helen, 'we had some really tricky and worrying times when Fay was reacting to things that we didn't understand. You must always listen to Jane and Eva, even if they say things you might not agree with at the time.'

'I know that,' said Emily simply. 'I trust them completely. You see,' she went on, 'Eva and Jane have already had to face unseen forces. I am from the next generation. The principles aren't new to me, although the detailing might be. When your mother was first affected, she was with people who were having to learn from scratch. Barnaby will be okay, because he has you, his parents and his grandparents. But like me, he has his own responsibility to keep alert to things that might be affecting him.' Here she turned to Barnaby. 'What did you think of them?' she asked.

'I can't really say. It's more what I felt and sensed. There's something far greater than words can express. And one thing is very clear to me.'

'What's that, Barnaby?' asked Harold.

'I can't begin to explain why, but it was very important to have read the book before I saw the spiral layout. If I were asked to explain that, the nearest I could get is to say that the book is somehow almost a key to the spirals. At the very least, the lessons embodied in it are a preparation. That's all I can say at the moment.'

Harold noticed that although Barnaby expressed himself very clearly, he looked completely exhausted.

'Perhaps we should wind up now,' Harold said, looking at his watch. 'It's after ten, and I think some of us are feeling pretty tired.'

Peter turned to Barnaby. 'Would you like to come back with us tonight?'

'I think he should,' said Harold firmly. 'I can come over and get you in the morning if you want, lad. That is, if you're awake.'

Barnaby collected his things, while Peter and Helen said goodbye to the others.

When he was ready, he said to Emily, 'If I don't come over tomorrow, I'll give you a ring in the evening. I want to hear how you are, and I'd like to talk to you about your trip to see Fay.' Then he left with Peter and Helen.

When they arrived back home, Jane and Emily stayed up talking for a while, and then Jane suggested that they both sleep in her bed, a proposal to which Emily did not hesitate to agree.

Jane waited until Emily was asleep before she allowed herself to doze. Then, just as she was falling asleep, she was certain that she heard Emily say, 'The coming together of Morna is part of the preparation for the reading of the spirals.' She forced herself awake again, switched on the bedside lamp, and scribbled this into a notebook that lay beside it.

Chapter Twenty-eight

Fay and Don were making preparations for the weekend, while looking forward to meeting Emily and Eva. Fay teased Don about the number of things that he had scattered round their 'library', but as was his habit, he took this well, and they enjoyed the resultant cheerful banter.

'My only sadness is that we haven't had a chance to read that book yet,' said Don. 'There's still no word from the search.'

'It's a bit soon, isn't it?' said Fay, as she flicked some imaginary dust from a shelf.

'Hey, I've already done that!'

'I know,' Fay admitted. 'I'm just finding something to do to fill the time. My mind's so fixed on seeing them tomorrow lunchtime. Try not to worry about the book, Don, at least we've had a talk with Helen and Peter about it.'

'Yes, that was good, but in some ways it made me feel even more frustrated about not having our own copy, particularly in view of the enormity of what took place at Harold's last Saturday evening.'

'Maybe we should phone Emily to ask if she'd be willing to bring Jane's with her.'

'Why didn't I think of that myself! I'll give her a ring straight away.'

'She'll be at work,' Fay reminded him.

'I'll phone this evening, then. Don't let me forget.'

Fay smiled. 'I don't think there's any likelihood of that.'

'After I've spoken to her, we'll do what we'd planned.'

'Yes, we must go through again everything Helen and Peter told us about the meeting at Harold's. There was so much, and I want to be as clear as I can be about it all for when Emily and Eva arrive tomorrow. I want to do my best for Morna, so I must have what little I know about the spirals organised in my mind.'

'I agree with all of that,' said Don. 'Why don't we make a start on it right now?'

'I'd like that.'

Don saw a look of anxiety flash across her face.

'Don,' she said, 'what if we don't seem to get anywhere this weekend? Do you think Emily will come again? I've been so sure that we'd be able to give Morna the final help she needs, but now I realise that perhaps I've been naïve about that.'

'Don't worry, Fay,' said Don. 'We all stuck together during your long illness, not knowing what we were trying to do, but all of us were committed to making sense of what was happening. We'll just do what we can. And I think that even if everything seems to shift this weekend in the way we hope, Emily will want to keep in touch.'

Fay relaxed. 'I think you're right, Don.'

That evening, Don's phone call to Emily resulted in her promising to bring Jane's copy of *Communications* with her, and also that she would ask Eva to bring hers.

By the end of the evening, Don and Fay felt satisfied that they had brought together everything they knew so far, and had discussed it thoroughly, ready for the next day.

Eva and Emily made an early start the following morning, and drew up at the end of the road that led to Don and Fay's house, well in advance of the agreed time.

'I think I'll give them a ring on my mobile,' said Eva. 'They seemed so keen to read some of the book as soon as possible. We could call round and let them have both copies, then go off for a walk somewhere. I'd like to stretch my legs before we join them. What do you think?'

'I think you should.'

Fay answered the phone after the first ring.

'Hello Eva... Oh, thank goodness... At first I thought you were phoning to say you couldn't come after all... Yes, of course, do come round... The book? Don will be delighted.'

Eva rang off, and drove the car slowly down the road to find an older couple standing at their front door, waiting.

'That must be them,' she said to Emily as she pulled up in front of the house. She could see that although Don's hair was pure white, there was little else about him that suggested that he was of advancing years. He stood very straight, and his frame looked strong and agile. Fay's hair was not completely white, and Eva wondered for a moment if someone had put a touch of colour into it.   She was a friendly-looking woman who appeared to be a little smaller than average height.

Fay threw her arms round Eva as she welcomed her in, and then embraced Emily in the same way. 'You'll have something to drink,' she said.

'No thanks, we have flasks in the car,' Emily replied. 'Could we use your bathroom, and then if you'd give us directions for a local walk, we'll go off for an hour or two.'

'Of course,' said Fay.

'Are you sure you wouldn't prefer to stay?' Don asked Eva.

'We're quite a bit earlier than planned, and we'd love to have a walk,' said Eva. She took her copy of *Communications* out of her bag and handed it to him. 'Here's my copy of the book. You'll have a chance to look at it while we're out.'

'Thanks *very* much,' said Don. 'I've tried so hard to get one, but still no luck.'

Emily reappeared, and when she saw Don almost caressing Eva's book, she said, 'Fay, I almost forgot, I've got Jane's copy here for you to look at.' She produced the book from her bag.

Don made a quick sketch of a local walk, and Emily and Eva set off.

'They seem such nice people,' said Eva as they walked towards the beginning of the first turn.

'I knew they had to be,' said Emily, 'but it's so good to meet them at last.'

'It must have been amazing to be involved with Fay at the time of her illness and all that lay behind it,' mused Eva. 'If it was during the months before Barnaby was born, you would have been about eighteen months old at the time.'

'This is something I haven't thought about properly yet,' said Emily slowly. 'The spirals were born when I should have been, and then when I wasn't much more than one, Fay became ill. But of course none of us had any knowledge of it until recently. Eva, I'm so looking forward to talking to them when we get back.'

'Me too,' Eva agreed. 'Don said this walk won't take us much more than an hour. That should be fine. They'll have had some time with the books, and then we can make a start.'

They walked along in silence, enjoying the scenery, and

occasionally pointing things out to one another. From time to time they consulted Don's sketch, but they found that the way was clearly marked, and they had no trouble getting back to the house.

When they arrived, Fay saw them through the window of the sitting room, and she hurried to let them in.

'I've read the first few chapters,' she said. 'It's such a beautiful story, and so well expressed. Reading it is quite a different experience from merely knowing a bit about it. Come into the dining room. Don and I laid out some lunch earlier this morning. Just choose what you want.'

Half and hour later they settled themselves in the sitting room.

'I'd like to come straight out with what's on my mind,' said Fay. 'I hope neither of you will mind.'

'That's fine,' said Eva. 'How about you, Emily?'

Emily nodded reassuringly.

Fay began. 'I've come to understand that what happened to me with Morna all those years ago is only part of the story. I feel embarrassed to admit that I've now realised that all this time I must have been clinging on to her through my relationship with her brooch.'

'It wasn't exactly *her* brooch,' said Emily.

'But I had wanted the copy of her brooch,' said Fay, 'and the feelings I've always had about it have been as if it were hers. Emily, since I heard about your dreams and about Beth Mace's story, I've become convinced that they are definitely about Morna's birth and her young life. I feel now I know that I'll be able to help her fully, instead of only in her death.'

'Why do you think she still needs help?' asked Eva.

'I don't think that she would have appeared in Emily's dreams if she didn't, and I don't think that drink would have come into Harold's hands – the drink that led to Emily "seeing" the girl again, and that time not in a dream.'

'I follow what you mean,' said Emily. 'And all this must be connected in some way to my link with the spirals.'

'Neither Fay nor I can claim any understanding of the spirals,' said Don, 'and we only have the knowledge that has been passed to us recently by Helen and Peter. But we want to learn more.'

'Did you bring a picture of them with you?' asked Fay.

'I'm afraid not,' said Eva.

Emily turned to Eva, and said with regret, 'I wish we had.'

'Don't worry,' said Eva. 'Now I know the way here, I'm sure we can come back some time and bring my copies with us.'

Don winked at Fay and said, 'I told you so.' To Eva and Emily he said, 'Fay was worried about whether or not she would feel that her work for Morna would be complete by the time you left this weekend. I told her that whether or not it was, I was sure you'd be willing to come back again.'

'If you want to ask me any questions about the spirals, I can try to answer them for you,' Emily offered.

'We would like that very much,' said Fay.

Don nodded, and said, 'Peter and Helen told us what they saw in Jane's diary, but tell us a little about the layout.'

Emily began. 'As you've probably gathered, there are nine individual spiral forms, one of which is a double spiral. The double one goes in the middle of the layout, and the others are arranged around it, alternating between one quite close to the central spiral and one at more of a distance.'

'Why do you think that is?' asked Fay almost whispering.

'I can't say,' replied Emily. 'But the nearest I ever got to knowing more was an experience I had in a dream. It was as if I were communicating with the spiral layout, using my hands.'

'Yes, Emily and Jane were staying with me at the time,' said Eva. 'I certainly believe that it's the closest connection anyone has had with the spirals so far.'

'Maybe you're going to be their interpreter,' said Fay, in a voice so low that Emily barely heard what she said. Then Fay said in clear tones, 'I wish they could help us with Morna.'

Until now, Emily had been concentrating entirely on the conversation, but her attention seemed to wander for a minute, and she caught sight of a photo in a frame that was standing on a shelf to one side of the fireplace.

'I know I'm changing the subject,' she said, 'but is that Helen and Peter on their wedding day?'

'Why yes, it is,' said Fay. 'Do you want to have a closer look?'

'Yes, please. The one I saw at the centre of their collage is much smaller. I can get a better view of the jacket from this one.'

Don passed it to her, and she studied it closely.

'There's quite a story behind how we found that jacket,' said

Don.

'It was more like being led to it,' Fay corrected him. 'Emily, I'll tell you all about it another time. But…' Fay hesitated. 'I don't know…' she said, half to herself.

'Are you wondering about offering to show it to Emily?' asked Don.

Fay looked at him gratefully. 'Yes, I am. Emily, would you like to see it?'

'Yes, I would… very much.'

'I'll go and get it,' said Fay.

She went into the hall, and Emily heard her going up the stairs. When she returned, she was carrying a garment in a protective cover. She unzipped it to reveal Helen's jacket.

Emily gasped. 'It's absolutely beautiful!' she exclaimed. She reached out tentatively.

'It's perfectly all right to touch it,' Fay encouraged her. She watched as Emily stroked the cream satin material upon which the jacket was based.

'It looks like a very rich satin,' said Eva admiring it. 'And the embroidery that covers it is very fine. It looks as if that's done in a kind of gold thread.'

Fay nodded.

'The scalloped edges are so lovely,' said Emily as she traced them, first round the end of each sleeve, and then up the front, round the neck and back down again.

'Either it's very old, or it's been based on an old design,' Eva guessed.

'We were told that it's a copy of one that was made for a young woman who was descended from a royal family,' Fay explained.

'It certainly fits the part,' said Eva. 'And it's so clever the way it's slightly padded throughout. It makes it lie properly, without being bulky.'

Fay opened her mouth as if to say something, but then shut it again. However, after a minute or two she said, 'Emily, would you like to try it on?'

'Oh! I mean… I don't think I could,' said Emily, startled.

'Why not?' said Fay. 'I think it would fit you.'

'It wouldn't be right,' said Emily hurriedly. 'It's Helen's.'

'Not entirely,' said Fay. 'Remember that the design belonged to someone else before her.'

It was then that something seemed to fall into place for Emily, and she said, 'Fay, I know it isn't right for me to put this on at the moment. I don't know exactly why. It's kind of you to offer. Perhaps if we'd asked Helen…' She stopped, took a deep breath and said, 'But please can I wear Morna's brooch for a while?'

Eva could see that Emily's face had drained of all its colour.

'Can I?' she repeated, almost desperately.

Don, too, had noted the colour of Emily's face.

'I'll just pop upstairs and get it for her. Okay, Fay?' he said.

Fay was busy fitting the jacket back into its cover and had not yet noticed the change in Emily. Don returned very quickly.

'Shall I help her to put it on, or will you?' he asked Fay.

Fay glanced up, saw the colour of Emily's face, and said firmly, 'I'll do it straight away, Don.' She took it out of its box and pinned it to the front of Emily's blouse. 'There,' she said firmly. 'Don, doesn't she look lovely with it on?'

'Yes, Fay. She looks beautiful!'

Emily put both her hands up to the brooch, and as she did, the colour began to return to her cheeks.

'Fay, it's so kind of you to lend it to me,' she said.

Eva marvelled at the way Don and Fay had responded to Emily's state. They could not have devised a more appropriate way had they had days to rehearse it. She said nothing, not wanting to risk disturbing the interaction.

'I think that you should wear it,' Fay suggested. 'I don't wear it very often myself these days, and you've waited a long time to see it again.'

'Yes, I have,' said Emily softly. 'A very long time.'

'Peter had it made for us,' said Fay calmly. 'We still need it, but not for much longer.'

Eva could see that Don had taken Fay's hand and was squeezing it gently. 'Take your time,' he whispered to her, so quietly that Eva wondered if he had really spoken. She noticed that Emily's skin had taken on a beautiful sheen, and that her face seemed to be glowing. In some ways it reminded her of Ellen's face, all those years ago, when she was being affected by the spirals.

Eva had no idea of how long she sat there watching the scene – Don and Fay standing, hand in hand, in front of Emily, who was sitting on the couch. What was taking place was out of any concept of time that she knew.

Then she noticed Emily begin to look very tired. Her eyes started to close, and she began to sag back into the sofa. Eva stood up and gently guided Emily's head down onto the seat of the sofa, where Fay had slipped a cushion. Don brought a blanket to cover her, and after watching her silently for a few more minutes, they moved quietly into the dining room, leaving the doors open so that they would be able to hear if she stirred.

There was no sound from her while they talked, then prepared and ate their meal, and then talked again.

Later, Eva said, 'I think I should sleep down here with her. Do you have something I could use?'

'We've got a blow-up mattress, and we can bring a duvet down for you,' Don suggested.

'That would be fine,' replied Eva. 'I'm sure she'll be all right, but I don't want her to wake up alone.'

'You're very wise,' said Fay. 'And don't hesitate to call us in the night if you need us.'

'Thanks very much,' Eva replied. 'I don't think I'll need to, but it means a lot to me to know that the offer's there.'

'Okay,' said Don, 'now I'll go and bring the things you need.'

He and Fay helped Eva to get her makeshift bed ready, then bade her goodnight, and went upstairs together.

Emily woke the next morning feeling refreshed. For a moment, she thought that she was in her own bed at home, but then she realised that she was on a sofa, and that she and Eva had come to visit Don and Fay. She looked around the room in the little light that the curtains allowed in, and was surprised to recognise their sitting room.

That's strange, she thought to herself. How is it that I'm sleeping down here? It was then she discovered that she was still fully dressed.

She heard a sound, and looking round, she could make out that someone was asleep under a duvet on the floor beside her.

'Eva?' she whispered.

The figure stirred, and Emily heard Eva's voice saying, 'Oh! It must be morning.'

'Eva, why are we sleeping down here?' asked Emily. 'I thought we were supposed to be upstairs.'

'I'll tell you in a minute,' Eva replied, her voice sounding muffled.

Emily continued. 'To tell you the truth, I've no memory of yesterday evening, and...' Here she clutched at her stomach, before finishing her sentence by saying, 'and actually, I feel terribly hungry.'

'I'm not surprised,' said Eva, who by now had emerged. 'You fell asleep so early that you missed your evening meal.'

'Goodness!' exclaimed Emily. 'I had no idea. No wonder I can't remember what happened in the evening.' She thought for a minute, and then said, 'Eva, I could do with a shower. Do you think we'll wake them if we get up now?'

'They told me not to worry about disturbing them,' said Eva truthfully. She opened the curtains a fraction, and looked at her watch. 'It's after eight. I think it should be okay.'

There was no sign of Don and Fay when Emily went upstairs. She noticed that the door of one of the rooms was shut, and she assumed that they were still asleep. She got ready as quickly as she could, and returned to Eva downstairs.

'Your turn now,' she told her.

Eva had been tidying her bed away. She had folded up the duvet and collapsed the inflatable mattress, and was putting everything in a neat pile in a corner of the room.

'I won't be long,' she said as she collected her wash bag and headed for the stairs.

Emily folded up the blanket under which she had slept, and added it to Eva's heap of bedding. Then she went into the kitchen, where she found a note from Don and Fay.

There's plenty in the cupboards and the fridge. Help yourselves. We've gone round to see Joan and Jim for a short time, but will be back soon. If you need anything that you can't find, phone us there.

Don and Fay

A phone number was written at the bottom of the message.

Eva joined her, and peered over her shoulder. 'I thought they were exceptionally quiet,' she commented. 'No wonder!'

Emily saw a jar of oatflakes. 'I think I'll start with a large bowl of these,' she said as she reached into the cupboard for a dish. She took her food to the dining room, and Eva joined her.

Don and Fay appeared only a few minutes later, when Emily was half way through her food.

'Hello again,' they said cheerfully. 'How are you this morning?'

'I feel fine,' said Emily. 'Sorry about last night. It seems I fell asleep quite early. Thanks for letting me sleep on your sofa.'

'That's okay,' said Fay. 'It's good to see you eating something. You must be very hungry.' She could see that Emily was wearing fresh clothes, and that she no longer had Morna's brooch pinned to her front, but she made no comment about this.

'Yes, I must have slept right through your meal last night.'

'You can make up for it this morning,' said Fay, smiling. She went to the kitchen, and put the kettle on. 'Anyone for a hot drink?' she called through the door.

'Some herb tea would be fine for me,' said Eva.

'Nothing for me, thanks,' said Emily. 'I'll get a glass of water, later.'

When Fay and Don joined them at the table, Emily said, 'By the way, when I went for a shower, I was a bit puzzled because I found I was wearing a brooch. Does anyone know where it came from?'

Fay and Don looked at each other, and Eva waited to see what they would say.

'I showed it to you last night,' said Fay calmly. 'You wanted to try it on, but you fell asleep so quickly afterwards that we decided it was best to leave it on you.'

'Thanks,' said Emily. 'It's so beautiful. It must be very special. I've left it in the spare room with all the books in it. I thought it would be safe there.'

'That was a good idea,' agreed Fay. 'I'll put it away later.'

Don addressed Eva and Emily. 'How long are you able to be with us today?'

Emily looked at Eva, who said, 'I think we ought to leave by two. I have some work to prepare this evening, and if we leave then, I'll have plenty of time.'

Don and Fay had finished their breakfast, but Emily was still eating a large banana.

'Don,' said Fay. 'I think we'll just take those things back upstairs.'

'Let us help,' said Emily immediately.

Fay hurried to deter her. 'No, no, dear, we'll be fine. There's not much, and we have to fit it into a particular shelf in the cupboard.'

Eva could see that Fay wanted to speak to Don in private, and she said, 'You and I can do the clearing up in the kitchen, Emily.'

'Thank you, dears, that would be a great help,' said Fay.

When she and Don reached the top of the stairs with the bedding, they went straight to their room, put the bedding on one side of the bed, and sat together on the other.

'What do you think?' Fay asked Don.

'She obviously has no conscious memory of what happened,' said Don. 'It reminds me of how you used to be, except for one big difference.'

'She's not agitated or upset,' Fay finished for him.

'The problem is to decide whether or not we tell her,' Don pondered.

'Exactly.'

'We had to with you, because you could become so distraught, and it was the only way of grounding that. More importantly, it was a part of keeping you safe.'

'Mm. At this stage, we don't know if Emily's safety is an issue.'

'Obviously Eva's like us in that she's not keen to tell Emily straight away what's happened.'

'And of course, none of us can tell exactly what's happened,' Fay reflected. 'We only know what we saw.' She was quiet for a minute, and then she said, 'Don, I've an idea.'

'Tell me.'

'I think I should show her the brooch again.'

'Do you think that's wise? What if something gets stirred up just when they're about to leave?'

'I've a hunch that it won't,' said Fay.

Don could see that she looked very confident as she said this, and he waited to see what else she might say.

'I think that it would have a good chance of completing what we came together for,' said Fay.

'Maybe we should speak to Eva first,' said Don cautiously.

'I don't think it's necessary. She knows we'll do what we think best. In any case, somewhere inside her Emily knows what's happening, it's just that she's not conscious of it yet. The change has been set in motion, and what has to happen will be quietly forming inside her.'

'How do you know?' asked Don. 'How can you be so certain?'

Fay looked at him pointedly. 'Don, surely you remember how in the past I would have this kind of certainty just when I was about to take an important step or say something that was a clue to the way forward?'

'Of course, I do, Fay. It's just…'

'What?'

'We hardly know Emily. She lives a long way from here, and I do feel responsible for her.'

Fay stood in front of him, took hold of both his arms, and looked straight into his eyes. 'Look, Don,' she said. 'She was born into the situation with the spirals, she's a friend of Barnaby's, she's met Helen and Peter, and she's come here with an intelligent and experienced older friend. What more could we want or need for her?'

Don hung his head, and said in a low voice, 'Fay, I think I'm remembering how terrible I felt when you were going through what you did years ago, and I was in the position of having to work away from home a lot of the time. You were here alone, and I had to depend on Joan and Jim to keep you safe. It was absolutely terrifying for me at times, and I often thought that I might lose you.'

Fay hugged him, and said, 'Thank goodness you've realised that. Now we can concentrate on the here and now and what's best for this situation.'

Don looked at her, and said, 'I think we should go and get the brooch now.'

Fay turned, and went to collect it from the room where Emily had left it, and they went together down the stairs.

Eva and Emily were deep in conversation at the dining table, and Fay and Don joined them.

'We were talking about Morna again,' said Eva. 'It seems right to me that we should keep thinking about the circumstances of her birth, her life and her death.'

'I agree,' said Fay. 'For one thing, if it weren't for her, it's extremely unlikely that we would be here together this weekend.'

'Yes,' said Don to Fay, 'at the very least, we've been given two new friends.' He turned to Eva and Emily. 'We do hope that you'll be able to come again soon. If you want, you can use us as a base for doing some exploring.'

'That's so kind of you,' said Emily. 'We'll remember that, won't we, Eva?'

'Yes, I'd like to see some of this part of the country,' Eva replied.

'Emily, you might like to come whenever Barnaby's at home,' Fay suggested.

'That's a really good idea,' said Emily brightly. 'I'd like that very much. I don't know what I'll be doing after the summer, but if I get free time that coincides with his, I may well take you up on your offer. Actually, that brings me to the other thing I wanted to speak to you about, Fay.'

'Oh, goodness, yes, we haven't spoken yet about the youth work I used to do. I've drawn up a list of a few people and their contact details for you. How about going through the list now, and I'll tell you a bit about each of them, and what we used to do together?'

The next hour was spent with Emily and Fay talking animatedly, while Eva and Don discussed places of local interest. By the time Emily and Fay had finished, Emily had made several pages of notes. She folded them, and put them in her bag.

'That's given me a lot to think about,' she announced. 'Thank you so much, Fay.'

Fay smiled at her, and said, 'Remember, there's a bed here for you if you want to meet any of these people, or indeed if you decide to work in this area for a while.'

'You're serious, aren't you?' said Emily. 'That's so kind of you.'

'We'd love to have you,' said Don sincerely.

'Oh, I nearly forgot,' said Fay. 'I brought that brooch back downstairs. I thought you might want to have another look at it.'

She unpinned it from where she had attached it inside the pocket of her dress, and put it on the dining table in front of them all.

'*Now* I remember what happened yesterday,' said Emily excitedly. 'How could I forget? We were looking at Helen's wedding jacket... When you said I could try it on, something started to stir inside me.'

'Can you put it into words?' asked Fay.

Emily thought for a few minutes, trying to work out how to say exactly how she'd felt.

'I desperately wanted to put something on, but not the jacket,' she said. 'I felt confused, because the jacket was the only thing in front of me. I remember thinking that I'd have to get Helen's agreement before I tried it on, but I knew that wasn't the real reason for not taking up your offer. In fact, part of me longed to put it on and feel what it was like, but I knew that I mustn't.'

'Would you like to try it on now?' asked Fay. 'I could easily go and get it.'

'I would love to try it sometime,' said Emily, 'but not now.'

'I'd certainly like to see you in it,' Fay remarked in a rather insistent way.

Don tried to catch Fay's eye. For some reason she was getting carried away, and he could see that this was taking things in the wrong direction.

But she did not look at him, and chattered on unchecked. 'I think it'll suit you. I'll speak to Helen about it. I'm sure she'll be interested to know how you look when you do eventually try it on.' Then she stopped, and seemed to gather herself. 'But let's get back to what you were trying to tell us.'

Don relaxed. He turned to Emily, and said, 'So you had the feeling that you mustn't try on the jacket. What do you think was the most pressing reason for that?'

'I...' Emily stopped as if her voice had seized up. She tried again, 'I...'

'Don't worry, dear,' said Fay. 'I'm sure it'll come to you in time. The important thing is that because you knew not to try the jacket on, you were able to think of the brooch.'

'Yes, that's right, Fay,' said Emily. 'And I found it difficult a few minutes ago when you were encouraging me to try it on.'

'I'm so sorry, Emily,' said Fay. 'I got carried away because I could see in my mind's eye how lovely you would look in it.'

'I could tell that,' said Emily, 'and that made it all the harder to resist. You see, I *must* concentrate on the brooch. Yesterday, once I was sure that I shouldn't try on the jacket, the brooch came into my mind straight away.'

'You went very pale,' said Eva, remembering her concern for Emily.

'I do remember feeling strange, and I suddenly felt desperate for the brooch. It was as if my life depended on it.'

'Your colour came back almost as soon as I pinned it onto your blouse,' said Fay.

'Ah,' said Emily, 'I can remember that now. It felt so wonderful.

I felt so… complete.'

'That sounds right,' said Don.

'What do you mean?' asked Emily.

Don glanced at Fay, who nodded, and he explained. 'You see, when Fay and I were talking on Friday, we wondered if something would happen this weekend to help to free Morna further. We think that what happened all those years ago in relation to Fay had freed Morna from the trauma of her death, but we hadn't realised that this was not enough. We now think that through you, Morna is being freed from the trauma of her conception and her birth, and the loss of her parents and of her name.'

'Oh, yes…' said Emily. 'Morna lost both her parents. Like me, she lost both her parents. But I had been wanted and loved. Morna didn't have a chance. She was misconceived, and she lost her parents when she was only a few weeks old. Her mother's husband saw to that.'

'And the culture that she was born into,' added Eva gently. 'Nowadays, her mother wouldn't have been forced to give her away. Her marriage might have broken up, but she wouldn't be forced to abandon her child.'

'But her mother's marriage was broken anyway,' said Emily. 'How could she ever look at her husband again?'

'I think she had certainly wanted to keep her baby,' Fay reflected. 'Otherwise she wouldn't have kept her pregnancy and the birth a secret. She must have been afraid that her husband would force her to get rid of the pregnancy.'

'Quite likely,' said Don.

'Her father must have loved her,' said Emily suddenly. 'Otherwise he wouldn't have had the brooch made for her. It was quite a big thing to do.' She reached forward, picked up the brooch, and started to toy with it. 'I don't know where my father is,' she whispered. 'But perhaps Morna didn't even know who her father was.'

Carefully, she replaced the brooch in the middle of the table.

There was a long silence.

It was broken finally when Emily turned to Eva, and said, 'Eva, we should be thinking about getting back now. I know it's bit earlier that we'd intended, but I think it's time.'

Fay and Don made no attempt to delay them, and instead Fay

said, 'It's been lovely having you both. Can we give you something to take to eat on the journey?'

'Thanks very much, and thanks for everything,' said Eva. 'Emily and I will get our things together.'

'We mustn't forget to give you your books,' said Fay.

Eva hesitated for a fraction of a second, before saying, 'If you want, I can leave my copy here for you.'

'That's a very generous offer,' said Don, 'and I think that both Fay and I feel tempted to take you up on it.'

'But we mustn't,' Fay added firmly.

'Yes, we must trust that somehow we'll get at least one copy for ourselves.'

Eva wondered whether or not to press them, but then said, 'Well, remember if that doesn't work out, the offer's there, and I'll find a way of getting it to you.'

Fay and Don looked at each other, and then Don said, 'I might take you up on that if we haven't got one by the time Emily comes back to see us.'

'And I promise I *will* come,' said Emily.

Fay and Don found the books, and then quickly made some sandwiches to give to Eva and Emily. Soon they were waving goodbye.

'It's a pity we didn't read beyond those first few chapters,' said Don with considerable regret.

'I've a feeling we don't have to worry about it,' Fay replied. 'And now I think we should give Joan and Jim a ring. They'll be waiting to hear how things have worked out. Maybe they'd like to come round.'

Emily felt very tired on the journey home. Eva made little attempt to initiate conversation, and she had a sense that Emily kept dozing from time to time.

When they neared Brookgate, Emily said, 'I'm quite glad we set off earlier than we'd intended. I think I need some time on my own to get used to everything.'

'Mm. Me too.'

Eva was about to drop Emily off at her house, when Emily said, 'Eva, would you mind if we went to yours first? I'd like to borrow your copies of the spirals.'

Eva felt thrown into a state of turmoil. She was happy to lend them to Emily, but not now, as she knew that it was entirely the wrong time.

'What's on your mind?'

'Nothing in particular,' said Emily airily.

Eva thought fast. 'I can drop them round this evening,' she said firmly. 'I'm tired from the driving, and need to get home.'

Emily looked as if she were about to protest. Eva said nothing as she drew her car up outside Emily's house, but made a mental note that she would phone Jane at the centre as soon as she got back. No, Jane would be very busy at this time on a Sunday afternoon, and she didn't want to worry her. She'd phone Harold. Yes, in any case, Harold would be the best person for this.

She waved to Emily, who glanced over her shoulder as she unlocked the front door to her house. Then she drove off. But she did not drive home. Instead, she went straight to Harold's house, and knocked on the door.

'Thank goodness you're in,' she said urgently.

'What's happened?' asked Harold, alarmed.

'Nothing yet,' Eva replied. 'But I'm worried.'

'Come in.'

'I think it's best if I don't try to tell you the whole story of the weekend,' explained Eva rapidly. 'What I should say now is that I'm pretty sure that on the way home Emily slipped into an odd state. She was very quiet and sleepy, and she said she was looking forward to having some time on her own to think about what had happened. Then, when we were nearly back, she asked me, in a rather strange voice, if I could take her to my house first, to pick up my copies of the spirals. I put her off, saying I'd bring them round this evening. To be perfectly frank with you, I don't think she should be left on her own, and I don't think that my staying with her would be the most helpful.'

'I agree,' said Harold decisively. 'You were with her through whatever happened at Fay's. It's better that she's with someone else now. I'll go down straight away.'

'I'll be at home,' said Eva. 'Don't hesitate to phone me.'

Harold grabbed his keys, and they went out together.

When he arrived at Jane and Emily's house, Harold found that the front door was locked, and would not yield to his key.

'Darn it!' he muttered under his breath. 'She'll have bolted it.

Eva was right, there's something amiss.'

He went round to try the back door, but found that it, too, would not budge. He considered calling to Emily, but decided against it. Maybe it would make matters worse. If she wasn't exactly acting strangely, she was certainly acting a little out of character, and it was important that he took this into account.

He decided to phone her, and took his mobile out of his pocket and keyed in the number. There was no reply.

Feeling temporarily defeated, he sat on a log to consider the position. Oh yes, there were ways that he could force an entry. He could go and get tools and lift one of the windows out, but that might alarm her. Then he had an idea.

'Why didn't I think of it before?' he asked his phone.

As quickly and quietly as he could, he made his way to the rear door of the other house and let himself in. Then, just as quietly, he moved to the door in the party wall. He could hear a movement on the other side, and for a moment he wondered if he might be too late. He gripped the handle, and opened it just in time, as on the other side Emily was standing there with the key.

'Hello,' he said calmly. 'How was your trip?'

Emily looked very startled, and Harold had the distinct impression that she had not at first recognised him.

'Hello,' she said carefully.

They stood looking at each other for a full minute before Harold said, 'I think I'll put the kettle on and we can have a chat.'

As they sat at the table, Harold came straight to the point. 'Eva called in to see me,' he said. 'She was a bit worried about you, so I came to check.'

Emily looked evasive. 'Why?'

'You didn't seem quite yourself,' said Harold cautiously. 'And I would agree that you don't.'

'That's nonsense,' said Emily.

Harold could see now that his direct approach wasn't going to help, and he changed tack.

He laughed heartily. 'Maybe I just wanted an excuse to come and see you and find out how things have gone.'

But he could see that this made even less of an impact on Emily, as she remained impervious to him. He felt at a loss as to what to do next, and wished that there was someone else there with him. He looked at the clock on the wall above Emily's head. One o'clock. It was at least five hours until Jane would come home. And then what? Her return wouldn't necessarily be the solution. Reluctantly, he accepted that he was stuck on his own with something that he didn't understand – something that unnerved him. He knew himself to be a man of courage and resourcefulness, but this had been predominantly in the physical and practical arena. Now he felt at sea. Maybe he should phone Eva? But that risked making things worse. He decided to do the most difficult thing that he could imagine, and that was to sit where he was and say nothing.

At first, Emily sat very still and silent, not looking at him, and appearing quite morose. Harold watched her, and said nothing. When at last she stirred, her movements were jerky and irritable.

'Why are you here? Why did you come?' she burst out.

Harold said nothing, and waited.

'There'll be trouble if they find you here,' she said angrily.

Harold noted that she did not look at him directly, but was surveying him out of the corner of her eyes, and her head was down between her hunched shoulders.

'Emily…' he began.

Emily jumped and looked over her shoulder, but seeing no one, she hissed, 'She's not here, but she'll be back soon, and then there'll be trouble.'

Harold tried again. 'Mor…'

But he had no chance to finish, as Emily spat at him, and said, 'Don't!' And she bared her teeth at him.

Harold had been hoping to connect with her, but clearly he was mistaken. He lapsed into silence again. He was totally at a loss as to what to do, and the two once more became frozen in a kind of tableau.

After a while the phone rang, but Emily seemed not to hear it, and Harold felt it was best not to answer it himself. He watched the minute hand of the clock. It crawled so slowly that each minute felt like an hour.

The phone rang again, and again he did not answer it. He searched his mind for something to do, but had no further inspiration, and remained seated, still and silent.

More time passed. Then he thought he heard someone at the front door. But there was no ring at the bell. Then there was a sound at the back door. This time he was certain. But the sound didn't last for long. Perhaps it was a stray dog sniffing around.

A few minutes later, Jane appeared in the kitchen. She took in the scene, and without pausing, said confidently, 'Emily! It's lovely to see you back. Eva rang me at work, and I thought I'd come straight down to see you.'

'Jane!' exclaimed Emily. She stood up and gave her a hug. 'It's been a really interesting time. I'm glad you've come, because I want to tell you all about it.'

Harold began to relax a little. So the phone call must have been Eva. Good for her. When she didn't get a reply, she must have known that something was very wrong, and had phoned Jane. Thank goodness he'd come down in the Land Rover. Jane would have seen it parked outside, and would have known that they were in. She, too, had managed to get in through the back door of the other house.

Emily looked at Harold. 'And you've come as well! That's good, I'll tell you both about it.'

'I'll just phone along to the centre,' said Jane. 'Emily, remember Malcolm, that new person I took on to help out on Sunday afternoons?'

'Of course, I do. He started last Sunday, and I liked him. I remember thinking what a good thing it had been to take on someone who's just retired.'

'Well, I asked him if there was any chance of him doing both afternoons this weekend, and he agreed. He's actually extremely competent. I'll give him a ring. I'm sure he'll hold the fort for an hour or so.'

After Jane had made the call, they moved to the sitting room, and Jane and Harold said very little, while Emily recounted the events of the weekend.

'That all sounds pretty big,' Jane commented when she had finished. 'How are you feeling now?'

'I'm fine,' Emily replied. 'I remember feeling a bit strange when Eva dropped me off. I'd been very sleepy on the journey. When we got here I'd asked her if I could borrow her copies of the spirals. I thought that once I'd had a rest I would like to spend some time making the layout while I was waiting for you to finish at work. She said she'd bring them round this evening. I remember feeling disappointed about that. No, as a matter of fact, I felt thwarted. How strange...   It was perfectly understandable that it wasn't convenient for her to get them straight away. After all, she'd already been driving for well over two hours. I came into the house, and now you two have come round.'

'I think that something else must have happened after you came in, Emily,' said Jane gently. 'I got here about three.'

Emily stared at Jane. 'But I was back here before one.' Her voice trembled a little.

'Can I be up front here?' asked Harold.

Jane looked uncertain, but Emily said, 'Tell me what you know, Harold. I'd rather know.'

'I was sitting in the kitchen with you from one, until Jane arrived.'

'But I've no recollection of that at all!' exclaimed Emily. 'I don't like this... First at Fay's, and now here. I don't like this at all.' She stopped for a few seconds, and then said, as if to reassure herself, 'But I'll probably remember in a little while. After all, I did at Fay's.'

Harold went on. 'With your permission, I'll carry on with what I was going to say.'

Again Jane looked uncertain, but Emily said, 'You must.'

'Now that I've heard the story of what took place at Fay's,' said Harold, 'I think I know what was going on here. At least, some of it. I think that when you didn't have either Jane or the spirals, you slipped into something else. And what I think you slipped into was a part of Charity's life – the part that she spent with her adoptive parents.'

Emily stared at Harold. 'Go on.'

'Eva had sensed that all was not well with you, and she called in to see me on her way home. I came straight down to see you, but I couldn't get in. Not only had you locked the front and the back doors, but also you'd bolted them.'

'What had I done that for? We only do that on dark evenings and at night.'

'You must have had a strong feeling that you had to do it, and I think that already you were being Charity. I think I had some sixth sense that told me that you thought that you were living in a small house, and instead of getting ready to take out one of the window frames...'

'One of the window frames!' Emily echoed.

'Let me finish,' said Harold. 'Instead of that, I went as quickly as

I could to the back door of the other side of your house and let myself in. After that I went to the communicating door as quickly as I could, because I sensed it was only a matter of time before you sealed yourself off by bolting that one as well.'

'Harold...' said Emily. 'You're amazing!'

Harold ignored her and continued. 'You were about to secure the door, but you made no move to stop me from coming in, and we went to the kitchen. You were pretty aggressive towards me when I tried to talk to you, so I soon stopped trying. You seemed to think that "Emily" was someone else who would be coming, and that there would be trouble when she came. Very significantly, you didn't want me to say the name "Morna". In fact, you spat at me when I tried.'

'I what!' exclaimed Emily.

'You spat at me,' Harold repeated with a twinkle in his eye. 'Oh, it's easy to say now, but I felt odd when it happened.'

'Is there anything else?' Emily asked carefully.

'I want to say that I think there's a good chance that Morna's adoptive mother was called Emily, and more importantly, I think that Morna's birth father visited her secretly when she was living as Charity with her adoptive parents.'

'You mean...' Emily began.

'Go on,' Harold encouraged her.

'You mean I was behaving as if I were Charity and you were my real father?'

'Yes, that's exactly what I mean. It fits like a glove.'

Emily put her head in her hands. 'Oh, I can't cope with all this. I feel all muddled up. My dad left me, and you're my dad now. No, you're not... I've got that wrong.'

'Take your time,' said Harold and Jane together.

'I just can't do it,' said Emily. 'My head's all full of dads and girls and other people.'

'Don't worry, it'll come right,' Jane assured her.

Emily looked at her. 'Jane, can you stay until I've got this sorted out? It's really hard.'

'I'm sure Malcolm can lock up if necessary, and he knows where to come with the keys.'

'Thanks.' Emily put her head in her hands again, but this time she seemed to be less agitated and more able to concentrate. Then she shivered. She looked up. 'Harold, I'm remembering being with you in the kitchen. I think I was about nine years old.'

'That would fit,' he agreed.

She put her head back in her hands yet again. 'George is my father. No, George was my father. Oh, I don't even know that.'

'Don't worry,' said Jane in soothing tones. 'Both of us find it really difficult that he was never found. He was, and is, your father.'

'George. Howard...'

Jane and Harold looked at each other, but said nothing.

'Howard is my father. No, he's not, it's Harold.' She shook her head, but this action did nothing to clarify her confusion, and she looked across at Harold helplessly.

He held her gaze, and said slowly and clearly, 'I think it would help us a lot if we knew the names of Charity's adoptive parents. At the moment, I guess the mother's name was Emily. And I want to say that from the first time I met you, I, Harold Barber, have wanted to be as much a father to you as I could be. But I'm not your birth father. George is your birth father.'

'Thanks, Harold,' said Emily gratefully. 'That really helps. You've explained it so clearly.'

'There's one thing I'd like to add,' said Jane. 'A moment ago, you said the name Howard.'

'When was that?'

'You'd just said George's name for a second time.'

'Yes,' said Harold, 'I noticed that too.'

'What do you think that means?' asked Emily.

'I wonder if it could be the name of Morna's birth father,' said Jane cautiously.

'I thought that,' said Harold.

'My head's beginning to swirl a bit again,' said Emily desperately. 'Could we write some of this down?'

'That's a very good idea,' Harold agreed.

Just then, the phone rang.

'I'll get it,' said Jane. She answered, and found that it was Malcolm. 'Hang on a minute,' she said to him. She turned to the others. 'Do you mind if I go up. I think he needs a hand with something.'

Harold looked at Emily. 'It's up to you.'

'That'll be fine, Jane,' she said. 'Thanks so much for coming. We'll see you soon.'

Jane left, and Harold wrote down a list of names and situations. Emily was finding it very difficult to concentrate. Sometimes things seemed clear, but then everything would scramble in her head. Harold tried to keep her involved, but in the end he wrote a few notes, and then suggested that they talked about something different for a while.

They were in the middle of discussing Harold's Soay sheep, when he said, 'I've just remembered, there were two phone calls this afternoon before Jane came. One would have been Eva, but I wonder who the other was?' He went to see if any message had been left, and he discovered that it had been Fay, calling to see if Emily had got back safely.

'That's kind of her,' said Emily when Harold told her. 'I'll try and remember to give her a ring this evening, once Jane's back. But I must phone Eva straight away to tell her not to bother bringing her spirals round this evening. I don't think it's the right time to be making the layout after all.'

Chapter Twenty-nine

'It was good to have that time with Joan and Jim yesterday,' Fay said to Don over breakfast. 'It's always so helpful to be able to talk things through.'

'And don't forget that they'd been sitting on the edge of their seats waiting to see us so they could hear about it all.'

Fay smiled across at him. 'It must have been frustrating for them. I can imagine how I would have felt if I'd had to wait like that.'

'You've always been a central player, and they have been the backup troops,' Don observed.

'That's not true,' Fay corrected him. 'We've always worked together, and where would I be now without their help?'

Don's expression became serious as he acknowledged again how worried he had been during the time he had been working away from home, almost entirely dependent on Joan and Jim to help Fay.

'And I hope Eva and Emily got back safely,' said Fay, some anxiety showing in her voice. 'I left that message, but we haven't heard anything yet.'

'Don't worry about it. They're busy people. I expect you'll hear from them before the week's out. By the way, I'm going to check to see if there's any news yet from Thome.'

'I still think it's a bit soon,' said Fay, smiling again.

'Aha!' said Don. 'You can see these things so well when it's about me, but when it's you, it's different.'

Fay slapped his arm playfully, and he went to the computer.

'You're wrong,' he called, as he saw a message appear. He opened it eagerly, and read:

Have identified a possible source, but the owner is uncertain about selling. Will keep you informed.
Phillip and Lynne Thome

'What's that supposed to mean?' he said crossly. 'I have to admit that I'm getting to the stage where I don't think I'd mind if Jim beat me to it. I just want to get my hands on a copy for us all.'

'Patience, Don,' Fay chided. 'These things unravel in their own time, and well you know it.'

'But knowing it doesn't take away my impatience. And I think I've got every reason to want to read the rest of it.'

'So have I,' said Fay quietly.

'All right, I take your point,' said Don grudgingly. 'Let's decide what we can do while we're waiting.'

'Why not send a message back, asking if we can have the contact details of the seller?' asked Fay suddenly.

Don stared at her. 'That's an excellent idea! Why didn't I think of it myself? I'll do it right away.'

Quickly he typed a message, and sent it off.

'Now I feel ready for the day,' he announced energetically. 'Let's go out somewhere nice.'

'Are you sure you don't want to hover by the computer to see if you get a quick reply,' Fay teased him.

'Actually, I don't think I do.'

'Where are we going, then?'

'Since we haven't decided, it'll have to be a mystery tour,' said Don.

Fay went to get her things. When she came back, she looked animated. 'I've an idea, Don,' she said.

'Your wish is my command. That is, if I want it too.'

'I've a strong impulse to go back to the place where we got Helen's wedding jacket.'

Don looked at her with a quizzical expression. 'I can certainly drive there, but what do you hope to find? The place might not exist any more.'

'I'm quite certain it's how I'd like to spend my time. If you don't want to, say so, and we'll choose something different.'

'I'm more than willing to go along with your idea. But before we set off, I want us to agree that it might be very disappointing.'

'From what I remember, it was a lovely run. Oh, I know that some of it is bound to have changed, and we may not even find the place, but the outing and the memories will be enough for me.'

Don drove at a leisurely pace, and Fay began to recount everything she remembered of the discovery of Helen's jacket.

'Fay, I'm glad you suggested this,' said Don. 'I remember very well how we found the old signet ring that you bought for me at *Courtyard Antiques.*' He laughed. 'I was astonished when I discovered that not only did it carry my initials, but also it fitted the ring finger of my right hand.'

'And if we hadn't had that experience, I don't think that when Helen was looking for something to wear for her wedding, we would have gone back to that particular courtyard of shops and ended up speaking to the woman in the linen shop who gave us the crucial phone number.'

Don continued the story. 'Once Helen had phoned and made an arrangement, I drove us all to the destination. But of course, Peter and I were excluded from then on. I felt pretty miffed, but Peter seemed to accept it. He and I strolled down the road, while you and Helen disappeared into that outstanding barn conversion. I remember it was huge.'

'At the time, it felt almost as if it were a natural sequence of events, but looking back on it, I've often wondered about it. Finding ourselves in that place with rails of exquisite clothes, and then Helen seeing the jacket, was extraordinary enough, but that the jacket fitted perfectly was beyond anything anyone could have expected.'

'Fay, would you mind getting the old map out? I'm not confident about the next few turns.'

Fay took the map from the glove compartment, and unfolded it to reveal their location. Don drew the car up at the side of the road, and studied it for a few minutes. Then he pointed out the route to Fay.

'Yes, I think I've got the hang of it now,' said Fay, 'but I'll make a couple of pencil marks.'

She circled two of the crucial junctions, and added arrows to indicate particular turns.

'There,' she said, 'we shouldn't have any problems now.'

But when they were still several miles from their destination, it became clear that much had changed.

'Acres of new houses,' Don remarked. 'And it looks as if this road's been realigned.'

Half an hour later, they had to admit that despite their best efforts they could not find the converted barn.

'I'm going to have to ask someone,' said Don.

He drew into a layby in front of a short row of shops.

'I'll try the post office. There should be someone there who knows. I'll be back in a minute.'

He bought a book of first class stamps, and asked the young female assistant for directions, but she looked at him blankly.

'I'm sorry. I've only just moved here. Hang on, I'll ask through at the back.'

She disappeared, and returned a few moments later with an older man.

'Yes, I remember that place well,' he said. 'I could never understand why they pulled it down. Beautiful it was. There's a hotel there now. Some of that modern rubbish.' He sniffed noisily.

'Can you give me directions?' asked Don.

The man lifted up a flap in the counter, and came into the front of the shop.

'Come out on the street, and I'll show you.'

When Don spoke to Fay, he said, 'I'm afraid it doesn't exist any more. There's an unappealing hotel on the site now. Do you still want to go?'

'Not really. I think I'd rather remember it the way it was. It seems completely built up around here now. All I remember is the place itself, surrounded by open countryside.'

'I agree,' said Don slowly. 'I knew there'd been quite a bit of development over here, but I'd no idea that it was so extensive, and that what we came here to see had completely gone.'

'But what happened to us hasn't gone,' Fay reflected. 'It lives on, and I have no doubt at all that there's more to be revealed.'

Don looked at her. He knew that yet again, Fay had made a pronouncement with the kind of certainty that confirmed its truth. 'And the first step is for me to get my hands on a copy of that book,' he said. 'Now we've accomplished our mission, let's get back and see if I've got a reply from the Thomes yet.'

Fay smiled. 'So long as you're aware that you'll probably be disappointed,' she said in a pompous voice, mimicking how Don himself could be.

Don pulled a face by screwing up his nose, and they both laughed.

On the way back, Fay continued to mull over the events of more than twenty years earlier that had led them to this place, and had resulted in their finding Helen's wedding jacket.

'I still haven't worked out what that young man meant when he gave it to us to take away,' said Fay.

'Yes, we never got any further with it, did we? It's remained a puzzle. But who knows, maybe the next generation will find the key to it.'

'I'd never thought of that before,' said Fay. 'I'd always thought it was up to us and Helen and Peter to work it out. But maybe you're right. Now, let me think... What exactly did he say?'

'One thing that surprised me was that no money exchanged hands.'

'Yes, we were only to go back and give money if we learned later that we should.'

'Well, if you learn now, you won't be able to,' said Don wryly.

'Don't joke about it, Don,' said Fay sharply.

'I wasn't.'

'Sorry, I'm feeling upset about it.'

'Actually, so am I,' Don stated baldly.

'The young man told us that the jacket was a copy of one that was created specially for a young bride of royal descent, who bore many children and lived with good health into old age.'

'I remember all that. Of course, you couldn't tell me anything until after the wedding, because Peter and I weren't allowed to know about the jacket until then. The other thing that stuck in my mind was that the young bride's husband was a good man. I thought it was very appropriate, because Peter's a good man too.'

'And Helen was told that she'd chosen the jacket because it was part of her destiny, and that the price should reflect that.'

'And you learned that Helen had a task of special significance to accomplish, and that you had to help her with it.'

'It was quite a while before we realised what that might mean,' said Fay.

'Well, one thing's certain.'

'What's that?'

'There's no doubt in my mind that you and Helen have accomplished your task... and some. Not only have you helped to nourish Barnaby in every way, but also you've put tremendous amounts of energy into helping Helen's large extended family.'

'I would have done that anyway,' said Fay quietly. 'And I couldn't have done it without your support.'

'And there's all that youth work you've been involved in,' Don added.

'But I think that the task goes on, Don,' said Fay. 'We're trying to bring all the parts of Morna together now.'

'I know, and I think we're not doing too badly with that, if I may say so.'

'Don,' said Fay urgently, 'Emily's part of the task, too.'

'What makes you think that?'

'There's something that's trying to come together in her, but it isn't to do with things having been hidden away.'

'I think I follow you, but go on.'

'Like Barnaby, all the people who've cared for Emily in her growing up years have done everything they can to remain honest and genuine in their relationship with her, so there's nothing that she has to reclaim about her own past. What's happening to her now is that she's trying to reach for her real purpose...'

'... and that could involve going through some profound experiences that we might have to help her with,' Don finished for her.

'The first step is to make sure that Morna's life is peeled away from her,' said Fay confidently. 'I think we made a good start over the weekend. But if there's any of it still attached to her, it'll be using her energy in ways that aren't helpful to either her or Morna. When she's freed from that, she'll be able to see what direction to follow. And I feel convinced that the spirals are part of that. At the moment, I think she's confused. She's trying to move forward, but there's something pulling her back at the same time.'

'All the more reason to get back home and see if I've got a reply from the Thomes,' said Don decisively. 'I want to immerse myself in that book.'

'You're right, Don. If that book is some kind of gateway to the spirals, for Emily's sake we both need to understand it inside and out. This evening I'm going to phone her again. I feel uneasy that we haven't heard back from her yet, and I'd rather phone and run the risk of sounding overly concerned, than not phone and fail to be involved when I'm needed.'

It was early afternoon when they returned home, and Don went straight to the computer.

'Fay, there *is* a message from them,' he called.

Fay appeared instantly. 'Tell me what it says.'

'There's a name and a daytime phone number,' he replied. 'And from that I can see it can't be all that far from here.'

'I think you should try straight away, Don.'

Don picked up the phone. His hand was trembling slightly, but he barely noticed. He could hear the phone at the other end ring several times, and he was about to accept that there was no answer, when he heard a voice say, 'Hello, Max Barnes speaking.'

'Hello, Mr Barnes. I was given your number by Phillip Thome.'

'Ah, yes. I've often done business with him in recent years.'

'He says you have a copy of *Communications* by Frances Ianson, but that it might not be for sale.'

'Yes, that's right. I'm gradually sorting through my late uncle's library of books. It's a huge task. I have a copy of that book, but it's in a section of the library that I haven't got to yet. Can I get back to you in a few months? I'll be able to let you know then.'

Fay saw Don's knuckles turn white as he gripped the phone, and she saw the effort he had to make to sound relaxed.

'I was hoping that I might be able to source a copy sooner than that,' he said smoothly. 'Is there any chance that you could look at the book now and make a decision?'

There was a silence at the end of the phone.

'Hello?' said Don, trying not to sound desperate.

'I think that should be possible. Can you give me your name and number, and I'll get back to you some time this evening?'

Don dictated the information slowly and clearly.

'Ah, I see you aren't too far from here.'

'That's right,' said Don. 'I'll look forward to your call.'

Fay watched as Don put down the phone. He took out his handkerchief, and mopped his brow.

'Well done!' she said. 'I take it he's phoning back this evening to say one way or the other.'

'That's right, but I'm not sure how I'm going to spend the time between now and then.'

Chapter Thirty

Jane had left Emily to sleep in that morning. She had managed to persuade her not to set her alarm clock, reminding her that Monday was usually the quietest day at the centre. Emily had made only a token objection, and had then agreed to stay at home for at least the morning. In the end, they had arranged that she would phone Jane at lunchtime to see if she was needed or not.

She woke just after ten, feeling refreshed, but with her head full of the events of the weekend, and she was glad that she wasn't at work. There was so much else to think about. She was surprised to find that she was missing Barnaby, and she wished that she could have at least phoned him.

After she had eaten some breakfast, she wandered around the house, unable to settle to anything until she had the idea of doing some clearing up in the garden. She phoned Jane, who was encouraging of her plan. She found a pair of thick gloves, put on her boots, and went to fetch a spade from one of the outhouses. She soon found that the rhythm of her movements allowed her to relax, and she was able to think about one subject at a time from the mass that was waiting to be teased out.

It was so good that Harold and Jane had helped her yesterday with all those people who had crowded into her mind, past and present, and she felt that this at least had been properly ordered for her. But where did all that fit into everything else? And what was everything else? Determinedly, she marked out a patch of garden, and focussed all her energy upon clearing it. She deposited the uprooted weeds into one of the compost bins, and more and more bare earth appeared as she worked. She reflected on how this simple task was ideal for her. It was clear to her what action she should take, and the results were immediately obvious, and of value.

She wished that she could be as clear as this about the direction of her life. But as the hours passed, and the cleared patch of earth extended further and further, she felt less troubled by thoughts of needing to make any particular decisions. She had work at the centre for as long as she wanted, and Fay had given her some contacts about youth work. With everything else that was going on, surely that was enough for now.

She turned her mind to Barnaby. He would be going home in only a few weeks' time. She felt again the pang of missing him that she had felt earlier that day, and instinctively clutched at her solar plexus. How strange. Throughout all the time that had passed since she had first met him, she had never felt that she missed him. She wondered what it would be like when he wasn't at Overton any more. Maybe she would definitely go and visit Fay again when he was at home with his parents. And there was that jacket. Why had Fay been so keen for her to try it on? She had to admit to herself that in a way she wished now that she had. It was so beautiful.

'Maybe I'll speak to Helen about it soon,' she said aloud, and then jumped at the sound of her voice. She resumed her work. 'And I must phone Fay. I forgot yesterday evening.'

She worked on. At length she realised that she was feeling hungry. She took off her glove to look at her watch, and found that it was already three thirty. She put away her tools, cleaned herself, and then went to the kitchen to make something to eat.

She had almost finished when the phone rang. She thought it might be Jane, but the voice at the other end was Fay's.

'I was going to phone you back yesterday evening,' said Emily, 'but there was so much going on, it slipped my mind.'

'Don't worry about that. I just thought I'd phone again in case you didn't get my message. I've been thinking about you, and wondering how you've been.'

'Actually, it would be good to talk to you about what happened after I got back,' said Emily. 'Have you got a few minutes?'

'I've got plenty of time. We're not going anywhere now. We were out earlier today. As a matter of fact, we decided to go and look at the place where Helen and I got the jacket all those years ago, but we found it was pulled down a long time ago, and the whole area is built up now. I must admit that I was quite disappointed. The other bit of news is that Don's expecting a phone call this evening that will tell him whether or not he can buy a copy of *Communications*. The owner of it, Max Barnes, was bequeathed a private library of books, and it's one of the titles in the many shelves he has yet to assess.'

'How interesting. I must tell Eva and Jane.' Emily hesitated.

'Fay, did you say "Barnes"?' she asked.

'Yes, Max Barnes.'

Slowly and deliberately, Emily said, 'One of the original group of people who studied that book was called Edmund Barnes. He was a professor of archaeology. He must be dead by now, as he was quite a bit older than the others.'

'I'll tell Don as soon as I'm off the phone,' said Fay excitedly. 'Max said that he had inherited his uncle's library. It does sound as if his uncle was the professor. But tell me your news. There's obviously something important.'

Emily went on to recount her experiences, and how Harold and Jane had sat with her afterwards so that they could piece together as best they could what had been happening to her.

When she had finished, Fay said, 'So it's no wonder I had a gnawing feeling inside that I had to contact you. I tried my best to convince myself that I was just being like a mother hen, but my instinct was right. And you say that you were deep in that state when I phoned yesterday and left a message.'

'Yes, I didn't hear the phone, and I only got your message later.'

'Emily, I was talking to Don about you when we were coming back from our trip today. I was talking about you and your life.' She paused for a moment before continuing. 'I've got a strong feeling that if we can somehow bring Morna together, both of us will move forward. Oh, I wish I could find a way of putting it all into words more clearly.'

'I know what you mean,' said Emily. 'There are things affecting us and those around us. We can sense them but haven't yet got a language for them. It's a relief to be talking about this, even if we can't describe it properly.'

'It's coming,' said Fay. 'Nearly every time I talk about it all, something falls into place a bit more. I remember it was like that when I had that illness before Barnaby was born. I wasn't so aware of it then, because I was the one who was experiencing most of the strange states. It was a struggle for us all, I can tell you.'

'When Jane and Eva speak about the spirals and their effects they say the same kind of thing, but of course it was Ellen who was the most affected then. Fay, do you think it's me who's the most affected at the moment?'

'It seems like it,' said Fay. 'But don't worry about it. So long as we all stick together, we'll make sense of it.'

'So do you think it's all right for me to keep working here for now?'

'Most certainly. In fact, I think it's the best place for you. After all, you're involved in something that's far bigger than any of us can see. It's important that you stay in a job that you know well and that you're good at. You're with Jane, you see a lot of Harold and Eva, and you're quite near Helen and Peter. It's a shame that Barnaby won't be at Overton for much longer, but you know you can phone us here any time. Now, I mean that. Day or night, just lift the phone. It's important.'

'Thanks,' said Emily. She felt the kind of relief that she hadn't felt for a very long time. Although overall her life had not been stressed outwardly, inwardly she was now certain that she had been under an enormous stress of a very particular kind. And it was this stress that was starting to shift. 'I know that meeting you has been the next step,' she said.

'Yes, I agree, and I can feel that it's the next step for me, too. Our connection is allowing Morna to come together. Her path is at last unravelling, and this is clearing the way for us. Emily, I still feel so embarrassed when I think of how I clung to that brooch for years.'

'Don't be, Fay,' said Emily. 'It was important that you did. It kept hope alive for Morna. She'd had to wait a long time, and she had to wait again until I began to connect with her, and you and I came together.'

'We may have more to do for her,' said Fay. 'We'll see.'

'I know, but I don't want to think about that at the moment. Fay, I had a strange feeling about Barnaby today. Can I tell you about it?'

'Of course you can.'

'For the first time I missed him. I wanted to talk to him, but he's at work, and when I was thinking about that, I realised how much I'll miss him when he leaves Overton.'

'That's all right,' said Fay. 'It's good that you're feeling like that. It means the time's right.'

'What do you mean?'

'If you'd missed him before, the feelings would have got in the way of the other important things you had to do.'

'Oh, I think I see…'

'Yes, first you and I have had to begin the final contribution to

295

Morna, and you had to think not only about her father, but also about your own father, and about Harold, before you were ready to think about Barnaby in a closer way. And we don't yet know what the meaning of that closeness will be.'

'I think you have some sense of it,' said Emily astutely. 'Otherwise you wouldn't have been so keen to show me Helen's jacket and then go on your trip today. As well as feeling disappointed, did anything else come out of that?'

Fay was taken by surprise when Emily's voice suddenly gained strength as she asked her this.

'Well, actually...' she said.

'I need to know,' said Emily determinedly.

'We were talking about how we found the jacket, and what the young man had said when he handed it to us. I began to see that there was something in it that had yet to happen.'

'Please can you tell me everything about it?' asked Emily urgently. 'I *must* know.'

'I think it's best if I start right from the beginning,' said Fay, 'although you'll know some of it already.'

When she had finished, Emily said, 'No wonder I wanted to hear everything about it straight away. This makes me understand so much more about Barnaby and about Helen and Peter's special family. But how choosing that jacket was part of Helen's destiny... and the strange statement about payment...' Her voice trailed off.

'I think we shouldn't worry that we don't understand that yet,' said Fay. 'But supposing it was Helen's destiny to meet you, then it was really she who brought you to me.'

'And because of me she met the spirals.'

'We'll just have to take things a step at a time and see where we go.'

'Fay, I know that I'm getting closer to wanting to concentrate on the spirals again,' Emily confided. 'I know now that yesterday was the wrong time, and that it was right that Harold and Jane came instead. But while I was working in the garden they seemed to be in the back of my mind all the time.'

'Maybe it's something to do with the last chapter in *Communications*,' Fay suggested.

'I thought you hadn't had time to read to the end,' said Emily, surprised.

Fay laughed. 'I must confess it's one of my habits. I nearly always look at the final chapter of a book when I first pick it up. Don and I were reading it together, but then he had to go off and see to something. I took the opportunity to look at it then.'

'So you've read the part where the son clears the garden and plants things in spiral patterns?' said Emily.

'Yes.'

'I can't say one way or the other if that's why the spirals were in my mind. That would certainly be the simplest explanation. If so, then maybe it's because I'm preparing for something. I don't think I'll be planting things in spiral patterns, though.'

Then Fay said, 'But you're certainly clearing the way for something in more ways than one. Emily, do you mind if we finish for now? Don's hovering around anxiously, in case Max Barnes tries to ring him. Personally, I think it's still a bit early to expect his call, but I think I should go for now.'

'That's fine. I've got a lot to think about,' Emily replied. 'And if anything else comes to mind, I'll phone you later this evening.'

'I'll tell you what,' said Fay. 'I'll ring back once Don's heard from Max. I'd like to let you know whether or not we've had any success, and we can continue our conversation then if you want.'

'That's a very good idea,' said Emily. 'Speak to you later.'

When Emily put the phone down, her mind seemed to be crystal clear. She was certain that the next step was to concentrate her energies on considering how to approach the spirals. Yes, when Jane came back, she would tell her about her conversation with Fay, and they could phone Eva to see when she could come across with her spirals. Then they could make the layout again.

But minutes later, her mind was filled again with what seemed to be a bombardment of fragments. Of what, she didn't know. But she was certain that it was crucial for her to find out. She did not lose her grasp of the importance of directing her focus upon the spirals, but she realised that the fragments meant there was more preparation to be done before she and the spirals became one.

Again her mind cleared. So she knew the goal at last. She and the spirals must become one. But what did that actually mean, and how was it to be achieved?

'I haven't a clue,' she said aloud. But as soon as she heard her words, she became aware of several things that she sensed could well be clues. She grabbed a piece of paper, and began to scribble furiously.

Ask Jane if I can have a bit more time off work. I could work half days.
Must talk to Helen about jacket.
Will Don get the book? Is fundamental that he and Fay study it.
Must speak to Barnaby about everything that's been happening.
When I next lay out the spiral patterns I need to be certain about who should be with me.

That evening, she and Jane were clearing the kitchen so that they could sit down for a long chat, when the phone rang. Emily answered it to find an ecstatic Don on the other end.

'Max Barnes called round out of the blue,' he said. 'He'd looked out the book, and decided that since he was just passing our door this evening on his way to visit a colleague, he'd drop it in. He wouldn't take any money. It's on long-term loan at the moment.'

'It's like the man who handed the jacket to Fay and Helen.'

'Correct,' replied Don. 'Emily, Fay's waiting to speak to you, so I'll hand her across.'

'Hello dear,' said Fay. 'How are you?'

'I'm fine, thanks. Some things have started falling into place, and Jane and I are about to have a long chat.'

'That's good. We've just phoned Joan and Jim. They're coming round now. They're expecting Paul and Diana to be home quite soon, and are eager to get every bit of news they can, so that they can bring them up to date. What a surprise they'll have. Let us know how you get on.'

By the end of the evening, Jane and Emily had made some decisions. Emily would work mornings-only for the following few days, and having decided this, she had phoned Barnaby to see if they could meet on Wednesday afternoon. This had resulted in a plan that she would go to Overton and stay on into the evening, when she would be able to speak to Helen and Peter.

'There's one more thing we need to sort out at the moment,' said Jane. 'We need to get together with Eva and Harold very soon. It's crucial that they know everything.'

'I hope they can come tomorrow evening, so that I see them

before I go across to Overton.'

'That's a good idea,' said Jane, 'and on a practical front we'll have a chance to ask Harold if he can take you there and collect you afterwards.'

Emily bristled. 'What do you mean? I'm not a child.'

'Morna is a child,' said Jane patiently, 'and we've got to be careful.'

'Oh! Jane, I'm sorry.'

'That's all right,' Jane reassured her. 'We had to be watchful about Ellen, and by all accounts, everyone had to be watchful about Fay. With what's happening with you now, it's better for us to be extra-careful.'

'Do you think we could phone Eva and Harold now?' asked Emily uncertainly.

'It's a bit late, but I think they'd both prefer that we got in touch straight away.'

Jane made the calls, and found that her intuition had been correct. In fact, both Harold and Eva had been wondering how soon they could all get together.

Chapter Thirty-one

When Emily went into work on Tuesday morning, she felt as if she hadn't been there for a very long time. Her duties felt surprisingly unfamiliar, and there were times when she had to ask Jane for guidance. Jane was not surprised that Emily had this difficulty. In fact, what surprised her was that overall Emily coped as well as she did.

The afternoon came, and Emily was more than glad to make her way back to the house. Every time she had tried to put her mind to something practical that morning, she had struggled against an overwhelming feeling that all she wanted to think about was the spirals, and how to prepare for them. She made herself eat something, and then settled down with a large notebook and a pen.

'The double spiral is not only central in the layout, but it's very important in its own right,' she murmured. 'I've known that for a long time, and I found that Ellen knew it, too. The double spiral has come into my mind in relation to Barnaby, his parents, and the girl who I am now sure is Morna.' She paused, and then said decisively, 'I'm going to sit here and think about doubles.'

She began to write:

It affected me when I learned that Fay had called Helen and Diana "the twins". There's the story of the spirals and there's the story of what happened to Fay, and these stories have been gradually coming together since I met Barnaby.
The spirals were born when I should have been, and Barnaby was born on Helen and Peter's wedding day.
Barnaby and I have some kind of connection other than just as two people.
Morna and I both lost both our parents. Fay and I have somehow been two parts of Morna, and now they're coming together.

She put down her pen, and said, 'I can't begin to grasp what all this means, but I don't think I need to yet. And I'm really looking forward to talking to the others this evening.'

She took her pad again, and wrote:

Jane was the conduit for the spirals.

'Is that true? I don't know, but it's something I want to think about.'

The coming together of Morna is part of the preparation for the reading of the spirals.

'I'm certain about that,' she pronounced confidently.

It seems now that the jacket has something to do with what we're all trying to understand.

Helen and Peter thought that the lessons that can be learned from the book are important to the spirals.

Jane wondered if the spiral layout is a 2-D plan for a 3-D entity.

'I'm sure she's right about that. When I remember that dream I had at Eva's when I was young, I've no doubt that I was involved with something in more than two dimensions.

How am I ever to understand the language? The spirals spoke to me, but I couldn't understand what they were telling me.

Then a voice seemed to speak to her. 'You and the spirals must become one.'

Although she knew that there was no one there, Emily could not help but look around her. The voice had been so clear and so distinct. Where had it come from? Yet whatever the source of the voice, she knew that her question had been answered. She had already known that she and the spirals must become one, but now she knew that it was in order to understand the language of the spirals that this must take place.

She leaned back in her chair, and shut her eyes. This afternoon marked the end of something that she'd been struggling with for a very long time, and the beginning of wherever she was to go next.

She felt very tired, but at the same time she felt... Felt what? Renewed. Yes, that was it. But what that meant, she didn't know. For now, all she had to do was to focus her mind on the preparation, and upon the spirals.

She could see them in her mind's eye, exactly as they appeared in Jane's diary. She loved their familiar forms. She never ceased to wonder at the intricate pen strokes that made up the direction of each. How anyone could ever have devised something so complex and so beautiful she did not know. Their beauty lay not only in the visual impact of them, but also in the effect they had on anyone who looked at them. There were no solid lines in any of them, only minute pen strokes. She loved following the tiny side branches that appeared in places, some of them ending in miniature spirals. And each spiral had a flow of its own. How this was conveyed was a mystery to her. Maybe it was the way that the pen strokes had been applied, or maybe it was something else. Anticlockwise or clockwise. The double spiral consisted of one of each direction. And the positioning of each spiral with its unique flow was crucial when constructing the layout.

So, if the layout were indeed a diagram, it had allowed her to experience these flows as having three, or perhaps even more dimensions. And this had become accessible to her in her dream. But now what?

That book... It must be a key to the language. Possibly a manual? But it can't be. It's a story. The story could provide a key to the code. But what code?

Here Emily's mind began to circle, and each time it asked the same questions and tried out the same answers, getting nowhere.

'I've got to get out of this,' she said desperately. 'There's something else...' Then a thought struck her. 'Maybe the final key will come from the people who know this book. Helen and Peter, Barnaby, Harold, Jane, Eva and Ellen. And Adam of course, although I've never met him. And there were others who were involved. I must remember to tell Jane about Professor Barnes' nephew, Max, who lent his copy to Don and Fay. Maybe there's a clue there as well. I wish I'd told her just after I spoke to Fay.

'The book... The mother was alone. She could get no real help, and had to rely entirely on her own resources. But despite that, she made the crucial link with her son. I'm not alone, but maybe I am alone in that I'm the only one who can make the crucial link with the spirals. Yes, that might be it. That might be a parallel between her and me. And when she made the link, her son became calm. In his peaceful state he made spirals in the garden, and little instruments that he hung in trees for the wind to play. None of this could ever have been achieved without her fortitude.'

She paused for several minutes before continuing.

'The good people who have read the book have been affected by it, and this is important in itself. Many of them are people who have come together because I met Barnaby – a meeting that has led to Fay's story and the spirals beginning to come together and merge. But we have to bring the parts of Morna together.'

It was then that Emily felt as if her whole being filled with the most beautiful kind of sound, far beyond anything that was imaginable, and she knew that she was now the closest that she had ever been to the meaning and purpose of the spirals.

She sat there, perfectly still. There seemed to be no dimension of time.

Eva drove straight from work to Harold's house, and together they met Jane, who was in the process of locking up at the centre.

'I've had quite a lot on at work,' Eva commented as the three walked down the road together to Jane's house. 'It's been quite hard to clear my mind on the drive across here, but I think I've about done it. I expect it's more difficult for you, Jane.'

'You're probably right. I had a number of calls just before closing time that I could have done without. Don't get me wrong, they weren't unpleasant, but they took up a lot of thinking space, when I needed it for our gathering.'

'I'm the lucky one,' said Harold. 'I put everything away about an hour ago, and sat thinking about everything that's happened since I first met you all.'

'I'm glad one of us is in the right place at least,' Jane commented wryly.

When they reached the house, she said, 'Come on round the back, I've only the back door key with me today.'

She took out her key, and unlocked the door.

'That's strange,' she said. 'It isn't like Emily to leave lights on in the daytime.' She pressed the kitchen switch, and the light came on.

'It wasn't on,' said Eva unnecessarily. 'But I can see why you thought it was. It seems to be very light in here. I wonder what's causing it.'

'Light seems to be pouring through the door from the sitting room,' said Harold, bemused.

'What an unusual effect,' said Eva. 'Maybe it's the angle the sunlight is striking the front of the house.'

Jane glanced at her, saying, 'I'm not so sure. Eva, don't you remember the light that we saw around Ellen?'

'Oh yes, Jane, but there's much more of this, and it seems to be pouring everywhere.'

'It's very quiet in here,' whispered Jane worriedly. 'I wonder where Emily is. I hope she's all right.' She looked around, while Harold went into the sitting room. 'Well, at least I can see she's had something to eat.'

When Harold entered the sitting room, he was overwhelmed by a sensation of being engulfed in light of a purity that he had never before known. He could not speak. All he could do was to stay where he was, and he was aware of nothing but the light.

'Harold, is she in there?' called Jane.

Hearing no reply, Eva and Jane hurried to the door of the sitting room, where they were hit by an intense flow of something that neither of them could see. They backed away from the door.

'It seems to be an intense flow of energy,' Eva whispered.

'What do you think we should do?' Jane whispered back urgently.

'I don't think we should risk disturbing anything,' said Eva. 'I think that Emily and Harold must be in there.'

'But do you think they'll be all right?' asked Jane anxiously.

'I think the only danger would be in disturbing what's happening,' Eva replied. 'Cutting it short could push either or both of them into a kind of exhaustion that could be too much for them.'

'How do you know? How can you be sure?'

'I haven't experienced anything like this myself before,' said Eva. 'I've read about similar things, although nothing exactly the same.'

'I'm terribly worried,' said Jane.

'So am I,' said Eva, 'although perhaps not in the same way as you are. Like I said, my greatest concern is that nothing is done that will disturb them. Is anyone else likely to come?'

'Not that I know of.'

'What about the phone?'

'Do you think it would be a problem if it rang?'

'I wouldn't want to risk it.'

'Then I'll disconnect it.'

'Excellent.'

While Jane was doing this, Eva thought fast. It was imperative that no one entered the house and disturbed this.

When Jane returned, Eva said, 'I think that one of us should stay here, and the other should sit at the gate, in case anyone comes. We can take it in turns.'

'Okay. How about changing over after fifteen minutes, if nothing's shifted.'

'Good!'

'I'll go to the gate, because I'll know anyone who comes and be able to head them off. And since you know more than I do about this kind of thing, I think it's best that you're in here.'

'I take your point. Maybe when we change over we shouldn't stay in that phase for long.'

'Five minutes?'

'Right.'

Jane left, picked up a log from outside the back door, and sat on it next to the gate, while Eva stood a few feet away from the sitting room door. She wished that she could predict what might happen, but she knew that all she could do was wait, and be there. She felt more confident now that she knew Jane had disconnected the phone and would stop any intrusion from outside, and she began to feel calmer.

How strange, she thought. At first I was worried that I'd find it hard to stand here for a long time, but now my body feels very comfortable. In fact, it's almost as if I'm becoming weightless. That can't be, but it's definitely the sensation.

Another few minutes passed, and then Eva felt herself being drawn towards the door to the sitting room. It was almost as if she were floating. That can't be so, she told herself. It must be an illusion. But she knew that she wasn't moving her legs, although she was closer and closer to the door.

As she passed through the door, she became engulfed in light and sound of a purity that she had never known before. Fleetingly, she remembered the last gathering with the spirals, years ago in Ellen's house, and how everyone had been deeply affected, each in their own way. But then the memory seemed to disappear behind her as she was drawn further into the room. She supposed that although she could not see anything or anyone, Harold and Emily must be there somewhere.

Fifteen minutes had passed, and outside, Jane looked down the road in both directions before running round to the back of the house and in through the door. She hurried through the kitchen, expecting to see Eva outside the door of the sitting room, but there was no one there. Maybe she's in the bathroom, she thought. I'll give her a minute. Time ticked past, but there was no sound, and no sign at all of Eva.

Cautiously, she approached the door of the sitting room, and carefully peered round it. She had a sense of becoming weightless, and instinctively she clutched the doorframe. She could just make out the shapes of three people standing in the room. But they weren't standing... Instead they seemed to be floating, but in an upright position. They were bathed in something that was filling the room. It could not be described as pure light. It was something far beyond that, and she knew that she was perceiving it with her whole body and not just with her vision.

Her struggle to remain attached to the doorframe was almost defeating her. She could feel her strength ebbing, and being replaced by something that was a different kind of energy. She longed to give herself up to it, but at the same time knew that she must not. She had to be a witness to this, and must somehow remain grounded by the doorframe.

How long she managed to cling on to that frame she had no idea, and she only just managed to retain her grasp of it. She bit her lip until she tasted blood, and she tried counting backwards from the highest number that her mind could seize upon.

At length, her struggles were rewarded. She felt a slight increase in the strength of her hands, her feet felt as if they were firmly planted on the floor, and the pull from the room reduced considerably.

More time passed. How long she did not know, but slowly she felt more returned to her ordinary self. At the same time, she could begin to identify the three shapes as Harold, Eva and Emily, and these shapes gradually became more distinct, until they looked entirely like the people she knew.

Another few minutes passed, and she could sense the exact

moment when Emily became able to see her standing there.

'Oh good, Jane, you've come at last,' she said. 'But why are you clinging to the doorframe like that? You'll hurt your hands. Come and sit down. I think Harold and Eva have been here for a while already. Did something happen at work to hold you back?'

Although Emily looked like herself, Jane could see that there was something ethereal about her, and she decided that it was safer to stay attached to the doorframe for a little longer.

'It's all right,' said Jane. 'I'll stay here for another few minutes. Then I'll join you. But you're right, I am hanging on to this rather tightly. Silly of me, I'll lean up against it instead. Eva and Harold and I all came along together, but I decided to sit in the sun at the gate for a little while. I've had quite a hard afternoon, and needed to unwind a little. I took a log to sit on.'

Then Harold spoke. 'I came in first.'

Jane noticed with relief that he looked reassuringly substantial, and entirely himself.

Harold continued. 'Emily, you looked so beautiful when I came in, my dear. I felt rooted to the spot. You had a kind of "other worldliness" about you. I expect it's because we're all getting nearer and nearer to whatever it is that we have to discover. Eva came and joined us later.'

'Yes,' said Eva. 'You two looked so calm and complete together that I just stood and watched you for a while. Then I came into the room and joined you.'

'I want to make a quick phone call,' said Jane as calmly as she could. 'I've a feeling that perhaps we should see if Helen and Peter and Barnaby can come across and join us tonight. They might not be free, of course, but I'll give them a call.'

She backed out of the room, reconnected the phone, and quickly keyed in the number. What should she do if there weren't in? But she did not have to find an answer, as she heard Peter's voice.

'Peter,' she said urgently. 'It's Jane here. I can't explain anything at the moment, but could you possibly come across with Helen and Barnaby?'

'We're about to have our meal,' he replied. 'But I think we could come after that. We'll be about an hour, I should think.'

Jane tried not to scream. 'Please,' she said. 'Now.'

Peter realised that this was no time for anything other than action.

'We'll be with you in half an hour. Here's my mobile number. Helen will have my phone. Ring us any time.'

Jane felt tears welling up in her eyes. She grasped that there was no danger, but she could no longer bear to be on her own with this. It was too big.

She wiped her eyes with her handkerchief, and went back to the sitting room, where the others were sitting, deep in conversation.

'They'll be here soon,' she said. 'Does anyone want a glass of water?'

Emily stood up. 'I'd like one. I'll come and give you a hand.'

Once in the kitchen, Emily surprised Jane by saying, 'I don't think that the others have remembered enough of what happened yet.' She added calmly, 'But I think they probably will, given time.'

'When did you come back fully?' asked Jane. She had to work hard to hide the fact that she felt completely staggered by what Emily had said.

'It was just after I pointed out to you that you were likely to hurt yourself if you kept on clutching the doorframe.' Emily hugged her aunt. 'Dear Jane,' she said, 'you might not think it, but you have a soul like a rock. Without you, I could not have been where I went today, and Harold and Eva could not have seen me there.'

'It was extremely hard for me,' said Jane, her voice trembling, and her legs shaking. 'I think I'll have to sit down for a minute.' She almost fell on to one of the kitchen chairs. 'Can you give me any idea of how it came about?'

'It would take too long. Let's get some water for the others, and when Helen, Peter and Barnie arrive, I'll see what's appropriate to say. I promise that if I find it's not right to talk to them yet about it, I'll go to bed with you tonight and tell you what I can.'

Jane felt the vibrations in her legs ease, and she watched as Emily collected a tray, filled a jug with water, and positioned it and some glasses on the tray.

'Come on,' said Emily. 'Let's go back in. It'll be fine.'

In the sitting room, they rejoined Harold and Eva, who were exchanging comments about how radiant Emily was looking.

'I think it was something to do with the fact that I wasn't at work this afternoon,' said Emily, choosing her words carefully. 'When the others arrive, I'd like to tell you all a bit about how I spent my time. It should be easy enough, because I made quite a few notes. Jane and

Harold, it was so good on Sunday evening when you helped me to sort out what was going on in my mind. Without that I don't think I could have got so far today.'

Fleetingly, Jane wished that she had advised Emily to occupy her time differently since she came back from seeing Fay and Don, but she dismissed the idea as quickly, knowing that it had come from a momentary weakness. Of course they had done the right thing on Sunday, and of course they had done the right things since. It was just that she had felt extremely stressed by what had taken place this evening.

She allowed herself to connect with what Emily was planning, and asked, 'Shall I go and get the things we wrote down on Sunday evening?'

'Don't worry,' Emily replied. 'I'll run up and get them. They're beside my bed.'

Jane waited anxiously until Emily returned, and she was much reassured when she saw that she was still her ordinary self.

Not long after this, there was a rattling sound at the back of the house, and Helen's voice called out, 'We're here!'

'Come on in,' Jane called back, as she stood up to go and greet them.

She found Helen and Barnaby standing in the kitchen, each bearing a large casserole dish.

'We thought we'd bring it across,' said Helen cheerfully. 'There should be plenty to go round. I often do double quantities. Barnaby's got the baked potatoes, and I've got the bean stew. Peter's locking up the car. He'll be with us in a minute.'

Peter came into the kitchen, and gave each of Jane and Emily a penetrating look, before saying casually, 'How about making a start on the food?'

'We'll be a bit cramped if we all try to squeeze in here,' Jane commented.

'Why don't we use the large soup dishes and eat in the sitting room?' Emily suggested.

'Good idea,' agreed Jane.

Soon they were all enjoying Helen's creation.

'I've got plenty of fruit we can share afterwards,' said Jane. 'I didn't think I was hungry, but I was wrong.'

As the meal drew to a close, Helen said, 'I ought to say that I had a long talk with my mum last night, so we know quite a bit about what's been happening.'

'Good for Extra-gran!' said Barnaby, beaming across at Emily. 'By the way, when I spoke to her she informed me that you thought you'd miss me when I leave Overton.'

Emily looked slightly uncomfortable, but said, 'Yes, I will.'

'That was a great relief to me, because I'd been thinking the same,' said Barnaby with his cheerful expression unchanged. 'It isn't just that we get on well together, is it? With all that's going on here, we can't possibly be out of touch.'

'Yes,' agreed Helen, 'so we've all promised that we'll put our heads together to see what can be done.'

'There's the phone,' said Emily, trying to sound positive.

'But that's not enough,' Barnaby stated baldly. 'Not when we're handling things like this.'

Here Peter interrupted. 'I think we should cut the preliminaries.' He addressed Emily directly and said, 'Fay, Don, Helen and myself have all agreed that we'll do what we can to make sure you two see each other at least once a month. We can contribute to the cost of travel, and we can help with lifts. I'm sure that Paul and Diana will do the same.'

'Yes, Mum and Dad are bound to want to help,' said Barnaby. 'By the way, Emily, you're the only person who's ever called me Barnie apart from Joan, my real gran.'

'I didn't know I'd called you that,' said Emily with surprise. Then she looked round the others and said, 'I think we should get on to what you all came to hear. I take it now that everyone has some idea of what I went through on Sunday evening, but I'll run through the notes quickly.' She picked up the sheet of paper that she'd brought from her bedroom and read from it.

When she had finished, she laid it to one side, and said, 'It was really this that cleared the way to what happened to me this afternoon. I came in from work and sat down to try to clear my head, and the first thing that happened was that I started to think about the importance of the double spiral. Then I realised that there have been a number of things recently that are in pairs, and that join together. For example, there's Fay and I joining to help Morna.'

'When you started talking about pairs, I thought of me and Diana being "twins",' said Helen. 'We came together to make a twin pair for my mum.'

'Yes, I thought of that one, too,' said Emily.

'And there's the connection between you and me,' said Barnaby. 'A lot has started to come together since we met. In fact the whole thing is huge. The story about what happened before I was born is huge in its own right. And it's been running alongside the story of the spirals. Then the two stories have started merging to make one massive story.'

'And it's still unfolding,' said Jane.

'These examples, and more, were things I wanted to discuss this evening with Harold and Eva,' Emily explained. 'I wrote them down, and then something else came into my mind – the words "Jane was a conduit for the spirals". I wrote that down because I wanted to talk about it to see what everyone else thought.'

'It fits everything I know,' said Eva quietly.

'I'm glad you see it that way,' said Emily. 'It feels more and more right to me, but it's good that you feel the same, because you saw the spirals soon after they first appeared.'

'Remember that you were there at the time, too,' said Jane suddenly.

'But I wasn't born,' Emily objected. 'What do you mean?'

'Just because you weren't born doesn't mean that you didn't exist,' Jane pointed out.'

'How could I fail to realise that?' said Emily. 'I can't believe I could be so dense.'

'There's a lot on your mind,' said Peter, 'and that's an understatement.'

Jane continued. 'I saw Clare quite a bit through her pregnancy, so you'd have had some idea of how she reacted to my presence, and even what kind of vibrations my voice made.' She laughed. 'I remember how we used to measure how big she got towards the end, and I was the one who put the tape measure round you both.'

'So I wonder why I waited inside her for another thirteen days after the spirals came,' Emily pondered.

'We may never know the answer to that,' said Jane. 'I think the important thing is to bear in mind that you and I have been closely involved since your conception, and that's bound to have an effect on the connection between us, and any thoughts you have about the spirals.'

'What else is on your list?' asked Eva.

Emily looked at her pad. 'The next thing that came to me was the coming together of Morna through me and Fay. I'm absolutely certain that's been part of the preparation for me to be able to read the spirals. I know I'm not there yet, but I'm much closer, now that Morna has come together.' She turned to Helen and said, 'And I'm sure that your jacket is important.'

'Ah, yes,' said Helen. 'I believe that you and Fay have spoken about how it came into my life, and what the young man said to us when we got it from him. I've always been puzzled by part of that whole experience, but now that you've come into our lives, it's starting to fall into place.'

'I feel that way, too,' Peter agreed. 'There's something coming together that had been left hanging.'

'Emily, when are you going to try it on?' asked Helen.

'I don't know,' said Emily.

'I think you should next time you go to see Fay,' said Helen. She chuckled ruefully. 'As you've probably realised, I've broadened out a bit since I was married, and there's no hope of it fitting me now, even if I had occasion to wear it. I've a hunch that it's going to fit you perfectly. And I'd take it further than that. I think this is part of what the young man meant would happen. Don't worry about trying to explain any of that to Mum, because she and I have discussed it already.'

'Helen,' said Emily, 'I thought that you and Peter had a really good grasp of the meaning of *Communications* after you'd read it. Can you remember exactly what you said?'

'That book impacted on me so strongly that I'll never forget it,' said Peter. 'I can't remember exactly what we said about it, but it's bound to have included admiration for the qualities of the mother. For a start, she had intelligence, persistence, and determination in the face of terrible adversity. The climax came through her real committed love for her son – love that resulted in an authentic union and communion between them.'

'Yes,' said Helen, 'and both Peter and I felt that we'd learned from the book in a way we want to put into practice.'

Emily turned to Jane. 'After that, I started to think about how you'd wondered if the spiral layout might be a plan for something that is actually three-dimensional. I thought about how that fits so well with my dream experience of the spirals when we were staying at Eva's.'

'Ah, yes. I remember so well how you showed that to me. You were clearly working with a three-dimensional entity. And that was how you'd been before, when I watched your hands moving over the spiral layout in the night at Eva's.'

'I remember that after telling you about my dream experience, I wondered how on earth I was ever going to understand their language. They had spoken to me, but I couldn't understand.'

'Yes, I remember how you were quite upset about that at the time.'

'And then there was what happened to me when I looked at the spiral layout at Harold's. I so wanted to merge with the spirals in intense joy, and I was convinced that my whole body would read them. But then I heard those words "not yet".'

'You were shaking all over with the effort of holding back,' said Jane.

Emily went on. 'The last thing I wrote was because I was wondering how on earth I was going to understand the spirals. I could not understand their language. Then I heard a voice say, "You and the spirals must become as one". Very soon after that my head filled with pictures of all the tiny details of the spirals, and as I traced them in my mind's eye, all the things I'd been writing down seemed to come together. It was then that I began to wonder if the spiral entity had a multitude of dimensions.'

'I'd never considered that,' said Eva quietly. 'You could be on to something.'

Emily went on. 'I knew how important it was that we're in this together, and it seemed to be crucial that you all understood the real meaning of the book. I toyed with the idea that the book was a kind of code that would lead to an understanding of the spirals. It was after that I was bathed in wonderful sound, and I passed through the veil into perfect light.'

The others sat in stunned silence. There were so many questions, yet in truth there were none.

'My experience then was something that I have no way of communicating,' said Emily.

It was now that Harold began to remember what had happened to him. 'Yes,' he said, 'I was drawn by the sound until I could see you in the light. There's no way of describing that sound. You've got to hear it, yet it's impossible to hear.'

'And I joined you,' said Eva, also remembering. 'I was just behind you, Harold.'

Jane began to cry. 'It was so hard,' she sobbed. 'I wanted to come, too, but I thought that if I did, there would be no way back for any of us.'

'You were perfectly right,' said Emily. She paused. 'It would not have been a tragedy if we hadn't been able to come back, but it would have been wrong. We still have work to do.'

'What exactly is that?' asked Harold.

'I can't tell,' said Emily. 'All I know is that it will be given to us.' She stopped for a moment, appearing as if she were listening intently. Then she continued. 'I will learn how to merge with the spirals, and I will learn their song. That way we will know.'

'Emily,' said Jane seriously. 'Please will you promise me one thing? I want to be sure that until you're more experienced you'll always tell someone before you start. It's crucial that you're securely connected to at least one of us at times like that.'

'Don't worry,' Emily replied. 'I know that now.'

Peter cleared his throat. 'I'm very sorry to have to interrupt our evening, but Helen and I must get back soon.'

Helen looked as if she were about to protest. She struggled, looked at her watch, and then said, 'We could stay for another half hour, but after that we really must leave.'

'I have news of Adam,' Harold announced. 'And it couldn't have come at a better time as far as I'm concerned.'

'And curiously, things are firming up about a visit from Ellen,' said Eva.

'I can't wait to see them both,' said Jane with considerable feeling. 'Ideally, we need them to be here together, and soon.'

'Adam's passing through at the end of the week, and he'll be staying with me over Friday night,' said Harold. 'After that, he might be able to arrange a weekend, but it's still a bit up in the air. What news is there of Ellen?'

'She's driving down on Friday afternoon, and is staying with me over the weekend,' said Eva. 'I only heard this morning, just before I left for work.'

'So we've got them both on Friday evening,' said Emily slowly, taking in what she had heard. 'And they are the other pair.'

Everyone fell silent.

At length, Harold said decisively, 'I'm going to get back in touch with Adam and tell him he's got to stay for the weekend. He can change whatever he'd planned, and when I tell him why, I don't think he'll object.'

Peter turned to Helen. 'We're available for most of the weekend, aren't we?'

Helen nodded.

Next he spoke to Barnaby. 'Do you want to come back with us tonight, or do you want to stay here?'

Jane could see that Barnaby was struggling, as if finding it difficult to breathe. 'You're welcome to sleep here if you want,' she assured him.

'No, the lad's coming with me,' said Harold firmly. His face was set with determination.

Barnaby managed to say, 'I mustn't be far away from Emily. Peter, do you mind if stay here for now?'

'I'm sure we'll manage,' Peter replied kindly.

Harold's tone softened. 'I'll lend you some pyjamas. You'll rattle around inside them, but they'll do for now.'

Emily started to giggle at the thought of Barnaby looking like a clown, and this punctured the tension for all of them.

Everyone soon went their separate ways, and she and Jane were left together.

'Can I sleep with you?' Emily asked.

'I was just about to suggest it,' Jane replied, smiling.

They went upstairs, arm in arm.

Chapter Thirty-two

Harold appeared at the centre at lunchtime the next day, looking triumphant.

'I've fixed it!' he said. 'Adam will be with us over the weekend.'

'What did he say?' asked Jane, who looked delighted.

'When I told him what had been going on, he said that wild horses wouldn't keep him away.'

'Did you tell him that Ellen's coming?' asked Emily.

'Of course,' Harold replied loftily, 'and I think he'll be spending quite a bit of time with her on the phone before then.'

'I'll ring her myself this evening,' said Jane, 'and I expect Eva will speak to her, too.'

'Harold, could you ask Barnaby if he'll come down to our house this evening?' asked Emily.

'I think I know the answer to that, but I'll ask him anyway,' said Harold, smiling. 'I've plenty to get on with.'

After Harold had gone, Jane said, 'I'm a bit behind here. Do you mind if I come back after tea. Do you think you and Barnaby will be okay on your own? You can phone me any time, though.'

'That's fine. Barnie and I have got plenty to talk about, and I'll probably ring Fay while he's there.'

Barnaby called for Emily at the garden centre in time to walk her down the road for lunch.

'Harold told me to come now, so you wouldn't be on your own in the afternoon,' he explained. 'Would it be all right if I phone Fay from your house? I expect Helen and Peter will ring her this evening, but I want to talk to her as soon as possible.'

'That's exactly what was in my mind. Let's do it first.'

But there was no reply when they rang.

'Never mind, we can try later,' said Emily, but she wished she didn't have to wait.

'My parents will be back home very soon,' said Barnaby.

'Do they know anything of what's being going on in their

absence?'

'Officially, no.'

'What do you mean by that?'

'I mean that everyone has been waiting until they're home before telling them any details, but we all know that they'll have sensed there's something in the wind.'

'Why do you say that?'

'Through all Fay's difficulties when she was ill, no one told Helen's brother, Jack, what was happening, because he was working hard abroad. When they eventually sent him an e-mail to say there was a lot to catch up on when he came back for my parents' wedding, he told them that he had known that there was something afoot. I didn't want to contact Mum and Dad about any of what's been happening recently, not because I don't want to worry them, but because I'd find it too difficult to explain it all in a phone conversation.'

'Won't you want to see them as soon as they're back?'

'I'd rather be here,' said Barnaby. 'Fay, Don, Joan and Jim will explain what they know, and we can take it from there. If they want to see me, I'm sure they would come here.'

'I'm going to try Fay again,' said Emily. 'I don't feel I can settle until I've spoken to her.'

Still there was no reply, but this time she left a message.

'Barnie,' she said suddenly, 'what do you think about me trying on Helen's jacket?'

Without hesitation he said, 'I want you to... very much.'

'Then I'll certainly try it on when I next go to Fay's,' said Emily.

'I think you'll look lovely in it,' said Barnaby confidently.

Emily felt startled. Barnaby had never before said anything personal like this, and although it sounded nice, it felt very strange.

'Actually... I wasn't thinking about how I'd look. I was thinking about the meaning of it, and where that might take me in my task of being able to read the spirals.'

'For me, your looking lovely will be an important part of that,' said Barnaby, gazing at her intently.

Emily looked away quickly, grabbed the kettle, and filled it with water. 'I'm really thirsty,' she said. 'Would you like something?'

They were sitting sipping from their steaming mugs when the phone rang. Emily jumped, and then grabbed it.

'Thank goodness!' she exclaimed. 'Barnie, it's Fay.'

'Emily,' said Fay urgently. 'What is it, dear?'

'Fay, so much has happened...' Emily burst into tears, and handed the phone to Barnaby.

'It's all right, Fay,' Barnaby reassured her. 'But there was so much yesterday that it'll take a while to bring you up to date.'

'I'll get Don on the extension,' said Fay quickly. 'We'd been out for some shopping, and then I got Emily's message and rang straight away.'

'Emily, shall I make a start?' asked Barnaby.

'Please,' said Emily between sobs.

She listened while Barnaby explained everything slowly and methodically to Fay and Don. She marvelled at his clarity, his precision and his composure. She became aware that Fay and Don asked no questions, since Barnaby's discourse was never interrupted.

When he had finished, she asked to speak to them.

'I'm so excited for you, dear,' said Fay. 'You are getting closer and closer to it.'

'If I weren't so full of questions and uncertainties, I'd be feeling excited for all of us,' said Emily, cheered by hearing Fay's voice.

'I know, but everything will come clear in time,' Fay soothed. 'Your task is greater than mine. Mine was only a beginning, and yours is far beyond that.'

'But I don't know what it is,' Emily protested tearfully.

'Oh, yes, you do,' said Fay. 'You have to read the spirals, and they will tell you what we must do.'

Don's voice came on the line. 'And all of us must help you to develop until you can read them.'

'Yes, dear,' said Fay. 'Now, I'd like to talk to you again about Morna. Do you think you could do that?'

'Yes, yes, of course,' Emily replied, as if nothing else in her life mattered at all.

'I want to be sure that our shared purpose for Morna is complete. We have come together because she needed that, but also because both of us would be held back if we were still involved with her. I no longer cling on to her through my brooch, and we must be sure that the resonance of her early life peels away from you, so that you can become more clearly yourself, and your real purpose can be discovered. Our shared work for Morna is something that meant that we had to come together, and now we must grow on.'

Emily dropped the phone and fell to the floor, where she curled up tightly in a ball.

Barnaby grabbed the phone. 'Talk me through this,' he said tersely. Rapidly he explained what had happened.

'Hold the phone by her ear,' Fay instructed.

Emily did not move as Barnaby positioned it.

Fay waited a minute to be sure that he was ready, and then began to speak. 'Morna, a wrongness forced you into being. What you came for is complete. It's all right for you to leave now. Your purpose lies elsewhere.'

Emily remained motionless. Barnaby was just about to speak to Fay and Don again, when he became aware that something was happening to her. It was as if she was surrounded by an amber-coloured aura. He watched, transfixed, as the aura collected itself into a vortex above her head, hovered there for a moment, and then vanished.

He became aware that he could hear Fay's voice whispering, 'Tell me what's happening, Barnaby.'

He moved the phone away from Emily, and said, 'It's all right, Fay. Just stay there, and I'll tell you later what's happening.'

He could see Emily begin to stir. Slowly she uncurled her body, and rubbed her eyes. Then she saw him.

'Oh, Barnie,' she said. 'I had such a beautiful dream. There were amazing colours, surging and flowing.' She stopped. 'Why on earth am I lying on the kitchen floor?'

'I'll tell you in a minute,' he replied. Then he said to Don and Fay, 'I'll ring back in a while.'

'That's all right,' said Don. 'We'll be here.'

Barnaby put the phone down. 'Sit on this chair, and I'll explain,' he said gently.

Emily's eyes opened wider and wider as he told her exactly what he had witnessed.

He finished by asking, 'How do you feel?'

'Ready,' said Emily. 'Oh,' her hand flew to her mouth, 'why did I say that?'

'Don't let's worry about it. It must be the right answer,' said Barnaby. 'And now let's speak to Don and Fay again.'

Soon, Emily and Fay were deep in conversation, at the end of which Fay said confidently, 'I think the next step is the jacket.'

'Barnie wants to see me in it,' said Emily shyly.

'We do, too, dear,' said Fay warmly.

'But there's something here that's far beyond straightforward pleasure,' said Don. 'Emily and Barnaby are the next generation of the task, and the wearing of the jacket will set a seal on that.'

'When Barnie and I are pledged, we will come to know our destiny, and the spirals will instruct us,' Emily told Fay and Don.

'That's it!' said Fay. 'And it won't be long now before you know their language.'

'Ellen and Adam will be here this weekend,' said Emily, 'and Helen and Peter will come across from Overton.'

'All being well, Paul and Diana should be back,' said Don, 'and we'll tell them everything. You must let us know when all of you are gathering together, and the six of us will do the same here, so that you can be sure you can contact us at any time.'

'Barnie and I will keep you up to date,' said Emily before she rang off.

After that, Barnaby and she wrapped their arms around each other and held each other closely for a long time.

When at length they moved apart, Emily held on to Barnaby's hand and said, 'I'm going to get Jane's diary. I want us to sit looking at the spirals together for a while.'

'Are you sure that's a sensible thing to be doing at the moment?' asked Barnaby worriedly.

Emily looked at him aghast. 'Barnie,' she almost shouted, 'it's the *only* thing to do.'

Barnaby seemed to jerk out of something, and said, 'Let's go and get it together.'

He waited on the landing while Emily went into Jane's room and collected it from the bedside table. Then they went to the sitting room and sat closely together on the couch, studying the spirals. When they finally reached the double spiral, they sat for a long time in complete silence as they both stared at it.

At length, Emily said, 'I've known for a long time that this is very special, and Ellen knew before that, but today I feel it even more.'

'You've got to remember that I'm pretty new to this,' said Barnaby, 'and I'm only beginning to become acquainted with the spirals. But what I'm very aware of is a change in you.'

'What is it, Barnie?

'When we were looking at the double spiral together, I could feel something shift inside you. That's all I can say.'

'I felt it too, Barnie,' said Emily, almost reverently. 'And I don't have the same feeling of urgency about reading them, because I'm beginning to know that they are me. We *are* one, and the time will come soon when I can speak them, and sing their song.'

'What I am very aware of is the need to know our task,' said Barnaby. 'It is the task that was begun by Fay, and is now ours.'

'It's all right, Barnie, the "spiral me" will tell us soon.'

Although Jane returned quite late that evening, she sat up with Emily and Barnaby, determined to follow everything that had happened. She had been unable to contact Harold, but he came just after ten to collect Barnaby, and he stayed on.

It was nearly eleven when he stood up to leave.

'We've got to get together tomorrow evening,' he said. 'Everything's happening fast, and we must keep track of it all.'

'Emily and I will speak to Fay and Don again tomorrow afternoon,' said Barnaby, 'and I must phone Helen and Peter in their lunch break.'

'I'll keep Adam up to date,' said Harold, 'and I'll make sure that Eva's with us in the evening.'

'Thanks,' said Jane gratefully. 'I've got so much to see to at the centre at the moment, and I don't want it to get on top of me.'

'Jane,' said Emily, 'do you think I shouldn't be off in the afternoon, then?'

'There's no question of you working after lunchtime,' replied Jane firmly. 'Your real work is elsewhere, and you must be free to pursue that. I've arranged for Malcolm to do some extra hours, and he should be able to take some of the load in the office. He's proving to be a real asset, and he's only too willing to help out when he can.'

'Harold,' said Emily, 'can you be sure to ask Eva to bring her copy of the spiral layout.'

'Don't worry, I'd already decided that,' Harold replied, touching her arm.

How strange, thought Emily. He's never done anything like that before. Yes, he would touch her if he was helping her to do something, but never in this kind of way. But of course, it wasn't strange, it was right.

Then Harold and Barnaby left. Emily found it hard to watch Barnaby go away, and when he waved to her from the Land Rover, she could see that his face showed something of what she herself was feeling.

Chapter Thirty-three

To Emily's surprise, she found that the morning at the garden centre passed easily, and she had plenty of energy and concentration to go about her responsibilities. She had thought that she would be quite tired, but she felt no trace of weariness or stress. She missed Barnaby very much, but was content, knowing that she would see him again very soon.

Again he came to meet her, and her face lit up as soon as she saw him.

As they strolled down the road together, Barnaby said, 'I phoned Peter before I came to get you. Helen was in with a patient, but I told him everything, and he will relay it to her. They intend to speak to Fay and Don this evening. He told me that they've got a temp at the desk for a couple of weeks, so that leaves me free to be here.'

Emily heaved a sigh of relief. 'I'm so glad to hear that, Barnie,' she said. 'We do need to be together.'

'Yes, I know,' he replied seriously. 'If it were just our feelings, I would find it hard enough to be apart, but our task makes it imperative that we are together for now.'

They joined hands as they walked along.

In the house, Emily picked up the phone saying, 'I want to speak to Fay straight away.' Soon she was deep in conversation, discussing the events of the previous day.'

'I'm certain that Morna's left us now,' said Fay. 'Everything feels very clear at this end. The brooch is a lovely piece of jewellery, and that's all.'

'I'm sure things have shifted for me, too, Fay,' said Emily. 'I have plenty of energy, and my connection with the spirals is focussing. I feel quite calm about it, and I know that the final merging with them is inevitable.' Her voice changed and became softer. 'Barnie and I are merging, too.'

'I know, dear,' said Fay, her voice showing intense pleasure. 'I've been wondering how to get the jacket to you.'

'Oh, but we don't need to have it yet,' said Emily.

'But you do,' said Fay.

'I don't understand,' said Emily, very puzzled. The only thing that mattered to her now was the spirals. Barnie was here with her, and this evening she would be with the spiral layout with the others. What more could she want or need?

'It is necessary,' Fay insisted.

'Then how are we to get it here?' asked Emily worriedly. 'It's a five-hour round trip.'

'Don and I will discuss it. We must get it to you before the weekend, when the others will be with you.'

'I'll talk to Harold and Eva about it this evening,' Emily promised. 'There must be a way.'

Barnaby and Emily spent the rest of the afternoon quietly together. They were surprised and pleased when Jane arrived home early.

'You put your feet up, and we'll make you something nice to eat,' Emily insisted. 'We want you to be rested for this evening.'

'Harold is bringing Eva at seven,' Jane told them.

'Why's that?' asked Emily.

Jane chuckled. 'He's a bit like a mother hen at the moment. He wants to be sure everyone's all right, and I think he wants a bit of time on his own with her.'

By the time they had finished eating, it was nearly seven, and the others arrived ahead of time.

'It's good to see you, Eva,' said Emily emotionally, hugging her. 'Everything's happening so fast.'

'Can I get you something to drink?' Barnaby asked them politely.

'Some water would be nice,' Eva replied.

'Nothing for me, thanks, lad,' said Harold.

When they were all settled, Eva asked Emily, 'Shall we lay out the spirals together?'

Together... The word resonated in Emily's mind. Aloud she said, 'Together... I am to become as one with the spirals. Morna has come together and left us. Together, Fay and I made that possible. Barnaby and I are close, and we have come together because of the next phase of the task. And now, Eva and I will create the spiral layout together.'

'Emily, we've got to tell them about this afternoon,' Barnaby reminded her.

'Oh... yes... of course we must.'

The others listened carefully while Barnaby and Emily related the events of the afternoon.

'I'm so glad that you managed to contact Fay and Don,' said Eva.

'Yes,' said Jane, 'it was the right time, and absolutely essential.'

Harold said nothing, but appeared to be calm and thoughtful.

A look of contentment spread across Emily's face. 'So now the way is cleared for me to concentrate all my energies towards the spirals.'

Barnaby touched her hand. 'Before you make the layout,' he said, 'we should make some decision about the jacket.'

'That's where I come in,' said Harold.

'You can't possibly go across for it,' said Emily. 'It's too much to ask.'

'I would if it was necessary.' He paused, clearly enjoying creating a feeling of suspense, before continuing, pacing his words slowly and deliberately. 'I happen to know that on his way here, Adam will be passing not far from Fay and Don's. I'll get in touch with him tomorrow, and he can collect the jacket.'

Emily stared at him. 'Everything's falling into place,' she said quietly.

'Yes,' replied Harold, 'and I'll be meeting Ellen at last. The few times she's visited, I've not been around. If I'd known then what I know now, I'd have made the time to see her.'

'You weren't ready, and so it wouldn't have been the right time' said Emily, smiling across at him.

'I want to give Fay a quick ring about the jacket,' said Barnaby. 'Is that all right, everyone?'

'I think you should,' said Jane.

'Eva and I will start making the layout,' said Emily.

Eva produced the large brown envelope, and slipped the ten sheets of paper out of it. Carefully following the small diagram of the layout, she and Emily laid out the sheets.

While she worked, Eva said, 'I remember the first time I did this. I knew nothing then of what it would lead to.'

Barnaby slipped quietly back into the room, and sat down.

'Eva, it feels so right to be doing this with you,' said Emily dreamily.

Jane noticed straight away that her voice had changed, and she signalled to everyone to say nothing.

The spiral layout complete, Eva moved back into her seat, but Emily stayed kneeling on the floor. With her eyes shut, her arms outstretched, and her hands palms downwards, she moved as if she were working with something that was about half a metre above the layout.

Jane could see that this time she was making intricate movements with her fingers, as well as changing the shape and angle of her hands, and each hand moved in its own individual way.

Emily's breathing was very slow and deep, so much so that at times Barnaby thought she might not be breathing at all.

She worked in this way for a full ten minutes before a change took place. It was Harold who saw it first. Her lips began to move slightly, and by gesturing, he alerted the others to this. Then her mouth opened a little, her lips continuing their movements.

After this, Emily began to emit a kind of song, but it was a song that sounded like no other that anyone had ever heard before. The changes in rhythm and pitch were strange, and almost eerie, but in a way that drew them all closer to her. They moved from their seats and joined her on the floor, as close to her as they could be without touching her.

Then the words of the song began to flow from Emily's mouth – joyful words, that were filled with a sense of purpose. The message was clear, yet it was language that was new to them, the words of which no one recognised.

No one had any idea of the length of time they sat with Emily, watching her and listening.

The song gradually grew quieter and quieter, until the sound became inaudible, and all that was left was the minimal movement of Emily's lips. Then her hands slowly became still, and she lay down on the floor, next to the spirals, and fell asleep.

Silently, the others returned to their chairs and waited, not wanting to disturb her, lest they interrupt a process that none of them yet understood.

As time passed, Harold leaned back in his chair, and began to doze. Barnaby was sitting on the edge of his chair, scrutinising Emily carefully. It seemed as if he hardly dared to blink, in case he missed something. Jane began to write in a small notebook, and from time to time, Eva gestured to her to indicate things she might have missed.

At length, Harold woke with a jerk, and Jane, who was sitting closest to him, put her hand on his arm to steady him. He looked at his watch, opened his mouth to say something, and shut it again quickly when he realised that Emily was still asleep on the floor. Instead, he caught Jane's full attention, and pointed vigorously towards his watch. It was past eleven.

'I know,' she mouthed. She pointed towards Emily, and shook her head at Harold.

They waited until eleven thirty, and then Harold stood up very carefully, took Eva by the hand, and tiptoed from the room with her.

In the kitchen, he said, 'I'm going to take you home. You've got work tomorrow, and you'll be in no fit state to drive.'

Eva did not resist him. She knew that what he said made every sense, although it felt entirely wrong to be leaving the others.

Harold dropped her off at her house, having first promised to be at home at lunchtime the following day, so that she could phone him for any news.

'And I'll take good care of your spirals,' he assured her.

When he returned to Jane's house, the scene was very different. Emily was sitting in a chair, sipping a hot drink, and she, Jane and Barnaby were talking animatedly.

'Harold, I'm glad you're back,' said Emily. 'While we were waiting for you, Jane and Barnaby have been telling me what they saw happening, and I've got so much to tell you all.'

'Go ahead,' said Harold.

'I remember laying out the spirals with Eva, but then everything changed. It was as if the spirals were filling me up. At the same time I seemed to be sinking into them, and I entered a state where I didn't know myself as separate from them. When it began, it was like the feeling I've had diving off a high diving board, only much more intense and joyous. It's impossible to convey how full of joy I felt.

'And while I was in that state, I knew in a flash why George had been my dad, and why he had taught me everything he had. I knew why I'd gone to uni, and why I'd been drawn to study everything I did study. All of that had been a preparation for my task.'

'What is our task, Emily?' asked Barnaby quietly.

'We will be guided by the song of the spiral language,' Emily told him. 'I have already learned that the world's destruction around us can be transformed into something beautiful and right. I must learn more and more, so that I can transmit what has to be done. That's my destiny. Everything so far has been a preparation. Our task is to enable me in it.'

'I feel very humbled to be a part of this,' said Harold, bowing his head. When he raised it again, he added, 'Practical, as always, I have to remind us that we have other things that we have to see to, day-to-day. We've got to look after ourselves so that we can do them, alongside helping Emily with what she's learning.' He turned to Barnaby. 'Come on, lad. It's bed for us.'

'No!' said Barnaby, in strangled tones. 'I can't be apart from Emily.'

Harold stared at him, as if seeing a different person.

'Let him be in one of our spare rooms tonight, Harold,' said Jane, trying hard to persuade him.

'I hope I'll be with you again tonight, Jane,' said Emily.

'I'd assumed that,' Jane replied, touching her arm.

'See you all in the morning,' said Harold, gruffly. He stood up and walked out briskly.

Chapter Thirty-four

The rest of the week passed uneventfully. Barnaby and Emily spent as many hours together as they could, turning over everything that had happened since they first met, and thinking about what the future might hold. There was the enormity of the coming weekend to consider, and there was the longer-term future to bear in mind. Although neither of them could begin to guess how life would evolve for them, they were sure that they belonged together, and they wanted to make definite plans for keeping in touch once Barnaby was back at university, knowing that whatever they decided, the others were willing to help them.

Harold had no difficulty in getting Adam to agree to collect the jacket from Fay. In fact, he was not only eager to help, but also he was keen to meet Fay and Don, given what he had learned about them from Harold.

By late Friday afternoon, Jane was at home, ready for Ellen's arrival. Eva had said that she would join them as soon as she could.

Barnaby was at Harold's house, preparing a meal for Adam's arrival. He was looking forward to meeting him. He knew that there was much he wanted to ask him about how his connection with Ellen had originated, although he realised that there might not be a suitable opportunity.

Harold came in, and found Barnaby stirring a large pan of soup. He sniffed the air appreciatively.

'Good work, lad!' he exclaimed.

'It's just a repeat of the parsnip,' said Barnaby modestly.

Harold winked at him. 'Takes me back to my childhood days,' he confided. 'My mother was a dab hand at this kind of thing.'

'It's the least I can do to repay you for having me to stay,' said Barnaby politely.

'Nonsense,' said Harold. 'It's a pleasure having you here, and you must stay whenever you come back to visit Emily.'

'Thank you. But I don't know where Emily will be.'

Harold's face fell. He could not conceal his distress at the thought of her absence. He had managed to get used to her being at university, but then he had always known that she would be back for some time each holiday. To his consternation, he realised that over the last weeks he had fallen into allowing himself to feel that she was back home for good. This conversation had forced him to accept that when she left next time, the situation would be very different.

To give Harold time to gather himself, Barnaby concentrated on the soup.

Harold reached for the newspaper, saying, 'Well, lad, you're welcome to stay here any time, whatever the reason.'

Barnaby continued the food preparation, while Harold behaved as if he were studying the newspaper. In reality, his eyes could not focus on the print, and instead threatened to fill with tears. He blew his nose irritably, and concentrated on the immediate future. It was selfish of him to think of Emily as if her continued presence here was central to his happiness. After all they had been through together, he knew very well that his role in her life was to enable her. He must not do or say anything to hold her back.

He pushed the paper away, and stood up. No one knew what would happen this weekend. Adam would be here soon, and he would have the jacket with him. Ellen and Eva would go to Jane's, and tomorrow he would meet Ellen for the first time. In the evening, Helen and Peter would come.

Aloud he said, 'We haven't decided yet which house we're going to use tomorrow evening.'

'I think Jane and Emily have been assuming that we'll join them there,' said Barnaby.

'All right, lad. We can check with them tomorrow, though.'

There was a ring at the door, and Harold rushed to the hall, saying, 'That'll be Adam.'

Barnaby lifted the pan off the ring, and followed Harold, arriving just as he opened the door to reveal a man who was carrying a bag designed for transporting suits. He could see that he was about his own height, although he was broader across the shoulders. The wrinkles that appeared on his face as he smiled were suggestive of someone in their sixties, but his brown hair showed no sign of greying.

'Adam!' said Harold, grinning from ear to ear. He took Adam's spare hand, crushed it in his, and pumped it up and down excitedly.

'It's good to see you. How was your journey?'

'Fine, thanks,' Adam replied. 'I had a clear run.' He nodded in the direction of Barnaby and asked, 'Are you going to introduce me?'

'This is Barnaby, of course,' said Harold. 'Come on in, and you can get to know each other.'

As Adam came into the hall, he held out his hand to Barnaby and shook it warmly. 'It's good to meet you.'

'I've been looking forward to meeting you,' said Barnaby. 'Since I began to learn about the spirals, your name has often been in the conversations, and as you'll know from Harold, I've recently become directly involved with them through Emily.'

'Don't stand in the hall. Come and sit down,' Harold instructed.

'Shall I take this and hang it up?' asked Barnaby, pointing to the bag that Adam was carrying.

'I've been given strict orders not to let it out of my sight,' said Adam, smiling, 'but I know it'll be in good hands if I give to you. It's the jacket, of course.'

Barnaby took the bag almost reverently. 'I'll hang it at the back of the door of the room where I'm sleeping,' he said.

He carried it carefully to his room. The bag felt lighter than he had expected, but he realised that was due to the fact that it contained only a ladies jacket, and not a man's suit. Tempted to open the bag and look at the jacket, he lingered on in his room, wrestling with his impulse. The more he thought about it, the more he knew it would be wrong for him to open it. He decided that the right thing would be to hand it to Helen, when he saw her the following evening. After all, it was hers.

When he joined the others, they were deep in conversation about Harold's pigs.

'Would you like a drink of something, Adam?' he asked.

'I'm fine, thanks,' replied Adam. 'Come and sit down. Harold and I need to talk about his rare breeds project some time, but far more important is what's happening with the spirals. Although I've known Harold for a very long time, our meetings have always been about farming, so it was a complete shock to me when he phoned and told me what had been happening here.'

'It's taken a good few hours to bring you up to date,' said Harold, 'and I learned a lot from what you had to tell me. Oh, yes, Jane and Eva had told me the story right from the beginning, but everyone has a different angle on things.'

'It's been on my mind almost constantly since you first phoned about it,' said Adam, 'and since then, I've spent a long time on the phone to Ellen. When you told me about this weekend, I just cancelled everything else, to clear both Saturday and Sunday. It's obvious that things are coming to a climax, and we must all be together.'

'If you'd planned to leave here on Saturday morning, I was going to make sure you couldn't,' Harold pronounced bluntly.

Adam looked at Harold's still burly frame, and knew that this was no idle threat.

'I assure you that such a course of action will be entirely unnecessary,' he said with mock politeness.

Barnaby stared at them both, and then started to laugh. The thought of Harold penning Adam in, as if he were a difficult steer that was trying to escape, was too much for him. His hilarity broke through the need for any more preliminaries, and soon the three were deep in discussion about what might happen the following evening.

'The size of this is mind-blowing,' said Adam. 'The original effect of the spirals on Ellen and how she linked to me was huge, but what's happening now is far, far, beyond that.'

'And it's not just the bringing together of two very complicated situations from around the time I was born,' Barnaby observed. 'That, in itself, would be monumental, but something is forming now that involves us all in the safety of people in general. Emily is at the centre of that, and I'm right beside her.'

'That's right, lad,' said Harold, 'and I'm doing my best to hold up the rear, but none of us have much clue about what we're doing.'

'That's the scary bit,' remarked Barnaby. 'For most of it, we've got to respond to whatever comes, and there's little preparation we can do, except to be determined to be as open as we can to it.'

'Harold, you were so right to get in touch with me,' said Adam. 'The more of us who can be here who have had any involvement, the better. And I was lucky to have a reason to go and see Fay and Don. In the end, I arranged to set off early this morning, so that I could spend time with them, rather than merely collecting the jacket. Hearing first-hand about the part of Morna's life that came into the open through Fay brought it into much sharper relief for me.'

'And I'm glad you've met my extra-gran,' said Barnaby. 'Did

they tell you that they're getting together with my parents and grandparents tomorrow, so that they'll all be at the end of the same phone if we need them?'

'Yes, they explained all that,' said Adam. 'And because of that I've got a greater appreciation of your background. Your upbringing has certainly been a preparation for something important.'

'That's right. I've seen from the beginning that you've got an old head on young shoulders, lad,' said Harold.

Then Adam said, 'Do you mind if I give Jane a quick ring? Ellen should have arrived by now, but I'd like to check.'

Just then, the phone rang. Harold picked it up to find that it was Jane.

'I thought I'd better let you know that Ellen arrived a minute or two ago. Is Adam with you yet?'

'Yes,' replied Harold, 'and we've been having a long talk.'

Barnaby caught his eye. 'Can I have a word with Emily?' he asked.

Soon he was speaking to her. 'Adam brought the jacket, and I've hung the bag up in my room ... No, I haven't looked at it ... I thought the best thing would be if I give it to Helen when she comes tomorrow evening ... Yes... See you soon.' He handed the phone back to Harold.

'Emily,' he said, 'tell Jane I'll phone her later this evening, and we'll decide about tomorrow. It strikes me that we'll need more than the evening, and we'd best spend some time together in the afternoon as well.'

Emily looked flushed when she put the phone down.

'I've longed for everyone to be together, and now it's about to happen, I don't know what I feel,' she said. She knew she was profoundly grateful that she was sitting with three women who had known her all of her life, and who had as much grasp as anyone ever could of what she was facing.

'Try not to worry,' Ellen advised. 'You're in good hands. In comparison with what is happening with you, what happened to me was only a start. It seemed pretty big at the time, and having Eva and Jane with me in it was crucial.'

'I know it's daunting,' said Eva, 'but at least we're all in it together, and we'll keep close watch over you, and try to be ready to

333

act in whatever way is right.'

'I know I'm not your mother, and never will be,' said Jane, 'but I'll keep doing everything in my power to help you to live a life that's right for you, and I know that what's happening at the moment is absolutely right.'

'Jane,' said Emily, fighting back tears, 'is it all right if I sleep with you again tonight?'

'Of course, it's all right,' Jane assured her. 'I was assuming that's what we'd do. I don't like the idea of you sleeping on your own at the moment.'

'Jane's right,' said Eva. 'I think you shouldn't be on your own at all over the next few days. It isn't just for your safety, it's because you might need to communicate something to one of us at any time.'

'I would support that,' said Ellen. 'I certainly needed that, and it was hard for us all each time I went home, because I lived alone.'

'I wonder if Helen and Peter would be willing to come across after lunch, and spend the rest of the day with us,' mused Jane.

'I don't think that'll be a problem,' said Emily. 'They said they'd keep the weekend clear.'

'I'll give them a ring now,' said Jane decisively.

Not long afterwards, she had fixed that Helen and Peter would join them around two the following afternoon.

'That's a huge relief,' said Emily. 'I realise that I want some time with Helen, talking about the jacket, and trying it on.' She now looked calm, and added confidently, 'That must happen before I can connect with the spirals again.'

The rest of the evening passed quickly as they talked over the many details of what had taken place since Emily first met Barnaby.

When Jane eventually glanced across at the clock, she exclaimed, 'Goodness! It's well after ten. I'd better ring Harold. He must have forgotten.'

She tried his number, but there was no reply.

'What on earth can have happened?' she said, alarmed.

'I expect he's showing off his pigs,' said Emily, unconcerned.

Jane chuckled. 'You're probably right.'

It turned out to be so, and when Harold phoned later, he was very apologetic.

'Just went out to give them a look over,' he said. 'But one thing led to another, and we must have been out for an hour or so. Is anything wrong at your end?'

'No, we're fine,' Jane reassured him. 'I want to let you know that Helen and Peter are coming here for two tomorrow. And Emily says she needs time with Helen and the jacket. One of us will come along in the morning to pick it up.'

Harold did not object to this plan, although he sensed that Barnaby was going to find it difficult to let it go before seeing Emily again.

When Barnaby eventually went to bed that night, he lay awake for many hours, thinking about the day that was to come. He was grateful to share his room with the jacket. As yet, he did not know how his relationship with Emily would develop, but the jacket was at the centre of it.

Chapter Thirty-five

'Come on, Helen. We mustn't be late,' said Peter.

'I know, Peter,' said Helen, almost desperately, 'but there's something I've got to bring with me, and I can't think what it is.'

'You don't need anything,' said Peter firmly. 'The only important thing is to get there safely, and at the right time.'

Still Helen lingered.

'There's something, Peter,' she said. 'I know, I'll phone Mum.'

Peter gave in, and sat down. 'If we're going to be later than two, we can stop on the way and phone them to let them know,' he said.

Helen gave a sigh of relief when Fay answered the phone.

'What is it, dear?' she asked. 'You sound flustered.'

'We're just setting off so that Emily and I can have some time with my jacket,' Helen explained.

'Oh, good,' Fay replied. 'I hoped you would do that. It needs to happen before this evening, and the sooner the better.'

'But you don't understand, Mum,' Helen said, her desperation showing very clearly.

'I'm so sorry. Tell me what's the matter.'

'There's something else... Oh! *Now* I know. I knew if I spoke to you I'd remember. I've got to take the head cover.'

'That's right, dear. I was so glad that you had it made for your outfit. It was such a wonderful surprise.'

'It was out of respect for your experiences when you were learning about Morna's life.'

'I know, dear. I remember when I first described the design of it to you. It was so distinctive. And by the way, I put my pearls in with the jacket. They are in a cloth bag that I tied round the hanger.'

'Thanks, Mum. Yes, I'll tell Emily. I loved wearing them for the "something borrowed". Look, I'll ring off now. We're running a bit late. Speak to you later.'

Helen rushed upstairs, collected the head cover from her 'sentimental items' drawer, and returned as quickly as she could.

'I'm ready now, Peter,' she said. 'I'm sorry about the delay.'

He put his hand on her arm. 'I'm sorry I was so impatient,' he said. 'I wanted to be sure that there were no hitches, and in my haste, I nearly contributed to one.'

As it turned out, they were not as late as he had feared, and he drew their car up outside Jane's house just after two. She had heard it, and was there at the door to welcome them.

'Ellen's looking forward to meeting you,' she said, as she gave each of them a hug.

After they had greeted one another, Ellen said, 'Just go ahead. I've got most of the background now, and the jacket's here and waiting.'

'Yes,' said Jane, 'I went up earlier to collect it.' There was a twinkle in her eye as she added, 'I got the impression that Barnaby wasn't keen to let it come here on its own, but I insisted that this was a "women only" event, except for Peter.'

'Are you sure?' asked Peter.

'Yes,' said Emily. 'I want you to be here, too.'

'Then this is a great honour for me,' he said, smiling. 'As you all know, I was excluded from the first event of this kind, many years ago.'

Helen picked up the jacket in its bag from where it lay on a chair. She slowly unzipped the bag, lifted it out, and handed it to Emily.

'Here you are,' she said. 'Mum's pearls are in the little bag here.' She pointed to it, and then produced the head cover. 'I'll help you to put this on,' she said. 'I nearly forgot to bring it.'

'Thank you so much,' said Emily. 'I thought it would just be the jacket that I would try on. Are you sure that you feel all right about the other things?'

'I don't just feel all right about them,' Helen assured her. 'I know they're essential.'

'I think I'd better go and change out of my jeans,' said Emily. 'I'll be back in a minute.'

She went upstairs, and when she returned she was wearing a long summer skirt made out of light brown cheesecloth, and a close-fitting white vest.

'I know it's not ideal,' she said, 'but it's the best I could come up with.'

Helen looked at Peter meaningfully. He nodded knowingly.

'Emily,' she said slowly, 'it could hardly be any better. Your skirt's a cheesecloth version of the material that Fay's outfit was made of.'

'Sackcloth...' mused Emily. 'Morna... She brought us together, and we brought her together.'

Jane and Eva watched her closely, as she slipped into a kind of reverie.

But she stayed there for only a moment, before saying, 'Please could you help me with the jacket, Helen?'

She slipped one arm in, and Helen helped her with the other, before standing back to admire the effect.

'Just as I thought, it's perfect,' she whispered. 'And now the pearls and the head cover.'

Deftly she fixed the clasp of the pearls behind Emily's neck, and then arranged the head cover.

'I wish Fay could see you now,' she said softly.

'And I wish Clare could see you, Emily,' said Jane.

A tear slid down Emily's cheek as she said, 'My dad... Jane, do you think we'll *ever* know what happened to him?'

'I don't know, Emily,' Jane replied, 'but I'll never give up hoping.'

'I know that if he were here now, he'd want to take a photograph of you,' said Peter. 'I happen to have brought my digital camera. Would you mind if I take some pictures?'

'Peter, that would be lovely,' said Helen. 'What a good idea! We can e-mail them to Mum and Dad.'

'Helen,' said Peter gently, 'I was asking Emily.'

'Yes, I knew that, but I was so excited for Mum and Dad. They'd love to be here now and see Emily, and photos would be the next best thing.'

Emily looked thoughtful. 'Can we wait for a bit? I think it'll be all right, but first I need time to get used to being dressed like this.' She fell quiet for a while, and then said, 'I'd like to speak to Fay. Helen, do you think it would be all right to phone her now?'

'I was about to suggest it,' Helen replied. 'It's my guess that she's sitting there at this very moment, hoping that you'll call.'

Emily soon discovered that Helen was correct, as Fay answered the phone saying, 'Emily! I was hoping that you'd ring. Everyone's here. Paul and Diana have just been speaking to Barnaby. They're very excited by all the news.'

338

'The jacket feels so... right,' said Emily. 'And... thank you for putting the pearls in with it.'

'I wanted you to have the full effect,' said Fay.

Emily went on. 'Peter has offered to take photos.'

'Tell him from us that he must,' Fay encouraged. 'We'd love to see you.'

'I'll say goodbye for now, then,' said Emily shyly.

'I'd like you to come outside into the garden,' suggested Peter. 'The light is good there, and there's a choice of background.'

'I'm finding the waiting really hard,' said Barnaby with uncharacteristic impatience.

'The time will come soon enough,' said Harold.

'And we've got other things that we must talk about first,' Adam pointed out.

'All I can think about is seeing Emily... in Helen's jacket,' Barnaby insisted.

'Well, you can't at the moment, and that's all there is to it,' said Harold flatly.

'Let's put our minds to this evening,' said Adam. 'Apart from Emily and the spirals, there will be eight people there – three of us, and Jane, Eva, Ellen, Peter and Helen. This number of people should provide a good stabilising atmosphere.'

'I agree,' said Harold.

'And there's the phone link to Fay's house,' said Barnaby. 'It probably means more to me that to anyone else, though.'

'You may be right, lad,' said Harold, 'but I'm not far behind you. And there's Emily.' He stopped and considered, before saying, 'Look, we hadn't made a final decision about where we're eating. I'm in favour of getting that out of the way before we get together.'

'I think you're right there,' agreed Adam. 'As far as I see the general picture, we'll join them around seven. You will meet Ellen, and I'll speak to Helen and Peter. Half an hour should be long enough for that. Then we'll be ready for Eva and Emily to make the spiral layout.'

'Sounds good,' said Harold. 'I'll phone in a while and see what the others say. Now, what are we going to have to watch out for?'

'Everything,' said Barnaby starkly. 'Absolutely everything. That's just the point. We can't predict what's going to happen, so it could be anything.'

Adam looked solemn. 'You've put it very clearly, Barnaby, and there's not much else to say.'

Harold reached for the phone. He spoke to Jane, and soon the arrangements were finalised.

'That's it!' he said. 'Anyone for a stroll down the road to have a look at my Soay sheep?'

'I'm your man,' said Adam. 'I want to know exactly how you reclaimed the land, and how things have been going.'

'Do you mind if I stay here, Harold?' asked Barnaby.

'That's fine, lad. We'll see you in a while.'

Barnaby heard the front door shut, but then open again almost immediately, and Harold came back into the room.

'Just come back to pick up my mobile,' he said casually. 'Phone me any time.' And then he left once more.

Alone, Barnaby soon found that solitude had been exactly what he needed. He pottered round the kitchen, slowly ordering the utensils and generally clearing up. This suited him well, and he found that his thoughts settled into a coherent pattern about the evening to come. By the time Harold and Adam returned, he felt restored.

There was just time for a long drink and a cold meal of substantial open sandwiches. After this they walked down the road together to Jane's house, where they found that the others were looking out for them.

Ellen greeted Adam affectionately, and he introduced her to Harold and Barnaby.

Peter and Helen expressed their pleasure on meeting Adam. Barnaby had noticed straight away that there was no sign of the jacket, and he asked Peter what had happened to it.

Peter smiled, and explained that the others had whisked it away upstairs before his arrival. 'I'm used to that sort of thing,' he added candidly. 'I was very surprised that I was allowed to be in on it this afternoon.'

'We've organised enough seats for everyone,' said Jane loudly. 'Sit down when you're ready. Then I think we should have some quiet time before Eva and Emily work on the spiral layout.'

Peter spoke again. 'Before we begin, I want to say that the others are definitely at Fay and Don's house now.'

'Perhaps as a start we should run through what happened the last time,' suggested Barnaby wisely.

'Good lad,' said Harold. 'Everyone's been told, but you're right, we should go through it while we're all together, before we go ahead with anything else.'

'Barnaby, would you like to lead it?' Peter asked.

Barnaby began to speak, and everyone listened in complete silence.

When he had finished, Emily said, 'I've got something I want to add. It's about this afternoon. I've been thinking of how it's affected me. Helen, wearing your jacket and head cover and Fay's pearls, just like you did on your wedding day, had a very profound effect on me. I couldn't put it into words at the time, and it's no wonder, because there are several layers to it. At first I felt as if I was getting married, and that Peter was standing in for my dad. But I had no husband, so it wasn't a wedding of that sort. Then I began to see that it was in part a celebration that set the seal on the coming together of Morna. The parts of her are wedded, and she is gone. This freed me to come together within myself, and this afternoon was a celebration of that wedding too. That has set the seal on the final preparation for me and the spirals to come together in the fullest sense. Oh, I know that, like a wedding between people, the greater part of the coming together will emerge and develop. But there is nothing that stands in the way of my union with them now.'

She looked at Barnaby and continued. 'Barnaby, you will be my eternal companion.'

'Yes,' he replied, 'I will be with you throughout.'

'Eva,' said Emily with great dignity, 'I'm ready now.'

Eva slipped the sheets out of their brown envelope, and together they arranged them with care and precision.

No one spoke.

When it was complete, Eva slipped backwards into her chair.

At first, Emily knelt, motionless, beside the layout, her eyes shut and her hands clasped in her lap. As time passed, Jane thought that it seemed as if she might be in a kind of trance.

Then, very slowly, her fingers unfurled, and she stretched out her hands, palms downwards, in front of her, and began her now-familiar movements over the spiral layout. Eva was aware of watching her lips intently, but thus far could see no movement.

Her silent movements continued – each hand sensing, scanning, reading and manipulating the invisible. As before they seemed to be working independently, but as time went on, they worked together, before returning to a more independent mode. This sequence was repeated several times, until finally, her hands moved with an obviously shared purpose.

Ellen became aware that there was an escalating intensity in these movements, and she knew that something was about to happen that none of them had ever witnessed before. That's strange, she thought. I can't see the ends of Emily's fingers. She blinked her eyes, but this made no difference. In fact, now she could see no fingers at all. Quickly, she glanced round the others, and saw that they were blinking or rubbing their eyes, and she knew then that what she saw was not an illusion.

Emily's hands disappeared. Her outstretched arms were still clearly visible, but she seemed to be reaching into something, and her arms were rapidly becoming shorter.

Jane was sitting next to Harold, and she put her hand firmly on his arm only just in time, as he was about to lean forward to grab Emily.

'No' she mouthed silently.

He looked at Adam, as if pleading for help. Adam shook his head very slightly, clearly indicating that Harold should do nothing.

Emily reached further, and her arms and head disappeared.

Barnaby was clutching the arms of his chair so hard that his knuckles turned white. His teeth were clamped tightly together in an effort to remain motionless.

Then the rest of Emily's body surged forward and disappeared.

Completely stunned, everyone stared at where she had been only moments before. It was as if they were fixed as a tableau, suspended in time. Adam and Ellen were holding hands, Jane still had her hand on Harold's arm, Barnaby was in his chair, Helen and Peter had linked arms and Eva was close to Jane's other side. Each person was in a state of intense concentration, as if trying to recreate Emily's visible presence.

It was Jane who heard something first, although she wondered if she were imagining it. No, it was definitely that sound, but as if coming from a very long way off. She glanced round the others, but they were unchanged, and she guessed that they could not hear it yet.

Then it grew a little louder, and Barnaby stirred from his fixed position. Still very quiet and distant, the sound increased. One by one the others sensed it, too, and began to shift from their rigid positions.

Some minutes later, Jane, Eva, Harold and Barnaby knew without any doubt that this was the sound that they had first heard only very recently. It was the song that had come from Emily's lips. It was here again, but Emily had gone. Yet maybe she was still there, lost to their eyes, vibrating in other dimensions.

The sound intensified until it filled the room. It was indescribably beautiful, and completely overwhelming.

Barnaby looked at his fingers. They felt strange, and straight away he could see that they were vibrating. He was fascinated by this, and studied it for a while before looking round the room. There he saw that, one by one, each of the others had the same experience. Jane's hand fell from Harold's arm, Peter and Helen unlinked their arms, and Adam's hand dropped from his grasp of Ellen's.

The intensity of the vibrations seemed to come in waves – waves that reminded Barnaby of the gentle ebb and flow of the tide on a sandy beach on a calm day, with sunlight glimmering on the water.

The song began to transform, and beautiful yet incomprehensible words formed from its sound. They could see clear water falling from wonderful crystal rocks, birds with iridescent plumage flying past, shoals of gleaming fish, mountain tops covered with unblemished snow, field upon field of healthy crops and grazing animals, and forests of ancient trees. Sounds of the wind rushing through trees, waves breaking on the shore, and birdsong of every kind filled the room.

Then this sensory feast seemed to distil into a swirling mass of pure white light just above the spiral layout, and from this Emily began to materialise, covered in tiny pinpoints of light from all colours of the spectrum. As she emerged, rivers of pure light seemed to pour off her and disappear through the spiral drawings beneath.

She spoke quietly. The flow of her words was constant, and what she said was full of meaning that was instantly comprehensible to everyone, yet the language itself was unrecognisable.

Barnaby was so glad to see her again, and he had an irresistible urge to reach out to her. But he knew that he must not touch her, lest he disturbed the state that she was in. Instead, he reached out to Jane, who was sitting near to him. She took him into her arms and held him tightly for a moment before releasing her embrace.

Emily continued to radiate images and sounds of wholeness, as if this would go on forever. Indeed, its continuity and constancy left Harold beginning to wonder if this was a new life that they had all stumbled into. He had no idea how much time had passed, and had no need or wish to know.

Jane felt full of joy. Emily was not only safe, but she had transformed. And from that state, she had tapped into wonders that defied description, and which she brought to them in abundance. Clare and George's beloved daughter had reached the beginning of her final purpose.

Beyond the Veil by Mirabelle Maslin
ISBN 0-9549551-4-5   £8.99

Spiral patterns, a strange tape of music from Russia, a 'blank' book and an oddly-carved walking stick…

Ellen encounters Adam, a young widower, and a chain of mysterious and unpredictable events begins to weave their lives together.   Chance, contingency and coincidence all play a part – involving them with friends in profound experiences, and lifting the pall of loss that has been affecting both their lives.

Against a backdrop of music, plant lore, mysterious writing and archaeology, the author touches on deeper issues of bereavement, friendship, illness and the impact of objects from the past on our lives. Altered states, heightened sensitivities and unseen communications are explored, as is the importance of caring and mutual understanding.

The story culminates in an experience of spiritual ecstasy, leading separate paths to an unusual and satisfying convergence.

Order from your local bookshop, amazon, or from the Augur Press website www.augurpress.com

Fay by Mirabelle Maslin
ISBN 0-9549551-3-7   £8.99

Fay is suffering from a mysterious illness.   Her family and friends are concerned about her.   In her vulnerable state, she begins to be affected by something more than intuition, and at first no one can make sense of it.

Alongside the preparation for her daughter's wedding, she is drawn into new situations together with resonances of lives that are long past, and at last the central meaning of her struggles begins to emerge.

Order from your local bookshop, amazon, or from the Augur Press website www.augurpress.com

Also available from Augur Press

The Poetry Catchers   £7.99   978-0-9549551-9-9
by Pupils from Craigton Primary School

Beyond the Veil by Mirabelle Maslin   £8.99   0-9549551-4-5

Fay by Mirabelle Maslin   £8.99   0-9549551-3-7

Hemiplegic Utopia: Manc Style   £6.99   978-0-9549551-7-5
by Lee Seymour

Carl and other writings   £5.99   0-9549551-2-9
by Mirabelle Maslin

Letters to my Paper Lover   £7.99   0-9549551-1-0
by Fleur Soignon

On a Dog Lead by Mirabelle Maslin   £6.99   978-0-9549551-5-1

Poems of Wartime Years by W N Taylor   £4.99   978-0-9549551-6-8

For ages 8-14 years (and adult readers too):
Tracy by Mirabelle Maslin   £6.95   0-9549551-0-2

Postage and packing – £1.00 per title
Ordering:
By phone   +44 (0) 131 440 1690
By post   Delf House, 52, Penicuik Road, Roslin, Midlothian
           EH25 9LH   UK
By fax   +44 (0) 131 448 0990
By e-mail   info@augurpress.com
Online   www.augurpress.com   (credit cards accepted)

Cheques payable to Augur Press
Prices and availability subject to change without notice

When placing your order, please mention if you do not wish to receive
any additional information

www.augurpress.com

Mirabelle Maslin
ON A DOG LEAD

Mirabelle Maslin
CARL AND OTHER WRITINGS

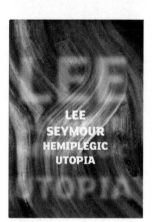

LEE
SEYMOUR
HEMIPLEGIC
UTOPIA

Letters to my Paper Lover
FLEUR SOIGNON

Poems of Wartime Years
W N Taylor

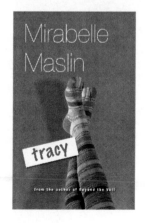

Mirabelle
Maslin

tracy

from the author of Beyond the Veil

Poetry Catchers by The Pupils of Craigton Primary
ISBN 978-0-9549551-9-9   £7.99

Craigton Primary is an inner-city school in Glasgow, Scotland. It has over 200 poetry-mad pupils, and it is the first school in Glasgow to have its own poetry library!

All of us have written a poem for this wonderful book.

We have picked our favourite poems, and we hope that you enjoy reading them as much as we have enjoyed writing them.

We have been inspired by Michael Rosen and our poetry-loving teacher, Mrs McCay.

Some of the poems will bring a tear to your eye, and others will make you cry with laughter.

Why don't you open the book and see what's inside?

Order from your local bookshop, amazon, or from the Augur Press website www.augurpress.com

Lightning Source UK Ltd.
Milton Keynes UK
29 July 2010
157577UK00001B/4/P